Remnants

Anneliese Ronda

Copyright © 2014 Anneliese Ronda
All rights reserved.
ISBN: 1497464943
ISBN-13: 978-1497464940

To my Mother

I

– Persian Empire, 540 BC –

Remember, O Lord, what has happened to us; look and see our disgrace. Joy is gone from our hearts; our dancing has turned to mourning. The crown has fallen from our head.

Woe to us, for we have sinned! Because of this our hearts are faint, because of these things our eyes grow dim for Mount Zion, which lies desolate, with jackals prowling in it.

You, O Lord, reign forever; Your throne endures from generation to generation.

Why do You always forget us?

Why do You forsake us so long?

Restore us to Yourself, O Lord, that we may return; renew our days of old, unless You have utterly rejected us and are angry with us beyond measure.

– Lamentations 5

Chapter I

Mustard Seed

The scent of the rosemary hanging from the rafters did little to mask the bitter reek of death that clung to the dark room. There was a man in the house, knelt facedown and frozen on a mat in the middle of the empty floor.

Kefira had left as soon as she'd seen this. Her back was against the wall outside, breathing hard beside the bricks as she stared at the door she had left open, still swaying. It creaked against the rattling drone of cicadas and cackle of chickens. Aside from that, no sound was heard save for her own breathing. No sound from inside. No sound of pursuit.

"Hello?" the girl asked, hands tugging tightly at the corners of her shawl. She peeled herself from the wall, and moved a little closer to the door. A smell like ill-fermented grapes wafted out of the opening, and no reply came. That man was dead.

Her stomach was a cold knot as she forced herself to look inside again. No movement in the shadows. She turned her head and looked about the land; there was no sign of anyone, only a smattering of thin trees and dusty hills. No stones to mark out the property of any neighbors, and no herds. This small mud-brick dwelling and the trail that ran alongside the creek were the only betrayals that men walked this country. And the only man here was dead.

"Why is your master dead, little goat?" Kefira inquired of the frail creature tied to a stake at her feet, voice trembling. She knelt to put a thin arm around its neck. It bleated in her ear and began chewing on her dark hair. She pulled away, putting a chastising hand to its muzzle. "Stop it," she whispered.

It had been a stroke of luck to find the tied-up goat in her travels that afternoon, until she realized that it'd come from the lone house below the hill. It was her duty as a good Jew to barter in order to obtain something, such as a goat, instead of outright stealing it, as it was her duty as a good Jew to give a goat to a priest to make a sacrifice to Jehovah for all the times she had disregarded that first statute. Yes, the yellow-eyed creature gnawing on the hem of her robes would pay for all the times she'd filled her hollow stomach with bread that was not hers. All she had to do was find a priest, and the penance could be made; never mind that she hadn't seen a priest of Jehovah walking in Persia for half a dozen years.

"Would it still be stealing if I were to take you when your master is gone?" She looked inside again, unease like thorns underfoot. She put a hand on the mantle and peered around the dark interior. There was very little inside by way of furnishings, so the dominating shape of the dead man clutched her gaze all the more. The smell — the sight — it made her eyes burn and water.

Yet Kefira still stepped inside. She wielded a branch; whatever asp or beast that killed the man may yet be hidden. Upon her entrance, the goat abandoned her, cantering off to the chickens that were scraping around the bush. Undeterred, the girl swept around the room with her weapon pointed at the shadows, unoccupied hand clutching her sleeve to her nose.

Still there was no movement. Kefira looked back at the door, the rectangle of golden light it threw onto the floor and the corner of the man's mat. There were sandals on his wizened feet, and he was clothed in long robes of simple black and white fabric. On his head, a black band secured a shawl over grey hair. This all struck her as familiar. Hadn't her father dressed like that? All the men in her village?

Of course, this was no one from her village; though he'd passed away only recently, this man was very, very old, and everyone from her village had died a while ago. Still clutching her nose, she knelt in front of the wrinkled figure and stared hard at him. He was another Jew, though, he had to be. She looked at the thin trail of scarlet that leaked from his lips into his hoary beard, the wrinkles on his face so much like the streaks in the sand of a turbulent river. He looked ancient. Perhaps he'd just knelt to pray one day and never got up.

But what was he doing so far away from other people? Judging by the few furnishings in his room, she guessed he lived alone. But how could he ever have fended for himself at his age?

She angled away from the body, naked feet pressing into the cold, soft dirt as she straightened. Her umber eyes roved over the room, and, feeling quite ashamed even as she did it, examined the wares in his house. There was no food, she saw, much to her disheartenment. But there were crumbs that suggested rodents got to what stores there had been. Besides the mat the dead man knelt upon, there was only a bedroll, a staff, and a table. And the table was bare, save for a few brittle cylinders of parchment and old linen: scrolls, from what she could tell by their inscriptions, wrapped in oilcloth, sitting in a bowl of stone. It struck her as strange that another commoner, this man, was in the possession of scrolls; perhaps he could read. She stood a moment appraising the documents – weighing what price she could get from them against how convenient they would be for her to carry. She had no suitable rucksack to tow them in. Bread could be bound to her back in the confines of her clothing, but these brittle, long things could only crack and come asunder with such treatment.

So, frowning, she set them down; there was nothing valuable therein fit to be taken. The only bounty was the lone goat outside and maybe a chicken if she could grab one. She wondered where the rest of the goat's herd had gotten off to. Judging by the creature's youth, it had to have a sire somewhere. But maybe they'd abandoned the bound creature and the land after their shepherd ceased tending them.

Kefira sighed, as her stomach audibly reminded her of its vacancy. She'd feed herself soon enough. But she couldn't leave yet. She faced the old man again, plugging her nose. She would have to bury him. Though she couldn't do rites like a priest, she would at least give him the common respect of a burial. He was a fellow Jew, after all.

So the girl removed the scrolls from the bowl, and went outside to dig with it. The frost had melted since that morning, as the old winter sun had thrown its warmth upon the packed earth, but still the ground could not be called soft. She used some water from the brook to soften a place and scraped away at the dirt.

Despite the use of her makeshift shovel, her fingernails were still blackened after almost an hour. Most of her time was spent glaring with envy at the chickens, who scraped away so easily at the ground with their yellow claws. Another portion of her time was spent bashing the shrieking cockerel away from her whenever she passed by him to get to the creek. By the time she had anything remotely like a grave dug, she'd sweated through her clothing, and her arms were almost unresponsive. She straightened up, setting the soiled bowl aside to stretch out her aching back. "God in Heaven, I pray you find this a suitable grave for your son." Maybe Adonai would smile upon her for this paid respect. Anyone else might have looted the clothes off the man's body, and left his disgraced shell to rot in the open.

On unsteady legs, the girl went back inside to bring out the man. She did not touch him, however, instead dragging him out on his mat. She could only speculate how many days she would be unclean if she touched the dead. Maybe she was already unclean, for entering the tomb that had been his house, or touching what he had touched. She did not rightly remember all the statutes of uncleanliness learned in her childhood. So she just satisfied herself with the fact that she simply did not contact the body itself.

It required effort to move. Many times the mat sounded as though it would rip as she pulled it, but in the end she made it to the hole without incident.

She was about to roll his body into the ditch, but before she did, something occurred to her about the man's posture. His face was bent down to his knees, as though praying, as she'd thought he was earlier. His eyes were shut as such. But amidst the folds of his robes his hands were cupped against his chest, around something.

The girl got her stick back from the house; curiosity overcoming her better judgment, she used it to roll him onto his side, where around the small something he lay curled. She prodded open his stiff, stubborn hands, to reveal – a chicken egg. A very large chicken egg. Her eyes went to the hens scuffling about the trees.

Could the man have been preparing to eat it, even as he prayed to his death? The idea didn't sit right in her mind, but that did not keep her from pinching it from his grasp – it was rather heavy – and setting it on the ground at her side. If she determined it was not very old, she could make supper out of it to accompany her loaves. And then she paused. She probably ought to try and remember the rules regarding eating something off of a dead thing. She recalled a story about a man whom God had gifted with great strength, who had disobeyed God by eating honey from a dead lion. But he had also been a Nazirite, and so was specifically not allowed to do very many things, if she remembered correctly, and so perhaps she was not restricted in the same way; and in any case, the honey was from a hive inside the lion's very carcass – this egg was from the man's hands, which did not appear to be festering. She shot a glance at the egg, and her stomach growled. Perhaps Jehovah would make an exception for her.

She looked up at the sky, the slowly descending sun. Spurred by the threat of dusk, she covered the old man's body in a solid layer of earth and rocks, sending a prayer after his spirit to God. Then she left, leashed goat in tow. It was a last minute decision not to stay in his home for the night. It was too unnerving to be in the house of a dead person she did not know. And anyway, there might be other wanderers seeking shelter, and she did not want them to stumble upon her. The woefully bleating goat did not seem to reach the same conclusion, however, and gave her an earful the whole way as it tried to turn back to its home; for a starving kid, it seemed to have the strength of a wily hound as it pulled against the rope.

Despite this, Kefira managed to go sufficiently far upstream, that the house was only a half-obscured lump in the distance. She'd found a suitable enough place to rest against a slanted tree, aside a clearing. The brook still wove nearby and there was ample grass to make a bed out of, and she picketed the goat where it had access to both. For her own bed, she pulled up some of the foliage to act as a cushion beneath the fabric she used as a blanket, and got out the bread from the confines of her clothing. The warmth of their baking had long-since abandoned the four flat loaves, but they smelled just as good as when she'd stolen them – yesterday morning. She'd been passing through a village and happened by a vendor of baked goods. Having had nothing but roots and well water to sustain her for the past week, it had been impossible not to steal the food. Kefira liked to justify it as involuntary charity on the baker's part. He didn't know that, in throwing that jar after her, he'd nearly taken the head off of a starving orphan.

She'd felt a little guilty at the turmoil she'd caused him, and was very frightened by the uproar in the village that resulted, but she'd gotten used to it. She'd been eating what was not hers for the past few years of her short life. At first she'd tried bartering, and she'd tried begging, but those means quickly soured when she realized that some men wanted more than a hopeful smile and open palm to make them feel generous. So now it was her lot to travel from village to village, and run away with whatever she could to sustain herself without getting into too much trouble.

The girl had eaten half way through a piece of bread before stowing it all away for later. She was still hungry, of course, but hunger was constant. She only needed to stave it off frequently enough to keep on waking up.

She was thirsty, however. Leaving her bed behind, she crawled in the orange-cast shadows to reach the stream that glimmered in the setting sun. Now that darkness was falling and warmth was fading, her sweat cooled on her body, the salty brine on her robes chafing her skin. She rinsed off her dirt-clogged fingernails as she stooped to drink. The water was lukewarm on her lips as she slurped, the taste of stony dirt cool welcome on her bitter tongue.

But suddenly it burned in her throat as she inhaled a gasp, startled by movement in the water. Something beneath her had plunked from the creek.

Or into it. She looked, coughing, into the sandy bank, to see a round shape the size of a fist amidst the stones. It was a dark shade of red that was almost black, and was dappled in a spray of coppery yellow. Was it gold? Did gold come in rocks?

She picked it up, quickly, only to find that it was the egg again. It had slipped from her clothing, where she'd forgotten it. She rolled a sleeve over its surface, to get the moisture from its shell. But before she returned it to its place in her robes, she paused. Perhaps she should eat it. It was certainly a chicken's egg. She saw no great nests of raptors anywhere, in any case, so it had to be clean to eat. She sat back on her haunches and smelled it. Its odor was reminiscent of iron and dry feathers. It was fresh, certainly. The girl brushed a finger over its smooth surface as she considered its merit; she hefted it in her palm. It was very heavy. She could only imagine how good it would be to taste, and there was so much of it, too.

It still struck her as odd that it was so large – and round, rounder than anything she'd seen come from fowl, and its girth was only just contained by her palm. She'd heard tell before that hens sometimes laid eggs the size of a man's fist; she guessed this was just evidence of that legend.

The girl tapped the egg against a rock. She could break a hole in the shell and drink the yolk from there. Her stomach roared in an exultant anticipation; it had been a long time since she'd tasted anything like meat. And egg was the second best thing.

The only problem was that the egg didn't break. She felt the shell vibrate against her fingers with the tap she'd given it. But when she ran her fingers over the surface, she felt no cracks. She tried again, a little harder this time. The egg gave a resonant peal, but nothing else.

Maybe it was not an egg at all, but a stone. It could have been a precious jewel that the man had held in his death, a charm. Kefira squinted at the object in the half-light. The white dish of the moon was coming up now, even as the sun's last rays were dissipating on the horizon. It was getting hard to see.

With a frustrated sigh, Kefira crawled back to her bed. She didn't want to get lost as night fell just because she was sitting perplexed by a stone, or an egg, or whatever it was. The girl nestled herself into her blanket, the round thing still in hand, trying to explain it to herself.

Perhaps it was indeed a gemstone, a geode. It could be sold and she would come away a much happier person for it. But her fingers persisted to feel it, and the softness of its surface, and the idea withered away. No, never had she felt a rock this smooth; never had she felt an egg this smooth either, for that matter. She held it up before her face in-between her palms, as she lay on her back. The pomegranate shape was silhouetted against the stars — it was so very large.

A feet-chilling possibility entered her mind, slowly gnawing its way to her consciousness as she stared. It could very well be a dragon's egg. But that was impossible — the smallest Persian beast was a Siyudūrai, and even its egg was larger than a man's head.

She set the egg aside in the grass, feeling rather frightened. Despite all logic, the thought persisted. How stupid was she, to have thought that an egg that size and color could belong to a chicken? It was almost half the size of a chicken's whole chest, anyway. It could never be mustered by so small a fowl. If anything, it was a vulture's egg, and even that was dubious. She didn't know any bird's egg to be red and yellow in color. *Perhaps the old man dyed eggs*, came a feeble rationalization that she quickly dismissed. No. She picked up the egg again. She held it in front of her face, blue moonlight glinting off of its lustrous surface.

She would have rather liked to see what produced this egg. Perhaps she would, and perhaps it would only be a great bird, and she would have nothing to worry about. But perhaps it would be a dragon, coming back to recover her stolen offspring. And then perhaps the dragon would take her goat, too. She looked warily at the form lying in the grass.

If she could confirm that it was a dragon's, though, she could get more gold from it than she could carry. She held the egg to her throat, hearing her mind race, pounding between her ears. If only she could find someone with enough money to pay for one. Perhaps there would be a merchant in the metropolises around the Mazandaran Sea; she was heading there anyway, after all. Follow this creek east, to the Atrak River, follow that north, and she'd be able to immerse herself in the life-sustaining commerce and faceless rabble of the city – a vagrant orphan's paradise. She'd be able to live for the rest of her life off of the money gained by selling a dragon egg.

Provided this egg was not mothered by one who was very covetous of her brood. It would be most dreadful, most dreadful indeed – she smelled the egg shell again – if the parent of this egg sniffed her out as a thief and snatched her egg back. Certainly, if it was the spawn of a viper, its mother could be pinned with a stick, and if it were a pup, the jackal that came for it could be scared off. But dragons – Kefira was sure those could not be skirted or deterred by a fistful of rocks. She'd never seen one up close before, but they had to be great indeed, to be used as mounts by the king's warriors. A few times before in her travels, she'd seen an asmanaba passing by like a flock of birds in the sky, detachments from the Asman Kāra scouting Persia's borders. They did not look so very big from where she was on the ground, but she'd heard that there were dragons that outsized whole market squares.

Of course, whatever produced this egg could not be so very large as that. This was a small egg, and so its mother – could she only be the size of a horse? Like a shaghāl, the jackal dragons like giant lizards? It could be a shaghāl egg. She hoped it wasn't. She'd heard dreadful tales about those marauding beasts.

But her imagination was carrying away her senses. She'd been walking safely for days in this country, Hyrcania. She'd not encountered any droppings or tracks that suggested she would be troubled by any dragons at all. She put the egg back into her robes, careful not to harm it; but now she was sure she couldn't, she guiltily recalled, after having gone so far as to hit it against rocks. She would just try to keep it warm; perhaps the thing inside was still quite alive, and needed a little help. Kefira clutched it against her chest, shutting her eyes.

The light of morning would assuage her fears, she knew. It would illuminate the egg's shell before her appraising eyes once more, and bring her to find that her skin was yet not clawed by vengeful dragons. She strove to find solace in that as she descended into slumber. If it were not for the fatigue owed to the day's labor and her hunger, she would not have been able to fall asleep at all.

She woke before it was light outside. Well before it was light; there was not even a hint of blue in the eastern sky, and she could no longer see the moon. As she blinked in to consciousness, she realized that the stars were covered, too. It was so very dark.

A sound like thunder rumbled above her, and she started, now quite awake, waiting for lightning to flash. Storm clouds must have rolled in overnight.

Though no bursts of light came, and she smelled no rain. Just acrid, warm air blowing on her face. She blinked, fighting for her eyes to adjust to the dark. All she could perceive was sound and smell – the ripple of the brook and throaty wind. The aroma of what could only be a breeze from the house she'd just abandoned. But no, this scent was raw and meaty.

Kefira sat up, alarmed by this change in her surroundings. Had she sleepwalked back to the old man's home? That would explain the darkness and the smell.

The groggy wheels in her head stopped turning as a snort abruptly split the air above her head. "Do you not see me?" a voice rasped.

Kefira jerked her gaze up, and up, and up – to stare into the green glimmer of large eyes. Her breath halted.

"Ah, now you do," came the words, with a harsh, clipped accent. "Now speak up, girl. What are you doing out here alone?" As it spoke, more of the fetid air blew into her face, and she saw, as her eyes adjusted, the black shape of great a head and jaws – large enough to bite her in half at the hips. Kefira scrambled back on all fours, as thick saliva from its maw dripped to the ground to hiss like a snake. The inhuman voice emerged once more from deep in its gullet. "Well?"

Kefira did not want to displease this beast by any means, and so responded – or tried to. But her voice caught dry in her throat, and she could no more speak than fit a camel through the mouth of a goblet.

The beast exhaled, much like a discontented horse. It brought back its head and looked down at her disdainfully, studying her. It lifted a talon from the darkness, claws like scimitars – and the girl flinched, collapsing on her back in a wretched attempt at evasion.

Yet it wasn't Kefira the appendage made for, but its own neck. Her eyes followed its movement. "Do you see this?" it hissed. It was pointing out cloth rigging, much like a scarf, swathing its neck and shoulders. "According to your customs, this means I have a man. I do not think he woult like me to hurt another of his kin. So you can speak ant I will not kill you." It eyed her. "What are you doing all alone?"

Words – any words at all, she was vying to give them up to the beast, and she finally found breath with which to speak. "I am... a traveler, an orphan, Master Dragon," she replied simply. She felt a little foolish for titling him thus, but she could not withdraw the address.

The dragon huffed, hopefully in amusement. "Very goot, so you can speak. Now tell me why you are alone. It is dangerous in the wilterness at night." It lowered its head to be eyelevel, and as it did, the stars reappeared to shine upon its scales. Its face was broad like that of a viper, but it had horns that crowned its head and spined its thick neck. Taut frills fringed its jaws where it was not covered in spikes. She would be drinking in the brutishly regal sight if she wasn't so busy avoiding its slaver as it dripped to sizzle and bubble on the ground.

"I told you... I am just travelling. I know it's dangerous," she stammered finally. "There are dragons like you."

The beast's teeth and eyes shone with avarice as it sneered, "That eat little girls, like you. How unfortunate for the little orphan."

Kefira felt her heart lurch. "But you said you had a rider - "

He brought his head back again. "Oh, that is what I sait, but maybe it was a lie to make you speak. Maybe this rigging is arount my neck because I just attackt a merchant caravan and fount their linen stores quite becoming." It turned its head so that one of its eyes could scan her face, slit-pupil dilating and narrowing as though to measure her response.

But she could not tell whether he was serious or jesting. Her jaw trembled. "What are you called, dragon? I'd like to know the name of my murderer."

"Oh, murterer, that is a harsh way to put it." She heard it exhale a rattling breath – a laugh. "But you *dit* do me the courtesy of calling me by *master* and a *who*, so I suppose I will oblige you. I am Mār," it said. "If you woult return the honor, I woult like to know the name of my supper, so if it pleases you..."

The girl managed to give the dragon her name through clenched teeth. "Kefira," she said, and her chin trembled even as she raised it in defiance.

"Mār! Where did you get off to?"

There was another voice. Kefira stared as the dragon lifted its head to call back: "I am only right here, brother."

Brother? Was there another beast? Kefira felt the bark of the tree behind her press into her back, as she scanned the darkness on either side of her for an escape route. If she moved fast enough, she could get under cover of the trees, where it would be hard for the tall beasts to pursue her. Her cold feet pressed against the ground, and she clutched her blanket in a hand, ready to move.

But there was more talking. "The house was empty. I could find nothing but a goat."

"A goat! Truly?" Mār perked up at the unseen newcomer's words. His demeanor now was like that of a great puppy.

"Only half of one, really; an underfed kid." And then the silhouette of a man came into sight, dragging the bleating shape of her goat into the clearing. Kefira's breath froze. A man! That was worse than another dragon – and he had the goat! Her eyes darted to where she'd tied the creature, and she felt for the end of the rope; it'd been chewed through.

Verdict striking her, she objected, "That is mine!" indignant words coming out more like a whine than declaration. She scrambled to her feet, clutching her bedroll, back to the tree. He was going to give the goat to the dragon; she knew it!

Through the darkness, she saw the man turn to her, utter a note of surprise, and look in-between her and the beast. "Mār! You were not doing this girl mischief, were you?" he demanded, with the voice of a young Persian.

"I was merely acquainting myself," the dragon muttered in reply.

The man sighed, "Of *course* you were," and Kefira heard the goat squall as he picked it up. She stepped back, feet going cold as he approached.

"Stay away," she said, the threat halting in her throat as she saw the glimmer of the goats yellow eyes before the man's face.

"Forgive me," and the man stopped. He hoisted the moaning creature and said, "This goat is yours?"

Kefira nodded and then answered with a soft, "Yes."

"Please forgive us – the place down there is your husband's, then, as well. It had looked as though there was no one there, and I'd just wanted to see if I could feed my beast."

Kefira took his explanation rather dubiously – the making of such slipshod excuses was familiar to her, so she suspected what this man was. "It is alright," she replied reservedly. "I fled as soon as I heard your dragon. My husband will understand." Playing into this man's ploy would behoove her. Let him think she was not alone. For she *was* alone, and began to feel a hot nausea inside her in the proximity of these two. The man seemed civil enough, but that could easily be a ruse. She made herself step forward a little. "I will take my goat back, please."

There was a displeased huff above them from Mār, a sound that no more heartened her than it did the goat thence returned squirming to her arms.

"Hush, Mār, it is her animal," the Persian laughed. His voice was good-natured, but she could tell there was a hint of concealed irritation in it. Of course; she'd deprived his beast of a meal. Kefira straightened, arms a little tighter about the goat as the man turned back to her. "My name is Rakhshan. What's yours?"

"I'm Kefira," she said in a less amiable tone. She felt the tree against her back again, and she paid more heed to the darkness around her than the dark shapes before her. She should leave soon.

"Well met, Kefira. Where are your servants?" There was the question, the prying inquiry to discover how very alone she was. "Did they leave you when they heard my friend?"

Kefira set her jaw, feeling the wiry hair of the goat's neck on her face. "Yes, they did. But I'll be fine." She wanted this stranger to stop pretending to be concerned.

The man scratched his head beneath the cloth that swaddled him in a cowl; was he so discomfited by her lack of cordiality? That was not so bad a sign. Or maybe it was just that he had a dagger hiding in his headband. Whatever it was, Kefira could hardly see him at all, so was only left to conjecture. "Very well," he said. "I will return you to your house, then."

There was an ambiguous sort of sound from above – Mār snorting. Kefira flushed and replied, "No, I'm more than capable of doing that myself, thank you." Holding the goat on one hip, she was already winding her blanket around her arm, stooping very quickly to grab the rest of her things and stuff them into the roll.

Mār stepped back a pace, and she saw the Persian shrug at her decline as moonlight flooded past the dragon's shoulder. Flat blue light fell upon them, and she could look up to see that the man's face was not wholly unpleasant. He was handsome – deceptively handsome, she saw, as starlight illuminated the chiseled planes on his face, past the folds of his keffiyeh scarf. His golden eyes were on her as she picked herself up again. With the newfound light, she could now see how very tall he was.

That didn't make her feel any better, as the weight of the goat and her provisions seemed to grow in her arms. Neither did Mār's lowering head, as it stooped to his rider, Rakhshan. "She smells of dragon," he whispered as quietly as a thing of his size could.

Kefira blinked, and reached past the goat to feel the lump in her clothing, over her chest.

The man didn't say anything at first, and for a moment, Kefira believed he was going to make a move to rob her then and there, but he only said to Mār, "Are you sure it's not you?" But he was still looking at her.

"No, I smell *far* better." The dragon put back his ruff in distaste.

Before the man could broach her, she quickly defended, "Yours is the only dragon I've ever seen up close before."

Kefira had to nearly crush the goat in her arms to keep it from fleeing, as it protested violently against Mār's descending head. To her unease, the dragon stuck his dripping muzzle up to the bundle of her belongings, and herself. His nostrils flared as he inhaled. "Shallots and breat – and youngling," he proclaimed with satisfaction, raising his head again to peer down and measure their reactions. In the silence and the moonlight, a trail of saliva gleamed as it trailed from the bone razors jutting from his maw.

She could see now that this discovery had very much piqued the Persian. He stood even taller, arms taut at his sides. "Do you have a dragon egg with you?"

Under both their expectant gazes, Kefira felt her heart pump out heat that made even her bare feet begin to sweat. She shrugged, arms straining with the weight of her burdens as she edged a little closer to the trees. "I have an egg, but it is far too small to be a dragon's." But she didn't move to bring it out and show them. That she would't do even if her hands were not full.

"Let me look at it," the man said, and the leather soles of his feet padded a little closer. She did not like how eager he'd grown all of the sudden.

"So that you can take it from me?" Kefira narrowed her eyes, half-turning away from him. "If it is truly a dragon egg, then I need never go wanting again." She was ready to drop everything and run at this point, if they decided to insist, but the Persian stopped and raised his hands, showing her his palms. "I'm sorry." But he sounded more vexed than apologetic. "Does it belong to your husband?"

"No, it is my own."

"How about I speak with your husband. Where is he?"

"He is away," she replied, and regretted the lie even as she said it. The last word ended with a swallow. Her large, dark eyes searched the Persian's face, but he seemed indifferent to the admission of her isolation; only more irritation lined his face. "Very well. Will you tell me where you found it?"

"The egg?" she said slowly, regaining herself. "Why do you want to know?"

"Well, if it is a dragon egg, then it is invaluable," he explained, "to Persia, and the Asman Kāra."

"So you're a soldier, then?" she observed dubiously. "You seem rather more like a thief in search of a bounty, to me."

And now he seemed not to try so hard to hide his exasperation. He stepped forward with a groan. "Please, why are you being so difficult, girl?"

Kefira felt the hidden egg in her clothes as she readjusted the goat in her arms. "Forgive me if I am a little suspicious. You just seem very intent upon a chicken's egg, is all."

"Well, if you would just let me see it, or answer my questions," the man began.

"Answer me first, please," Kefira broke him off, and asked bluntly, "You are a thief, yes? You were stealing my goat."

Mār seemed to chuckle overhead, and Rakhshan's posture stiffened with unease. There was silence for a moment, before he said, "And I am very sorry about that."

"Right, but are you a thief? A bandit?" Kefira persisted.

Finally he inclined his head and admitted, "Of sorts."

Kefira straightened a little. "Good, then we may speak as equals." She took a breath before confessing, "I found it on a dead man."

She saw the Persian's brow knit, and then he crossed his arms; he didn't speak for a moment, before saying, "Then you yourself are a thief and a liar. Tell me that the lump by the river bank is not that body, and that house not his."

Kefira blanched. That seemed a very immature, a very scornful way to respond to her revelation. She was speechless for a moment, but before she could open her mouth to make an objection, the dragon spoke up, too. "Ant that means there are no servants ant no husbant, ant that is not your goat at all!"

Kefira hoisted the animal defiantly, exclaiming, "Why does that matter? That does not mean that - "

Rakhshan uttered a scathing laugh himself. "Since when can a common urchin afford a dowry? I thought you were too young, in any case, the way your voice squeaks."

Flustered by their sudden rebuke, Kefira pressed her lips together, and gave up on the pretense herself. Huffily, she rejoindered, "Well, you cannot be much older than I am."

Rakhshan put his hands on his hips. "I have ten and nine years."

"You're only four years my elder," she said defensively. "So I wouldn't go around calling people young."

The man shook his head dismissively, waving a perturbed hand. "That doesn't even matter. When did you get the egg?"

Back to the egg. Kefira felt the hair on the back of her neck prickle. "That's hardly any of your business." He was so fixed upon it. He wanted it for himself, she was sure. She felt tree bark rub her through her sleeve as she began backing away. "I'm going, now."

"Wait, not just yet."

The insistence in his voice stopped her. He'd stepped forward, and was within lunging distance. As she stared at him, Kefira felt her fingers stiffen around the heavy goat. Could she drop it if she needed to run?

"Oh, yes," Mār was intoning, now. "The wilterness is full of ill-willt strangers. *Hartly* a place for a youngling like you."

Kefira felt heat flood to her face, helpless anger rising. "I was just fine before you two came along. I think I can take care of myself."

"Please – I'm sorry if I was prying," Rakhshan mollified slowly, "but an egg is of utmost importance."

"It is a chicken's egg, the size of a rock. Let it go, and let me be."

"Very well, then," Mār sighed. He nodded to her, eyes gleaming. "Give me the goat, ant I will make sure that my man does not bother you further."

Kefira looked at him sidelong, even as Rakhshan protested. Perhaps she should. But she didn't trust herself to speak. She needed the goat, and so held it tighter.

"Oh, it is not even yours, you little thief," the dragon snapped at her reticence, patience lost. "Give it to me, or I shall swallow you right along with it."

"Give it a rest, Mār," Rakhshan said.

Kefira argued past him. "But it isn't yours, either! I must make a sacrifice with it. You would not want to interfere with God, would you?" And the dragon only replied with a derisive snort.

"I'll be on my way, now," Kefira said finally. "Good night to you both."

"Wait!" Rakhshan offered, "Perhaps we can make an arrangement. My dragon is hungry. If you let us have the goat, we will ferry you to wherever you wish."

"There is nowhere I want to go," she said mulishly.

"Why so stubborn, girl?" the dragon asked contemptuously, ruff flaring. His teeth dripped with the burning spit. "My rider has given you a hantsome offer, but it is clear you will not have it! So let us see how far your precious goat gets to your mighty Got when its bearer is turnt to meat!"

But Rakhshan staved him off before Kefira could so much as gasp. "Shut up, you ugly cretin," he said, putting a hand onto the beast's foreleg. "Stop barking things you don't mean."

"Oh, but I do mean it, Rakhshan."

Kefira, eyes burning from the dragon's breath, glared at them both in their dispute. That Mār was truly a loathsome sort. And his rider, the Persian, was only better because he was more proficient at masking his frustration. For certainly both their tempers were very short with her, now. She thought about turning around and leaving them then and there, but Rakhshan had turned back to her. He looked at her earnestly. "Look, girl – Kefira – are you sure that you cannot give up the animal? For any reason?"

"Yes, I'm sorry. To you, too," she looked flintily up at the dragon. She even meant it, a little. She knew what it was like to be hungry. "But I really need it."

Mār just hissed halfheartedly, turning his head away and glancing down at his rider as though he expected him to do something about the stingy girl. But Rakhshan just patted his foreleg. "Well," he said, "You can go another day without a bite, can't you, Snake? You're as tough as any of the Immortals." The compliment raised the dragon's frills a bit, but he looked no less hungry. The Persian looked at Kefira. "Are you sure, then, that there is no where you would like to be taken?"

The resurgence of this offer caught Kefira off guard. She felt the goat's ear flick over her face as she stared at the man and he continued to say, "You would not need to give us – your offering."

The girl waited a moment before responding, suspicious of the favor. "Well," she began, "I was going to get to the Atrak to find a place to stay, by nightfall tomorrow..."

"You will not reach the river by then," the man interrupted, before she could walk through the rest of her plan.

She blinked. "How do you know? Do you have a map?"

"I do, as a matter of fact. Getting here from there will take you almost a week on foot. Were you going to cross over to Dahae, thence?"

Kefira swallowed, confounded by his approximation. Would it truly be that long a travel? For a moment, she searched his dark face for sign of a jest, before recovering and saying, "Um, no – I was going to go north, to the sea."

"That would be two weeks on foot, girl," he said rather pompously.

And she didn't like the condescension in his voice. "Well, I daresay you could know better without a map," she defended. She was still incredulous: maps were most uncommon – a single one created only by the arduous laboring of many surveyors, cartographers, and scribes. Only the rich or fortunate possessed them.

She gazed at him doubtfully behind her goat. He was a little handsome, but that was the only fine quality he possessed; his riding leathers and tunic were disheveled in a very boyish fashion, and dirty. He shouldn't have a map, at all. "How did you come by one, anyway?"

"That's hardly any of your business," he replied smugly, as he turned away to Mār.

Kefira huffed, seething at his smugness as he flipped the tail of his scarf over his shoulder, pulling it back over his head. And then she turned away herself. Her eyes found the dark horizon, still dismayed by his reckoning of her course. She wanted to ask him if he was very sure about his estimate, but refused. He would just take the opportunity to make her plan sound even more ridiculous. Maybe it was ridiculous anyway, but she didn't need anyone else to know it.

She became aware of a conversation going on between the rider and dragon. When she turned back around, the dragon was nodding rather sullenly, Rakhshan saying, "Let us take you there. It would only be a day or two, flying."

Kefira stood still, arms crossed over blanket and animal. She looked cagily at both Mār and Rakhshan. "What do you expect me to owe you in return?" she asked, voice hard. Her hand went to the concealed egg, even as her legs grew uncomfortably hot. She did not know the man. She couldn't expect him to be generous without any avail to himself.

"Naught but the civility of your company," the man said, bringing a snort of disgust from the dragon. "We are not going anywhere in particular. The Mazandaran wouldn't be out of the way."

Kefira was more than taken aback. He could not truly be offering this out of the goodness of his heart. He was a thief. But still, if a three week journey, fraught with threat of disorientation and hunger, could be shortened to only a couple days, how could she wave the opportunity away? She pensively stroked the wiry hair of the goat trembling in her arms. "Your offer is difficult to ignore," she admitted, eyeing him warily.

"Though not too difficult, of course," Mār interjected eagerly. "You may feel free to decline ant be on your way, ant we woult think no worse of you."

"But I will, if you do not mind," Kefira decided aloud, "go with you." She didn't look at them as she said it. She didn't want them to know how irresistible their service was to her, so she maintained control of her jumping voice. *Let them think that you have all the time and food in the world, that you don't even have to go with them.* She glanced at Rakhshan, to measure the effect of her words.

He was smiling, a short, jaunty expression. "We leave in the morning, then," he said simply.

Kefira breathed a little, now. "Alright," she accepted slowly. She hefted the goat that had become a deadweight in her arms. Had she truly just accepted the company of this brigand and his dragon?

"You may sleep alongside Mār if you like," the brigand offered, at which his dragon intoned, "No, you may not!" The narrowing of his pupil told Kefira that he'd not anticipated this second act of charity.

"Hush," the man said, and then continued to her, "Anyway, it'd be much warmer than going off into the bushes."

Kefira looked at the dragon, then to the brush, and to the man who was offering. "No, thank you," she said. "I am content with the bushes." She gingerly set down the goat and her pack to roll out her blanket again, behind the tree. When she glanced up to make sure that the man was staying away, her eyes fell upon the silver lump of the goat. It hadn't gotten up.

The girl dropped to her knees with an astonished cry. She prodded it, its emaciated belly, its face, but it didn't respond. "It's dead!" she cried, voice tight. Her eyes darted over the bands of the ribs, the froth on its mouth – had it been distress that made its starved heart give out?

A sharp exhale from the dragon caused her to look up in fear; she saw Rakhshan, expression a little remorseful. "Does the offering not work if the creature is dead?" the man asked dubiously. "Mār, put your head over the creek – you're dripping acid everywhere."

Kefira held the young creature's face in her lap, devastated. "No, of course it does not work," she sniffed. This man must be a complete ignoramus; even the Persians had to use live animals to do service to their Ahura Mazda. But she doubted if this man had ever been leagues within any sort of priest in his life, so his obliviousness could only be expected. She looked up at him, and then to the dragon, who was grinning venomously over the brook. "You may eat it," she stood herself up and away from the little creature.

"Oh, yes!" Mār exclaimed, moving forward with steps that rocked the ground. "I shoult hope so!"

Rakhshan stepped in front of him, though. "You are sure?" he asked her.

Kefira just nodded, and already her back was turned to them. No sooner had she affirmed the decision than she heard the snap of teeth behind her, and a spitting, boiling sound. She glanced over her shoulder, tugging the corners of her shawl as she saw the dragon eat. Behind Mār's locked teeth, saliva roiled at the blackening corpse in his maw. She smelled the salty foam of blood and acrid bile, and covered her nose. With a few jerks of his head, the dragon swallowed, and the dripping once-goat was gone.

She looked down to see the ground smoking where his drool had slithered.

The goat was gone.

Kefira turned away again. "I am going to sleep," she murmured, voice low.

Rakhshan stepped up behind her as she began to retreat into the trees. He stopped a few paces away, arms folded behind his back. "I am sorry – I guess you've not seen that before."

"It's alright. I'm going to sleep, now," she repeated.

"You're sure you want to do it over there?"

"Yes, I'm sure."

"Very well, then. Don't get eaten by scorpions."

"Goodnight," she finally banished him, sitting back with her bedroll and swaddled bread. She glanced beyond the tree to watch him disappear into the dark beside the hillock of the dragon.

And then she curled up and sighed. How could she have agreed to travel with the likes of them? She looked over at the brigands again, and heard a quiet conversation as the dragon curled up around his rider. There was a whistle in the wind as his wings shifted in the air. Now, for all his caustic ferocity, Mār only looked like a great bird, gathering its young under wing.

As she settled into her own rather cold blanket, something hard pressed up against her ribcage. She sat up and found the lump. It was the egg, of course. She stroked it with a finger, and instinctively prayed as she did. Adonai should be thanked for its discovery, and for her this supposed ferrying to the Northern Sea, no matter how questionable her current company.

After her prayers, she held the egg for a little longer. When she rubbed it against her face to feel its softness, she felt how very cool it was. It needed to be warmed, didn't it? She slipped it down the nape of her clothing and undergarment, to hold it close to her chest. A mix of fear and excitement filled her as she thought of the prospect of it hatching.

If for some reason this Rakhshan and Mār insisted that this small egg belonged to a dragon, she would not quash her hopes of it just yet. It could very well hatch to be a great and regal creature. Hopefully not a dragon as beastly as Mār, but a dragon no less.

She half-expected then to feel the tapping of a confined hatchling inside, but no such activity was forthcoming. So she stayed all the more wakeful, as an expectant mother waiting for the kicks of a child in her womb.

The moon roamed the sky, as her fingertips rested on the shell. But she felt nothing before succumbing to sleep.

Chapter II
Spiral City

The first thing Kefira did upon waking was secure once more her shawl to her head. She was of course not married, so the act was not necessary, but it'd always done her good to feign the protection of espousal.

Of course this guise was already useless to the two laying nearby – they'd called her bluff already. Despite that however, she still found herself tucking her dark tresses beneath the violet cloth. She didn't like for anyone to see her uncovered anyway, let alone such crude characters as the brigands.

Shadows of gold spilled around her as the sun crested the horizon. Though her blanket was damp with dew, she still clutched it around her as she sat up in the cold morning light. Her back was to the tree, and she hadn't yet looked past the bushes to see if either of the thieves were awake. The only activity she heard was sleep-breathing, the heavy hiss of the dragon. No birds chirped nearby. She imagined she knew why.

Kefira got to her feet, rubbing her back where a root had bored into it in sleep. She rolled up her blanket and set it down, before peering past the tree at her new companions. She almost jumped. It looked as though a hill had grown up from the ground overnight. The green and dusty brown hide of Mār was like a scaly knoll, rising and falling with breath. How much greater he was in daylight! He was curled up in his sleep, leathery dark-striped wings folded against his flanks, yet even in repose his visage was frightful; she could smell his acrid odor from where she stood. As yet, she didn't see his rider.

Kefira looked around warily in the growing light, through the brush and along the gilded creek, from where she could see it past the dragon. No one was up and around, that she could tell, but perhaps the man was just hidden by the dragon.

Out of caution, she peered at the land behind her. Empty scrubland. Distantly she saw a fox cantering off, a chicken in its mouth, amidst the scraggly trees. No man.

Her hand wandered to the egg, and she looked back at the snoring monster. Perhaps she should leave now. It'd been brash, accepting their service. It was a decision driven solely by sloth, to take up their offer of ferrying. She could walk to the Mazandaran just as well as fly, no matter how long it took. She didn't need the company of a rogue and an uncouth dragon to get there.

But still, her feet did not agree with her. They only took her the distance she required to relieve herself; beyond that, she found she could not leave the thieves behind. She could only move forward, bare soles skimming over brambles and rocks to reach the creek. She moved soundlessly, careful not to rouse the dragon as she passed. She saw now that the man was there too, sleeping sprawled halfway under his wing. His shoulder-length hair was strewn, loosed from its tie, around his head. He didn't look overly threatening in the light – rather more like a boy than a man, if not for his stature and the dark stubble on his face. Kefira left them both asleep, to kneel by the creek. Then she looked back at them, thought better of her location, and decided to go farther upstream behind the dragon.

There she sat stooping over the water, demurely removing her shawl. She hung it over her shoulder before splashing water onto her face. Shivering from the jolt, she rubbed her face and eyes, oil and dust streaming from her chin. She blinked at the warped reflection she saw, fingers pulling on her face; her skin had the look and feel of the craftsmanship of a tanner.

Shoving away the rising feeling of dissatisfaction, she pushed her hair back from her face, to take in a few long swallows of water. Despite her efforts, some of her hair trailed in the current. This made her consider washing her hair, as she felt its stringy tangles against her fingertips. It was a veritable mane, her hair, dark and matted. She pulled a leaf from it, and then another. And then she started vehemently combing its extensive locks, fingers impatient. Its unkempt length was somewhere in-between one and two cubits, longer than her arm. She couldn't remember the last time it'd been cut. The time since its last rinse, at least, she knew to be more than a week. The pungent, bready scent of old sweat had long-since returned.

But she would not wash it. She didn't want to, with the nearby sleepers, for she couldn't cover it in her shawl as it dried, and it would cling cold to her face until the sun was shining down. She could wait a day or two until she was at the sea, and could perhaps find one of the fabled bathhouses, and use a bar of sapo.

But until then, she just splashed her face before submerging her feet. The water was cool over the appendages as she rubbed the dirt off her soles. They were like the paws of a hound, tough and numbed to the pain of sharp rocks and hot sand. Most unattractive they were, but she would rather have unfeminine feet than walk around upon bruises and cuts everywhere she went.

She was rubbing between her toes when a pair of sandals crunched a little ways off. Rakhshan was up, stooping at the creek himself.

Seeing him, the girl took her feet from of the water, dried off her hands on her skirts, and got promptly to her feet. She wished it was night again, that the darkness could conceal her once more. Not that she was ashamed of her appearance; rather, she simply did not like the attention daylight could bring her, now. She threw the shawl upon her head.

His golden eyes were friendly, however. "Good morning," he said. Water dripped from his hair as he tied it back.

She muttered a greeting in reply, shaking grit from her robes before treading back to her tree. He didn't persist in the pleasantries, much to her relief, and he still knelt at the water. The dragon was yet asleep. She sat back down beside her wound up blanket, the hair on the back of her neck relaxing a little. From the bedroll she withdrew the bound-up bread. She pulled up the half-eaten loaf from last night and indulged. There was also a late-blooming abal bush nearby, and she began to pluck off some of the furry red berries.

The strip of flatbread hung from her mouth as she stretched over to the plant, feeling the bristly fruits against her palm as she picked as many as she could carry. She turned her head when a sound reached her – the harrumphing of the dragon. She could see Rakhshan prodding him awake with his feet. She looked back to her harvest and stuffed some of the berries in her breads' swaddling, before lying back against the tree and teething on the rest.

"I'll trade you some jerked venison for a bite of bread."

Kefira looked up quite abashed to see that the Persian was standing aside the tree. She swallowed what was in her mouth, and found the remaining piece of her breakfast with her hand. He had red strips of dried meat in his grasp, and was chewing on one.

And then she looked resentfully down at her own piece of bread; of course, anyone in possession of a map certainly also had meat at their disposal. Her mouth watered, despite herself. "No, thank you," she said. She was cross that he'd snuck up on her like that. "I don't think that's a very fair trade." Indeed it was not; he would be getting the poor end of the deal, too.

"Fairness is a matter of perspective," the man said with a shrug. "Say, perhaps, that I have meat very often and am very sick of it, and value it beneath bread. You, however, being an underfed vagrant, of course would take a single meal of meat over any amount of loaves. That, I think, would make the trade fair. Though, if you are not open to giving me any bread in exchange, I shall have to content myself with mere berries." And he himself began picking the fruit.

Kefira watched him, rather dumbstruck. Had he insulted her and offered her charity in the same turn of speech? She pulled her knees up to her chest and stared at him, while rather stingily eating the last bite of her bread. The morning light cast ruddy shadows on his angular face; he was smiling a little, but that expression was gone by the time he'd gotten what he wanted off the bush and asked, "How fares the egg?"

"It fares well," she replied, quite perturbed by the question. "You may not see it, if that is what you are getting at."

"No, no," he waved, looking away and scooping a fistful of fruit into his mouth. "Just keep it warm."

"I am," she said, folding her arms against her chest where it resided. But before he began to move back to the clearing, she asked, "Did you hatch your dragon yourself?"

"Yes," he said.

She felt the hard surface of the egg under her clothes. "All dragons do not drool as he does, correct?"

The man laughed a little. "No, they do not. He is only an Azhi Dahaki. That is acid that comes from his mouth."

"Acid?"

"It is liquid fire. It burns away whatever it touches."

Kefira blanched. "Oh." She'd heard of Azhi Dahaki dragons, come to think of it. It was a breed that roamed the wilderness of Persia, almost exclusively feral. It was a menace to the villages of men, untamed. Mār was rather a menace anyway, but at least he seemed to be checked by Rakhshan. As the man returned to his dragon, she stole a look after him, and saw the places on the dirt where the beast's spit had scorched. Curdled black spots pockmarked the ground, and there was a particularly vicious scar where his head had rested in sleep.

The Azhi Dahaki was gazing at her now, with a cold emerald orange eye. His spittle trailed like thin yellow webbing from his crooked, toothy jaws. He and Rakhshan were conversing, and she did not care to listen. She was still a little mad at herself for not accepting the man's offer of the venison. She hadn't tasted meat in a long time, and her cursory refusal to take his now seemed foolhardy.

But she wasn't about to ask him if the proposal still stood. That would make her even more a fool. Instead she just watched from the bushes, rather hungrily, as the man and the dragon did things with the dragon's scarf. Indeed, it did appear to be some form of rigging; it coiled around the spikes on the dragon's neck, and was secured with leather thongs in places. The fabric it was composed of was patchwork, and she guessed that material had been added on and repaired as the dragon had grown. Some of it appeared to be the same cloth the Persian's own clothes were cut from. The dragon's forelegs slipped into a pair of leather-braced loops, and rings of fabric hung loose on his back in-between his wings. Kefira watched as Rakhshan wove and tied off both ends of the long strip of rigging in their own respective places at his neck and keel. It was more complex a process than Kefira thought bore thinking of. She hoped that whatever hatched out of her egg would know how to handle such matters by itself.

"Girl – is that cloth you have very old?" The Persian was asking her a question.

"What?" she asked, uncomprehending.

"You need your own rigging to stay upon Mār," he explained. "Do you think that the cloth you have would hold if we used it for your harness?"

"Maybe – I'm not sure." She looked at the bundle uneasily, remembering once more that she was apparently going to fly with them. "It is holding my things, already, though."

"That is just as well that it will not work." Mār lowered his head, teeth borne in a derisive smile. "You may as well not come at all now; though I suppose that if you insist, I am sure it woult be just as safe for you two to share a harness," he advised rather unhelpfully.

And Rakhshan pounded him with a fist. "Shut up, you overgrown newt."

The overgrown newt rumbled defensively, frightening grin still playing on his maw.

Kefira didn't like the dragon's sense of humor. Face hot and stomach full of mortar, she took her things out of her cloth and stood to throw the wadded fabric over to the pair. "Just take it."

Mār exhaled a rattling laugh, holding his head high once more. Rakhshan stooped to pick up the fabric and clambered up the Azhi Dahaki's back. With a few practiced knots, he added the drab grey fabric around his own loop.

She heard the dragon cluck disapprovingly. "Alas, there is not enough to make a secont pair of leg loops. Oh, well, I'm sure the girl can steal some more for us, shoult we pass a tailor."

"You are very disagreeable," Kefira said, stepping into the clearing with her bread tucked in a bundle under her arm.

The dragon didn't dignify her with an answer as Rakhshan shot him a look. The man said from his back, "I can keep your bread with my things." He pointed to a pair of fabric bags from where they were tied to hang beneath Mār's chest. "You can put it in one of those – the foremost."

Kefira looked at both him and the dragon dubiously as she approached. She did not want the man to be in possession of her only means of sustenance; but neither did she want to shove the bread to lay in her clothing, either, should it fall out or heat her up as the day grew warmer.

So despite herself, she relented, biting her lip as she skirted up to the dragon's side, holding her bundle to her chest.

Wings shifted like dry leaves above, as she swallowed. The beast's undercarriage resided well above her head, broad bone-colored scales running the length of his belly, with leathery folds of hide where legs met his trunk; a trio of camels could walk side by side beneath the dragon and never touch him.

Tied to straps on his breast was the luggage Rakhshan had pointed out, but they were out of reach; and she didn't want to leap for them with Mār looking on so contemptuously.

She was about to say something, but the man had already noticed her hesitancy and had slid down. He reached up to untie a corner of the first bundle, and held out his hand for her bread, which she submitted. In it went with the rest. Kefira felt her heart sink. Now she wanted it back.

"We should get going, now," and the way Rakhshan said it made it sound like more than a suggestion. Kefira nodded mutely and followed the man to where he deftly clambered up the dragon's foreleg. She looked on, at a loss as to how she'd make it up herself. There were no handholds aside from the cords of fabric bound well out of her reach. Rakhshan's voice sounded past the dragon's high shoulder, "Mār, be a gentleman and help her up."

"Very well," the dragon sighed. Kefira balked as he lifted a talon and said, "Don't you run off, little girl."

But she did flinch, the dragon's threat notwithstanding, when his clawed fingers encompassed her waist and lifted her off the ground. She was too taken aback to protest with anything but a gasp. His grip was not gentle, and there was grit between the scales of his palm. He set her promptly upon his back, where Rakhshan was standing. And then he let go — seemingly as anxious to break the contact as she'd been.

She teetered, bare feet pressing into ridged scales. The sudden elevation had made her head spin. The ground swayed beneath the dragon like a boat on a river — but sudden pressure on her arm came to steady her. "Be careful."

It was Rakhshan, his hand clasping her elbow, looking down at her with his amber eyes. She stared for a moment, astonished, before jerking her arm away. "Thank you," she said stiffly. Her eyes went back to the ground; not for the first time that day, she wondered what it would take to leave and get out on her own again.

Rakhshan stepped back a pace, looking at her sidelong before pointing at the base of Mār's neck and saying, "Sit here."

Kefira looked at the horns protruding along the dragon's spine, the cords of muscle thicker than a tree trunk. She saw various apparatus in the rigging that she guessed was supposed to harness her in place; but she knew not the first thing about strapping herself in. And anyway — how could she straddle the neck in the confines of a robe? She would have to pull her skirts up, and situate them somehow that she showed the least shin possible. She chewed on her lip.

"Here, let me help you," Rakhshan said.

Before his hand could fall upon her shoulder to direct her, she was already crouching in place. She looked perturbed. "Why must I sit in front?" she asked unhappily. She did not want to be so intimately bestriding the dragon, let alone have the man in a like manner behind her.

Rakhshan raised his eyebrows, and his voice was filled with all the patronizing he would use to address a particularly slow child. "So that you do not go flying from Mār's back as soon as he takes off," he said simply. "If you do something foolish, or the fabric you're using breaks, then I will make sure that you do not go plummeting to your death."

"Yes, for you can be sure that I will not try to catch you," Mār purred.

Kefira did not feel reassured. But she sat, despite herself. She kept her legs bent up, so as not to have to rearrange her robe. She turned her head to see the Persian. "What do I do, now?" she asked.

"I'll show you," he said, kneeling as he started to point at things and give directions. "See that strap, the loop there? There's one on both sides. Pull that up and put your legs through, just like that. Now, with that, the cloth you gave us, pass it over your back and put your arms over; that's your brace. It will keep you from being pulled back." And he continued until she was all over with rigging. By the time she finally looked back at him, she saw that he was already finished himself, and sandals hissed over scales as his feet slid into the leg loops along with hers. Proximity thus increased dramatically, she could smell the smoky-sweet cardamom and salty leather of his aura. "Sorry," he said casually, as she practically hugged Mār's neck to get away from him. The dragon laughed.

Her heart palpitated, as scales and ridges of bone pressed against her face. It was then that she was very sure she did not want to travel with them any longer. If flying meant being in such a manner with the both of them, then she would do better with her own two feet. Her heart stuttered again. She blinked. No, it was not her heart that was moving.

She placed her hands over the egg. "It is - " she began, voice breaking.

"What?" Rakhshan exclaimed. "Do you mean the egg?" Mār swung his head around, a flicker of interest in his eyes.

Kefira felt the cold of dread suffuse her legs, like melting ice. "Yes," she replied haltingly. Hatching – was it hatching? She wondered how valuable hatchlings were compared to eggs. Did the value depreciate? "Is it coming out?" she asked him, mouth dry.

"Maybe," the man said. "You should let me see it. Take it out, to see if it is breaking the shell."

Kefira knew that she did not want them to see the egg. It would not be very hard for them to swipe it from her. Through the linen of her bodice she could feel the hard shell, twitching against her fingers. She heard no cracks or peeps. But still – she felt it moving. "No, it wasn't anything at all, never mind," she murmured. "My skin is playing tricks on me. Why don't we fly, now? Maybe it will have started hatching when we get to the sea."

There was a flinty sort of look on the Persian's face. She knew then that he didn't believe her. She swallowed, hands tight.

The man said, "You heard her, Mār. Go ahead and take off."

Kefira blinked at him.

The Azhi Dahaki's eyes narrowed keenly. "Very well. Brace yourself, laties."

After this discourse, the last direction Kefira thought she should be going was down. But the dragon had lowered itself like a prowling cat, shoulders inclining to the ground. She clutched the shuddering egg, even as, in swift afterthought, she secured her shawl to her head with a knot. And then the brief moment of silence before the tumult was exhausted. The dragon vaulted upwards.

The ground was thrust away, even as Kefira's insides smashed downwards together. There was a loud *whooosh* as his wings beat the air, skimming the earth in a wreath of dust – a sudden cold wind pressed upon her face. A whine escaped her clenched teeth, the dragon continuing to row with his wings, every upward jolt sending blood pounding into her toes.

Rakhshan's arms were over her shoulders, grasping a portion of the rigging around Mār's neck. She felt the strain of his legs behind her own, and the hardness of his chest against her back as they went very nearly vertical. And then she didn't notice any of this, as her ears split with pain. She put her hands to them with a cry.

"That's just your ears popping, you're not dying," Rakhshan shouted.

It felt as though she was. Never had she ever moved so fast – she could hardly draw breath – the entire world was a blur of blue and green, and her momentum was at the mercy of the dragon's wingbeats. Cold nausea emanated from her astonished innards, when they finally began to recover. Mār had slowed in his ascent, and was beginning to level off. His wingbeats were not so jagged or frequent. She finally felt herself able to breathe.

"Put our backs to the sun, Mār!" Rakhshan called over the roaring air. She could see the cords in the dragon's neck flex as his low-hanging head bobbed; he banked, and Kefira's arms tightened on the straps that bound her. As of yet, her eyes refused to look down at the panorama of the world sliding around beneath them. The hills were nothing more than tossed linen, wrinkled and covered in tiny green beads, and the sight spun around sickeningly as Mār did. She jerked her eyes away, putting a hand to her mouth.

"Why are we going west?" she made herself ask.

"What?"

"Why are we going west?" she repeated, louder.

"The coast of the sea is closer to us on its southwestern stretch than the southeastern. We will get to the cities faster that way."

She didn't argue. She found that flying was considerably more comfortable with her eyes shut and head pressed against the dragon's neck. With the arm that had least entangled itself in the rigging, she touched the egg. It felt like a second heartbeat. It was still moving. An ill feeling pressed into the back of her throat.

They landed at noon, and when Kefira slid from the dragon's back, after falling and crawling back to her stiff legs, she promptly went to a bush to let herself vomit.

Often in her life she went a few days without eating, or eating very little, and having any food at all after such starving periods provoked the reflex to throw up. Of course, she grew to control the instinct most of the time, for retching always meant the loss of a meal.

But now, she could not control it. The vertigo of the landing had been too much for her.

"Are you alright?" the man called from his dragon.

She wiped her mouth. "Yes," she said slowly. "Why did we stop?"

"Because I'm *exhaustet*, of course," the dragon tossed his head melodramatically. "You must weigh a thousand talents, you portly girl."

Kefira huffed indignantly – she couldn't weigh more than *two*, soaking wet and holding a millstone. But before she could retort, Rakhshan punched the dragon from where he stood between his forelegs. "Shut up, you drooling oaf." He looked at her. "Midday meal," he explained.

"But that is so wasteful!" she cried. She never ate midday.

"You don't have to eat if you don't want to," Rakhshan said perfunctorily. He was fumbling with one of the luggage slings overhead. He grabbed a few of the bundles. She recognized one of them to be hers. "Do you mind sharing?" he asked her.

"Yes," she said. "It is mine. It will feed me when I get to the sea." And as she spoke, the man unwrapped the bundle and took out a loaf, splitting it in half. "What are you doing?" she asked, outraged. "That is mine!"

"But it was someone else's before you stole it." The man

handed her half of the loaf. He bit into the other half.

Kefira snatched it from his hand. Simmering, she said, "You oughtn't steal from the *less* fortunate, at least." She wanted to strike him, but she figured the attempt would only make his smile wider.

He wrapped up the bundle and put it back overhead before walking to sit on a rock with the rest of his meal. She followed him, fuming, and he said, "But you're not less fortunate."

Kefira stared, uncomprehending.

Rakhshan smiled, simpering. "We are *both* favored equally in heaven – both suffered to live by the graciousness of the gods," he said with pious rancor.

The girl frowned, defeated, fingernails digging into the bread in her hand. She could tell by the tone of his voice that he did not mean what he said.

She looked up from her clenched toes when his hand crossed her vision. It was holding a strip of dried meat. She stared at it. "Have this as compensation for the bread, girl."

It was beyond compensation. She grit her teeth. "I do not need your charity, rogue."

"But you're already getting it, girl." He said, looking at Mār, who had long-since fallen upon a seized hare. "And my name is Rakhshan, remember?"

"And mine is *Kefira*, not *girl*."

"Duly noted, girl. Now have this." And he tossed the meat at her.

She was not stupid enough to let it fall. It felt like gold in her thin hands. She licked her chapped lips, gazing at it, and then at him. "Is this," she asked reluctantly, "from a cloven-hoofed animal?"

His eyebrows raised and lips crooked as he said, "Oh, so you're *that* sort. Yes, it's antelope, killed and cured myself." He scratched his dark-stubbled jaw speculatively.

"Oh, she is a *Jew*, how quaint," Mār said, after swallowing his kill. "You don't see many of those. Like five-legget lambs."

Kefira turned her back on them to eat behind a rock.

She heard the dragon say, "I do not understant why you do not eat your own breat, brother. Hers must be quite stale."

And she heard Rakhshan laugh.

They flew again, afterwards. Beforehand, though, Rakhshan had asked her about the egg — it'd stopped moving since the meal — "Has the egg cracked at all? Or do you trust me enough yet to grace me with its sight?" to which she replied, "If you think that I shall ever trust you, you shall be sorely disappointed."

And the egg hadn't cracked, not even since they'd started flying again. And they flew into the sun, now; its orange light made her shut her eyes, for Mār flew with his head down, and she had nothing to cast a shadow over her.

The golden orb touched the teeth of a nearing mountain range. "Why haven't we turned north yet?" she'd shouted into the wind. She hadn't yet seen Rakhshan look at whatever map he had, and they'd been going west all day. "Do you know where we are?" she asked.

"Better than you do," Rakhshan said simply, much to her unenlightened chagrin.

She shut up. The whole day thus far had made her cross.

Time passed. Everything seemed to be going at an unbearably slow pace, despite the swift wind tousling Kefira's hair beneath her shawl. Until at once, she opened her eyes to the sight of green scales, tinged yellow with sunset. The egg. *Crack.*

She uttered a cry, and felt Rakhshan stiffen behind her. "It's the egg, isn't it?" he asked.

"No - " she tried to stave off. But her hands were at her chest, and they felt crackling.

"Please stop lying," he sighed, and there was a newfound tenseness in his voice. "Mār, did you hear that?"

"I'm moving," the dragon said with an edge, wingbeats rolling at less a languid pace.

Kefira looked around, dark eyes flitting about. The mountains were beneath them, now, and there was a valley, gilded with a lumpy spiral-shaped striation ahead. No ocean was in sight, but the dragon was beginning to descend. Her fingers were fast about the egg. "Where are we going? Why are we stopping here? The egg is fine," she said all-too-quickly to Rakhshan.

But he did not reply. When she turned to look at him, his close face was expressionless save for a firmness about the mouth. His eyes didn't meet hers.

She looked away, back to the spiral on the ground. She saw walls, and buildings – it was a city. A very large city. A flock of birds flitted over it. No – not birds, dragons, rising. She saw grey ones, and a sinewy white beast at the head. She gasped. "Rakhshan, they are going to attack us!"

"No, they're not going to attack us," he said.

"Do their riders want to speak with us, then?" She could think of no other explanation for their growing proximity.

Rakhshan didn't answer, and the illness she felt grew. "Rakhshan – will you not take me to the sea? We don't need to detour here, we have enough food," she said. The egg twitched. Another crack sounded. "Please, the egg is shaking again," she finally admitted. She could make out the green of the eyes on the white dragon's long face. The beard of its rider. "Let it not hatch in the city!"

The Persian raised his hand, cupping it around his mouth like a funnel, and shouted past her with ear-bursting strength, "We cannot wait to land, take us directly to Deioces at once!" He took in a breath before adding, "And send someone to get the rider immediately!"

The man on the white dragon shouted to another on a grey beast. One of the smaller dragons peeled away, and the rest of the asmanaba became a cloud about Mār. The Azhi Dahaki was letting himself be herded by them to a gap in the growing buildings.

"Rakhshan!" she cried. "What is the matter? Where are you taking me?" She spun on him. He ignored her, even after receiving a blow to the shoulder.

    She clenched fistfuls of his tunic. "What is going on?"

Chapter III
Bounty Forsaken

Kefira sat small against the wall of the great room, unable to disappear in the shadows of gold, cast warm by the torches. The egg quavered against her fingertips as she glared at the two men speaking with increasing heat before her. Her cheek was bleeding from where she'd bitten it, and she sucked on her gums as she listened to what she only half-believed. There was a man, as large and imposing as a warhorse, covered in red and indigo raiment, talking with Rakhshan – whom she'd just learned to be a mercenary.

"You know that Shaza'eil was still in Bagastana when you got here. I had to send out my swiftest Siyudūrai to fetch him, and still he won't be here in time for the hatching," the man she knew to be Deioces grit. His fist threatened to pull out his black silver-shot beard as he gazed exasperated at Rakhshan. "The very *least* you could have done was contact one of the others and send him to inform us of your find."

"It is not that far between that city and Hangmatana," the younger man defended. "It will do that pompous Babylonian good to be in a rush for once; I can't help it if the creature's hatching, anyway."

With her eyes Kefira shot daggers at the Persian; ever since they'd been rushed from Mār's back into this stately hall, he'd treated her as though she did not exist. The only one who was not completely ignoring her was the lord Deioces. And he was looking disdainfully down at her now. "Never mind him or the hatchling - *you* should have taken it from the spaka from the start. She could be nothing but a hindrance on the wing, and you could have gotten here with hours to spare, otherwise."

"Well, all you wanted was the Hardlā egg – and egg it still is – by the end of the fortnight. And I brought it. So you are going to keep your oath, are you not?"

"Don't test me, boy," the man growled. And then he spun on Kefira, who was still hugging her knees beside a servant. "Stand up girl, where is it?"

"I will not let you have it," she said, voice as taut as a bowstring. There was fear in her eyes as she met his gaze, and saw the expression on his stony yellow face.

Rakhshan loomed behind him, looking down upon her. "Kefira," he said, "It is worth a thousand talents of gold."

Her eyes froze on the jewelry that encrusted the fist of the lord. "What?" The word came out choked.

"Yes," he said, and there was urgency in his voice. "I will give you a sum of my bounty, just give him the egg."

She glared wrathfully up at Rakhshan. "I would not take anything from the likes of you," she snapped, clutching the egg all the tighter.

Her fiery gaze was broken when Deioces stepped in front of him, and brought a hairy arm down to jerk her to her feet. "I said stand, girl!" he snarled. "Where is it?"

"She has nothing to do with this, Lord. I will get it for you." Rakhshan's voice behind him.

But the man would not have it. He jerked her hands away from the egg himself, and she gasped as she felt her throat crush beneath his arm, as she was driven into the wall. She couldn't utter a cry as his cold hand thrust into her bodice. And then he had the egg in his fist, just as quickly withdrawing from her.

She fell to her knees, clutching her neck, trying to breathe. When the Persian moved to put a hand on her arm, she deflected him with an out-flung hand. Her breath came raw and icy and painful, eyes dripping to wet the tiled floor.

"Why did you do that? I said I'd handle it!" Rakhshan snapped above her, to the lord.

"If you worried for her safety, you shouldn't have brought her here." The other man replied. Kefira saw before her eyes the light of his rings dancing on the ground as he held up the egg. "Bind the egg, now," he ordered his men. "Break it and I'll have you hung in a trice."

Kefira felt an aching pop as her throat popped back into shape, and her wind returned. Only for a second did she remain on the ground to regain her breath before scrambling to her feet like a stunned animal. She glared at the mercenary to stave off what aid he might offer. The egg had already been handed off to armored men and servants – one was sowing leather strips around it. She bit into her knuckle, horrified.

"Now, I hope you didn't expect your pet to have an easy time of it, coming here." And Deioces was not talking to her. His arms were folded before him, as he looked at Rakhshan.

"What do you mean?" he replied. He'd just been gazing after the imprisoned egg.

"That *girl* you brought with you. Certainly you know that she, seeing what she has, cannot be allowed to go about spreading tell of this to her ilk."

"You do not mean death."

"Well, I thought that simply removing her tongue would be sufficient, but now that you mention it, death would be a much more reliable solution."

Rakhshan didn't speak, and Kefira looked up at them, unable to breathe.

"Do what you will with the girl," the mercenary finally conceded. "I came here for your coin purse." There was an iron edge to his voice. The girl stared at him, and he did not meet her eyes.

"And coin you will receive," the lord replied, looking pleased that he received no argument. He waved a hand to one of his men. "Meran, take her away to a detainment cell. Rakhshan, your reward will be waiting for you in my treasury shortly."

Kefira was led out in a daze, every footstep as insubstantial as fog. The bound egg wobbled on a red cushion in the corner of her eye. The little egg. Worth more than a hundred thousand times its weight in gold. Leaving her hands like vapor, condemning them to shackles.

She was going to die.

A rope bound her wrist to the guard walking impassively beside her. He led her down endless halls, the tile cold underfoot. The only sound to be heard was the tromping of the soldier's boots, for the sound of her tears came only when the guard's feet hit the ground, so that he could not hear her cry.

It did not seem as though it should make sense, that a girl who had once spent her days shepherding her father's flock in the northern hills should end her short life in a dark prison cell fit for a murderer.

Torchlight from the post of a distant sentinel only illuminated half of her tiny square of Sheol, and that it did poorly. She could only just make out the bucket in the corner that smelled of old excrement, and the straw scattered about in a half-hearted attempt to stave off the chill from the ground. Her hands were cold on the rusty bars before her. Her face was pressed into them, as she shut her eyes.

Upon being put into the cell, after recovering her breath and weeping for a while, she'd come to the consensus that she'd be able to fit her entire narrow body through the bars, save for her head.

She let her hands fall to tug at the corners of her shawl, pulling it closer about her face. And then she drew it up to mop up the brine around her eyes. Kefira did not like to cry; but when she could not help it, it was the fabric of the shawl that took her tears. How often she'd employed it for that purpose, in the past few years. Ever since her mother had pulled the purple scarf from the loom to bestow it upon the shoulders of her little daughter, it had been Kefira's most precious possession. And it'd become even more so, since its maker and its maker's husband had perished.

Her home had been a small village; she hadn't thought it small when she was little, with the high-ceilinged herb-smelling room where she slept with her mother and father and cooked and played, and the green slopes where dwelt the sheep, and the great stories that the story teller, the rabbi, brought to life with his great voice and great words. The grand history of their since-fallen people he told; he spoke of bold warriors and golden temples and riches and favor and milk and honey, the story of the god who shepherded a nation. No, her town hadn't seemed small then. But neither a pile of kindling seems small to the mouse that lives there, until she watches it burn.

She'd just returned from the hills after a day of watching the sheep, bearing a wounded lamb on her shoulders; it'd broken its leg. She didn't know how, though she did know that her father would know how to heal it. But when she crested the rise that overlooked the half-a-dozen houses of their settlement, she saw that nothing but ash and smoldering ruins remained.

Fire. That was all she knew. No explanation. No reason for it. It had not even been the season of fire, summer.

Five years later, here she was. From a promising young shepherd girl of integrity, and 'smiled upon by Jehovah,' everyone had said – to a street-rat and a thief, condemned to die for what she did not understand.

She would like to ask God where the time had gone. And where a lot more than that had gone. But she could not expect to hear from Him until she gave Him a goat. And there were no goats around.

Only the cacophonous reek of moldering hay, unwashed bodies and corroding metal. But she did not think she would have to endure it for long, if the lord Deioces went through with what he said.

After a time, boots thumped down the hall, pausing on occasion, with an accompanied scraping sound. Kefira opened her eyes, and craned her head to look; down the way, the silhouette of a man stood before a torch. He was carrying some things. She could make out no more.

There was the sound of breathing in the cells beside her; someone howled in the distance. She pulled back from the bars and sat against the wall, hugging her knees. The footsteps came to her, and a tall expressionless man tossed a hunk of bread to her through the grate, and bent, nudging a clay cup through with his foot.

Kefira looked hollowly up at him before he passed on, clutching the bread to her lap. When he left, she scooted forward to pick up the cup. There was water in it.

She drank the water, but did not eat the bread. She set it aside. She did not feel like eating. A fool like her did not deserve to eat anyway. There had been no Jewish law that she'd ever followed as strictly as her own personal rule: trust no one. It'd taken her a few scrapes and poor choices to learn the statute as a newly-orphaned girl, but it'd steered her truer than any other commandment since. But the one time – the one time she'd chosen to neglect the law by trusting Rakhshan – for yes, she *had* trusted him, at least more than anyone else in a long time – she was stabbed in the back. She should have left him while the poor goat was still alive. Then she would have the gift for God, and He would be pleased with her, and she could have kept the egg, too.

But she could not think of these excruciating what-ifs. She pressed her fists into her eyes and tried to quiet her spirit.

The passage of time had no face. The only proof that she was not frozen in darkness was the occasional anguished sound from a neighboring cell. These came at irregular intervals and sounded different every time, carried on the thin musty air, and so she guessed that time still passed, that the sun still moved in the sky outside. Eventually a second meal came, as additional proof. Was it midday? Or was this supper? She could not tell, and did not make to ask. Her back had seemed to melt into the cracks of the stone wall, and she was not inclined to move from where she was sitting.

The footsteps sounded again; certainly it could not be time for another meal. The echo was distant, but coming closer. Her stomach growled, as her eyes went to the abandoned chunks of bread, but she just pulled her legs all the closer. Let them give her more. It would not make a difference if she did not eat; perhaps starving would be a better death than being put up to hang on a spike. Most certainly it would be. But then a frightening thought came to her: what if that was someone coming for her now? What if it was time for her to be hung? For certainly, she could not hear the person stopping to administer rations.

She heard the mutter of conversation in the distance. Her heart wavered. Then two pairs of footsteps began moving down the hall. Oh, no. O, God. No, they could not be coming for her yet. It was too horrific to be borne; she could not die, not yet, not after striving against death for all these years.

But tears did not come to her eyes. Her gaze was fixed on the floor, completely impassive. A shadow fell over the stone. Two, and the light was blocked from her eyes. She made herself look up. A pair of men stood by her cell, red shadows in the half-light.

"Kefira." But it was a voice she recognized.

She jumped to her feet, fingers clenching into fists. She didn't know what to say, except to snarl at him. Rakhshan stepped back to let the guard next to the door; there was a jingle as the man fumbled with a ring of keys.

"What do you want?" she spat. She lunged forward, to wrap her arms through the two panels of grate that made up partition and door. The cell couldn't open. Whatever this wicked man wanted, she would not let him open the door. She wound her arms tight about the bars.

"I'm sorry about before. I hadn't anticipated the consequences." His half-expository words were clipped, short, as he glanced at the guard.

"You're *sorry*? I do not care! Leave me be, you devil!" she spat.

"I will not. You are needed elsewhere. The orders of the Satrap." He raised a hand, and upon it flashed a gilded signet ring.

"The Satrap?" she asked.

"Deioces, the Satrap of Media – that is where we are, the

province of Media," the man said, once more talking to her as though she were very stupid.

"He is - the Satrap of Media had you steal the egg?" she gasped, indignity rising within her. Certainly, the ruler of a state could not dirty his hands with such an endeavor.

"Don't waste your breath on that," he hushed her. He looked on as the jailer unlocked the door. "Come on, move your arms."

"No! I want to stay in here."

"No you don't, come on," Rakhshan said. He looked at the guard. "I'll take it from here, my good man. Thank you for your assistance."

It took no great effort for the Persian to open the door past the grip of her thin arms. When the hinges creaked and he was at the threshold, she jumped back. Her ankle bumped against the bucket, and the wall pressed into her spine. She lifted her arms to hover as fists beneath her chin. "Get out of here," she threatened. "Leave me be."

"I'm very sorry," the man repeated. His voice was less callous. "I did not know that you'd wanted the egg."

"That is because you could only see what *you* wanted," she snapped in reply. "Now leave; you've done enough to harm me."

"I'm not going to harm you," he said, and there was a hurt sort of frustration in his expression. "Stop griping. You're going to leave this place, alright?"

"I don't want to," she said. "Not with you."

He lifted a hand. In it was a bundle. "Get into something decent," he said simply, shoving the fabrics to her.

"I do not want this," she said. But even in the darkness she could feel how fine the linen was.

"Just put it on."

"I'm not going to."

Rakhshan ran a hand through his hair. "Stop acting like such a child. Throw it on over what you're wearing, and let's go."

"I am not going with you, not anywhere!" she exclaimed.

"Shh – be quiet. You'd not rather die, would you?"

"I would."

"You don't mean that."

Kefira was already pulling the loose sleeves over her stained clothing, winding the fabric over her old garb. She glared up at Rakhshan. And then she tied the belt around her waist. "I don't see why he wants me dead," she said simply. "I don't suppose you'd tell me?"

"In time. Are you ready?"

"In time? I don't intend to stay with you long enough for there to be anything *in time*."

"What I meant was – *now*'s just not a good time to be telling you things," he explained crossly. "Are you coming?"

"Where are you going?"

"*We* are going to where they took the egg."

"What? Why?"

"Because."

Kefira frowned. "I don't like you." Her fingers dug into her crossed arms as she stared at him, wishing he would explain more.

"I don't really care, at this juncture," he said, grabbing her arm and leading her out of the cell.

The Satrap had misplaced his trust in the mercenary, just as she had. The gold that flashed on his hand was a signet ring from the hand of Deioces, the Lord of Persia's imperial Media. Rakhshan used the ring liberally on any guards that questioned their presence in the bowels of the palace. Kefira watched with a newly skeptical eye as he worked his charismatic affectations on those who questioned him; he'd gotten new clothes, too, and so looked less like the vagabond that he was. As a matter of fact, he looked as though he positively belonged in the court they were skirting. She could only imagine what *she* looked like: a mangy hound with silver collar, an imposter. But she hid well behind the mercenary, and so evaded most suspicion.

Still, she was nervous. She could only imagine what this so-called rescue was leading up to. He'd mentioned the egg. But it was not as though they could get it back! If it was as valuable as he'd said, then no amount of fancy words or flourish of signet ring would convince the thousands of guards stationed about it to be off. Yet still, this feeble promise of the egg kept her from slinking off when they finally emerged into the light of day.

A broad patio lined with tall, manicured cypress trees opened up before them, stretching gradually into the rabble of a bazaar. The flat rooftops of buildings descended from sight, and looming in the sky over the city was a swathe of rock, a mountain, stretching across the valley. There was snow on it – she hardly ever saw snow on top of mountains, anywhere.

She asked the man at her side, "Where are we going?"

"Not to Mount Alvand," he said, glancing at where she was looking. "To the barracks. Shaza'eil will be landing there shortly to attend the hatching. He'll get the egg, if we don't hurry."

"Who is he?" she growled. "A Babylonian?" She did not like the idea of such a man getting her egg. She walked after Rakhshan as he started forward again.

"That he is," Rakhshan replied. "He's the son of a man with whom the Satrap has a contract, surrounding the egg. Don't know much beyond that." And then they were nearing people, entering the crowded streets of the marketplace. As they were absorbed into the throng, the man held her arm again. "Stay close."

She jerked away. "Stop touching me. I'll be fine."

"Alright, alright, just stay close."

"Do you think it's already hatched?" she asked him, scampering past a cart of all-too tempting fruit. "What about the egg – why is it so valuable?"

"One question at a time, and not so loud. Come on," the man said, keeping his eyes before them. "No, it can't have hatched, the infernal man had it bound," he explained resentfully. And then he looked at her. "You've heard of the Hardlā dragon, have you not?"

She shook her head.

"Oh, that's odd. Well, it is a breed of your nation, so you should know. It's rather valuable – there are not many of its kind, since Israel fell."

"And that's the only reason it's valuable?"

"No, but I won't explain here."

She followed him closely out of the congested streets, feeling children buffet her legs; servants of the wealthy went hither and thither from booth to booth, getting their morning's allotment of food. Of course – talking openly about this *Hardlā* where others could hear would not be wise. She wondered hungrily what the significance of the tiny egg was. Could it breathe fire? The Persians already had a flame-tongued Thu'ban, and so did the Babylonians, with their beastly Khumbaba. And certainly no regal breed of Israel's would have the grisly acid-drool of the Azhi Dahaki. What could come so special from such a minuscule egg? As the crowd around them grew thinner and they became more solitary, she wanted to press him further on the matter. But he was picking up speed as the street curved downhill and split into two; he took the left side, which doubled back in the direction they'd come, to a lower tier of the city. She followed, watching as the buildings that surrounded them grew fewer and fewer. The street was broadening, the shops and houses giving way to a large clearing, where resided a vast building.

"Here we are," Rakhshan said with a triumphant smile.

Kefira's eyes flittered about to capture the scene before her. It was a rectangular structure, the barracks, or rather, a whole compilation of rectangular structures; pillars throughout stretched up and down like the legs on a centipede. The compound appeared to be set apart from the surrounding city, though its organized spread had no walls. It was not the uniformity and formal appearance, in all its lofty height, that was striking to her, however. What stopped her in her tracks was the sprawl of dragons that surrounded the place like straw around eggs in a nest.

"How do we get in?" she breathed. Her hesitation had pulled Rakhshan up short. The barracks and its dragons were still a great long distance away, but the great glittering beasts were frightening even from there.

"The same way we left the Satrap's," the man said, raising his ringed hand. "Come along, the beasts are quite tame. And asleep," he added with no small amount of amusement, upon noticing her fear. She reluctantly followed him as he continued on. "We must make haste; I think I see the Barid who'd fetched the Babylonian."

The girl had to walk almost at a jog to keep up with his long strides. Her eyes roved over the scaly mounds of dragon to look for a messenger beast – one of the smaller grey ones, it would be, she guessed; that was what Siyudūrai looked like, if she remembered correctly. And certainly there was one, which had only just collapsed into an exhausted heap aside a greater dragon, flanks heaving. As she and the mercenary drew closer, she could make out white foam on its jowls.

Kefira shrank as close as she could to Rakhshan without touching him. Being around Mār was one thing, but to be amongst all these dragons, many of which were even greater in size, was almost wholly unbearable. Her head swam – and her mind went to the bread she'd left in her prison cell. Perhaps she would faint.

But no – she righted herself, blinking feverishly while stealing glances at the dragons, which were largely asleep, as she passed. There were dragons the color of weathered rock, and dragons the color of a storm cloud, and one that was as pure white as the full moon. She recognized it from her previous flight – the one that had herded them down to the Satrap's residence. It was a lot more graceful looking than Mār, slender and long-snouted; it was almost pretty. Its yellow-green eyes opened astutely upon her passing. She jerked her gaze away and hurried after Rakhshan.

The man looked back at her, with half a mocking smile on his face. "If you think it would dissuade any dragons from eating you, you may feel free hold my arm."

"I will do no such thing," she looked away dourly.

"Very well." And he walked on at a higher pace, for now his dragon was in sight. Her head felt as though it was full of tumbling air, as hunger wracked her again, but she kept pace.

"Shaza'eil's gotten here, right, Mār?" he asked his dragon upon arrival.

The Azhi Dahaki raised his head, looking first at Rakhshan, and then at Kefira. He muttered, looking narrowly at his rider, "I thought you't gotten rit of her."

"Sorry to disappoint you," Kefira growled at the dragon.

Rakhshan shook his head. "Mār."

"Yes, yes, he came," the green beast answered, looking testily at Kefira, as spittle dripped sullenly from his maw.

"We're going to go in after him, alright? Stay alert for us," Rakhshan said.

"What do you intent to do? *Kill* him?"

"Of course not, keep your voice down," the Persian said. "Just be ready to fly, if we need to leave."

Kefira looked at Rakhshan, taken aback. What *did* he intend? Did he truly have a plan for recovering the egg? She chewed on her lip doubtfully.

"I'll be ready. Did you make your meeting, anyway?" the dragon asked him.

"There were higher priorities."

Mār seemed to balk, staring at Rakhshan, before snorting disgustedly. She saw an angry sort of incredulity in his emerald eyes. "Oh, you *are* a fool."

Rakhshan just patted him on the foreleg before he turned away.

Kefira looked back at the dragon, uncertain of what had passed between the two, as she followed the Rider. When she returned her gaze ahead, the building loomed even closer, many dark slots of windows gazing down at them; she saw statue-still sentries standing at many, robes rustling in the wind. But, to her surprise, she was not filled with arrow shafts upon breaching the threshold after

Rakhshan. The soldiers that guarded entry to the hall let the ring-bearing Persian and his companion pass.

Rakhshan smiled at her when they were beyond them, and lengthened his stride: a procession could be made out in the hall before them. As they rounded corners, she could see the long, curly hair of two Babylonian guards and a dignitary, amidst a dispatch of Persian soldiers, and hear their sandaled footsteps on the tile.

"What are we going to do when we get there?" she whispered to Rakhshan.

"Hope Deioces hasn't discovered my fraudulence any time soon. When we get to the egg, we'll tell Shaza'eil we're his representatives to oversee the hatching."

"What if they find out you're lying?"

"I am not. The Satrap sent me because he wanted to make sure I wasn't breaking you out of prison during the hatching."

"Well, he failed if that was his goal." Kefira frowned. "Why did he not do anything about your time before the hatching?"

"I was supposed to be elsewhere, doing something much more desirable than freeing you." He smiled bitterly.

"Oh." Kefira did not comprehend.

They went up a flight of stairs, seeing as they reached the second floor that the procession had entered a broad-doored room. Four of the guards peeled away to stand outside and seal the entrance. Kefira shrank beside Rakhshan as they approached. They casually brandished the silver ends of their spears.

Rakhshan gestured a greeting to them, and showed them the signet ring. "We were sent by the Satrap to observe the hatching."

Kefira watched with shallow breath as the sentries' eyes slid from the ring, to the man, to her. She averted her eyes, to stare at Rakhshan's ring, feeling the blood in her veins slacken with nausea.

The spears before them lifted, however, and the door was pushed open. Kefira blinked, even as Rakhshan said to her with the tone of a well-bred patron, "Now, rein in your tongue. You ought not speak here." She obeyed, meekly settling behind him when he entered the room and bowed; everyone was surrounding the room's sole furnishing: a pedestal which bore on a cushion the leather-bound shape of the egg.

Kefira backed up to the wall, hoping to be hidden despite the flickering glow of torches dancing on the windowless span. None of the men were paying attention to her, the straw-hewn doll in the corner, but certainly they would notice the disarray of her hair and dark complexion and smell if she came too close, despite the fine array she'd thrown on. So badly, though, she wanted to step past Rakhshan, to look at the egg, to grab it and run, but she knew doing so would be futile. She looked at the back of the head of the mercenary, wondering what he was up to. He did nothing now, he was listening to the men speaking, and seemed to have no great plan for retrieving the egg.

Kefira stifled an impatient huff, eyes moving to the tall man whom she guessed intended to have her egg. He was not in heavy leather scale-mail like his guards, though light armor showed beneath the scarlet, gold, and purple of his robes. He had an angular face, with a sharp nose, and swathing his chin was a coiffed beard curled in tiny corkscrews of the Babylonian fashion. He looked as refined as a cut gemstone, and she would call him handsome, if not for his flat, dark eyes that reminded her of a jackal.

There was a dagger in his hand, and she saw a large ruby glinting in its gilded hilt. She swallowed, looking at Rakhshan, who paid no attention to her. What was the knife for?

Her question was answered when the man turned to the egg.

Rakhshan's hand was on her arm before she could jump. She swallowed a gasp, watching as the blade slid beneath the constricting straps over the egg – only to pull up and sever them.

She let out a quiet breath of relief, stepping back. But then she moved forward just as quickly, to look past a burly man in armor – for the egg had crumbled. A stain spread on the cushion, where a small shape uncurled amidst the fragments of shell. The whole room, even the stoic sentries, seemed to forget to breathe.

But it was not even the size of a falcon. Kefira squinted, incredulous; only a wispy lizard it appeared to be, though its scales glittered like gold and topaz. Its waist was thinner than the tail of a cat, tiny talons no greater than the ends of her fingers. It had a long, serpentine neck, with which it slowly hoisted its head to peer around the room. She saw the tiniest of teeth glimmer in torchlight as it opened its maw to yawn.

"Hardlā." The silence was broken as the man, Shaza'eil, addressed the creature. Kefira's eyes were jerked from the dragonling to look at him. The clipped voice sounded again, only in a tongue that she did not understand. Kefira felt her heart gradually begin to pound, unpleasant heat beneath her arms. She looked at Rakhshan. His eyes were averted from hers. She had half a mind to shake him, to get him to look at her and tell her what was going on, what he planned, but her breath was frozen.

Her eyes returned to the scene before her. The Babylonian queried once more, "Hardlā," more insistently this time, and Kefira realized that he was trying to coax the creature to converse. In answer, the dragonling looked at him and squawked.

At first the man looked bewildered, but then his narrow eyebrows converged. He spoke again in the foreign language, and the Hardlā just stared, looking at him for a little while before sweeping its face across the room. Kefira swallowed as its large yellow eyes came to rest upon her. It chirruped.

Shaza'eil snapped his fingers, promptly retrieving the creature's attention. His voice was a little higher as he addressed it. But the dragon did not return any words.

"It is not speaking," Rakhshan said plainly. She could see he was surprised.

Kefira didn't know that it was not common for dragons not to be able to speak straight out of the shell. She looked between him and the dragon, wondering, dreading – was it a runt of sorts? They did not kill runt dragons, did they? They would not do that to a thing so rare.

She was chewing on her fingernails, listening with mute dismay as Shaza'eil spoke more feverishly this time, stepping closer to the small dragon, snapping his fingers once more – it'd been looking at her again. "Get that girl out of here," he ordered. "She has no reason to attend this."

Kefira felt her heart jump to her throat, as quite suddenly the room's attention had been thrust upon her. She stepped closer to Rakhshan, desperate to shrink away. The Persian raised his hand, gold ring gleaming, and said, "Forgive me sir, but she is with me, Deioces's representative."

"I know who you are; what is she?"

Her thumb tasted bad, but her teeth dug into it anyway, as she looked between Rakhshan and the emissary. For once, the mercenary seemed to struggle a bit before saying, "My wife."

If she had the strength, her thumb would have come off upon that statement. She gritted her teeth, staring at him incredulously, but caught herself before snapping a denial.

A look of regal contempt fell upon both husband and wife as Shaza'eil digested this lie. He raised an eyebrow. "How quaint," he said simply, acid in his tone. "I pity the man whose wife will not stay at home to attend to his children and his supper." He looked her over with an un-impressed, scornful eye and Kefira chewed her tongue to keep from retorting.

"I will be sure to beat her severely when we return to my home; for you, my lord," Rakhshan said with utmost sincerity. The girl looked at him, unsure if he was serious. Then she hung her head to hide the smile that crept upon her face, knowing that laughter would not be appropriate.

"Irony does not become you, mercenary," Shaza'eil dismissed him distastefully.

All their attention was diverted as the creature's wings snapped open, tiny sails of wine and orange, the color of sunset. One of the guards flinched as it leapt like a feline from its perch. The circle of people quickly rearranged itself to surround the delicate creature as it padded about on uncertain, dainty feet, meandering. Its head craned on its neck to survey those present; Shaza'eil seemed disturbed past words that its gaze hardly lingered upon himself.

Its star-like eyes shone upon Kefira, where it finally rested, limber tail threshing over the floor. She looked down at it, not quite believing that it was truly looking at her. Her hands pressed to her lips to suppress a sound of wonderment. She looked at Rakhshan, who had the barest hint of a smile on his face as he watched the Hardlā.

She took an astonished step back as the flutter of wings rapped the air before her, and she felt a tug upon her garments. Dumbstruck, she brought a hand to feel the warm, scaly body of the dragon striving to reach her shoulder.

"What is it doing?"

Kefira straightened as it wound around her neck like a garland, disappearing into her hair. Wonder mingled with fear as she stared at Rakhshan. "What do I do?" she couldn't help but ask aloud, terrified at the shade of red the emissary's face was turning.

"Remove it, get it off," Shaza'eil demanded. "You have no business touching it."

"I did not mean to - " she said, sweat gleaming on her palm as she reached for the dragonling. And then she stopped, for it'd wound all the tighter about her.

"Of course you did not, now hand it over."

Rakhshan stepped to her side now, and said, "Let me help." But Kefira clenched her shawl over her head as he made to remove it, taking a step back. She felt the dragon's tiny claws cold on her skin, heard the creature trill. "Kefira," Rakhshan said, sighing with exasperation.

"I don't want anyone to hurt it," she found herself saying, looking warily at all of them. The guards had all at once become more attentive, the two Babylonians eyeing their charge expectantly.

Shaza'eil himself glared at her and the dragonling icily, and his white teeth shone from a grimace. "It cannot speak," he said, as though to himself. "A curse. Mercenary," he snapped at Rakhshan. "Are there priests of Tiamat in this city?"

"I imagine there is a small number."

"They ought to have been summoned to pray over the egg; why were they not present?"

Rakhshan blinked, and shrugged. "I do not arrange the affairs of hatchings. I believe you should have thought of your goddess earlier, before you cut the bindings."

A furious expression flashed over the Babylonian's face before Rakhshan added, "But why not summon them now, their prayers may ameliorate the spirits that cursed the dragon. Or if perhaps there is a shrine nearby, we may go there."

Kefira felt the motion of the dragon as it scrabbled around and around her neck, the scales of its belly grazing her skin. She put up a hand to settle it as she listened nauseously to the discussion. At her touch, the dragon stopped. But that was only a brief reprieve, for then it was moving again, and she felt it slither down her back, inside her robes. Her lips pressed together, and she stifled a sound of astonishment. She wanted to feel around for it, to stop it from roving, but did not allow herself to move.

Instead, her hands went to her neck, and she felt around in her hair, and looked at Rakhshan with a gasp. "It is no longer here," she said. She cast about, feigning to search the ground.

The man started, looking at her neck. "By the gods, you did not lose it, did you?"

The room fell silent for a moment, and Kefira's head swam, before Shaza'eil cried out a curse. "Where is it!" And everyone looked towards the door, which of course was not open, and then to the light of the surrounding torches, to detect the tiny truant. Words of *where could it have gotten off to?* and reprimand for her foolishness sprang up like wildfire, and the girl grew ice cold. Rakhshan joined in the search; she watched him as he took a torch from the wall and started combing the floor and corners with the other men. She hoped that this was what he'd wanted.

The girl shivered as the creature squirmed throughout her clothing, talons cold against her skin – she prayed that its motion could not be seen. She tried to stand as still as possible – no use in pretending to look around for it. But she almost doubled over as it suddenly slithered up her belly, and squirmed beneath her undergarment, in the alcove of her chest. She stifled a gasp, and found herself leaning against the wall. It took all her willpower not to reach down her collar and remove it then and there. Instead she just stood, rather paralyzed, hoping that no one noticed her distress.

"It is small enough to have gotten beneath the door, is it not?" She heard Rakhshan say.

"We must widen the search – it cannot be let loose!" Shaza'eil fumed. He dispatched all but two of the Persian guards: "Go, and inform the men outside. You two, stay and search in here."

Kefira let herself breathe a little as Rakhshan came up beside her; his eyes met hers briefly, and emphatically she blinked – *I hope you know what's going on.* Despite her lightheadedness, she was almost relaxing, now, for she was no longer under the suspicious eye of the Babylonian. The rabble of the search was spreading; the tall double doors were open, spilling white light into the room. She stepped next to Rakhshan, trying to insist all but verbally that they make their exit.

And he had the same mind. They were moving forward, the mercenary looking rather like he intended to join the spreading of the search outside, and she was moving right behind him. She held her chin with a hand, to discreetly feel with her wrist the dormant creature over heart. It was still there, and no longer moved. She chewed her lip.

"Do not leave, yet," a voice commanded from behind, when her feet felt the warm stone of the threshold. She turned around, as did Rakhshan, almost confrontationally. She could see the impatience pent up in his back.

It was Shaza'eil. He strode forward, past his guards, and he was looking at her. "The creature just *jumped* from your shoulders, is that it?" he asked.

Kefira felt her insides shiver under his scrutiny. "Yes, sir. Or – I do not know rightly what happened, it was just not there," she tried.

Rakhshan stepped forward. "You do not mean to accuse my wife of stealing, do you?" he asked reproachfully. "She is simple," he gestured to her, "and incapable of such insolence. I assure you she would not have been let to come, if I knew her to be wicked."

"You are one to talk, mercenary," Shaza'eil scoffed. He looked them both over and then looked to the guard on his right. "Search him."

Kefira saw Rakhshan's lips flatten as he said, "I have nothing to hide." He cast a fleeting glance at her, and stood silently as the man approached.

Kefira herself looked in horror upon the guard as he patted his hands over Rakhshan's body – certainly she would not be dealt with so! She felt herself take a step back into the hallway.

"Not so fast, girl," Shaza'eil said, mouth twisted in an imperial scowl. "Swiftly, find a maidservant," he ordered his other man.

Kefira didn't move, except to lean against the railing along the hall, eyes wide. The open air of the courtyard behind her felt all too inviting. They were going to find out. Ought she jump down, and see if she could run? She looked over her shoulder, to the soldiers drilling on the patio, to the hall below that led to the dragon square. Her eyes went to Rakhshan, who was being felt between the legs, and looked away.

"You are looking very nervous, girl," Shaza'eil said. "If all is as your husband says, then you have nothing to worry about."

Her mouth and lips were dry. She did not respond. Almost she wished to pull the dragonling out and give it to the man, and end the trouble – then her sentence of thievery might be waived. But now – they would most certainly discover the creature on her.

A maidservant from the kitchens came up the stairs, goaded to a jog by the guard that'd retrieved her.

"My lord," she said to the Babylonian.

"Search her person, woman," he said. "Conceal nothing you find."

Kefira swallowed, trying not to flinch away at the obedient woman's approach. She was older than her, but not by much, and had large eyes that told Kefira that she was just as flustered as she.

"There is nothing on him," the guard who'd searched Rakhshan concluded.

"I thank you for noticing," the mercenary said bitterly, and his eyes went to Kefira; there was tension in them. His hand was on the railing, the tendons of his fingers taut; she wondered if he had a mind to jump down. He could abort this ruse as soon as he liked, and leave her to her troubles.

He certainly would.

Like a soul condemned, she returned her eyes to the woman who knelt now before her. Her hands went up past the hair of her ankles, and all of Kefira's muscles became as taut as harp strings. She stared down at the floor past the woman, unable to look at her jury, or her accomplice. She shut her eyes as the maid with her hands tentatively searched her lower regions, Kefira's skirts draped over her elbows. Her mind reeled, mortified that these men had to be watching. It was all she could do not to kick the woman away; she'd never been so touched in her life.

The woman arranged the hem of Kefira's robes back into order, and straightened, glancing wordlessly at her face before meekly patting her hips, waist, stomach, upward.

Kefira felt blood surge sickeningly through her head as the search ascended, and her elbows pressed against the railing to keep herself upright. She was going to be found out. In a matter of moments. Dear God, she was going to be found out.

Her underarms were felt, and the maid's hands converged inward over her chest, where the dragon resided. Kefira shut her eyes, every nerve in her body frozen. The hands moved up; shoulders, neck, hair.

"She has nothing but her clothes, my lord," the woman said, stepping away.

The Babylonian blinked, and she could see well-hidden shock in his eyes. "She has nothing?" he repeated. "There were no lumps in the clothing? No foreign body?"

"No, my lord."

"Search her again."

She did, and came to the same conclusion.

"May we leave, now?" Rakhshan asked. "I have business to attend elsewhere."

Kefira, speechlessly watching the dismissed maidservant leave, stepped to the mercenary's side. Her head pounded; she looked at no one, even as Shaza'eil growled, "Go, then." He turned away with a vicious grin. "Word has already been sent, however; no one will enter or leave the city until the Hardlā is found."

"I will enforce the word myself, worthy Shaza'eil."

And, as though in a trance, Kefira finally followed the mercenary from the barracks.

"You *do* have it, yes?" the man asked, voice low, as they emerged into the dragon yard.

Kefira brushed her knuckles over the place the dragon rested. "I do," she said quietly. "Though it does not stand to reason that I should."

Rakhshan smiled broadly, like one emerging from a den of lions. "Come, let's return to Mār."

"When I lookt over at the criminals being hung in the square down yonter, ant dit not see you there, I guesst you't not been caught," the dragon said upon their arrival. In a lower ring of the city, tall stakes could be seen, erected with the bodies of dead men on their summits. Kefira looked away as a raven descended upon one. "You have the egg, yes? I smell it. It has hatcht," he said sharply. "I cannot believe you got it."

"I am full of miracles, brother," Rakhshan said smugly.

"You are full of something," the dragon concluded. He looked down at Kefira, who had long-since collapsed to her knees, reveling silently in what had just occurred. Her head still hurt, and her stomach was aflame. "Let it out, where do you have it?" he asked.

"Where *did* you hide it?" Rakhshan asked her.

"It hid itself," she said simply, disinclined to reveal its location.

"Oh, a clever little one," Mār grinned bitterly. "Out with you, hatchling."

"No, not here, Mār. We ought to leave soon, in any case."

"We? Leave? But we cannot leave the city," Kefira looked up; the return of the word *'we'* did not please her. "I would rather part company with you here, if that is permissible," she said sourly, getting to her feet.

"Oh, you think it is *that* way," the Azhi Dahaki grinned bitterly. "How atorable."

"What do you mean?" she turned on him. "Mayn't I go? Our business together is done, I think. You've quite repaid me for your *betrayal*," she said to Rakhshan.

"No, it is *you* who are indebtet now, little girl," the green dragon grinned. "Do you know where Rakhshan dit *not* get to go when he went to save your skin?"

"Shut up, Mār," the Persian said, eyes flinty. "Kefira, you move to the far side of Mār, sit under his wing. The less people see you the better."

Kefira took a tentative step towards the dragon, looking at Rakhshan warily. "Are you going somewhere?"

"I'm going to the bazaar; we need food."

We. Kefira blinked. "Alright," she said slowly.

"Rakhshan," Mār said. "Mehrnaz is here, too, and Arsham. I spoke with them when you were gone."

Kefira saw sparks alight in the man's eyes, and he cast about. His gaze came to rest upon a great yellow shape surrounded by a half a dozen sleeping beasts. It took Kefira a minute to realize that what she saw was a colossal dragon, not a mountain of gold coins. She stared.

"I will go to speak with them, too," Rakhshan said, and there was eagerness in his stride as he set off.

"Be back swiftly."

Kefira watched him depart with no small amount of misgivings, as she put her hands over the tiny hidden dragon. It was not moving, except for the expansion of its chest; she sighed, incredulous that the maidservant had missed it; Kefira was not in the least buxom, there was no alcove of flesh where the dragonling could be concealed. How had the woman missed it? She watched from behind Mār's foreleg – the dragon was quite content not to speak – as dispatches of guards went discreetly from barracks to barracks. She could very well guess what they were doing.

"Why is no one ringing an alarm, or sounding a horn, if the loss of the dragon is so important?" she asked the Azhi Dahaki.

"No one is allowt to know that this important dragon is here."

"Why is that?"

"The Satrap's dealings with Babylon concerning its export," he said shortly, "that is not quite lawful, given the Hartlā's importance. If the King or any other important sort of person knew that so *precious* a beast was being dealt away to a rival empire, merely to fatten one man's pocket, there woult be bloot spillt."

Kefira touched the sleeping hatchling. "Why is it so very important?"

"I'm sure you'll figure that out in time," the dragon answered with an exasperated sigh.

"Tell me why," she pleaded. There was no reason for him to be so discreet.

"I'll let Rakhshan do that, if he wants." The dragon did not relent. He lifted his head, to peer away, and Kefira guessed that he looked after the way his rider had taken; she couldn't look past his bulk. She wondered if the man would take very long talking with this *Mehrnaz* and *Arsham*. She wished he would hurry and get their provisions, that they could move on. To where, she did not know. She wondered what they intended.

She looked up at the reticent Mār, who'd lowered his head to the earth in repose. She ought to leave now, it occurred to her. There was no time more opportune than this; there was no reason to stay with these unlawful people. With half a mind, she stood, yet looking at the dragon. He did not seem to notice or care that she'd gotten up. She took a step back, feeling a smile creep up on her lips.

And then Mār raised his head, alert, craning it larboard to look at what she could not see. She stood still, and then padded around to see what had aroused him.

She heard Rakhshan's voice before she could see him: "Deioces knows, Mār. Quickly, put us up."

"What?" Mār hissed, frills flattening.

"Hurry," Rakhshan snapped quietly. "Kefira, come on."

The girl didn't move, taken aback.

"Come on, there are guards waiting for us to leave the dragon yard, we must hurry."

"But – we cannot fly," Kefira stammered, taking a step back.

Mār turned to her, having already put his rider on his back, looking down at her narrowly. "You think that the law daunts me, girl?" Before she could make her escape, he picked her up and the ground disappeared underfoot; once more she was atop his shoulders. She looked down in desolation. She could not jump.

Rakhshan pulled her down to sit. "Hurry up and bind yourself," he urged, and dumbly she did so. Once more, she was sitting between a rogue and a dragon.

"Do not let them fly!"

She heard a voice, many voices, now; they were noticed. Dragons were rousing, men were running. When she turned her head to look, the sight was jerked away, and the Azhi Dahaki, without even waiting for Rakhshan's cry of, "Fly, Mār!" was going skyward.

Chapter IV
Dragon of Israel

Pursuit was lost by nothing short of a miracle. The only sound besides dragon wings whistling past high above was the warble of a nearby bird, oblivious to the mossy statue that Mār had become. Kefira crouched still with Rakhshan beneath the lowered bulk of the dragon, none of them daring to breathe, or move, or blink. Past the Azhi Dahaki's lowered wings, Kefira saw large shadows sweep. Her hands trembled, holding the tiny hatchling to her chest. A dragon cried out overhead.

But their tent, Mār, did not hold still for eternity. The sun continued in its journey across the sky, and sounds of the hunt diminished. Kefira saw the dragon's wings droop, his tail lower, his belly heave a sigh. She released the hold her teeth had upon her finger when his head lowered to see them beneath his chest, and he said to Rakhshan, "They have gone on to the next valley."

Kefira dug her palms into her eyes, relief flooding her. The mercenary asked, "What was their number?"

"Greater than when we left Hangmatana at first. There were eight," the dragon said uneasily. "They probably know what you two *did*."

"Certainly they do not," the girl protested, voice higher in pitch than she was proud of. "They cannot know, they did not see us take him."

"Who flees but the guilty, girl?" Mār replied, snorting.

"I never returned this, either, and that airs rather on the side of capital offense," Rakhshan muttered in understatement, twisting the Satrap's ring on his finger. "Though I doubt the lord gives a fig for this, compared to the heaps of gold he lost from misplacing his dragon."

"Oh, to the wint with that little devil," Mār rasped, lowering his head, as the exertion of his flight caught up with him. Kefira could see white froth in the corners of his already dripping maw as he panted. They'd flown straight from the city, past the ridges that bordered the basin, to dive into woodlands on the other side for the few precious seconds they could not be seen by their pursuers. Skinny, silver boughs of acacia stretched like a canopy high above them, a number of them broken by Mār's hasty descent. The dragon ousted her from beneath him with a talon and said, "Now where is it, this object of all my pains? We dit not lose him in our little flight, dit we?"

Kefira said, "No," but was reticent to coax the creature from where it resided against her chest. But despite her better judgment, she turned around and pulled forth the nape of her bosom, to see the little creature curled up inside. It appeared as wine-soaked bronze, squinting into the sunlight with its yellow eyes. "Hello, little one. Would you like to come out now?" she asked.

It regarded her quietly for a moment, and she heard Rakhshan behind her ask, "How does it fare?"

Kefira watched as the creature climbed languidly from the confines of her clothing, to sit upon her shoulder and look back at her companions, burgundy-streaked wings shuffling against its back. "Goodly, I think," she replied quietly. "Hello," she found herself repeating, as the creature looked at her.

"I coult kill it with a *sneeze*," Mār scoffed.

"Be quiet," Kefira snapped, spinning on her heel to face them, holding a protective hand over her little hatchling.

"They certainly were not lying about its size," Rakhshan quipped to his dragon.

"Yet I dit not think it woult be *this* small at first."

"Stop talking about him like he's not here," Kefira said defensively. But she stopped glaring at them quickly, for the dragonling leapt atop her hand, and wrapped itself around it like a bracelet, claws resting on her palm, neck thrust between her fingers. She laughed.

"It may be mute, Mār," Rakhshan intoned a little quieter.

"Truly?"

"It has not spoken yet."

Then the greater dragon chuckled. "It woult be most ironic if so renownt a beast was an invalit."

Kefira clutched the hatchling to her chest. "You ought not say such things! He is perfectly sound." And as she said this, the hatchling in question thrust its mouth over her little finger. She stifled a sound of surprise.

"That perfectly sount little creature seems to have a mint to eat his new master," Mār scoffed.

"May I see it, Kefira?" Rakhshan asked, approaching.

"How come?" the girl replied, as she removed her fingertip from the creature's maw. She found herself looking at the man sidelong, cagey once more.

"I want to tell its gender."

Kefira looked at the hatchling winding around her wrist. "Oh," she said, "very well." She was a little curious, too. "How do you tell?"

Rakhshan took the dragonling in his hand, palm over its shoulders, gripping around its forelegs and the base of its neck. The little creature seemed to go limp – though gave them an earful of squawking – as the man then flipped it belly-up in his hands, splaying its legs upwards.

"Be careful!" the girl protested.

"I'm not hurting it. I have done this before," said Rakhshan, as he looked at the underside of the dragonling.

She made herself relax a little, and followed his eyes. She saw no distinguishing parts on its loins. In fact, she saw nothing at all, really. There were no orifices to be made out whatsoever of the Hardlā's nether region, only folds of leathery skin and smooth scales. She blinked, breath halting for a moment – perhaps it *was* an invalid. Even hounds had outlets and various organs there, but with this dragon she only saw the flat planes of the underbelly scales going in a row down its stomach. "How does one tell?" she asked hesitantly. "I see nothing."

Rakhshan did not seem to hear her. "Our Hardlā is a little boy," he said simply, smiling at Mār and then to her, as he flipped the outraged dragonling back on its right side.

"What? He is? How do you know?" she repeated, jumping. "You are jesting, there was nothing there. He is not a neuter, is he?" Certainly, Rakhshan was just telling her these things to make her believe that there was nothing wrong with it.

The dragonling squealed again as Rakhshan flipped him on his back once more. "He's *not* a neuter," the man sighed at her. "Stop your fretting. See this?" He pointed to one of the broad scales along the dragonling's belly, the back-most of the scales between his hindlegs. "That is his vent; if he were female, it would be wider. And see the inside of his thighs." Kefira looked as the man straightened out one of her dragon's legs, indicating a nigh-unperceivable slit on the inside of his ankle; inside it appeared as though therein resided bone, or even a claw. There was one on both sides. "He has spurs. Only male dragons have those. Are you satisfied?" he asked her, eyebrows raising emphatically.

"Uh, yes," she said, rather overwhelmed by his knowledge.

"Oh, joy," the man replied, releasing his hold on the hatchling, whence it promptly flipped onto its feet and leapt to Kefira's shoulder with an indignant hiss.

"Heavens above," Mār was laughing bitterly. "If the Satrap ant that Babylonian man fint out that they let a *male* Hartlā slip through their fingers — I hope we may get out of the satrapy soon." And then, as though by afterthought, he cast a glance at the evening sky.

Rakhshan snorted. "Leaving, yes, that is a wise notion." He straightened, casting about their surroundings, peering around at the ridges that made up their valley through the tall trees. "But firstly, the hatchling needs to eat. Mār cannot go without being seen, and soon it will be too dark for me to hunt anything."

As he thought aloud, the Azhi Dahaki said, "I saw a pont nearby, when we flew in. You Jews can eat fish, yes?" he asked Kefira wryly.

"Certainly," Kefira scoffed. "'Any creature of the water that has fins and scales, those you may eat, be it of the sea or of rivers,'" she quoted pompously.

"Oh, you will be a cruel mistress to him," Mār sighed, "I can see it now, you *flogging* the poor beast whenever he sticks his snout in a hole after a rabbit. What a torturt soul he will be, *never* to have the taste of pig."

"Shut up, you great oaf," Rakhshan swatted his dragon, and shot the riled Kefira a look that told her engaging in warfare with the dragon was not worth it. "Which way was the pond?" he asked Mār.

"Down there a ways," the dragon indicated with the point of his muzzle.

"Very good, stay here while we fish. We'll be back shortly," Rakhshan said. "Keep an eye out for any search parties."

Kefira balked. "I can fish on my own, you know, I'm not stupid." The dragonling chirped on her shoulder.

"I didn't say you were stupid," Rakhshan said, and she saw him rummage through his things and pull a knife from a sheath. "But I doubt you'd be so skinny if you could actually *catch* anything."

But even the mighty hunter Rakhshan had a hard time pegging any fish; the pond was not very large, and its water murky, so its inhabitants were small and quick and hard to see; if it was not for the evening bugs dancing upon the water's surface to draw the hungry fish up, they'd not have seen any at all. Within minutes the Persian had fashioned a makeshift spear – a straight branch he'd found and sharpened. Kefira watched him work, disinclined to help him after his arrogant words. He'd taken off his sandals and rolled up his pants to his knees, and stood still in the water for a while, standing still except to swat bugs away on occasion. It would have all been very boring, if her dragon was not roving about her and the landscape, making a spectacle of himself as he discovered the height of trees, and the motion of pebbles, and her toes. He nibbled on the latter – and when dissuaded by a startled yelp from her, went about nosing rocks. For a moment she watched him struggle to flip over a rock the size of a pomegranate, only to look away abruptly as she heard a splash and a string of curses from Rakhshan.

"I thought you would be better at that, the way you talked," she commented sardonically at the vexed man, as he missed another fish.

"Oh, be quiet," the Persian grit through his teeth, fixing his eyes on the water again.

Kefira smiled, glad to rankle him now, as she returned to watching her dragon. He'd flipped over the rock now, after long last. Then she jumped to her feet, crying out in horror. The hatchling looked up at her with large eyes, crouching in fright over the earthworm he was eating.

"What is the matter?" she heard Rakhshan say.

"No, you mustn't do that!" she protested, kneeling before her startled dragon. "No, you must not eat vermin!" She picked up the twitching remains of the unclean thing and tossed it away into the water. The hatchling looked after it, and then turned his little face to her, eyes still wide. "I am sorry," she said, quieter now. "Very sorry, I did not mean to scare you. It is alright. It is just that worms are unhealthy."

He stared up at her. And then rolled the rock back over in its place. Kefira pressed her lips together sheepishly, afraid she had scared him. "Worry not, that man over there is going to catch you something delicious to eat. You will not be hungry for long." She stroked a finger along his back, and his head craned downwards; she pouted, still unnerved that he'd taken so vulgar a course of action.

Then there was a wet sort of choking sound, and Kefira, in a panic, lifted his head to face her. Before she could ask if he was alright, she noticed a slime of spit up on the ground at his feet. "You spit it up? Did it make you sick?" He just blinked up at her, two pairs of eyelids flicking over his topaz eyes.

She stared at him for a moment, uncomprehending, and she

heard Rakhshan behind her say, "I caught one. I told you I would," rather huffily.

"Only one?" she quipped with a smile.

He handed her the fish.

"Thank you." She turned to her dragonling. "Here, this will be good for you." The fish was thin and not even the length of her hand, roughly the size of the dragonling's whole torso. He eyed the twitching thing appreciatively – of course it was more appetizing than a worm, even as it gaped up at him.

Yet the hatchling did not take a move towards it. "Will he not eat the fish whole?" she asked.

As though by way of answer, the hatchling promptly took the offering up in his claws and started eating its head. As Kefira paled and grimaced at the spectacle, Rakhshan laughed and said, "It does not look as though he's having any trouble to me."

As darkness fell, they decided to settle for the night at their original landing place. It was not ideal, as there was no crag or cleft of rock to shelter alongside, and the trees above were only thick enough to hide themselves from the most cursory passing of the eye. Rakhshan had never gotten to the marketplace in Hangmatana, so their meal was a small one of leftover bread and what green things they could forage in the dark.

"Sleep over here, for once," Rakhshan had said, when Kefira had unrolled her blanket a few trees away. "You *and* your dragon will catch cold if you keep up your childish demurring."

"I'm not demurring," she said, frowning as she picked up her bedroll and reluctantly moved closer to the two mercenaries. She looked dubiously up at the half-asleep Azhi Dahaki, and the rider who sat between his curled forelegs.

"Of course you're not. Just cuddle up to our friend Mār a bit and you'll be warm for the night."

"He'll roll over and squish me - us." The hatchling nibbled softly on her ear. "On purpose."

"Not with the Hardlā, he won't. He's worth a lot of gold."

"I see," Kefira said dryly. But she only stood measuring Rakhshan and his dragon for a moment before tentatively walking behind Mār's foreleg. "You don't mind if I sleep here, do you?" she asked him hesitantly.

The dragon blinked, coming out of his stupor, and turned his head to her. "If you must."

It was indeed warmer, lying next to the great dragon. The grass was not all over in growing dew, and any sort of night-chilling breeze was broken by his hulk. A wing drooped like a canopy overhead. For all of his caustic pomp, the dragon was not a horrible sort of thing to sleep next to.

And apparently, her hatchling felt the same way about her. He'd made a nest of her hair, fish-gorged body curling up against her neck amidst a warm tangle of her tresses. At first she'd objected to this venue for his sleep, his tail draped over her neck and around her face, but he seemed to like it very much, and after a few futile attempts to get him to move, she relented, and settled to petting him with a finger. He seemed to purr.

"I'm glad to have you," she realized aloud, after a while. "You're a very pleasant sort of creature, even if a little pesky on occasion," she whispered to him with a smile. "And a clever one, too, I guess," she added. "You hid awful well today. It's a miracle they didn't catch us." She felt soft scales rub against her finger. She'd never thought that she would actually keep the egg, let alone what hatched out of it. By all rights, she should have been put up on a pike that evening, at the Satrap's whim. But she was here, in the grass with a little dragon.

For that she supposed Rakhshan could be owed.

But she did not open her mouth to thank him. In any case, he was probably already asleep, just as she should be, and her dragonling already was. So she shut her eyes and slowly followed their suit.

"Yonatan," she said as she woke up, with the dragonling

standing on her face. He was larger — had he doubled in size? She sat up, and he tumbled like a kitten into her lap.

"What?" Rakhshan was already awake, sitting atop Mār's foreleg above her, looking at his map.

Kefira pet the dragonling's belly, the length of his tail whipping lazily to and fro in the air. "Yonatan," she repeated. "I think that is what I will name him."

"Does that mean *'daft and dumb'* in your language?" Mār scoffed; he was awake.

Kefira turned her head to glare at him. "It *means* 'Gift from God.'"

"I'm pretty sure that technically he was a gift from *me*, but you know, who is counting." Rakhshan shrugged. But as he saw his companion begin to seethe, he ameliorated, "No, no, I'm just jesting, it is a lovely name, truly."

Kefira chewed her lip, looking ruefully at her Yonatan as she asked him, "*You* do not mind the name, do you? You know that it is a good name. Yoni." Yonatan just gazed up at her with his great yellow eyes.

"He's gotten bigger. His legs are as thick as a finger, now," the Persian observed.

"Yes, I did not know they could grow so fast!" Kefira said. "How large will he be, all grown up? Big enough for me to ride?"

"Let us not get into that, yet," Mār sighed, heaving himself onto his feet and sending his rider tumbling to the ground.

They broke their fast with the remainder of the bread they had. Kefira did not finish her share, only stowing half of it away for safekeeping, in the confines of her robes. "It seems a little rash to eat the last of the food while we're in hiding in the middle of the forest." According to Rakhshan, they were not to fly at all, even to get farther away from the city of their pursuers.

"I'm not a moron. There's a village nearby, I'll get some more food there." Rakhshan was rummaging through his things again, strapping on his sandals, and organizing some sort of bundle for himself.

"What are you doing? Are you going now?"

"There is nothing better to do. I'll be back soon."

"May I come with you?" she asked. "I might stay there, then, while you and Mār went on your way to do whatever other sorts of mercenary business you're into."

Rakhshan looked at her hard before speaking. "You certainly are naïve."

"What?"

"With a dragon, you don't think that you'll still be able to go on living life as an urchin from now on, do you?"

"I don't know what else I'd be," she replied slowly.

Rakhshan just raised his eyebrows – as though he was being ever-surprised by the depth of her foolishness - and said, "Just stay here with Mār for now. He'll tell you why what you're saying right now is so stupid, and then when I return, we can be on our way."

Kefira did not like anything he just said. Firstly, she was not wholly sure that Mār would not eat her and Yonatan as soon as Rakhshan left sight; secondly, Rakhshan's assertion of *'we'* and 'on *our* way,' galled her. She did not think she should like to go anywhere further with them, never mind the man having rescued her yesterday. She could not imagine where and for what purpose he intended her to travel with them.

But she did not complain, biting her tongue. Perhaps Mār would enlighten her a little, and alleviate her of some of her apparent stupidity. "Goodbye, then," she said to Rakhshan, as he assessed the surrounding landscape and set out in a westerly direction.

"Do not kill each other while father's away," he replied with a wave, not looking over his shoulder.

"You're stupid," she muttered.

"Be careful, Rakhshan," Mār hissed after him.

And then the three were left quiet beneath the crisscrossing shadows of the trees. Kefira was sitting cross-legged, weaving grass as she watched Yonatan scramble about a fallen tree. She looked sidelong at the Azhi Dahaki, who had not yet spoken. In fact, his head was on the ground and eyes half-lidded, as if he were contemplating dozing off.

"You're supposed to tell me why I am a fool, are you not?" she asked him. "Do not fall asleep already."

The dragon exhaled huskily through his nostrils, shifting his head to look at her. "Do not tell me what to do, girl. I will tell you why you are a fool when I am goot ant reaty, ant I will give you an earful at that." He turned his eyes to look at the oblivious Hardlā hatchling.

Kefira halted her fingers over her braid of grass, and picked up a stick, throwing it before Mār's face. "Stop being such a sluggard. Your rider wanted you to tell me, so *I* am not commanding you, it is he."

A growl of annoyance emitted from the dragon's throat, raising Yonatan's head before the hatchling leapt primly to Kefira's side, tail stiff behind him. Mār looked at both of them before sighing, "You quarrelsome little brat." But he did relent. "I suppose you *must* know."

The girl did not say anything, but held her breath, hoping he would continue. She stroked Yonatan's back as she watched the older dragon.

"He is one of only a few of his breet, the Hartlā of olt Israel," Mār said slowly, spittle running from his chin to sear the earth. "Ant when I say a few, I am meaning a number smaller than that of your fingers on one hant. No one is very sure how many remain, since the utter demolition of your nation," he explained. "But there were not even so great a many to begin with, for the female Hartlā's season comes only a few times a century. But as soon as the Assyrians, the Babylonians, swept in and killt your people, many of his kint were lost as well."

"Why have I never heard of a Hardlā before?" Kefira protested. "If they are so very great, I ought to have heard stories of them when I was little." It disturbed her that a creature of her own nation could be lost along with her ancestors. She rested a warm hand upon Yonatan.

"How do you expect me to know?" scoffed Mār. "Do not interrupt me, I will tell you what I was tolt; you can keep your questions for someone who cares."

Kefira fell silent.

"Anyway, me ant Rakhshan ant a few others were employt to recover this youngling's egg. Apparently Babylon fount out that there was an egg hitten somewhere in the countrysite of Metia, ant so the Satrap here decidet to fill his pockets while they endeavort to fint it."

"But why did they want to kill me for it, for finding him?" the girl asked, looking at her dragon as he flitted away again. "Certainly he is desired for more than his rarity."

Mār seemed displeased by her interruption, but appeared to swallow the displeasure, raising his thorny head. She rolled back a little on her haunches, before he finally said, "His is a very large breet, to put it shortly." The words came bitterly from the Azhi Dahaki's mouth. "Even the colossal Tiamat of Babylon's ranks will be dwarfed in comparison."

The cord Kefira was making was clenched in a fist now, as she turned to look at her little Yonatan. He was trying to scale a tree, thin talons splayed over the silver trunk. She faced Mār. "You jest. Even the egg of the *smallest* Persian breed is greater than his was. A Siyudūrai's is no smaller than a man's head, no? Yet Yonatan's egg fit in my hand." She looked helplessly up at the dragon.

He rolled his eyes. "You think I woult waste my time pulling wool over your eyes? You are not *that* amusing a runt."

Kefira gaped up at him. "But – how large is a Tiamat? Is that not a goddess of Babylon?"

"They namt a breet after her." Mār explained curtly, "It is five times my size," and shuffled his talons.

The girl stared at him for a moment, before moving her eyes quickly to assess the size. Mār was as long as one of the trees was tall: about as high as a building with four stories. If the number of fingers on one hand was five, and the dragon before her one fifth of a Tiamat at his size... She imagined his length that many times, stretching over the land before her, and swallowed.

"Yes, yes, your little Yonatan will not stay little for very long, to be sure," Mār grinned crookedly.

Kefira looked at the dragonling carousing in the brush, and back at the Azhi Dahaki. "How much greater will he be than a Tiamat?" she asked, voice small.

"He will be greater," Mār replied evasively.

"He will be the size of a mountain," Kefira breathed.

"Not quite."

The scale was dizzying; if she surmised correctly, when Yonatan was fully grown, Mār could only ever be the length of his tail, if that. He and the dragons of the barracks in Hangmatana had been the very largest things Kefira had ever seen, and to hear that Yonatan would dwarf them was unthinkable. "How will I ever keep him fed?" she blurted, horrorstruck. Short of constant hunting, there was no way beyond stealing livestock for a girl like her to maintain a beast so large. "He will be as large as the barracks himself!"

"That is a bit of an exaggeration," Mār said wryly. "He will only be about twice the size of a Gantarewa – you may have seen one, the gilt beast in Hangmatana – and a couple of those can fit in the dragon yard."

"Do you speak of the Mehrnaz that Rakhshan went to visit with?"

"Yes," Mār replied shortly, suddenly averting his gaze.

Kefira paused. "A Gandarewa. I have heard of those." It was the largest breed of dragon in Persia.

"I'm sure you have."

"Do they need very much feeding? How much do you think I'll need to feed Yonatan?" she asked him, fingers knotting the grass.

"Do not worry about that. We are going someplace that woult be happy to feet him."

"*We?*" Kefira frowned. "Where is that?"

"I think Rakhshan means for us to go to Parutrauga."

"Parudrauga!" Kefira exclaimed, mortified. "But that is all the way South, to the ocean, Al-Khaleej, on the coast of Gedrosia!" The distance made her head spin. "And it is full of wicked and wayward men!"

"Exactly." Mār sounded pleased. "There are people we can trust, there."

"What?"

"How many lawless men do you know that woult turn in one of their brethren?"

Kefira curled her lip. "You two turned *me* in."

"We turnt in the *egg* – *you* just happent to be attacht to it," Mār smirked, and then just as quickly his expression soured. "Ant why are *you* complaining? Rakhshan *broke you out* after, dit he not?"

"I guess so," Kefira muttered, looking down at her hands, where she was wrathfully weaving. He *had* saved her from execution, true, yet she still did not feel as though she'd left her prison. She glanced at Mār, and then at Yonatan, who was loping back over to her. He leapt atop her shoulder, and she already felt his greater weight as he wobbled, tail waving. She stroked his neck and looked at Mār. "I would like to just leave you two and go on my own way," the girl told him. "Though I do not suppose you two have a mind to let me."

"Oh, *no one* sait anything about keeping you against your will." The Azhi Dahaki leered down at her, a glimmer in his eye. "Though," he said, looking off aloofly, "even if you *dit* leave us, you woult be hart-presst to fint prey suitable for your beast, let alone a hiding place from your newfount enemies."

Kefira stared up at him, jaw trembling a little, as she grasped his words. She gazed at Yonatan, who was chewing on a strand of her hair. Newfound enemies. "So they will not stop looking for him?" she asked quietly.

"*I* certainly woult not, if I were them," Mār said. "I myself woult want to *kill* you for your insolence."

Kefira swallowed, feeling the cold radiating from the Azhi Dahaki. There was none of the violence his words suggested present in his eyes, but his gaze was icy and indifferent. "But – you and Rakhshan," she began, trying to keep a quaver from entering her voice, "You will – you're making me go with you, so that Yonatan can be fed and sheltered?"

"We're not *making* you," the dragon purred.

Kefira glared at him. "*Why* do you want me and Yonatan to be safe?"

"Rakhshan does; I do not care," Mār clarified.

The girl was seething inside. "Very well, why does *Rakhshan* want us to be safe?"

The dragon tilted his head, looking at her like she was a trussed rabbit. "To make sure that saving you was not a wastet effort, I think," he said simply. "As of yesterday, you owe him more than your life."

Rakhshan returned when the sun was at its apex. Kefira was tying her grass braid around Yonatan's neck when he came into the clearing and handed her a piece of dried meat. "You can eat goat, can you not?" he asked.

Surprised, she nodded, and tore the strip, giving one half to Yonatan and stowing away the other. She looked up at Rakhshan, who had more meat and other things slung over his shoulder in a piece of cloth. "Is all of that food?" she asked.

"Yes."

"How did you afford it?"

He held up a yellow half-circlet. "I sold part of the ring."

There was a rasping sound that could only be a chortle from Mār. "Oh, the Satrap will be *very* pleast by your stewartship of his capital."

Kefira didn't say any more. Her mouth was watering, but she'd long since lost her appetite, so she just sat still and pet the dragonling in her lap, watching as the man slung the bundles into

Mār's rigging, and thence continued to pack up their things.

"Where are we going to after this?" she asked him, not looking up from where Yonatan was rolling in her lap.

"Out of the valley is what I aim for," Rakhshan said, straightening beside his prone dragon.

"Where after that? I take it I must go with you," she said rather stonily.

"If you'd like to. We go where it will be safe for us to lie low for a while, until this Hardlā business has died out."

Kefira looked at him appraisingly for a moment before speaking. "Parudrauga?" she asked him.

He turned to look at her, a question on his face. And then he looked at his dragon, who had just released an exasperated sigh. "Yes," he said finally. "That's where we're headed."

"That place is the capitol city of debauchery." Kefira glared at him. "I imagine devils run there in the thousands. If I go there, I will be stabbed to death or turned into a prostitute on the first day," she said in a matter-of-fact tone. Yonatan hissed, as though to second her.

She heard Rakhshan snort. "You believe in too many wives tales. Nothing like that would happen to you if you came with us."

Kefira relented, and said nothing more. She ought not make too much of a fuss – for she was still not wholly sure she wouldn't run off from these fools the first chance she got.

The dragons were watered at the pond, before they set out. The water wasn't clear enough for human consumption, and Rakhshan had refilled waterskins at the village's well, so only the dragons needed sating. Mār nudged Yonatan forward with a talon, insisting he drink first. "If he drank any acit, it woult eat straight through his precious skull," he said, not sparing the details, even as a thread of drool dripped from his maw.

"More or less," Rakhshan concurred.

As her dragonling drank his fill, Kefira asked, half-accusatorily, "Why does it not eat through *your* skull?"

The dragon shot back, "For the same reason the juices in your belly keep from harming you, so the Greeks say." She of course knew nothing on the subject of science, and was well silenced. Yonatan finished and bounced back to her, and the Azhi Dahaki stepped forward and took great gulps from the pond. Even from a few paces away she could see his syrupy slaver mingling bitterly with the water. A fish floated up from the depths of the water nearby, motionless.

"We're going to travel south on foot to the other side of the valley," Rakhshan explained peremptorily.

"Which means I will be carrying you all," Mār sighed.

"That's correct, mighty steed."

"I hate walking," the dragon harrumphed.

"Well, we can fly tomorrow once we get past those mountains," Rakhshan said, pointing to the rocky hedge to the south. He looked at Kefira. "That is Media's border against the satrapy of Elam. Once there, Deioces should not have immediate jurisdiction, and we will be harder to pursue."

The girl nodded slowly, gathering Yonatan up in her arms.

"So I take it you will be joining us?" Rakhshan asked her.

"At least for now," she said warily.

The man just nodded.

Kefira found that she didn't like Mār walking any more than he himself did. His gait was uneven, and he swayed slightly, tail swinging side to side as he strode beneath the trees. There was at least a sort of smoothness present when gliding through the air; right now it felt as though she was mounted on a barrel constantly teetering in the water. She would have forced herself to fall asleep, Yonatan curled comfortably about her neck, to escape the nausea of the constant motion, but the man behind her hardly allowed for such a luxury. Without the wind to pull them backwards, there was nothing keeping Rakhshan from fitting quite snugly against her back, a proximity she'd not known for years. So she'd refused staying seated at Mār's neck at all, until the man ameliorated the indecency of the situation by straddling his dragon's shoulder blades, a healthy distance from the flustered girl.

Little conversation was had throughout the traversal. Mār was quiet, except to laugh on occasion, when he noticed Kefira doing something he thought to be stupid; Yonatan was asleep, and Rakhshan absorbed in scanning the horizon. Kefira wanted to converse with neither of the mercenaries, and could not speak with Yonatan, so she stayed quiet as well. So the silence made only louder the sound of grit and bracken crunching beneath the dragon's feet. The girl could not shake how much like the grinding of dry teeth and bones the sound became.

The mountains became quite palpable before them, low and jagged like a spine, russet-grey slopes reaching ever closer towards them. The peaks before them were only really high enough to be a nuisance. Whereas Mount Alvand behind them was engorged and white-capped, these mountains were short and about as wintry as the Sinai Desert. "We'll get over those tomorrow," Rakhshan had interrupted one of their prolonged silences. The sun was cresting the mountains to the west.

"I fint that agreeable," Mār sighed, readily lowering himself to the ground as soon as he'd been given reason to halt. They settled at the base of the range's foothills; their surroundings had gradually changed from forest to rolling hills, with only a few trees to offer cover. They had only seen two dragons that day, flying overhead while they were still under the cover of forest canopy; they resided beneath one of the broad trees now, for what meager shelter it could offer. Surrounding them were beige sweeps of dirt, sprinkled with swathes of dusty green grass, gilded in stark red flowers. Kefira had never seen blossoms so bright in color. Yonatan had never seen flowers in general, and so these blooms amused him for the better part of an hour, as Mār ventured to hunt, low fling in the evening light.

By some miracle, the dragon returned with an antelope, and tore off a leg for Yonatan. The hatchling had grown to the size of a large cat over the course of the day. She had to ask Rakhshan more than once as to whether or not this was normal growth, before she could relax as she watched her dragon eat. Though it was very nearly larger than he was, he devoured the whole haunch with gluttonous delight.

After a dinner of fresh bread and dried fruit – Kefira still stowed away all the meat she acquired – she retired with Yonatan on the other side of the tree from their companions. As she unrolled her blanket, Kefira noted with dissatisfaction that her dragonling was all over with blood. "Oh, you are all filthy, Yoni," she frowned at him. She peeled away the topmost layer of her clothing – the fancy stuff Rakhshan had given her when they were leaving Hangmatana – it'd been causing her to sweat all day, with its added warmth, and so it would do no harm to employ it now to clean her dragon. She used it as a rag to wipe, but mostly just smear around, the reeking blood from the little one. She frowned at her handiwork. "Well, I guess we can clean you up better when we find some water," she sighed.

"You're not very good at cleaning things, for a girl," Rakhshan said.

She stiffened where she was kneeling. "You're stupid," she turned around to glare at him. He was holding a waterskin.

"Give me that," he said, taking the gore-smeared garment from her hand. He promptly folded it onto a clean side and poured some of the skin's contents onto it. "Now use it." He smiled sardonically, holding it out to her.

Kefira took it wordlessly, looking at him sidelong before wiping her Yonatan's face once more. She peered close at her dragon's scales; the blood was removed – and he smelled good. "There is wine on this," she said suddenly, looking at Rakhshan with surprise.

"I thought it would be a shame for any of that blood to get on you," the man shrugged as he turned around to leave.

Kefira looked at the makeshift rag once more, and then at his receding form. "Thank you," she said quietly.

"Goodnight," he replied.

"Goodnight," said she.

Yonatan curled around her like a necklace in sleep, a wreathe smelling of spice and bitter sweetness. Kefira kept the washcloth garment beside her head, offering with the coppery smell of its blood also the smell of wine. She'd not smelled wine in a long time, except for on the breath of unsafe men. Wine did not bubble from springs or flow from rivers; why Rakhshan would deign to use it for something as common as cleaning she could not venture a guess.

She stroked Yonatan as she looked at the stars through the black shadows of tree boughs. She could see the moon, full now, a yellow dish in the sky. Seen through the crisscrossing silhouettes of branches above, it appeared to be a shattered dish. The girl felt the tremble of the dragonling's heart pulsing against her fingertips. "Things are going to be very different from now on, Jehovah," she whispered. She heard Yonatan exhale, warm breath stirring her hair. "I hope You did right by this."

Chapter V
Debtor to a Thief

The mountain range was broader than it'd appeared. More than jagged lines on the map did the peaks prove to be, as broad and rigid as the scales along a dragon's back. With the thaw of old winter's rime, the dun, scrub-flecked mountains were spider-webbed in glittering threads of melted ice, trickling down crags and crevasses and slopes, to eventually reach the lowlands. The wind was strong and winter cold at these heights, numbing Kefira's face as they flew, even as she clutched her shawl tight about her head and covered her nose with a sleeve. Yonatan wormed about inside her clothing – he'd been stowed therein against her belly so that he would not blow away. His presence warmed her a little, yet still not enough that she *completely* shied from the form of Rakhshan at her back. Her core thus kept from freezing over, all that really concerned her was her bare feet, which she could no longer feel scraping over Mār's hide.

When the dry, cool sun was at its apex, they took a respite on a ridge, the Azhi Dahaki leaving to make a meal of a markhor, one of the goats of the mountain. Kefira let Yonatan out to wander the windswept slope, as she sat on a rock in the sun to morosely rub her feet. "You ought to get a pair of boots," Rakhshan remarked, handing her the nuts and bread that made their midday meal.

"I am not a warrior to put on such cumbersome things," Kefira frowned disdainfully. Anyway, she couldn't steal such commodities if she tried. Bread was different than the fine-tailored craftsmanship of a leatherworker.

"Well, you'll wish you'd had a mind to, soon, I think," Rakhshan said. "You'll get frostbitten if you're not careful, and your toes may fall off," he added, taking a casual drink from a waterskin.

Kefira halted over her aching feet, and gaped at him. "Surely not, what is frostbite? I've never heard of it." He was pulling her leg again. She vengefully chewed upon her almonds.

"I would not lie about so grave a thing. It happens when your flesh grows so cold that it dies, and breaks straight off of you."

Yonatan squawked at this, and Kefira heard his talons scrabble on her rock as he came to her side, gawking at Rakhshan. The girl stared at her feet, and she wiggled her cold toes. She looked up at the Persian. "You do not think – I do not have it, do I? Where can we get boots?"

"I'll get you some eventually. Perhaps we can at our next stop at a village."

"But what if my feet fall off before then?" Kefira pleaded, wrapping her feet up in her robes, glancing covetously at the man's own sandals. Who knew dragon riding could be so dangerous?

When she looked up again, his hand was upon her brow, ruffling her shawl and the hair beneath as he laughed. "Calm yourself, Kefira, your feet will not fall off! It would be an act of the gods for you to get frostbite here, anyway," he said, as she stared at him. "You can only get it far north east of us – there is a range of mountains there where you could drop the whole of Mount Alvand and never find it again." He smirked at her dumbfounded expression.

"Why did you scare me like that?" She glowered at him, smoothing her hair beneath her scarf. "Do not touch me again."

Rakhshan grinned roguishly at her. "Forgive me, but it is hard to resist scaring one so easily roused."

"You are stupid," Kefira said balefully, crossing her arms. "Will Mār return soon?" she asked, exasperated. "Yonatan is hungry."

Yonatan was sated when Mār finally returned, bearing one of the tawny, spiral-horned goats she'd seen climbing the mountain slopes. The little hatchling and grown some more, even since morning, now as long the span of both Kefira's arms. He fell upon his portion of the markhor with avid delight; she imagined he was bent on doubling his size by the time night fell.

In accompaniment with the midday meal, though she still

deemed it a wasteful repast, she also gnawed on a piece of jerky she'd stowed from the previous day. Yonatan had found the stash in her clothing during the flight and eaten all but one of the pieces before she could wrest it from him. It was wonderful, unspeakably wonderful, eating meat. Though the hard flesh did hurt her teeth, and she tasted blood from a cut on her wan gums, it was as refreshing as sanguine wine on her tongue. She chewed it until it was bland mush in her mouth, and even then persisted to roll it around over her tongue. She sat upon her feet, looking at Rakhshan who was studying his holy map.

"Why have we seen no patrols?" she asked him.

"We're probably behind them all," he replied absently. "They did not find us in the valley when we hid yesterday, and so I'm sure expected us to have moved on."

"I hope so."

When they set out again, she discovered her unease was not without cause. There were only a few ridges left for them to pass before leaving the mountains when two white dragons appeared behind them. There was not a cloud in the sky, no fog for them to emerge from, yet their materialization was as swift as though they'd come from thin air. "Where dit those Asteevs come from?" Mār snarled, more than taken aback, and Kefira heard Rakhshan curse most colorfully behind her – and with this sudden change of energy, she felt Yonatan go quite still.

"They found us!" Kefira felt her heart skip a beat, as she looked past Rakhshan to see the swiftly approaching white birds behind them. "What are we going to do?"

"Swiftly, Mār! Dive past the last ridge," Rakhshan shouted to him.

"I cannot – there are no trees to hite in!"

"Duzahk!" Another curse from Rakhshan. Kefira felt her entire body go cold with dread. They were going to be caught – for once, the mercenary did not know what to do. She held a hand over Yonatan. He was going to be taken and she would be killed. Perhaps it would be one of the dragons that killed her.

There was a roar beneath them, jarring Kefira to the bone. Rough dragon hide pressed into her face, her stomach lurching forward as Mār stopped in midair, wings sweeping backwards with a great *whoosh*. Her breath left her lungs with a cry as Rakhshan slammed into her. Yonatan yelped.

A mighty voice bellowed, "Land!" the command echoing from mountain to mountain. Kefira felt Mār's blood thrumming through his hide as he hovered; he was looking at something his riders could not see. Kefira glanced back to see that the two dragons were gaining on them.

"What in the Seven Hells, Mār?" Rakhshan cried.

Mutely, the dragon descended, spiraling downward in a nauseating whorl. Kefira shut her eyes, the black spinning around her until there was a crunch and a halt. They clung to a mountain face. Rakhshan was breathing hard behind her. They were all looking up at a great beast carved of gold.

A Gandarewa. It was easily twice, very nearly three times, the size of Mār, a monster looming above them. It glittered in the sun, wings spread to cover the sky, blinking with eyespots of red and blue. The dragon lowered her massive head on a thick, thorny neck; on her brow there was a scarlet patch of scales between two icy eyes.

"Good afternoon, brethren!" A less than genial voice called from above – decidedly not the dragon's. "You – a man, an Azhi Dahaki, and a girl – are the thieves and smugglers of the Satrap's dragon, no? Let me know now if this charge is unjust." Kefira's stricken eyes searched past the Gandarewa's unblinking gaze to see the figure of a man sitting at the base of the dragon's head.

"It is not."

Kefira turned around, baffled to see that Rakhshan had spoken. "*Now* you choose to speak plainly!" she hissed. He ignored her, and suddenly, she had the sinking feeling that she was about to be betrayed once again. She looked away, paling, arms over her hidden hatchling.

The white dragons, Asdeevs, were circling them now, two thin rings floating in the sky. Kefira looked past Mār at the Gandarewa and her rider, fingers knotting together.

"Well, how fortuitous that I have the right triad," the man above said. Squinting, she could make out that he had a silver-streaked beard, and was running a hand through it. "Rakhshan, my pupil."

Kefira heard the mercenary behind her smile. Taken aback, she asked, "Do you know him?"

"He was my mentor for the few weeks I spent in the Asman Kāra," the man explained quietly. "Until me and Mār found that the military life was not for us."

"Then will he let us pass?" Kefira cried, hope sparking up inside. They may actually get out of this! She looked with new eyes upon the Gandarewa spread before them.

"Not so fast," Rakhshan said. "Those two Asdeevs and their riders are not kith to us. Arsham's comrades do not know of our affiliation with him."

Kefira looked up at the two vigilant dragons wheeling above, and felt a lump in her throat.

Rakhshan promptly returned his attention to his master. "You know where we are headed, do you not?"

Despite the distance, Kefira could just make out a nod from the man above, Arsham. He motioned with his arm, and Kefira felt Rakhshan move behind her. "You are headed straight to prison and swift execution! Mehrnaz!"

His dragon's eyes lit up, and at the same time Kefira felt Rakhshan spur Mār. The wings of the great Gandarewa glowed with sunlight as she blotted out the sky, lunging from her place on the mountain to barrel down upon them, with a roar that pierced Kefira's ears. All of the muscles in her body clenched as Mār hurtled forward, the force of his speed sending her into Rakhshan's chest.

The Asdeevs shrieked as Mār disappeared beneath Mehrnaz;

Kefira's breath refused come as the Azhi Dahaki bounded up the tunnel of mountain rock and Gandarewa scales, as the great dragon soared above and past them.

Mār pushed away from the mountain top with a sickening upward spiral into empty space. On swivels of bone and sinewy muscle, his wings snapped forward to propel them through the air.

Kefira snatched a look back at the Asdeevs, and Arsham and Mehrnaz, to see that the Gandarewa had clumsily ensnared her wings with those of the Asdeevs, and heard her rider's distant voice calling to *get after those cursed mercenaries, blast you!*

But with renewed energy, Mār's wings scooped voraciously through the air, and they coursed past and over the remaining mountains. They were in Elam, and the asmanaba pursuing them was diminishing, diminishing, until the dragons could no longer be seen.

Rakhshan turned around to salute his unseen master, and Mār skreed triumphantly when they finally returned to flat earth. The dragon didn't even wait for his passengers to climb off before collapsing to the ground, breathless.

"Why did he attack us?" Kefira asked, watching fretfully as Yonatan unwound and emerged from her skirts. "I thought he was your friend."

"You are quite the little fool," Mār said.

"I think he rather more helped us than harmed us," Rakhshan replied simply. And he passed her a waterskin. "Have some water, you look ill."

They stayed the night beneath a stand of trees. The land of Elam was composed of yet more rugged mountains, with broad swathes of brown plains sweeping between. As far as the eye could see, where more mountains did not hem their vision, spidery green trees spotted the land, and where trees could not be seen, there were thickets, and where thickets could not be seen, there was sparse prairie. Kefira could see cultivated land, with fields of emergent barley and wheat stretching away from the homesteads that tended them. There was a river here in the basin, an ever-present entity in the distance, a strip of stark blue branching out into small canals for irrigation.

"We'll follow that river, Kārun, south for a while," Rakhshan said, as Kefira was yawning beside a hound-sized Yonatan in the fading light.

"Very well," she replied. She knew better than to give him her naïve input as to their course. Who knew for how long she would be accompanying them to their destination, in any case.

"I have never been to Parudrauga," she found herself saying. "Is it as all the rumors say it is? In the north, I met a boy once, who thought he could travel there on foot, I guess. He told me of all the prosperity and other such pleasurable things he would have as soon as he got there." It was only now that Kefira was a little older that she realized that the boy had been largely speaking of harlots. "Not all of those pleasurable things are unlawful, are they?" she asked skeptically. She'd hate for Yonatan to grow up in a place where there was brawling in the street, where brazen women were kissing men in public, where drunkards walked in the daytime. She shivered at the prospect.

"The rumors do not do the city justice," Rakhshan said simply and Kefira frowned at the esoteric response. More maddeningly, he added, "You shall see it when we get there."

"Very well," she replied disconsolately. She looked at Yonatan, whose eyes glimmered in the sunset light. "I guess we shall see when we get there, Yonatan," she crooned unhappily. And he blinked at her.

He was larger in the morning. Try as he might, he could not fit himself in the swaddling of Kefira's clothing anymore. She'd woken to him trying to slither into her robes by way of her skirts – much to her bewilderment, and to the mercenaries' amusement. She let Yonatan know that he could fit in her clothing no longer, and ought not try, unless perhaps, she added upon seeing his disconsolate expression, no one else was around.

Now Yonatan's wings dragged on the ground, as though he'd wilted. Kefira felt as though she'd sorrowed him, and remorsefully spent the next two days coaxing him back to heartiness with praise and raisins from her meals. When they embraced, his greater size was apparent. His long, swanlike neck curled at her chest, and by the end of the next couple days, his shoulders were as high as her waist; his talons were bigger than her own feet. In short, it was no longer comfortable for him or Mār to be borne dragonback.

"When can I ride him?" Kefira asked Rakhshan one day.

"Not for a while yet." He explained, "Only when a dragon's wings span eight times the height of their rider can they bear their rider in flight."

Now Yonatan's wings were not much greater than the spread of a tent. But he was beginning to glide, now; no longer able to leap from Kefira's shoulder, he was leaping from taller things – hills, trees, whatever he deigned to climb, and coursed like a kite through the air. Though he did not do this frequently, as he seemed to grow more sluggish, for all his graceful appearance. He was actually rather slowing their party down – cumbersome as he was to bear by Mār, and sleeping as frequently as he did. The only time he ever seemed truly awake was when he was eating – for eat he did.

"He neets to start hunting his *own* prey," grumbled Mār, after catching three red deer for the dragons to sup upon. "I grow weary of obliging his gluttony." Yonatan was eating almost as much as the older dragon was. The Azhi Dahaki claimed that this was only because he was an *adult* and could very well go on without so much to sustain him, and the similarity in their appetites was only because this little Hardlā was still in his youthful stage of pig-like greed.

"Give a child a cloak and they will be warm for a year. Teach a child to sow and they will be warm for a lifetime," Kefira opined simply, weary of his complaining.

"That saying sounts very stupit," the dragon replied disdainfully. "Now is not the time to lament your chilthoot, in any case."

"No, she has a good idea, Mār," Rakhshan had said. "Why do

you not teach Yonatan to hunt?"

"Then you may never hunt for him again," Kefira affirmed. "I think that sounds like a wonderful arrangement." And so the Azhi Dahaki was condemned to the task. While the dragons were thus engaged in the countryside, Rakhshan invited Kefira to join him in town to resupply. "May I get some sandals?" she asked hopefully.

"Of course."

She needed no more convincing. She was unwilling beyond anything to leave her dragon with the likes of Mār — but given the fact the older dragon hadn't yet made an attempt to slay Yonatan, she found enough solace to leave with Rakhshan that afternoon.

"Come with me, youngling," Mār drawled, as Yonatan lashed his tail, winding his neck around Kefira before they parted. "You will taste your first kill soon, and forget about her soon enough."

Yonatan hissed at him as he disentangled himself from his rider, and shook out his wings before reluctantly following — but not before Kefira could kiss him on the nose in parting.

It was reflexive, an unintended occurrence — she'd never kissed anyone save for her mother and father in her life, and she'd always done that in the appropriate veneer of the house — a kiss was not a thing for the public. She looked after Yonatan for a while as she left him, wondering. And then she peered at her travelling companion, sidelong. She hoped he did not think her uncouth.

"If passersby do not know that you travel with me, Kefira, they may think an unescorted girl like you is something that you're not," Rakhshan said, breaking the silence on the downriver trek. Kefira had been walking on the far side of the road, opposite of him.

At his comment, she sighed and yielded in trudging a little bit closer to the man. Certainly he did think her uncouth, she thought, before remembering what sort a person *he* was. "We've not even passed half a dozen people," she then objected. Farmers, mostly, with their donkeys laden with things bought or to be sold at market, or servants on errands. "You ought to stop meddling with me," she threatened, small fists balled.

"I'm sorry, I'm sorry," he feigned guilt, raising his hands defensively.

"Like a fox holed in a vineyard you are," she muttered, crossing her arms. She glanced past him, at the sky glaring down above the turquoise river. "How do you suppose the dragons fare?"

"I am quite sure Mār has not eaten Yonatan yet, if that is what you're asking."

"Yoni is too clever to fall for anything that brute would devise," Kefira retorted crossly.

"I hope he's clever."

Somehow Kefira did not think he was merely talking about avoiding wrath from the older dragon. "Do you not think he is?"

"Well, it's hard to tell."

"Just because he has not spoken yet?"

"Well, yes," Rakhshan replied. "It would be very queer indeed if he was truly mute."

Kefira looked down at her bare feet as they walked. Then, "You do not suppose he is cursed, do you?" She swallowed. "Perhaps Shaza'eil, that Babylonian, perhaps he cursed him!" she said, suddenly vindictive. "Certainly he would, if he could not have Yonatan for himself, he would have him cursed."

"Perhaps."

"Do you not believe in such things?" she asked, remembering his discourse about the gods, all those days ago.

"I find it hard to believe a mere man could invoke spirits, to inflict such a wound upon a being of flesh."

"But there *is* such thing as sorcery," Kefira insisted. "A long time ago, there was a man who was a witch, named Balaam," she said, recalling the story from her childhood. "His king wanted him to call upon evil spirits, to curse the Israelites, but God did not let him."

"That was an awful decent thing for God to do," replied the man.

Kefira knew that this pagan was not taking her seriously, and so did not press the story further – she did not remember much of the tale beyond what she'd said, anyway. In the growing silence, she felt her own words and said aloud, "I wonder why, if Yonatan is indeed cursed, why God did not stop it."

"Maybe he knew that Yonatan would be very obnoxious if he could talk, and so gave us the mercy of his silence."

"You are being very unkind!" Kefira snapped. Before she could stop herself, she struck Rakhshan in the arm. "You sound just like Mār!"

Rakhshan jerked his head to look at her, rubbing his arm, expression quizzical. For a second he looked angry, but then he just turned to continue walking, saying, "Yes, I suppose I did. I'm sorry."

Kefira didn't reply, following after him dejectedly. As they passed, she watched a fold of sheep grazing beneath some trees, under the eye of a shepherd nearby. She almost smiled at the familiar scene. It'd been a long time since she'd gotten close enough to pet a ewe's winter wool, or smell a young lamb's sweet breath.

"Is that what you did, before taking to life on the streets?"

"What?" she returned her eyes to Rakhshan.

"You were a little shepherdess, were you not?"

"I was," she replied. "I cared for my father's sheep while he worked in the fields."

"What made you leave?" asked Rakhshan. He was not looking at her; his eyes followed the river.

"They all died."

"Your family?"

"My village."

"Pestilence?"

"No."

"What happened?"

Kefira could still smell the smoke. She deferred. "I don't really know." And Rakhshan did not make fun of her for it. He seemed to have grown somber.

"What about you?" she found herself asking him. "Why are you a mercenary?"

"That is a good question." But he disclosed no more.

They bought more food at the town. It was strange for Kefira to be able to walk shamelessly up to the booth of a baker or a farmer, and pick out fruit and bread that could actually be paid for, courtesy of Rakhshan. It was a delightful feeling. She did not have to move furtively on her toes, or cling to the shadows of buildings, though it was still her natural inclination. Rakhshan had to assure her many times that she was at present not doing anything illegal, and did not need to skulk like a pilferer's monkey.

Despite that witticism, Rakhshan's tongue seemed otherwise less sharp. He, in general that evening, seemed to be acting a little different, a little strangely; not overtly so, not blatantly, but his manner was different nonetheless. He seemed to be acting with less care – he bumped into her when they perused the booths – and had to be reminded more than once that grabbing her arm was not her preferred means of getting her attention. Yet at the same time, he also seemed more aloof. Kefira guessed that perhaps their previous conversation bothered him somehow. Whatever the case, whenever he was not simpering or running into her, he seemed to be altogether quiet, pensive or put-out, as though perhaps he wished that she was not tagging along, which did not make very much sense to her at all.

Whatever ailed him, be it ill-humor or brain-fever, it didn't prevent him from taking her to the cobbler's. With her heart in her throat, Kefira was fitted with a pair of leather sandals. At first she was leery of letting anyone touch her, even just her feet, but the cobbler was a businesslike man, and the most forward he ever got was when he spoke to Rakhshan to ask for his pay. Pay he got, and with the Persian Kefira walked away, the soles of her feet never touching the ground. In-between the hot dirt and gravel of the street was a panel of tanned hide, strapped to her toes and her ankles.

"I can feel leather between my toes!" she marveled. "But I cannot feel the earth!"

"Keen observation," Rakhshan smiled. "How long has it been since you were last shod?"

Kefira's face colored, and she looked down. "A few years." Her last pair of sandals had been exhausted when she was twelve. It was the pair she'd worn when she left her village, the final remnants of her father's handiwork for her to bear. They only lasted her a dozen cycles of the moon before her travels had eroded them away. The year she turned twelve, celebrating her birth-day alone with a pilfered raisin cake, the final straps had finally given out. Anyway, her feet had long since outgrown them, even if she hadn't worn them to scraps. So she'd spent the evening of her birth-day trying to trade the wisps of leather for a warm place to sleep. No one wanted what she was offering, and in the end, her night was spent fleeing from a pair of drunkards. She'd been barefoot ever since.

They were finished at the market, and the sun was low in its descent. Rakhshan trod with their newfound provisions slung over his shoulder, and Kefira walked ahead of him, feeling as though she could traipse all the way to the sea in her new sandals.

"Do not forget," Rakhshan said, as they passed the well. She halted and looked over at the ring of stones that marked the shaft. The man handed her their waterskins and she set them alongside the well. With a creak, he lifted the wooden lid from the cistern and Kefira dropped the bucket therein. "I want to return to Yonatan before dark," she told him fretfully, as she waited to hear the bucket splash and submerge below. She began hoisting it up with the camel hair rope. "The sun is setting, and I want him to see my sandals."

"There will be plenty of time for him to see your sandals," Rakhshan laughed. "Here, let me help. For all our fuss, you are sure slow."

"But you do not want passersby to think you are a woman," Kefira insisted with mock sincerity. "It is *my* job to get water."

He rolled his eyes and lifted the dripping bucket, facing her. "Open up," he said.

She untied the opening to a waterskin and impatiently waited for him to fill it. With the advent of her sandals, she could quite audibly tap her feet, and he looked down at her with amusement over the bucket. With a few more breachings of the well, they filled the skins and Kefira could move freely again. The low, cactus-hemmed walls of the town were in sight, and she could see the road disappearing into the wilderness and to dusk.

"Hold on, Kefira." The man halted yet again.

The girl looked back, pausing midstride. "What is it, now?" she asked.

"You like cold dirt and rocks and roots in your back, do you not?"

"No," she said slowly. He was looking at a building, a pale, two-story affair, at the edge of the village, leaning upon a stable. She could smell the musky hay from where she stood.

"Then why do we not stay here?"

"What?"

"At this inn."

"I do not like inns," she protested, turning about to face him.

"Come on, just look at it," Rakhshan coaxed, raising an arm to gesture emphatically at the hostel. He pulled her to his side. "A roof overhead, a fire in the hearth – imagine, sleeping in a real bed."

Kefira grudgingly followed his gesture with her eyes. She removed herself from under his arm before admitting, "That does not sound... bad." She couldn't remember the last time she'd slept on anything but the ground. She looked sidelong at Rakhshan. "Would they let Yonatan, perhaps..." she trailed off, gazing at the prim, square holes of the windows.

"Not even in their stable. And anyway, we cannot risk him being seen, remember?" Looking speculatively at their prospect, the man jingled the coins in his belt pouch. "If you want to stay here, he and Mār would get along just as well."

Kefira didn't say anything.

"Your sandals will still be here in the morning for you to show your dragon," Rakhshan chided.

Kefira pursed her lips, looking down the road that led out of the village. "We ought to let them know, if we stay." The door of the building opened, and her companion stepped forward to meet the man who came out of it.

"Mār knows we may rest here," Rakhshan said over his shoulder, before turning to the innkeeper.

Kefira stood reluctantly by as she listened to the man greet her companion; Rakhshan asked for the price of one night's stay, stating that he and his young wife were passing through the country and needed a place to sleep. The innkeeper rubbed his hands together and named a price Kefira did not think was very fair. But Rakhshan agreed, and they were ushered inside. The girl followed slowly, with half a will, into the smell of baking bread.

She looked back as the door was shut, and she took a step closer to Rakhshan. They were in a small vestibule, lit golden with a fire, and the mercenary was exchanging money with the innkeeper. Kefira watched dubiously, still glancing at the door.

"Come on, Kefira," Rakhshan said. "He is taking us up." The two men were standing by the adobe slabs of a staircase. Kefira clutched the waterskins before herself and followed.

They climbed up into a narrow hallway, with dim windows open to the twilight on both ends. The innkeeper held a small oil lamp, which did more to illuminate the enclosure. On one side of the wall there was a wooden door, and the other three porticos were cloistered by curtains of old wool. The innkeeper broached the closest one of these, pulling back the veil to bid them entry. Rakhshan went in with a, "Thank you, friend," and accepted the offered lamp.

Kefira did not follow at first. She was waiting for the innkeeper to lead her to her own room. But then she remembered, and promptly entered after Rakhshan.

"There is a basin for you to wash in," the man said. "My wife will be in shortly to bring you supper. Please enjoy your stay."

"Thank you," Kefira said quietly, as he pulled the curtain shut.

Rakhshan was putting their things on the floor, receiving the waterskins from her to lay beneath a small table. The room was not much larger than a horse stall, with a window open to the street. A straw mattress strewn with a few blankets took up a good portion of the space.

"Now, this is relaxing, is it not?" Rakhshan asked, kneeling at a small table in the corner to splash water from a dish on his face.

Kefira skirted past him to look out the window and see the sun set. Frost was already on the ground in patches. She returned to sit against the wall beside the door. "It is warm," she said. The brick at her back seemed to radiate heat. She guessed the fire was somewhere below. "Did he say he was going to feed us?"

Rakhshan untied his sandals and crashed onto the bed. "Yes, indeed. That does not sound so bad, does it?" And then he seemed to catch himself and clamber off the bed. "You ought to have this," he said.

Kefira looked at the mattress, wistful, before returning her gaze to him. "No, I'm sure it was *you* who was so eager to sleep in one."

"Oh, stop being demure and just take it."

Guiltily, Kefira needed no more coaxing. After washing her face, she crawled upon the ample cushion. Straw poked from beneath the fabric, but to her it felt like sitting upon a cloud. She glanced at Rakhshan self-consciously, as she felt around the mattress, the linens. There was a pillow, soft and the smell of chicken feathers on it. The blankets were spun of wool; it looked as though a long time ago, they'd been dyed blue and yellow. But even though the colors were fading, they were soft and smooth and warmed to her touch. "This is nice," she murmured, remembering the feel and smell of her mother and father's bed.

"I told you," Rakhshan smiled.

There was a rapping outside the door, and the curtain opened to permit passage of a round-faced woman, who bore a pair of small boards. Kefira smelled food.

She swallowed, mouth hot, as the woman smiled and handed them each a plate before departing.

Kefira looked down at the board, and two loaves of flatbread and a mound of hot, vinegared vegetables steamed before her face. "If I eat this all, I will be sick," she said, gazing with wonder at the meal. She shut her eyes, to thank Adonai for merely the *smell* of the array.

"You needn't eat it all, if you do not like," Rakhshan laughed. "I will take some of your bread."

"No you will not," she said, taking up the first loaf in her teeth. The creamy dough was still hot, and she tasted the stone from whence it'd come. She exhaled sweetly from her nose. Fresh bread was a rare taste; often she was too busy fleeing the place of a loaf's baking to taste it straight from the cooking stones.

The vegetables were just as beguiling. Though they reminded her a little of the plants she ate on the road, they'd been stewed in savory brine, and warmed her fingertips as she scooped them up. "That woman is very kind to feed us," she said quietly between mouthfuls.

"This is what you get if you do not live your life avoiding people," Rakhshan said smugly. "Mankind is not all that bad."

Kefira privately agreed. After stuffing the remaining half of the first loaf in her mouth, the man passed her a cup. "Here, wash it down before you choke yourself."

She did, swallowing the lump with the swill. Bitterly it went down, and she needed multiple drinks to aid her. And then she winced, the taste of the liquid tingling her tongue. She drained the rest of the cup. A bitter drink, wine, but unsweet. She felt it thrum in her forehead, and wondered what the innkeepers had distilled to create such a draught.

The girl was looking down at her plate, teething the bitter taste on her tongue, watching briefly the remaining loaf of bread soak up the juices left from the since-departed greens, cup's cool clay surface against her hand. She felt quite content.

Then her face turned up, as Rakhshan's voice sounded again: "Are you going to finish that?" He was pointing at the bread.

She was full, stomach warm and thrumming. "You can have it," she conceded. The girl raised her arm to get the plate to the table. She pushed it to him, or tried to, realizing that it was a little out of reach, and mistily she leaned forward to move it to his side of the table, succeeding on the second attempt.

"Thank you," the man said, leaning back against the wall with the bread, little expression in his words or on his face.

Kefira bobbed her head in response, looking at her hands. And then at her feet. They still had their sandals on. She ought not sleep with sandals on. She began working her fingers at the straps, tugging here and there to try and get them loose. She'd once known how to put sandals on and off; she guessed that at some point she'd just forgotten, for they were not coming off now.

She looked up, startled, when Rakhshan leaned over, saying, "Here, let me help."

"I can do it just fine by myself," she said, watching with displeasure as he persisted in undoing the straps. "Don't touch me." But the protests were halfhearted, as though her tongue was disinclined to make them.

"Here, hold this," the man replied, unheeding of her protests. Into her hand he put his cup.

Kefira held it unhappily, and then, as he pulled off one of her sandals, she drank it out of spite, and set it aside. She would not hold his cup.

Both her sandals were off, and she moved to sit upon her feet, looking at the man across from her with vague disapproval. "Thank you," she said, blinking. Her head was abuzz, as though it were a tree with a warm soft breeze running through it. Like she was already half asleep. Had it been so long since she'd felt a bed?

She looked up tentatively, at Rakhshan, who seemed to be watching her, before she pulled one of the blankets about her shoulders. It was not threadbare or covered in grit and rootlets. It added to the placid warmth that made her limbs so heavy and comfortable. Before she knew it, she remembered that the first cup was in her hands, though she'd discarded the second. She looked at it, its interior shiny with residual liquid, its exterior lusterless and soft. The drink had been terrible, horrible, acrid on her tongue. She held it out to Rakhshan. "Can I have some more?"

He raised his eyebrows, and she saw a flatness about his mouth as he spoke, like the taught line of a snare. "More? You don't want to sicken yourself," he warned without conviction, pouring anyway, from a smallish pouch that made *glugging* sounds as it decanted.

Kefira stared into the cup when it was returned to her hands, the lamplight dancing orange on the liquid's surface. Perhaps she would make herself ill; she felt a little scalding in her stomach, but she was aware that her head felt very pleasant, very pleasant indeed. So she put her chapped lips to the rim. She drank more, and it seemed to burn with hearth fire down her throat. How bad it tasted. The girl grimaced at him. "This is not wine, is it?" she asked. She did not recognize the languid voice that pronounced the words.

Rakhshan made some sort of reply, and she put out the cup arm, and he refilled her. She drank. The feeling in her head was like a thousand silent tambourine dancers gliding over warm coals. She felt tired, as she drank and drank again.

At some point there was nothing left to be drunk, and Rakhshan got to his feet, and Kefira felt warm calloused hands; she took no more care for the cup as it rolled away from her.

Kefira awoke, sunlight glaring through the window. When she opened her eyes, they were on the illuminated ceiling, the rafters; the sight of gleaming wood grain splintered in her eyes. She blinked painfully, and sealed her eyes again. Her temples ached at the sound of birdsong, and her hands moved like lead to rub them.

The girl let her hands drop, and when she yawned, it came out as a groan that split the quiet of the room. There was drool on her chin.

She sat bolt upright, sending pain exploding into her head. Just as quickly, she dropped her face to the blankets over her knees, whimpering. Everything hurt.

She wiped her mouth. She tried to focus her gaze on a thread in a blanket that covered her, but even that was an effort. She squeezed her eyes shut. What had happened? Slowly, she lifted her head around to survey her surroundings. She squinted about a familiar room. The white of morning light made it look foreign. The floors were emptier, the masked doorway taller, the rumpled bed larger.

Perhaps it appeared so cavernous because she was the only one there.

She collapsed back onto the mattress, eyes agape over the ceiling. *Dear God*, she whispered hoarsely in her mind, as she clenched the blankets over her mouth. Then her hands flashed over herself, her neck, her chest, her legs. She was not naked; she sat up. Her aching eyes swept her surroundings as she bit into her knuckle. The blank white walls and empty straw-strewn floor glared into her eyes. *Rakhshan is gone. The provisions are gone.* Only her sandals remained, standing vigil at her bedside.

"Dear God," she prayed aloud, voice constricting to a choke. Upon the breath, she could feel her lungs begin to expand and contract with manic speed. She was hyperventilating, breath hissing through a dry, bitter reed. She tossed the blankets away, off of her, and clasped her arms above her head, trying to breathe. *He was gone. He'd taken everything.*

Hot tears burst into her eyes, and her teeth chattered. It was all she could do not to scream a curse aloud.

Wavering to her knees, Kefira pulled up the hems of her robe until her legs were borne. With shaking fingers she pulled away her undergarment. Her loins, she clutched them fearfully, as she searched the mattress, the blankets, the floor. But no red; there was no blood to be found.

At this, she knelt, her face to the straw. "O, God," she pleaded in a whisper. "Dear God!"

Her heart pounded in her ears like a hammer. She rubbed her running eyes and stared at the floor. What had he done? What had she done? She did not remember anything but supper. There was no blood – so it couldn't – it mustn't – it must not be what she thought it was. Yet he was gone. Everything was gone. The man had *left*.

Eyes watering, she sifted around the bed again, examined her clothes, every span of fabric. Though her sight was blurred, she saw no blood. No explanation. There was nothing but the pain in her skull and the quiet sandals to tell her that the last week had not been a dream.

By the time Kefira wound her undergarment back on, she'd stopped her tears from flowing. She was sucking air more evenly now, as she chewed on her knuckles; she could gather her bearings.

She was alone, yes, but she'd always been alone. She could bear that. Rakhshan was gone, yet the room and board were already paid for, and it was daylight out and safe for her to leave town. Though he'd taken the food and water, the man had left her with the sandals, and there was no immediate evidence to suggest that he'd taken advantage of her. She'd not have him, but she did have Yonatan.

She leapt to her feet with a cry. Yoni!

They – they were stealing him from her.

Her head swam, and she hardly noticed when she fell upon her back. Bright white boiled in her eyes, and she was crying again. "No, not him." They could not take everything from her. Take the food, take the sandals even, but not her Yonatan. Not the last remnant of her people.

Fabric swished, and a soft voice sounded: "Mistress, are you alright?"

The innkeeper's wife stood in the curtain.

Kefira couldn't reply, breath halted by her sudden appearance. Dismayed, she got to her knees and lurched to the washbasin, afraid to meet the woman's gaze. She scrubbed the salt from her eyes, rubbing her dripping nose with the water. When she opened her eyes, a hand held a cloth before her face. Kefira slowly took the offered towel, and dried herself.

"Are you alright?"

Kefira looked up at her sheepishly, meeting her small, shiny eyes. "Yes," said she.

"Very well, child." The woman did not appear to be convinced, but pressed no further. She handed her a cake of raisins and said, "Your husband awaits you at the wall."

Kefira's jaw dropped. She stared at the woman, wondering if she was a deceitful spirit in disguise. "He does not," she protested when she could get out words.

The woman gave the girl an odd look. "Oh," she began, "at least last I checked, he does." She lifted the arm with which Kefira bore the raisin cake and drew her to the window. "Do you not see him?"

Kefira clutched the cake and peered outside warily. Women were getting water at the well in the dawn light, and on the road that lead outside of the town was a familiar visage. He stood at the nigh corner of the open gate, against the wall.

"He is there," Kefira said fearfully.

"Are you sure that you are alright?" The woman frowned, looking worriedly at the girl.

Kefira shoved the raisin cake in her mouth as she sat to pull on her sandals. "This tastes good," she told the woman absently, as she worked to manage the straps.

"Thank you," she replied slowly, and stooped to aid the girl in her endeavor. "Here, let me help you."

"I'm sorry. I do not know how to tie them," Kefira said, standing swiftly as the woman finished. She tightened her garments over her shoulders and raced out the entryway into the narrow hall and stairs, soles slapping against brick as she descended.

Kefira reached the door, and the woman came puffing down the stairs in her wake. She stood now across the room, watching her with concern. Kefira turned to her, hastily. "Thank you – for your hospitality," she stammered, before opening the door to step into the street.

Rakhshan was not facing the inn, and could not see her approach. So Kefira had nothing to stop her when she halted midway across the street, deferring. He was standing rather still, arms folded, waterskins and the bag of their rations sitting at his feet. She was the distance of a stone's throw of him, and not sure she could go any farther.

So she stood, hugging her arms to herself, self-consciously noticing the flock of older girls and women conferring at the well, balancing jars on their heads. Some of them looked at her with curiosity, but there was no one else about to witness her reticence as she scuffed her shod heel in the dirt.

Perhaps she ought to turn away now. There was more than one gate in the village wall. She need not use this one. She need not cross paths with the deceitful vagrant before her.

And then Kefira drove her teeth into her bottom lip. No, of course she would go to him! Of course she would, after all the rogue had done. She would twist his ear and give him a piece of her mind, and make him return her to Yonatan, before he could have his way with him.

Her head hurt with the effort it took to drive herself forward, despite her newfound fire. She no longer cared to be furtive, and her sandals rasped over the ground as she stomped towards him. Hardly had he turned his face to look at her before she snapped, "You – bastard!"

Hands on his hips, he turned around with raised eyebrows. "Good morning to you, as well," he said, a sardonic edge in his voice.

He looked as though nothing had even happened, pert of expression, guileless of voice, clothes in order. "Good morning? Good morning?" Kefira stammered, trying to understand. She stared at him, baring her teeth. "What *happened* last night? Why did you leave?"

"What are you talking about?" Rakhshan's brow knit. "I left because you were sleeping in past cock's crow." He lowered himself to pick up their belongings.

Kefira stole up the waterskins, that she could stoop to meet his eyelevel. "I slept in because you made me drunk!"

"I made you drunk? You kept on *asking* to be refilled."

Kefira bit her tongue. Had she? Certainly, she had not. She would never let herself become merry, alone, with a *pagan*. She stomped her foot, stymied. "Then why did you have it in the first place, that drink? It was not wine – it was the draught of barbarians!"

Rakhshan squinted at her, as though she were evasive game fowl fluttering in the distance. "That flows like spring water where I come from," he answered simply. "Come on, the dragons are probably waiting."

Kefira could not believe him. He was deceiving her, even now! Even after she'd confronted him in his coercion, his yet-hidden intent to steal her dragon – he was acting as though – none of it was true? How stupid did this man think she was?

"You are a wicked man," she grit out between her teeth, glaring at him. She could say nothing more.

He shouldered the sack of rations, halfway turning around to face the road. "Do you have a fever?" he asked, flint in his expression.

She moved after him and shoved the waterskins into his back. "You were going to take advantage of me!" she seethed, piercing him with her dark, steely gaze.

There was a glimmer of recognition in his amber eyes. His countenance slackened, and he started turning away. "I don't know what makes you think that I would do that," he said, voice hollow.

"Yes, you do!" Kefira protested, voice rife with incredulity. "Mār, your dragon – he was right when he said that you were *only* keeping me around to pay back my debt!" she spat. "And now I suppose I am only *more* beholden to you, with your 'gift' of these sandals!"

Rakhshan had his back to her, and did not move.

She could not bear the silence, as it lingered like a death shroud. "Rakhshan," she cried, voice shrinking to a plea. "You didn't, did you?" she asked. Her jaw trembled, and she clenched her hands to her throat. The evidence in the room, the evidence on her person – she recounted it all, tried to remember any red she saw. Was there *any* place she did not look? She fixed her eyes to the back of the man's head. "You – you didn't?"

He did not speak.

"Rakhshan?"

"I did not," he answered without turning around.

The wave of relief that flooded her was palpable, and she closed her eyes, feeling her heavy head pulse. She was yet a virgin. He had not harmed her. Her eyes rose to his back, and she cooled; the bag of the food he'd purchased was slung over his shoulder. She squeezed the waterskins she held with tense fingers. "Were you going to?" The question refused to stay inside, and she bit her lip upon its utterance.

"What matters is that I did not," he said, replying more promptly this time, and he turned about to face her, looking at her squarely. His expression was as taut and featureless as a tanned hide, daring her to perseverate.

The girl swallowed, unsettled by his sudden directness. Her gaze wavered from his when she asked, "Will you not?"

The line of his jaw hardened beneath his stubble. "I will not," he replied.

She looked away, and combed her hair back from her face. "How much money did you lose by rescuing Yonatan and I?"

"That doesn't matter." He was turning away again. "Are you coming?" he asked.

Kefira stalked after him, steps slow and uncertain. She did not want to, but she followed. The air was quiet and still and cool, as the farmland gave way to wilderness. The river flowed stolidly on at their right. "I think I will leave you and Mār when Yonatan is big enough," she told Rakhshan quietly.

The man's expression disclosed nothing to her, as morning sunlight lit his back and left shadows on his face. "I suppose that makes sense," he replied simply.

Yes, it did. Kefira looked away from him, reaffixing the heavy waterskins in her thin arms. "You are a wicked man," she repeated.

"I am sorry," said he.

Chapter VI
Melted Gold

"I want you to deal with him unkindly, whenever you see him from now on," Kefira instructed Yonatan. His leathery chin rested on her collarbone, yellow eyes reflecting the light of the moon as he looked up at her. He cocked his head to the side, upon her words. She sank to his eyelevel, to where he floated on the sluggish waters of the Kārun River. "He is not a good man," she whispered to him, swirling her arms beneath the water, as its cool surface touched her chin. Yonatan blinked, and she shivered.

"I did not want to take a bath, but when you returned from hunting all over in blood, I wanted to wash you; and I've not gotten the chance for such repose in a long while," she continued quietly, to no real point. Having been alone for so very long a time, conversation was an unfamiliar thing, let alone a one sided dialogue where someone was actually listening; so it was with little skill she ambled on with her words, really saying all that came to mind in the moment that it did. Despite that, it was with patience Yonatan seemed to listen. She looked at him morosely. "I just wish we did not have to be so close to those mercenaries."

They were far upriver of them – far by foot, at least. Kefira had been only dubiously satisfied by the distance. But if a bath was her only excuse to get away from Rakhshan and alone with Yonatan, then so be it. Her dragon's wings had been an excellent veneer for disrobing, in any case. The span of them encircled her a little now, in the water. Somehow, he floated upon the river, though he was nearing the size of a pony. His head rose to gaze at her quizzically.

"That is what they are," she explained to him. "Mercenaries. They do unwholesome things for money." Yonatan blinked. "Money is – wealth. Shiny coins of gold and silver and bronze." The dragon's tongue flicked out, eyes gleaming appreciatively. She sighed. "You probably saw no end of fine things such as coin on the garments of that Babylonian from Hangmatana."

Yonatan's head bobbed, and he licked the air again.

"You're starting to make me wonder if *you* would do unwholesome things for money, the way you appear so eager..." Kefira began wryly, and then she trailed off. "You – you nodded to me, just a moment ago." She said, eagerly clasping his chin, to bring his face down to her level. "You understand."

Yonatan stared at her blankly, and words stopped coming out of her mouth. Yellow eyes trained expressionlessly on her, and he flicked out his tongue, the red fork darting before her face. Vacant. "You do understand, do you not?" Kefira asked, quieter.

Yonatan nodded.

She felt herself exhale, relieved. And then press her lips to his snout. "I was sure that you did," she murmured, even as her mind surged with exultation – he understood. Her mute hatchling was not a dumb beast, as the insufferable Mār had said.

"Khhhh..." Yonatan emitted a soft, humming growl – a sound like a purr – at her affection. He nuzzled into her chest, and she giggled and pushed him away. "That is not decent," she said. He crooned, and she embraced him about his neck, smooth dragon hide pressed to her chest. "You are a good dragon, Yonatan," she told him, standing back and wringing out her hair. He thrummed, and his tongue tip brushed her forehead.

She smiled, but the expression quickly grew somber. "You are growing very fast," she said. "You must eat well and much, that you may become as great as your kinsmen." He nodded, and purred, and she continued, "When you are large enough," she felt the mantle of his wing between her fingers, "I think we ought to leave our mercenary friends."

Yonatan's tail plashed through the water, and she saw his teeth gleam in the starlight. And she smiled. "Already you act fiercely so well. Rakhshan will think I have found another dragon when I return."

Yonatan blinked, lowering his head to her. She was chewing on her lip. He crooned. Kefira rested a reassuring hand beneath his jaw. "It is alright, Yoni, I am fine."

His gaze did not waver, question persisting despite her words. His scaly lips twitched, and she heard his tail shift. *Why?*

"I just think that we have been too kind to him – Rakhshan and his dragon," Kefira murmured bitterly. And Yonatan did not pry further.

The lagoon reverberated with the humming of insects; the tiny pests wheeled and swept over the placid water like drunken dancers, as small as stars. Their stage was flat and broad, reflecting the yellow haze of the morning sky and the sun that peaked from the horizon. The gilded water was as still as a mirror, save wherever a fish would choose to surface and suck air, whereupon a series of rings would resound from its mouth. When the dragons landed, the waters shuddered with all the colors of a butterfly's wings.

"Hallelu Yah." Kefira looked at the waters, at Yonatan's side. "I do not think I have seen any place so beautiful." She looked sidelong at Rakhshan, who was farther along the shore, where Mār entered the waters. She returned her gaze to Yonatan, who looked upon the sight as well. "I will tell you a verse I know. Of our people, describing how the beauty of Creation tells of the beauty of Jehovah-Jireh." The Hardlā crooned and nuzzled eagerly at her. "Yes, yes, I will tell you it! Let me try to remember."

The archaic words swelled up easier than she'd expected they would, upon her reminiscing. Yonatan crouched to listen, and she opened her mouth. "Praising the Lord: bowed earth, shimmered sea and streamed the rills. Flashed lightening, hail, through storm cloud's girth, God's herald wind cried through the hills," she recited softly. "In praise for the Lord let all the tossing seas halt, for His splendor is above all things, He alone can we exalt. He has raised up for His people a king set apart – loving mercy for the People close to His heart."

Yonatan nuzzled her gaily at the recital, eyes gleaming with admiration. Kefira smiled, a little sadly. "It is us," she said, "The Psalmist spoke of us, the Israelites – that's what was meant by 'People close to His heart.' God's heart." She traced the line of scales on his snout with a finger as she added, "Though I suppose we are still waiting upon that king."

"I did not know that you were a songstress." Rakhshan's voice from a distance.

Her face colored, and she rested her knuckles against Yonatan's foreleg. Without turning around, she said, "I am not. That is just a verse of my people."

"Get over here, Yonatan. You learn to fish, this day," was Mār's baleful call from the center of the lake.

Yonatan straightened unhappily, wings as stiff as a sack of broken sticks at his side. He looked down at Kefira, and then shot Rakhshan a glare that could have curdled milk, before thrashing his tail and entering the water.

"He's been a little less than courteous, as of late." Rakhshan remarked, not for the first time. It'd been a few days since Kefira's instruction to the dragonling concerning the mercenary, and they'd passed from Elam into the ridged, red-soiled lands of another satrapy beyond. Kefira had not yet made good on her promise to leave.

Nevertheless, she remained as distasteful as ever of her Persian companion. "Well, certainly I do not blame him," she said snappishly, looking the man askance.

Rakhshan pressed his lips together and did not reply; though somehow he managed to break past her protective aura of asperity to hand her a portion of the morning meal. She looked dubiously at the bread and a handful of raisins, and then to the man who now put his back to her, as stiff as a stilt-walker. "I did not tell him, just so you know."

He looked back at her.

"I did not tell him what you did, or what you had a mind to do," she elaborated sourly. "I'm sure you would be dead by now, if I had.

I think that makes us even."

The man turned away, and she heard him sigh.

"That does make us even, does it not? Certainly it would."

He didn't reply.

"How much money did you lose by saving Yonatan and I? You must tell me."

"I am not at liberty to say."

"Yes you are, you liar! Tell me!"

But he would not.

Where Mār was haunch-deep in the water, Yonatan's head craned up from where he bobbed upon the surface like a bronze swan, a good many spans away. The elder dragon had instructed the hatchling to stick his jaws beneath the water, voice carrying over the lake. "Lower your jaws, but keep your nostrils up – yes, like that, so that you don't get any water in them. Keep your craw open and be very still – but also wiggle about your tongue. No, not your whole snout, you fool, just your tongue." A dour Yonatan was soon following his instruction correctly, and Mār finished, "After a while, fish will be curious ant swim in, ant then you may eat them." He snorted. "Unless you're in the ocean, you do not get anything so very large or worth the wait, but I guess you must know how so that you do not starve when there are no antelope about."

"Why does he float?" Kefira found herself asking Rakhshan.

"Huh?" The man turned his head.

She looked away from him, to her dragon. "He is floating, on the water. Why does he not sink?"

"Dragons have an organ of sorts – the Greeks call it the Chamber of Flight. There is an air therein that keeps them light."

"Did you learn that at the Asman Kāra?"

"Indeed."

"Why did you leave there?"

"Where?"

"The Asman Kāra."

"Like I said, Mār and I were not cut out for such work."

"Such lawful work as peacekeeping and fighting off violent Bedouin slave-traders?"

He looked at her wryly. "I guess so," he said, not bothering to defend himself, to Kefira's surprise. She let the matter drop.

A yelp from Yonatan carried over the lake, and Kefira looked up to see him thresh his wings through the water, as though recoiling from it. Again, he cried out.

"Whatever is wrong? Dit a fish bite off your tongue?" asked Mār.

Yonatan snarled ferociously, whirling away from him and piercing the surface of the water with his jaws, his whole front half charging after with the surge of his wings. Kefira cried out as his tail thrashed above the water, as he seemed to be engaged in battle with some unseen combatant. Red froth splashed from the water and twinkled like a handful of rubies before it fell. "Yonatan! What is wrong?" she cried, leaping into the lake, gathering her skirts to her hips to wade after him.

"Get out of the water!" Mār snapped at her, and her heart burst as he leapt towards her, jaws wide. Then Rakhshan was there, sweeping her off her feet, even as a gnarled grey drake lunged up from the water and snapped at her retreating heels. The Azhi Dahaki made quick work of this creature, wrenching it from the water with his jaws and tossing the bubbling form away like a discus. Another great lizard took the dead one's place, and hissed in pursuit of the two humans.

Kefira was practically thrown onto shore when the man reached it, and he shoved her behind him to rip a blade from a sheath at his side.

A hissing breath left the gaping white mouth of the drake, as it slithered forth on short legs, huge tail dredging the mud. Kefira saw silver flash in Rakhshan's hand, but before he swung, Yonatan glittered upon them. The white and red splatter of the first reptile was strewn over the front of him. The other beast was finished quicker though, as with all his weight Yonatan fell upon it. The offending creature croaked its death cry. The skirmish was over, and the dragons loomed broodingly over the corpses.

Kefira let out a pent-up breath, as she looked upon her dragon. "You're safe," she gasped, leaning upon him. Her garments were no longer sufficient to wash the mess from his face. His head was almost as great as her torso. Blood dripped from his jaws. "Yonatan," she said. "Where are you hurt?"

Air hissed through his teeth, and he nuzzled his hindleg, low upon his foot. There was a wound on it, but nothing formidable, she saw. His toughened scales were merely bloody on the edges, where one of the drakes must have bitten him. "You're a tough one, my love. That should heal nicely. But don't scare me like that again," she chided, touching the wound with her hand.

She looked over at the corpse of the grey drake. "What is that? It looks like a small dragon." Though it had no wings. She looked over at Rakhshan, who was sheathing his sword.

"A crocodile. It is a small water-dragon they have farther south here," he explained shortly. "Are you alright?"

"I am fine," she said, moving to her feet, and gesturing towards the water. "Yoni needs his face washed. It isn't safe though, is it?" she asked dubiously.

Mār was glaring across the lake, at a bask of crocodiles emerging from the water on the opposite shore. "They woult be very stupit to attack again, while the crimson of their own lingers upon the waters."

Rakhshan nodded to her, although a little uneasily. "Go ahead."

Yonatan shook his head in the lapping waves, and Kefira scooped up water to rinse his face. He immersed his front, too, and soon all the signs of battle were washed away. They were not disturbed by the crocodiles, Kefira was pleased to find, as she rubbed the soft flesh beneath Yonatan's eye. The dragon persisted in looming above her like a mothering falcon, as though she'd been the one wounded and not him. "It is alright, Yonatan. I was not harmed," she assured him. And it was eerie to her as to why that was. She glanced at Rakhshan on the bank.

"Are you sure you're alright?" he inquired. Beside him, Mār began messily tearing away at one of the drakes. She saw him rend it open like a tome with his claws, spilling hot blood and white meat and black innards over the dusty shore.

"What?" she asked, swallowing.

"Are you alright? You were almost eaten by a bunch of crocodiles," he repeated.

"You've asked me that already." She pursed her lips. "I assure you, I'm fine." Reluctantly, she added, "But thank you for – dragging me away from them, I suppose."

He cracked a smile. "Holding a maiden away from dangerous devils is its own reward."

"Your words are not consoling me, mercenary," she said, a sardonic edge in her voice. "All things considered, you ought to abide by a simple 'you're welcome.'"

Like a peal of thunder, Yonatan's stomach rumbled above her. He looked at one of the crocodiles, and inquisitively scraped at its hide with a claw.

Kefira stepped forward sheepishly, in-between the dragon and the crocodile. Frowning, she said, "I'm sorry, it is not right." It had scales, but no fins; not kashrut. Yonatan just dug his claws deeper and rolled the corpse back into the lake.

Rakhshan looked as though he was about to protest on her verdict, but held his tongue. "It is alright," he said simply. "We shall find something else while we travel."

"Very well..." She felt guilty for depriving her dragon of a meal. It was not as though there was a rabbi or priest around to chastise them for not adhering to kashrut. Surely, if worse came to worse and they could find no more food, Jehovah would permit them to take some unclean food. But the idea made her stomach turn and she frowned. "When are we leaving this place?" she asked Rakhshan.

"I certainly see no reason we should stay," he said. He went up to the glutting Mār. "Are you ready?"

The Azhi Dahaki swept a talon over the exhausted remains of his meal, burying it in the caked earth. "Yes." And they departed the lakes.

It was late in the day when they flew over the temple, crowning the top of a hill, constructed of stones of a washed-out color, gilded in plates of gold that shone in the sinking red sun. Yonatan, who was flying alongside Mār, squawked and banked towards this sparkling diversion, and even from his distance, Kefira saw his pupils dilate and contract as he examined the sight. Mār noticed his stalling, and Kefira felt his wings lilt to dip towards the dragonling. "What is the matter?" he rumbled irritably, herding him back to their course. "It is only a temple." Yonatan replied with a coarse bray of protest, yet reluctantly returned to following the elder.

"I told him of the Temple of God, a few days ago. I hope he does not think that is what that was," Kefira explained to Rakhshan, after distastefully looking back at the high place and its occupants. "I'm sure *those* men are going to defile themselves with the shrine prostitutes."

"Yes, I do believe that was a temple of Ishtar," the man replied.

"I'm sure you are familiar with such places."

"Indeed, no. Remarkably, though I am a vagabond, I avoid even the carnal places of worship like plague." He cocked a wry smile at her. "I am not the harlot-monger that you seem think I am, even under the pretense of worship."

"Do you hate all gods?" Kefira found herself asking. "When you speak of any of them, you act as though you speak of the very Lord of the Flies."

"Beelzebub, Angra Mainyu, Hades," the man said, "Zeus, Spenta Mainyu, Baal, they're all the same to me."

Kefira chewed on her tongue. "You would not cast the Jehovah of my people with the lot of such consorts of the Devil, would you?"

"Not when you're here to box my ears for it."

Kefira scowled. "You vex me," she muttered. "Someday when your dragon is not looking, you shall be in for it."

"Of that I am sure."

That night they camped amidst a clump of hills, and upon their arrival, the Persian conceded with satisfaction, "We are making good time."

"Do we have very much farther to go?" Kefira asked nervously, looking at her weary Yonatan, who was stretching his mauve and gold frame across a hill. She tried to measure with his eyes the expanse of his wings.

"We haven't much longer. More than halfway there, I would guess." She saw him look at the map he'd brought out as he usually did in the evening, and trace his finger on it. "Once we get past those grey mountains there, we'll be in the green cedar forests of Carmania."

"Is the ocean nigh? Is it truly green there?" Kefira inquired, halting in her supping, bread and dried meat resting in her lap.

"Indeed it is, in places. Just like the Kārun River, back where we were a week past. There are a good many more rivers there, from the mountains, and tall trees of cedar grow there."

"Are we close to Parudrauga?"

"We've a few more days of travel, no more than half a fortnight, I would guess."

"I want to see the ocean," Kefira said quietly, by way of a response. That at least she did want to see. But she wanted to be gone before the mercenaries took them to Parudrauga. She glanced up at Yonatan, who had reclined behind her, and hung above her head the canopy of a wing.

"You shall see it even from a long way off. I imagine even when we hit the skies of Gedrosia it shall be in view. It is quite a sight."

"Is it truly like a great lake?" Kefira asked, as she scooted back to enfold herself in blanket and Yonatan's embrace, as he draped his tail over her lap.

"I suppose that is what it could be most compared to. But you shall have to see for yourself. Standing upon its shore is where one can best take in its splendor."

Kefira pet Yonatan's lowered face, looking into his liquid gold eyes as she said, "I'm sure that if Yonatan and I still deign to travel with you by then, we shall quite enjoy seeing it together."

The somnolent Mār snorted, even in his repose, and Rakhshan just shot her a pert look as he resettled the map in his lap.

The night unfolded like a black sheet of linen. Stars began to dapple the sky. She saw it past the fiery wine streaks on Yonatan's wing, the ground-up jewels of amethysts, diamonds, and jacinth sprinkled across the sky by the hand of God. Kefira wondered if that was truly how the sky was formed, if by flying up very high upon Yonatan's back, they could feel the wool the clouds were made of, the paint that composed sunsets, and the gemstones of the night sky. Well, she supposed that if the stars were indeed made of gems, then someone else with a dragon would have taken some down and become very rich by them, and she probably would have heard of it by now. Yet still, she wondered.

She looked at her dragon, who was not yet asleep; his head rested beside her bedroll. His scales reflected the orange light from the campfire, as did his dazzling eyes of topaz, as he peered up at the sky along with her.

"Yes, it is beautiful, love," she replied, and his lower eyelid rose in an expression of gladness.

"One woult think you two consultet spirits, the way you can speak without talking," Mār interjected from across the clearing, raising his head a ways to leer. "But, forgive me, you woult not practice anything against the Laws of Moses – my mistake."

"Shut up, Snake." Rakhshan batted at the dragon absentmindedly, without looking up. He was yet poring over the map by firelight.

"But it is a little queer, you must concete, brother," the dragon's voice lowered conspiratorially. "Ant unnerving."

"As is your breath, my friend."

Kefira was about to drift off to sleep, when she felt Yonatan's nose on her stomach, and she opened her eyes to look at him. He craned his face close to hers, inclining it to the left, that one of his eyes was square upon her. "What is it, Yonatan?" she murmured.

His pupil narrowed and broadened, like an indecisive eclipse of the sun. She saw the vague reflection of her own face in the black dish of his pupil. He looked as though he had when he was poring over the golden roof of the temple, though there was no happy tug at the corner of his jaws.

"There are such things as false gods, my love," she explained, coming to understand him slowly. "Idols of stone and wood and precious things that do not speak or make miracles. That was a temple of one of them. It was not the temple Solomon created, the one I told you of."

His gaze lingered, inquiring.

"Andonai's temple was destroyed by the Babylonians, many years ago." She frowned, and then when Yonatan raised his head and his pupils narrowed in distress, she added, "But Jehovah is not destroyed, love. His temple fell, Israel fell, but He is not destroyed. That I know because I would not have you, if He had not let me find you. I found you with one of our kinsmen, from a man of God. That is why I named you Yonatan – you are a gift from Him," she said, rubbing his nose.

He seemed pleased by this knowledge, and he rested his head once more by her side, looking up into the sky. "You are proof that He was not destroyed with the Temple, I think," she murmured, half to herself.

The dragon's eyes glimmered, glittering warmly upon her. She nestled closer to him, feeling his warm hide steady past her blanket. "You are a good friend, Yonatan," she told him. "Thank you for listening to me ramble."

His tongue flickered out, and he blinked. She felt him curl closer about her, tail glimmering with polished garnets and agate as he became a living nest for her.

Now that he was large enough, Yonatan was ensconcing her in sleep like a mother hen. Though at first it felt constricting, too dark and close to another being – she'd gotten used to it. And now, she loved the warmth and the presence of him. She'd never felt so safe.

The tapestry of his wing descended, but not before she could see Rakhshan by the fire; he'd not been looking at the map, though his eyes quickly returned to it upon her reflection of his gaze. His expression was unreadable. Kefira wondered if he'd been listening to them, about to make a rude comment about Adonai, perhaps.

But she held her tongue. Now it was dark. She could see vague firelight illuminate the veins in Yonatan's wing, and felt his foreleg above her head, his breathing at her side. She saw Rakhshan's silhouette as his sandals crunched towards Mār. Sleep descended upon them.

When she awoke, it was still dark. The yellow saucer of the moon hung above the black horizon, and the fire had died down to glowering embers. Was it midnight? It had to be late, for she could tell by the dissonance of peaceful sleep-breathing that everyone was asleep. All she knew was that she no longer wanted to be.

Kefira slowly unwound herself from her blanket, and carefully crawled from Yonatan's encircling limbs. Once out of his reach, she looked back at him momentarily, a small golden red hill that rose and fell with breath. Mār was a larger hill across from him, Rakhshan a fitfully sleeping bundle in the crook of his foreleg.

She left the perimeter of camp, pulling her shawl tight about her face against the damp chill. A shroud had fallen over her in sleep, descending like brimstone to burn up her dreams. The image of an inferno in the carven halls of the temple, as gold dripped from the ceiling – it plagued her – the fires spread to her village, her home. Devouring.

She'd thought she had seen the last of this nightmare when it hadn't resurfaced for two years – in the months that had followed her orphaning, this was all she saw in sleep. Slowly, it had gone from every night to every fortnight, to once a month until she hadn't seen it for years. Yet tonight it had lunged back.

She pressed her fists into her leaking eyes, trying to stem the sorrow that welled up within her, kicking rocks in her path. Truly, Yonatan was a sign that Jehovah still had an arm moving in the world, yet why had He ignored them until then? Israel. Why could He not have moved when they were being attacked, enslaved, killed, raped, destroyed by the Assyrians, the Babylonians? Why could He not have moved when her parents were consumed by a fire that came as reasonless as the wind?

She made herself sit beneath a lone tree, a few hills away from their dwelling. Its rough bark pressing into her back comforted her a little. But before long, she had to stand up again, and she ground her knuckles into its rough surface. She hated it when she became this way – when she asked questions that she could have no answer to. It made her feel as though she were drowning in fog.

"What are you doing to your fists?"

Kefira jumped, whirling around to see that Rakhshan was there, descending a rise a few paces aft.

"What are you doing here?" Kefira breathed, backing up to the tree as he sauntered over.

"I wanted to see this tree," he said, patting the bark. "No, you just looked upset when you got up, is all."

"What makes you think that having you follow me would make me any happier?" she growled, folding her hands behind her back. Her fingers seared with pain, and she felt numb skin peeling from them.

"What did you do to your hands?" he asked, ignoring her rejoinder. He reached for her elbow, but she backed away and snapped, "Last time you got me alone, I woke up with a headache that made my head feel like a tabor drum. You ought not be here."

In the moonlight she saw that there was something that appeared to be concern on his face; he backed up and defensively spread his hands. "I'm sorry, I'm sorry – what business is it of mine if the one I rescued from execution goes out at night to strike trees."

"I was not striking it," she denied quietly. Her arms were shaking; she looked away, and hugged them to her stomach. "I wish you would not continue to bother me."

"I wish you would not consider simple conversation a bother." The man sat down perfunctorily with his back to the tree, looking up at her as she stood. "Why do you not sit down?"

"I will do no such thing."

"I can see how your hands shake better from this angle. And that your right hand is bleeding a little."

"What business is it of yours?" she snapped, folding her hot hands beneath her throat. "Leave me alone, please."

"Why, so that you do not have to go looking for another tree? I think not."

"You are such an - insufferable mule," she growled.

"Why did you hurt yourself?"

"I did not."

He did not heed her. "It just seems like an awfully heathen thing to do. Though I suppose they use ceremonial blades and the like."

"Shut up," Kefira cried, but her voice was low. Though it sent pain up her arm, she swept her knuckles over her robes, to wipe away the blood that had not yet dried.

"Is that the sacrifice Jehovah requires if you do not bring him enough goats?"

Kefira grit her teeth, glaring down at him; she was wholly stunned by his brazenness. Anger rose up like a roused lion within her, but it stopped before her tongue, heating her fists. "I would kick you," she spat, "if it would not do mischief to these sandals."

Rakhshan looked up at her, unruffled. "I'm glad you came to that conclusion."

"You're a very unkind – a very wicked man," she told him.

"Kefira," he said.

"What?"

"You ought to sit down."

Kefira glared at the man, who was patting the ground at the base of the tree beside him. She bit her lip before relenting to sit – though not in the place he directed – upon a rock that jutted from the ground across from him. "Are you happy?" she asked him.

"Elated."

"You make no sense."

"I could say the same about you."

Kefira slouched, hands folded fitfully in her lap. "What is it that you want, Rakhshan?"

"Nothing."

She gazed at him skeptically from below a furrowed brow, and pulled her shawl tight over her head.

"Why do you always keep your hair covered?"

"What sort of question is that?"

"I don't know. I just wanted to say something before the silence grew too long."

Kefira cracked a smile of forbearance. "If you *must* know, it is the way of my people."

"I thought only married women covered their heads."

"I think it's best that people think I'm married," she said simply. "It worked for a while, when we first met."

Rakhshan let out a small chuckle. "You didn't trick me for a minute."

Kefira shot him a look. "Really? I was very sure I did."

The man shrugged. "It was obvious by your lack of cordiality that you were not a hostess or homemaker; no man in his right mind would ever take up so cold and societally incompetent a girl." He grinned. "You ought to brush up on your thespianism."

"You're very rude." She frowned, rubbing the cold flesh of her knuckles with a soft finger. "I needn't be fettered by the expectations of society, when it is composed wholly of those who do not even care to offer a hungry orphan bread."

"Yet you insist upon covering your head, a societal stricture."

"It is so that I do not catch any eyes."

"Your hair must truly be something then."

"It is not," she assured him flatly, hooking her fingers in its dark curls. "Why do you speak of it so persistently?"

"I do not mean to, I assure you."

"Are you perverse as well as wicked?"

"You grind my heart into the dust, little by little, whenever you call me such things." The man smiled mirthlessly. "No, I am not perverse, I'm sorry. Just curious, is all."

"Well, philosopher, I would appreciate it, if you *do* insist upon perseverating in conversation, a new topic of discussion."

Rakhshan let out a drawn out breath, as though pondering.

"But I shall choose it," Kefira added, catching herself before he could bring up any other sort of unwelcome matter. "You must tell me how much Yonatan and I owe you."

He looked at her sidelong. "You've been asking me that every chance you get."

"It is because I need to know."

"Why is it important to you? I do not think I very much regret the exchange."

Kefira was given pause. It was difficult to look at him, now. "Well," she said, stymied by his nonchalance, "I must know, that I may repay you, and be on my way." And then, upon recognizing her words she swallowed, eyes rising to meet his.

His expression was earnest, and weary. "Kefira," he said. And then he took in a deep breath. "It was eight hundred shekels of silver. That was how much money they offered to the one who could find the egg and bring it to the Satrap."

The girl almost choked. She gaped at him, wondering if she heard correctly. The sum was astounding – she'd never seen *two* shekels of silver together in one place in her entire life – let alone *eight hundred*. "Rakhshan," she breathed, when she'd finally regained her wind. "You – when I was in prison – you were supposed to get paid, then, yet you rescued me?"

"I guess that's how it happened."

"How could you?" She jumped to her feet, staring at him, hands balled into fists. "How could you do such a thing? I shall never be able to repay you!"

Rakhshan stood, leaning against the tree. "Well, at the time, I thought it was a good idea."

"It was not!" Kefira said, taking a step towards him. "What am I supposed to do, now?" Tears were springing to her eyes, but she refused to shed them, furious. "I cannot repay you. Not ever!"

Rakhshan seemed more than a little taken aback by her vehemence. He looked at her with concern. "Quite frankly," he said, "I believe any other young lady would have fawned over such a sum spent on their behalf."

Kefira whirled away from him, to pace a trench through the earth. "But – but that *sum* is no less than a *bride price* for a princess of the Nile!" she cried. "You are a fool!"

"Stop saying such things – it's as though you want me to regret not seeing you dangling from a spit in Hangmatana," he said with a wry laugh. "I think you are overreacting."

"You – you are *underreacting!*" she spat, turning on him. "Do you know what you've done to me? If even I were bound as maidservant to your family, my descendants would not be free of my debt for a hundred generations!"

"Well, you see," Rakhshan said tersely, "That would not work out very well anyway, as neither of us have a family."

Kefira paused, staring at him. Was he an orphan as well? Indeed, she never remembered him speaking of family.

"You know what I think," Rakhshan began. Kefira watched him as he spoke and took a step closer, before folding his arms behind his back and looking down at her. It was with the utmost casualness he suggested, "I think you ought to be my wife. I think that would make things even."

Kefira stared at him as though he'd just spit fire. She took a step back, arms tingling at her sides, as her face grew pale. Had he truly just suggested – what she heard? She met his gaze, eyes flinty, trying to read him. "Why – why is that?" came out as a sputter. Him, the man – Rakhshan – what a notion! She seethed, "So that you could molest me under the cover of the law?"

Now he took a step back, and she saw a wounded look flash across his face. "That was a very unkind thing to say," he finally managed. "No, for your information," he scowled, "*not* that I could molest you."

Kefira was quiet, guilt tugging at her stomach. Perhaps that was out of line. Chewing her lip, she steeled herself and said a little quieter, "Well, in any case, that was a very irrational thing for you to suggest."

He shrugged, looking away dejectedly. "I suppose so. Though it is always an option, if you're ever again wracked with conviction of your debt," he muttered.

"I don't understand you." Her cheeks flamed. "Why – why would you even suggest such a thing? It would avail you nothing."

"Just forget I asked, if you are so disgusted," he told her, lips curving upwards without any gladness. "Let us return, and pour some wine over your hands," he said. "Yonatan will be anxious if he wakes up and you are not there."

The girl straightened, looking away from him, as the aftershock of his words swept down her spine. Her face jerked towards him when she felt his hands on hers, saw her hand between his. He was looking at her knuckles.

She surprised herself when she did not recoil. "What are you doing?" she asked, voice shallow.

He let her have her hand back. "You are a little fool," he said; in the moonlight she could make out the melancholy laughter in his eyes.

She let out a sigh, and held her hands protectively to her chest. "A fool in the company of fools."

Chapter VII
Sleepless City

Kefira could now walk beneath Yonatan without her head grazing his scales, and at night, even furled, his wings spanned over her like a pavilion. Though he hadn't the elder dragon's weight, the serpentine length of him, swanlike neck and proudly carried tail, was now nearly as long as the Azhi Dahaki. His wings, set against the green of the tall trees, were the color of fire, dappled in burgundy and white; Kefira deemed them the appropriate length. He was almost two fortnights old.

"I want to ride Yonatan, now," she told Rakhshan, their first morning in the satrapy of Carmania. The dry wounds on her knuckles brushed against her chin as she informed him of her intentions. She'd not yet quite recovered from the encounter of nights past and so her eyes were cool on his. She was not imploring him by any means, she was collecting her rightful due.

"You sound as though you expect me to object," said he, promptly handing the girl her portion of the morning meal. He looked at her squarely, and then appraised the Hardlā swishing his tail behind her. Smiling pertly, he returned his gaze to her. "I'm not so greatly perverse a man to deny you the right to sit alone, aback your own dragon."

"*Thank* you, brother," came Mār, from his somnolence.

Kefira pressed her lips together, a laugh almost escaping. She looked up at him. "You are serious?" She was a little surprised, to be sure. When she recovered, she smiled a little. "Then it is truly a feat, Master Heathen, for you to set aside your wickedness and abide my will."

Rakhshan shot her a sardonic look and said, "Indeed, Mistress Kosher. We're going in to town today, and thence we can buy you some rigging to promote your crusade." Irony aside, he seemed to be measuring the breadth of Yonatan's chest, his neck, his shoulders, with his eyes. Kefira turned around to look up at the dragon, who seemed pleased with the Persian's words, though he dutifully glared down at him.

"We — not just us, yes?" Kefira intoned uneasily to Rakhshan. "I do not care to repeat out last excursion." Bitterness crept back into her voice. Yonatan's eyes sparked with curiosity.

"Oh — no — I mean yes," Rakhshan stammered, taken off balance by the mention. "Yes, the dragons will be able to accompany us in this town; it advocates the Asman Kāra." He glanced at her sidelong, lips tight. "That last excursion was nothing more than a black sheep."

"What black sheep? What happent?" Mār lifted his head. His green eyes flickered with impish yellow. "You't not spoken of any mishap, Rakhshan."

"Nothing happened, Mār." Kefira found herself intervening for the Persian, hastily. "The lout merely spilled a bucket from the well upon me, when we were filling the waterskins." She glanced at the man as she spoke.

There was a glimmer of surprise and then relief in his eyes, but he continued her tale without faltering. "Alas, I am as graceless as a newborn calf, and her robes took the brunt of it."

"Oh, that is amusing. I'm sure you dit it on purpose, too, clever boy, just to see her all wet," accepted Mār dismissively.

"You pig," Kefira shot at him, astonished, knotting her fingers together at her chest. And Rakhshan didn't even dignify him with a rejoinder.

That morning they prepared for travel; Rakhshan packed up the party's belongings below his dragon — for, indeed, he was really the only person of them who owned anything. As he worked, Kefira walked beneath the cedar trees with Yonatan. The dragon was large enough now that his wings brushed the thick grey trunks of the trees as they passed, and he had to lower his head to keep his neck from tangling amidst the branches.

"I'd wanted to, when you were big as you are now, to abscond from those mercenaries." Kefira found herself speaking to him. "You remember. Perhaps, when Rakhshan fits you with the riding cloths, we can be off on our own." Yonatan's topaz eyes glinted keenly at her.

"Do you agree?" she asked quietly, as though they might be overheard.

He touched his nose to her forehead and blinked. "I do not rightly understand," she replied. "Do you mean yes?"

The dragon's wings shuffled, and his gaze maintained hers.

She nodded, looking at the bright grass springing up from the rocks underfoot. "I am not so certain, as before, however," she told him. "About leaving." Though he lacked more character than she should like, Rakhshan had given her reason after reason for them to stay with him. His slick tongue had gotten them out of Hangmatana and past the asmanaba encounter on the border; that was a great benefit, even if she did not count the unsurmountable boon of the money attained from selling the signet ring, and his generous pocket. With all these things, she and Yonatan were quite well off. Never minding the other advantages, she had not eaten this good in years. She used to be able to count five rows of ribs from her breast to her navel, but the ridges were disappearing, now. She could not even wrap her thumb and forefinger around her ankles, anymore. There was no way to get around it; without the rogue and his dragon, they'd have none of his food, deceptive charisma, or money. And if she were to ever be able to ride Yonatan without falling off his back, she'd need rigging, which she'd have to steal without Rakhshan's coin purse. And though her fingers were natural pilferers, she'd never liked using them.

So what – if she left she would weave her own cloth? She had been with her mother only long enough to be competent with a needle and thread. But she had no loom, no yarn, nothing with which she could craft the textiles necessary to keep herself aback her dragon.

"I will not lie, he is a generous person," she murmured to

Yonatan. "Rakhshan is." She looked up at the dragon, halting in their procession. "When you hatched, I'd looked like I walked from the Valley of Bones, but – well, he has been kind, I suppose, to feed me so well."

Yonatan blinked. His smooth tongue flicked out across her cheekbone, and he gazed at her quietly. There was a little sadness in his eyes.

"We shall see if we want to leave later, after we have seen more," she said finally. "There is no reason to leave just yet." She thought about Parudrauga, their destination. "Perhaps when we cross over to Gedrosia we shall part ways."

They returned. "It is not foolish to bring Yonatan, is it?" Kefira asked Rakhshan, as an afterthought. "Will they be looking for him, do you think?"

"I do not know if word of his escape has been given this far south," the man speculated. "But the vagrant Hardlā would not be of common knowledge, anyway. I'm sure those who see him will think he is only a Thu'ban of odd color. There is nothing criminal about him to be worried over."

"No, nothing criminal at all." Mār assured. "With his large eyes and hitten teeth and gaily swinging tail, all the village chiltren will be on his back as soon as we lant."

"Very well…" Kefira rubbed the smooth muzzle of her dragon as he glared at the Azhi Dahaki.

They set off that morning, easterly instead of directly south – Rakhshan must have known where they were going; the gleaming slate mountains and the carpet of green trees led to some settlement in the distance. Mār's claws grazed the tops of the cedars, and Kefira could smell their aroma on the wind.

Yonatan was displeased to still have her riding with Mār for the time being. He flew before the dragon, twining through the clouds above with fervor. *Soon you will be on my back, and I will not carry you so closely to the ground,* she could almost hear him say.

"You ought to get into the habit of *not* being so reckless, if you want your little faerie to stay on your back," Mār called up to him, and the young dragon did a good deal less of showing off.

"It is there," Rakhshan said eventually, shouting into her ear that his dragon could hear. "Where the smoke is." There was a settlement nestled in the forest at the knees of a mountain.

Mār was pleased by its appearance, as his wings tilted to descend. "Goot. Now perhaps soon Yonatan will stop fussing, when we give him his girl."

Yonatan waited impatiently for Mār to land on the outskirts of town, at a rock outcropping on the slope above it next to a spatter of pale rocks, and he swooped down behind the Azhi Dahaki.

"Do not mess those up," the older dragon ordered, craning his neck to Yonatan as he obediently mince-stepped out of the rocks he'd landed upon.

"What is the matter?" Kefira demanded.

"Don't worry, that is just the mark that lets riders know that dragons are permitted in the village," Rakhshan clarified.

Kefira looked down from Mār's shoulder, to see that indeed the rocks were conformed into the shape of a character: three columned triangles with tapering line above them. "Is that the cuneiform letter for A?" she asked the man. "I did not think that 'dragon' began with an A," she said quizzically.

"It stands for Asman Kāra," Rakhshan laughed. "That is one of the few letters I remember from my schooling days."

Rather than having her slide off his shoulders, Mār promptly deposited Kefira to the ground with a talon. "Ant that, little girl," he said, "is the last time, I hope, I must have you on my back. Go to your dragon."

Yonatan was more than happy to receive her. He nuzzled her, crooning low.

"You are very sure it is safe for us to go?" Kefira asked Rakhshan once more, uneasily rubbing Yonatan's chin.

"Yes, but that doesn't mean we should linger." The man began down the slope with his dragon. "There is no telling what trouble might await us."

"Hmm, that sait," Mār intoned, halting with a swishing tail. "I ought not go."

"Are you cowardly, Mār?" asked Kefira goadingly, glad to have an arrow to fire against him.

"No, I dare say I am, little fool. But any wort about us woult speak of two dragons ant two menfolk; let us for our sake only be a man, a Thu'ban, and a girl. Fare well, brother," he said, already dismissing Rakhshan.

"Clever Snake," the man replied, patting the dripping muzzle of his beast. "Hunt for yourself. We won't be gone long."

And so they were, a man, a dragon, and a girl. Rakhshan assured her as they descended that Yonatan looked something like the Persian fire-breather that was his alias, and would not be observed as a Hardlā at all, though she was hardly assured. Yonatan seemed to feel her unease, and as they neared the town gates, he put her on his back. She did not know what he was doing at first; but then he was walking behind her, and she was halted in her tracks as he stuck his head and neck through her legs.

"Whoa," Rakhshan said, as she slid backwards down Yonatan's raised neck, down the smooth scales along his spine to rest upon his shoulders. Kefira recovered from her surprise and laughed in delight, before hurrying to rearrange her skirts. "Someone is a little impatient," the man chuckled. "We'll have you some rigging, in good time."

Rakhshan led them into town, Yonatan content to prance behind. Kefira was astonished and more than pleased to see that they attracted little attention on the streets. For these men, it seemed as though seeing a dragon in the street was no greater a deal than seeing a procession of camels – neither panic nor parade in their wake. The innocuous entrance did much to ease her nerves, and at least Yonatan was enjoying himself. It had been a long time since he'd been in a settlement, and then he'd never gotten a close look at the wood and clay architecture, or the running children, or the merchants hawking their wares.

For though it was not yet noon, a good portion of the shops and booths were open, as though the sight of newcomers had spurred the shopkeepers to open early. They all had at least one very interested customer, Yonatan, who would gaze over all their commodities with a covetous eye. Be it shells and beads or fruit and bread or scarves, the dragon lingered at every place there was something new to look at – much to the hurried Rakhshan's chagrin.

The shopkeepers were not overly wary of the dragon's close loitering, or at least were less anxious than the livestock and the dogs that had withdrawn into the alleyways to give the Hardlā way. The vendors, at least, were brave enough to bark commands and not fear at the dragon. "Off with you, Thu'ban," the butcher said, when Yonatan had parked himself in front of shanks of meat that were sported at his booth. The dragon recoiled his curious head from the swatting hand.

"No, no, love – Rakhshan is buying some for later, worry not – the rest is not ours," Kefira told her dragon quickly, before he became outraged at his treatment. Yonatan looked at her sidelong, gaze breaking from the gleaming, sanguine-scented carcasses hung tauntingly before him. Slowly, with a melodramatic sigh, he moved on after Rakhshan.

The next stop was a fabric vendor, who had an impressive array of textiles on display. White bolts of wool, linens dyed blue and green and yellow, yarn and multicolored spools of thread. He had bolts of rigging cloth, too, strong and thick fabric that came in varying lengths. The greatest span he had was fifty cubits. Rakhshan seemed dubious at the purchase, however; though the incredible length of that fabric could easily go to the depths of a well and back twice. "Certainly that should be enough," she said to him.

"When he is fully grown I'm sure we'll need to find more, but for now it ought to work," he consented, much to the merchant's pleasure. Rakhshan tossed the heavy bundle into her lap at they moved on to buy more rations.

They left the village no worse for the endeavor – no heralds in their wake crying of the bounty upon the heads of the Hardlā Thieves. Their food stores were restocked, Yonatan had his rigging. Before departing, she and Rakhshan refilled the waterskins, the man under the watchful and suspicious eye of her dragon, who was vigilant against the pernicious splashing, lest it should befall his rider again.

Mār was resting in the same place when they returned, chops bubbling with acid and the blood of a recent kill. "Dit we get the pup some new trappings?" he inquired, upon their arrival.

"Indeed we did!" Kefira exclaimed, beaming at her dragon, whose muscles seemed to be trembling with anticipation as he beheld the bundle in her lap.

Rakhshan nodded in response to his own dragon, and she remembered from whose purse the funds for their new furnishings had come. She thought fleetingly of thanking him, but withheld. "Would you show me how to put them on, Rakhshan?" she said instead.

He did, certainly enough. "You will have to get comfortable wearing a scarf from now on, little drake," Mār said, as Yonatan squirmed beneath the first layer of fabric. Loops were fashioned of the linen's length, slung like short sleeves through his forelegs, around his neck. "Only be glat you neetn't wear bit and britle, as must a donkey."

"It is not too uncomfortable, is it, love?" Kefira asked Yonatan, holding his head from where she now stood on the ground. The dragon blinked at her, and there was no great complaint in his eyes, though he was ever shifting his neck around its bonds. Rakhshan was scrambling over his back; Kefira had been too slow at following orders for his liking, and so he'd taken to rigging Yonatan out himself, which the Hardlā abided.

"As he's a Hebrew dragon, he hasn't any horns down his spine. I'm not accustomed to that," Rakhshan said, as he slung some of the fabric over Yonatan's breast. "Mār's are a good help when it comes to reinforcing the rider's straps."

Kefira glanced over to appraise Mār's rigging. Some of the fabric twined around his neck was tied taut or leather-bound upon the spines protruding from his scales. Yonatan had no such appendages. "I can still ride him, though, can I not?" she asked Rakhshan uneasily.

"Of course. It shall just take some more work. Anyway, you're so small you're not likely to be much of a burden upon the rigging." He was fiddling with the two loose ends of the fabric that remained, upon Yonatan's shoulders. "You can come on up, Kefira. I will show you how to work it."

"Very well," she said, and Yonatan placed her gingerly on his back.

"Sit down, right between his shoulders and neck," Rakhshan told her, as Yonatan turned his head with interest to watch their proceedings.

Kefira obeyed, cinching up her legs to preserve modesty, knees straddling Yonatan's neck. She raised her head to look up at Rakhshan, who stood above her. "And now?" she asked. The mess of swaddling on Yonatan's back seemed alien compared to Mār's.

Rakhshan knelt and reached down to pull a belt from beneath her legs, the ends of the fabric knotted together, and rested it across her lap. "Forgive me for touching you, again," he said promptly. The girl nodded her forbearance, and he smiled. "Now loop your legs into the bands down there, over his forelegs." Kefira did so, and lifted her arms as Rakhshan moved another strap – or, a number of other straps – to press into her back.

"Comfortable?"

"Yes," she said, patting Yonatan's flank as she exchanged glances with him.

"Good." Rakhshan stood and brushed his hands over his tunic. "You can hold on to the hand-strap there, so your arms don't flail about. Just be sure not to grab the band above it, unless you want to suffocate dear Yoni."

"Oh," Kefira said sheepishly, looking at the numerous loops around Yonatan's neck, withdrawing her hands. "Is it truly so dangerous?"

"It is only that the hand-strap does not loop over his throat, so it is safe to grab. Do not worry, you'll be fine." There was not much room on Yonatan's back, so the man jumped off at an angle past his wing. He turned around to look up at Kefira, shading his eyes from the sun. "Shall you be alright following Mār from now on?" he asked the both of them.

Yonatan snorted in a way that suggested he had no intention of anything like *following* the other dragon, and Kefira laughed a little, before growing solemn. "*Shall* I be alright?" She pressed her lips together uneasily. "Is it very difficult, flying?" she inquired, a little quietly.

"No, nothing really beyond what you did riding Mār. Just sit tight and hold on," Rakhshan reassured. Then he smirked. "The only difference I foresee is that you and I will probably be a little chillier from now on, without one another's company."

The girl balked. "If I had anything to throw at you besides my sandals, I would," she sniffed, though a laugh threatened to escape her. "Let us be off already," she banished the Persian. And then she bit her lip, staring at one of Yonatan's scales. Gedrosia. Parudrauga. Her eyes flickered to her dragon's yellow gaze. She was going to fly with him, now. They could leave, really, any time they wanted. Her fingers tightened over the hand-strap. They were not bound to Parudrauga any longer.

"Alright, alright, no need to be impatient," sighed the man melodramatically, as he was ushered by Mār to the seat on his back. "Let us be off."

"Deal gently in taking off, hatchling," Mār growled to Yonatan, who was now fidgeting eagerly, face to the sky. "You do not want your first flight together to ent up with us trying to scrape the girl's remnants from the grount." He straightened up his neck, lifted his wings, and drove his hindlegs into the earth. "Now, after me."

Yonatan pounded his wings as soon as Mār's talons left the ground, and Kefira felt the world sway around her as he reared. Hand-straps found insufficient to maintain her equilibrium, she embraced his neck, flinging her arms about him as he shoved himself into the sky. She let out a giddy cry, even as Yonatan tossed his head and emitted a falsetto roar. She felt his lungs swell beneath her, his heartbeat like a tabor drum as he made after Mār. Kefira saw Rakhshan turn around in his seat, put a fist to the air and whoop. She laughed, smiling against the smooth scales pressing into the side of her face. "You're wonderful, Yonatan," she told him, when she finally had wind to speak.

He keened, but shook out his wings, and she felt his whole body move as he lashed his tail. He was not yet satisfied with his praise. The whistle in Kefira's ears grew in pitch, as Yonatan's wingbeats grew deeper, plowing through the air like the hooves of stallions. The multitude of trees below were reduced to a singular blur of green. He was going faster, much faster, and the gap between he and Mār was closing.

The elder dragon raised his head from its vulture-like lull, to peer over his shoulder at Yonatan. Kefira could see his eye, glimmering with amusement. "You're yet to outstrip me, youngling," he called, and his wings stretched lazily to accommodate for the Hardlā upstart's approach. He'd not even been going half speed, and so now quite merrily increased his pace to spite his pursuer. Yonatan could not hope to be quick enough to catch him up.

Kefira patted the twitching muscles in her dragon's neck as he panted, reluctantly accepting his place behind the Azhi Dahaki. "Soon," she reassured him, "he will be the one left in your dust."

The next weeks went swiftly past. The mountains turned into hills which in turn fell into flat plains of dusky goat-leather land. They passed into it, and Kefira and Yonatan did not leave them. Food and water was scarce.

There were no mountains on the horizon, but every day they

flew there Kefira saw a new wonder in the rock beneath. Ridges of small mountains of rock that looked like teeth, stretches of white sand as flat as papyrus, spires of wind-eaten stone that rose to the sky like earth-hewn, windowless towers. The earth was yellow here, like ochre, and water came in hues of red and orange. There was little land to be farmed. There were few villages. And so Kefira told herself that it was unwise to go on alone, from here. Though vendors were less vulnerable to silver-tongued hagglers here, Rakhshan still kept them all full of meat and bread.

So they stayed with the mercenaries. Yonatan continued to grow. Kefira could only claim to be as tall as his knee, now; he also put on more weight, slowly leveling himself closer to the height of Mār's shoulders. Already he was longer than him, and was indeed quite smug about it, preening his wine and gold scales to a sheen.

There were other villages they passed that allowed dragons in, though now Yonatan was threatening to outgrow the street. The last town they visited, there were many other dragons – not all the pets of merchants. There were riders of the Asman Kāra there. Dissenting from their escort Rakhshan, Kefira had rounded a corner with Yonatan, only to discover that there were men in uniform there that recognized her dragon's breed.

They left promptly after that, and had to hide out two days from an aerial patrol thereafter – a difficult thing to do, as there were no trees or mountains in the immediate vicinity. That ordeal had put none of them in a good mood. They had shaken their pursuers in the end, however, but since avoided settlements altogether. "We'll just hunt and gather, from now on," Rakhshan sighed. "Though that shan't at all diminish our time on the road."

"Are we very far from Parudrauga, still?" Kefira inquired, a little hopeful.

"No," said he absently, poking the map to indicate. "We should be about here. I think we crossed into Gedrosia yesterday."

"Gedrosia already?" she gasped, looking at Yonatan, and then at Rakhshan's finger on the map. "It looks as though we could only be a day away – to Parudrauga," she said, stomach stirring anxiously.

"Indeed, yes. We'll see the white mountains that stand up from the Golden Desert tomorrow, I think. That means that our Promised Land is very close, only a little south and east of us," Rakhshan explained. He was looking at her, and she knew that he was appraising her reaction.

So the girl checked her anxiety. "I suppose we shall see the ocean soon, then," she said simply, staring at the campfire. She felt nauseous, and leaned back against Yonatan to move her gaze to the waning moon.

The next day, the empty blue sky deepened on the horizon. There appeared to be a dark indigo line beneath the panorama, standing up behind the porcelain earth. They passed the white ridges and the golden hot glow of dunes, and Kefira knew that they were close.

She saw it as the afternoon was drawing to a close, a smudge in the distance. Nestled in the heaps of wrinkled bone-white tablecloth crags, a stain. The girl knew without asking that this was Parudrauga.

The intake of Yonatan's breath thrummed beneath her, and he brayed with satisfaction, turning his head to gaze upon her. "Khhh!"

She couldn't help but smile at his enthusiasm, despite the little knot of dread that her stomach had become. She was looking upon, apparently, the singular place where Yonatan could grow up in safety. She could not tell by looking at it.

More than a little daunted, she looked past Yonatan's left wing, to see Rakhshan on Mār. Despite the distance, she could make out the grin on his face as he returned her gaze.

And then Yonatan's wings stopped beating, and he was still, as though holding his breath. He hovered, coasting on, and Kefira looked past his neck to see what he gazed upon.

The white earth of the coast had fallen away in tiers, alabaster cliffs descending into a field of solid blue. Kefira stared. As far as the eye could see – an endless plain of sparkling water that rippled like grass in the wind.

The air was not arid and tasteless – but cool, fresh, salty. She'd never smelled its like. Yonatan keened, and she saw in his eyes the endless expanse of turquoise, jade, and sapphire that shifted beneath them. Beyond the wind in her ears, there was only a pounding sound, a rhythmic rumble of surf, as she and Yonatan breathed in the sight.

She glanced back at Rakhshan, almost speechless. "This is – the ocean?" she shouted to him, astonished. The sun was descending upon it, lighting it up with fire.

"Yes!" he called in reply. "What you are gracing with your eyes is Al-Khaleej, the Great Gulf of Persia!"

"Yes, yes, it is very pretty," said Mār, who now tilted his wings away from the waters. "But you mayn't take it home with you, and there will be plenty of time to look at it when we're in Parutrauga. Come on, now, Yonatan."

The Hardlā uttered a protest, but followed. Both he and Kefira twisted their necks looking back upon the sight, now starboard to them. They kept flying up the coast until the sun had nearly departed, tinging the green-blue waters of the ocean with orange behind them. But before long, Kefira could not afford to look at the ocean. Her eyes were unable to leave the port city that grew before them. An acrid, sickly-sweet taste was entering her mouth; she swallowed. It was really right before them, Parudrauga. That was their destination.

As a building dread began to rise within her, she was rather thrown off when Rakhshan suddenly decided to make camp just a few leagues before it.

"Why have we stopped?" Kefira asked him after they landed; he was already beginning to make a fire from dry bushes, as the light dwindled.

He cracked armfuls of thin branches, and laid them in a pile, knocking flint stones together. Yellow sparks flew, illuminating his hands. "It is considered polite to knock on someone's door before entering their house. That is just what we're doing." Some of the sparks caught on the brush, and the tinder glowed. "It's too bad there are no great trees, here," he muttered, as the bushes began to send up great gasps of white smoke.

"I thought you said that you had friends here," Kefira said uneasily, watching his progress, as he tamped the writhing bushes back into place with a daring foot.

"I do have friends here. We're just making sure they know that our company of dragons isn't a reason for them fortify the city." He turned to Mār, who was brushing off the clay from the roots of more scrub to hand them to Rakhshan.

"Well, we ought to go there in time for Yonatan to eat. There's not been much prey or anything in the past few days." She looked nervously at her dragon, who was curled up, and looking past the distant cliffs to the spread of the ocean.

"There will be plenty to eat there, and we shall be there soon, worry not," said Rakhshan, who was still working the flames.

"Why are you making such a large fire?" she asked, realizing that the flames now came higher than her head, and gave off glaring heat and light, in the dusk.

"I'm knocking on the door, Kefira," he replied simply, before dropping another armful of dry branches upon the blaze.

"Oh." She looked back at the city. "It looks like they themselves have many fires built. Sacrificing their infants to Molech, I would guess."

"The temples mostly lie outside the city, in the high places of the hills surrounding. You shouldn't see too many dead babies," said Rakhshan, in a tone of utmost casualness.

"I do not want to see any at all!" cried Kefira, aghast at his nonchalance.

"Oh, do not fret, Kefira, I was only jesting." He swept dust from his hands and placed them on his hips. "There are – pagan sorts of worship, here, but it is not overly indiscreet, and often only visible in the country, except on holy days."

"Yes, because the Thu'ban that is the priest of Molech is not partial towards the crampt city streets," purred Mār, looking down at her with an eye that gleamed orange in the firelight.

Kefira blinked up at him, feeling Yonatan press into her back. "What do you mean?" she asked him. "A dragon is a priest?" And then she shivered, despite the heat of the fire. "You mean – a *dragon* burns the babies?" she exclaimed in horror.

"Kashayar Atash is his name, ant, yes, I believe that is how it goes," said the dragon in reply. He snorted with mock-disdain. "Very distasteful, I think, the whole business."

"How could – why would you take me to such a place, Rakhshan?" Kefira stood, looking fearfully upon him. "What other evils lie there that you are not speaking of?"

"I'm sorry," he said, voice earnest. "It is only a small cult that worship that god, as it is Babylonian. Mār is just being melodramatic," he shot a look at the dragon. "Like I said, you won't see any of Atash in the city – he's quite the recluse outside of ceremony. And the high places of Baal – with all of the harlots – those are outside the city."

"But the harlots who are *not* shrine-prostitutes, on the other hant, they line the street like broken chariot wheels," intoned the Azhi Dahaki, with venomous whimsy.

Yonatan rumbled, looking at Kefira with concern as she wordlessly drew back to lie against his foreleg. She looked at the city in the distance, all the glowing red lights. "For every minute that passes, it seems like a worse and worse idea to go there."

"We'll be staying at the barracks, Kefira. Nothing of that ilk shall reach us, there," said Rakhshan.

She had no time to argue. Mār had raised his head to peer at the sky above the city. "There is someone coming."

Kefira felt her seat shift as Yonatan brought his foreleg around to clutch her. Her fingers were cold on his scales. A low growl began to rise in his throat.

Rakhshan squinted to the sky, Kefira searched the stars as well.

"I see nothing," the man said. "It is a dragon, yes?"

"Yes. A Siyutūrai, by its speet," Mār opined, and then the frills about his head seemed to rise in pleasure.

Rakhshan seemed to come to the same conclusion, for he said, "Tahmour and Sorushe."

"Who are they?" Kefira asked uneasily, from where Yonatan was holding her.

"A few of our friends." Rakhshan got to his feet. "They are of the Asman Kāra, Barid couriers, but their sympathies do not lie with the military."

"Well, I suppose that is good for us…" she trailed off. "Is it safe for them to be about, if they are rebels as you and Mār are?"

"The Empire has no hold upon Parudrauga. It ran out the soldiers of the King a long time ago."

"Now the utter lawlessness of this place makes more sense," she said bitterly.

"When the shepherd is away, the sheep come out to play," quipped Rakhshan with a grin.

A few minutes later the humans could finally see the figures – a dragon and rider.

"Yonatan, look how you outsize him," she said proudly after her dragon had relaxed a little, and she made out the proportions of their visitors.

Mār countered her, apparently defensive of the beast. "That is Sorushe, ant yes, he is small, but he makes up for it in other ways, tenfolt."

One of the ways he made up for it was not in the arena of intellect, apparently, for as he landed, the gust from his grey wings sent the remainders of the fire scattering in every direction. Cinders took to the air like glowing shrikes, and Kefira jumped as Yonatan swiftly took to patting out a rogue ember that had landed upon her robe.

"Sorry, sorry!" the dragon piped, rearing sheepishly over the ground between Yonatan and Mār. The storm cloud blue length of him looked to be almost half Yonatan's size, and as high as a man at the shoulder, shaking his wings like a self-conscious kestrel.

His rider, Tahmour, slid down the Siyudūrai's back to the ground. "You're back!" he exclaimed, and he went to Rakhshan. He did not look much older than her companion himself. By comparison he was slighter and taller, like a reed, mangy black hair hanging from a loose tie on the back of his head, flyaway ends scattered over his red-skinned face. He and Rakhshan embraced, even as Sorushe chirpily greeted the Azhi Dahaki. Then he turned to look at them with large, pale grey eyes. "You're the great big Israeli dragon, are you not?" he inquired, and Yonatan nodded, taken aback by his forwardness.

"Well met," said the Siyudūrai, standing on his hindlegs to become quite eyelevel with him. "I am Sorushe, and that is my man, Tahmour." He glanced at the two men who were conferring alongside Mār. "What is your name? Is this your rider?" He crouched and looked at Kefira. "That is odd. He is a woman."

"Uh, yes," Kefira stammered, as Yonatan put a protective foreleg between her and the newcomer. "This is my Yonatan. My name is Kefira."

"Hello, Kefira. Myonatan is a strange name." He looked at the bigger dragon, cocking his head.

"No, uh," Kefira grimaced. "Not Myonatan," she explained, feeling rather awkward. "Yonatan is his name."

"Oh." The Barid dragon crouched like a pleased cat, conversationally lowering his head to her. "Very nice. How quaint, foreign names are."

The girl bit her tongue, raising an eyebrow. "Um, thank you, Sorushe."

Yonatan wasn't paying much attention, she noticed as she glanced up at him. He was looking past the grey dragon at the others, expression unreadable and golden eyes fixed. Without explanation, Kefira felt as though her stomach was filling with stones.

Sorushe raised his head to speak with Yonatan. "Have you any notion of how large you'll get, big fellow?" he asked him, pale eyes flashing like white crystal.

Yonatan returned his gaze now, and shook his head.

"Oh, that is just as well," replied the other dragon perfunctorily before looking down at Kefira. "Can he not speak?"

Kefira blushed for her dragon. "Not yet," she replied.

The Hardlā muttered wordlessly above her. "Khh..."

"Oh, worry not – your voice is just a late-bloomed rose, as my man's mistress likes to put it," Sorushe reassured him. "Tahmour?" He promptly turned his head to his rider. "Why don't we take them to the city, now?"

"Yes, yes, stop fretting, you overgrown sparrow." The messenger seemed to have finished catching up with Rakhshan, and then sauntered past his dragon to them, to her. He smiled with a wide mouth. "Greetings, my lady. Rakhshan's neglected introducing us."

Rakhshan himself jumped in, bowing with mock-formality. "Kefira, this is Tahmour of Sorushe, of the Eleventh Dispatch of Barid."

"At your service," said the man, bowing himself.

"And Tahmour, this is Kefira of Yonatan, of the Remnant of Israel," finished Rakhshan with a flourish.

Kefira looked at them both sidelong. "Hello," she replied slowly, with an awkward nod. "Forgive me if I don't know how to respond to such formalities."

"You have found us a keeper, Rakhshan. I fancy her already," said Tahmour with a chuckle, as he glanced up at Yonatan. "Now, I take it you're all hungry, let's be off already."

"A *keeper*..." Kefira repeated, shooting a suspicious look at Rakhshan after Tahmour had mounted.

The man shrugged. "He's got an odd way of words – you'll have to learn to ignore him," he said with a sheepish smile. "Now hop onto Yonatan, and we'll follow him into the city."

Kefira sighed. "I can tell already — you both are two pods from the same pomegranate. You don't happen to be brothers, do you?"

"Not by sire, no" said Rakhshan with a sardonic grin. "But both of us were raised by the same mother: the Streets of Parudrauga."

The great sprawl of the city was spilled over the coast like a child's toy blocks, buildings of clay that gleamed white in the starlight and orange from windows studding the plains before the ocean, climbing the surrounding hills, tumbling down the pale terraced cliffs to the sea. Dark things, motionless, hung in the waters of the bay, tethered to docks, white wings and many thin legs illuminated by the city glow. Lights were everywhere — hardly was there a dim window to be seen below, lamps of kindled yellow gleaming in the caverns of the buildings, the orifices sometimes half-lidded by the red veils of occupied prostitutes. Even with the wind rushing in her ears, Kefira could hear the noises of activity from below.

Amidst all the chaos there was one place the reveling city gave a wide berth. The dragon yard of the barracks, abandoned by all but one dragon: a massive golden creature sleeping against the building. As their company landed, Kefira recognized with mounting astonishment that it was greater than both Yonatan, Mār, and Sorushe combined.

"Mehrnaz!" the Azhi Dahaki exclaimed. "How ever dit you get here before we dit?"

And Kefira realized that she'd seen the dragon before — she was the same beast from the border of Elam. The Gandarewa raised her head. "One can travel much quicker while not in hiding, as you've been." She squinted at Yonatan. "He's gotten a little bigger," she said. "But we'll have to fatten you up, little Hardlā, or you will stay skin and bones forever."

Yonatan snorted indignantly, and slumped to the ground. His muscles were trembling. He was tired. Kefira dismounted him and looked at their surroundings warily. Buildings loomed up all around, but none were so great as the empty monolith of the barracks beside them. She placed a hand on Yonatan, uneasy. She had half a mind to hide beneath his wing. Looking around the city, eyes flitting from window to window, she wondered if this unholy place ever slept. It looked as though it had bright glowing eyes, thousands of them, open and awake. The air cackled with the sound of nocturnal activity: the clatter of dishes in a tavern, the laughter of late-night carousers, the haggling of merchants as women and pouches of alalega were dealt.

Her queasy absorption of the scenery was interrupted as a man, it was Arsham, she saw, came from the barracks' portico. Her eyes flitted about him, the lone occupant of the gaping hall. No guards were posted anywhere, no sign of anyone else. *The Empire has no hold here*, she remembered Rakhshan's words. This was the only place with more dark windows than not.

Rakhshan called out a greeting to his teacher, and both men went to meet the elder. Kefira stayed in the background, crouched against Yonatan. Perhaps while they were talking, they could strike up and leave, she thought fleetingly.

The three men spoke for a long time, and Kefira itched for the whole duration of the conversation. Sorushe didn't really talk to them as he had before, as he and the rest of the dragons seemed to be succumbing to sleep, and the Siyudūrai himself was now snoring loudly. But Yonatan seemed disinclined to drift off. He appeared perturbed, looking around at the city himself, when he wasn't looking at the men. He would nudge her, look at them, nudge her again, and gaze around the city. Kefira shared his restless mood, though she rather wanted to follow the suit of the snoring dragon. Exhaustion had seemed to seep from her very bones, upon reaching this city; weariness as though she'd fallen into a cistern and bumped her head. But she'd wait until the men invited her over or forgot her to make any noise about sleeping.

In the end, she was not forgotten. "Come now, Kefira, it is time to sup!" belted Arsham. It was well past suppertime, as far as Kefira could tell, but she got up and went to them anyway, hands clasped before her. She glanced up at Yonatan, who had gotten up and followed her. "Are we to stay in the barracks?" she inquired to Rakhshan. "Does it have accommodations?"

"There are more than enough bunkrooms to house us," he replied. "Separate ones, I might add, for your comfort. You can have a hundred cots to yourself, if you so desire."

"Oh," said she, a little surprised. "They must have had a great many soldiers living here."

"It was terrible," intoned Tahmour peevishly. "This place still reeks of them."

Before they entered the corridor that hollowed a network through the buildings, Kefira lilted back to her dragon. "I'll try staying in here, tonight," she told him. Yonatan hissed his disapproval. She blanched, a little guiltily. "I'm going to get to try sleeping on a cot," she said. "I'll be safe. And I shall come back to you tomorrow morning at first light, so that we may do our morning prayer together."

The Hardlā seemed to accept this, grudgingly. He looked back at the sleeping dragons in the courtyard, and then to the three men before him. Kefira saw his lips curl, writhing silently over his teeth, as his eyes glared like fire over them. Then he nudged Kefira, looking at her with grim satisfaction, as though to say, *there, now you are safe – I made sure of it.*

She smiled, planted a kiss on his muzzle, and said, "From whichever room I sleep in, I'll be sure to call you through the window, that you may sleep outside next to me."

"Khhh," he hissed with pleasure.

"I'll see you soon, love."

Hugging her elbows, she self-consciously joined the others, and Arsham greeted her. "It has been a while, girl. Glad to see that you're still with us."

She nodded and smiled out of politeness. Looking over her shoulder, she saw that Yonatan was curled up on the patio outside the corridor, watching them leave. She waved to him, and he blinked.

Kefira turned back, hugging her elbows tighter. Rakhshan and Arsham were enveloped in what appeared to be small talk – concerning their journey and Yonatan's growth – walking in front of Tahmour and her. The messenger tried a few times to engage her in conversation, but she was disinclined to oblige him, keeping her replies short and vague, and so he eventually gave up.

Supper was a handful of dates and nuts and a skin full of wine deposited into her hands by Arsham as soon as he showed her the room she was to sleep in. It was on the second floor, and there were a number of old, dusty cots therein; one of the cots had been swept clean however, and had bundles of cloth – blankets and a rudimentary pillow; this place was apparently hers. It smelled old and dry like sand. Alongside Tahmour, Arsham departed her with a goodnight and said, "I shall tell you of our situation when we break the fast tomorrow."

"What does he speak of?" Kefira asked Rakhshan, who lingered in the hallway after they left.

"Nothing to worry your dusty little head over," said he. "Go on in and get some rest, Kefira. I'll be in the bunkroom right next to yours, down there." He pointed to door down the hall, and stepped forward. He placed one of his hands upon her shoulder, which she stared at. "You're safe in the barracks, remember. I know you do not like the city, but Yonatan and I will keep you quite safe," he said. He removed his hand, ushering her into the room. "I'll be just down the way, if you need me – need anything," he finished stiltedly.

Kefira wrung her hands behind her back. "Very well. Thank you," she said quietly, as she entered. "Goodnight."

Rakhshan paused in the doorway. He looked as though he was not done speaking, but he only replied with a goodnight in kind, and handed her an oil lamp before stepping back into the hall.

Kefira waited a few moments before she moved again. She shut the door, and leaned her back against it in fatigue, looking around at the room's shadows. How long had it been since she was last alone? Not since she'd first found Yonatan's egg, not since she'd woken up alone in the inn.

She exhaled softly, as the lamp's light gilded the empty interior of the room. It illuminated a small circle around her, and the rest of the place was dark. She could not make out the end of the room. She looped an anxious finger around the lamp's handle and traversed the aisle between the cots. Alone she was, she was very sure of it, but still, she made certain. All was quiet in the room, a great contrast to the night outside. She found nothing but dust and cobwebs beneath the bunks, and saw nothing creeping in the rib-like rafters above. The girl was in solitude.

Kefira went to the window. "Yonatan," she called, voice low.

He was already beneath her window, looking up at her with anxiety, yellow eyes shining from the lamp in her hand. "Khhh…"

She smiled. "You found me, already!"

He lifted his head to the window, touched her face with a flicker of his tongue, and blinked slowly at her. And then he curled up below, sprawling like a great guardian lion, blinking up at her.

She leaned against the windowsill for a long time, looking down at him. Then, "I am going to sleep now, love." He raised his head and nodded somberly as his rider disappeared from the window. He stayed awake until he could hear the soft breathing above that meant his rider was sound asleep.

Chapter VIII
The Orchard

A shimmering wind-chime, the low murmur of warm wind through leaves.

And she heard voices. No, one voice. It was speaking words she could not make out.

Those were the only sounds.

Kefira opened her eyes, and she was surprised to see that she was on her feet and Rakhshan was standing in front of her. He was not the speaker, though.

They were standing close to each other, a cloth draped on their heads and blocking out the world around them. A cloth... it looked like a chuppah. What would a chuppah be doing draped over their heads? It was not a chuppah. A chuppah was for a bride and groom.

Yet it was upon their heads, she and Rakhshan's, a shared shawl over the both of them. What was it doing there?

The chime continued to make its glittering sound, and the voice continued speaking words she couldn't understand. She tried to make out the shape of the speaker by peering through the cloth, but there was no sight to see besides golden light past the chuppah. No, the cloth. She wanted to remove it, to look past, to separate herself from the gaze of the man before her. But she could not move.

There were golden flecks in the amber eyes of Rakhshan, as she flickered to holding his gaze. He was taller than her, and so the cloth hung over them like a lopsided tent, and secluded them from whatever the outside world was. There were no words exchanged between them. They just looked at one another. Kefira did not know why she did not speak, and did not know why he did not.

She most certainly did not know why, when the chimes diminished and the voice stopped speaking, that as soon as Rakhshan dipped to kiss her, she kissed him back.

❖

Kefira awoke with a start.

She was on the cot in her bunkroom, not in the golden place of her dream. Quite alone.

Her eyes fixed upon a crack in the dawn-lit ceiling, above the cedar rafters. She frowned at the hairs-breadth line, as her mind flooded fully with consciousness, ruminating.

That was a bad dream.

There was no fire and no melting temple, but – heat flooded her face, her lips as she bit them. Her stomach was queasy with shameful hot waves. It was not entirely horrible, now that she thought about it. But, no, that had been *Rakhshan*, the Persian, the mercenary, the pagan! She squirmed in revolt beneath the covers, stifling a cry of disgust. Such dreams – certainly, that apparition was unchaste! Where in her heart had it leaked from? She scowled at herself, twisting her blanket with anxious hands.

That chuppah.

It was a chuppah.

But why? Why one of those, of all things? Those were meant to be a canopy over the heads of a bride and groom, not draped upon two cohorts.

Kefira swallowed, mouth dry. Why did she have to be reminded once more of that man's stupid words? When he had so *ridiculously* proposed that becoming his wife would nullify her debt to him. Was that dream merely a reflection of that discourse? Certainly it was, for it had nothing to do with how she felt. She could hardly bear to touch Rakhshan, let alone touch him with her *lips*. He was very handsome, but that was the charm of a mischievous devil, if anything.

She would not marry him at all. She would marry no one, for that matter. She had no dowry and no family to receive a bride price, and she was not desirable for matrimony in any case. She would live for the rest of her life as an old maid of the streets, as a matter of fact – or maybe she could acquire some skill and become a midwife or maidservant. No, she would do neither, she realized. She would be Yonatan's rider, of course, wherever that took her.

That dream, she seethed inwardly. She tossed in her cot. It was morning, but she wanted more sleep. Perhaps she could have another dream, one that would erase the vivid memory of this one.

No, there would be no sleeping after this. She felt as though she'd been struck by lightning, and its white crackling tendrils shot throughout her like hot arrows. Yonatan. She would get up and go see him. He could take her mind off of it.

So she sat up, clutching her blankets about her shoulders. She sat still for a long time. It took her a few minutes of staring at the floor and nibbling a finger to realize that she had no energy to leave.

She wanted to fall back into the cot, nestle herself and disappear from the light into the blankets, sleep more, keep warm from the draft blowing in from the window. Perhaps she could bring the blankets down with her, when she went out to the dragon yard. It did not seem to be very warm out, yet, but when she reached Yonatan, she could stay warm at his side. There was only the matter of getting to him. She did not want to chance an encounter with Rakhshan in the hallway. Cruel fate would have it that as soon as she left her room, he would take it up in his head to get out of bed as well. She did not want to see him. She felt strange just thinking about him. Seeing him would make her feel more unpleasant. What a dream – him kissing her, her kissing him back, instead of giving him a slap! Her heart was so reckless, so merciless in its nightly theatrics. As if the nightmares of the burning Temple were not bad enough, now she had the visions of a wayward woman to haunt her.

She shook her head, running her fingers through the unkempt length of her dark hair, untangling it with weary fingers until it fell back in some semblance of neatness to her waist. Over it went her sun-bleached purple shawl, and she dragged herself out of the cot and went to the window. Parudrauga. Its expanse surrounded her, now, looking as though it'd been carved of old ivory from the hills. It was much quieter, now. Below, Yonatan lay prone, nestled against the barracks rampart. The morning sun glittered like dew upon his scales. "Good morning, love," she said, hoping that his sleep had been better than hers.

He raised his head promptly, eyes bright and awake. Had he slept?

"Would you help me down to you?" she asked him. "I feel too slothful to walk through the barracks." She smiled a little.

He had no objections to obliging her, and raised his head to her window. She realized with no small amount of satisfaction that his head was bigger than her whole body. He had grown, tremendously, as usual. With only a moment's hesitation, she clambered out the window to cling to his face, smooth scales warm against her palms. Gently, he lowered her to the earth, and adjusted his forelegs to accommodate her.

She smiled, feeling her peace return to her once more as she sat upon his foreleg. Only his eyes were concerned now, pupil dilating with interest. Could he sense her anxiety? He crooned to her, as she settled against him.

"I had a bad dream, Yonatan," she said simply, no desire to keep him ignorant.

Yonatan nodded. She saw a muscle around the hole that was his ear twitch.

"Did you hear?" she asked, a little surprised.

His head bobbed.

"Oh. Was I speaking in my sleep?" she winced, and he nodded again.

Odd. She did not remember speaking in her dream. She was pulled up from the thought as Yonatan nudged her and settled a searching gaze upon her, as though he were saying, *You may tell me it, if that would make you feel better.*

The girl grimaced. She could not imagine he would fancy the contents of her dream. "Just..." she began, a little uncertainly. Quieter, she said, "Well, it had Rakhshan in it."

Yonatan went still, expression stony. She felt the echoes of a growl reverberate in his chest.

She feared she was merely adding kindling to the fire, but did not hide from him what she had seen, not even sparing that, "we kissed." But this latter word did not seem to faze him, making his brows lift with curiosity.

"Oh, do not mind then. It is not important." What chaos would be wreaked if he knew what that meant?

He stuck his great muzzle against her chest, piercing her with an eye. He was not going to let this go. Kefira kicked herself for letting that detail slip to him. She looked up at him sheepishly. "It is a thing that married people do, mostly. You've not seen it yet, because it's not a proper thing to do outside of doors." She shot a dismal look at the city that surrounded them, adding in an undertone, "Though I'm sure in this place there are *many* public displays of it."

Yonatan bore his teeth, and curled a jealous talon around her. Kefira leaned against him. "It is alright, truly," she assuaged. "It was just a foolish dream."

She resolved to coax him out of his mood with the morning prayer. He could not recite any verses, of course, but listened attentively as she herself did. He watched her as well, looked at her folded hands as she knelt her face to them upon the ground. He never seemed to shut his eyes during prayer. She would have to teach him to.

"...as long as my soul is within me, I will thank you Adonai, my God, God of my ancestors, Lord of all souls. Blessed are you, Adonai, who restores the souls to our waking bodies in the morning," she finished the recitation. When she opened her eyes and looked up, Yonatan was gazing at her, contentment in his eyes.

"Someday you shall be able to say that, too," she assured him. "And until then, Adonai hears your heart." She sat back upon his leg, resting her head and hand on his chest. His heartbeat was like a drum, the pulse of a leviathan. She counted each thump, feeling her own pulse and his. Once, twice, thrice, four times, five. His heart beat once for every half dozen of hers. She wondered at this.

More tangible than his heartbeat was now a deep rumble from his belly. Yonatan shifted uncomfortably, looking at her hopefully. She smiled. "I shall see what the men have in the way of board."

Kefira got to her feet and Yonatan eagerly followed. She had to hurry with her steps to stay in front of him. They moved from the front of the barracks to the dragon yard. It was the quarters devoted wholly to dragons – there must be livestock kept for them to eat, somewhere. But she didn't see any animals besides Mār, who was drooling acid alongside the other sleeping dragons. She only heard the noises of livestock – but they were far away – herders bringing in their beasts for the market.

And then she saw a pen, on the far side of the barracks. It was empty, but the rumpled ground inside showed signs of previous, if not recent, occupation. There were goat droppings, grass struggling in trampled mud, dry hoof prints. Apparently when the Empire's military occupation had been driven out of Parudrauga, the livestock they'd provided for the dragons weren't supplied any more. She guessed that served the silly mercenaries right, but the justice didn't help her now.

"Rakhshan said that you were going to be fed well here. I'd like to see him make good of his promise," she said huffily to her dragon. "I'll go find someone about the food."

He nodded and nudged her eagerly towards the veranda, the hallway into the barracks, and watched keenly as she receded. Sorushe rolled in his sleep behind him.

Kefira tried to remember if she had seen the mess hall coming in the last night. It would be a big, long room, to be sure, to occupy soldiers as they took their meals, so it oughtn't be hard to find. The hallway was open on one side to the air, the barracks hollow with a drilling courtyard in the center, bordered by overgrown hedges and gardens. She peered across this square to the dark holes that were windows into rooms. The top floor had no windows looking in, she saw past the second story's railing. The mess hall would not be on the second floor anyway, she figured. It would be too impractical to build cooking fires there, so she limited her search to the bottom floor.

Try as she might to search it out, the mess hall did not make itself apparent to her. She recognized little of what she passed – it'd been dark last night, and she had no memory to instruct her of a path. There were some words carved into the stone in places that she passed – some of it was vandalism, but others were cleaner and uniform, as though set there to provide directions. But she could not make heads or tails of the letters.

So she glanced into windows as she passed, stale air meeting her face, no sign of occupation; she continued down the network, anxious. She was getting nowhere. She stopped, listening as the sounds of her last footfalls left her. Why hadn't she asked Arsham or Rakhshan where exactly the mess hall was, before retiring last night? Better yet, why hadn't they told her? She had half a mind to call out, to let them know that she was wondering around with all the direction-sense of a headless chicken. But what a fool she would look like if she needed them to help her find her way. She might just wait, listen, and hope to hear snatches of their voices floating from wherever they resided.

But Yonatan was depending on her, and who knew how much time waiting would take. So she retraced her steps back to the veranda. Yonatan was no longer lying at its entrance, and so she veered to the corridors that led to her room, up the stairs. She might regroup there and thence remember where she ought to go. Or perhaps Rakhshan was looking for her, to take her there himself.

Kefira came to this realization too late, for indeed, a figure was standing by her door when she rounded the corner. She swallowed. Rakhshan – she did *not* want to see him, not yet.

But the figure called out. "There you are, girl." It was Tahmour.

She almost let out a sigh of relief. A few tentative steps closer, she halted. "Yes," she replied. "I wanted to find one of you, so that Yonatan could be fed."

"Do not worry, the dragons just went hunting in the eastern

hills." The tall man sauntered forwards, and Kefira blanched as he took her by the shoulder and steered her down the hall, where she'd come. "Come on, Arsham and Rakh are already breaking the fast."

She stepped from under his hand and looked at him sidelong. "Very well," she replied tersely.

"Don't like being touched, do you?" observed the man casually. "Cannot say we're used to that, here. You must have had a rough time with Rakhshan." He grinned wolfishly. "Good luck living here long."

Kefira kept on walking beside him, as he apparently was taking her to the mess hall, but had put herself off a healthy distance from his arm. "I do not intend to live here *long.*"

"Oh, that's what you intend, but the city will grow on you, I'm sure." He grinned crookedly. "But who knows, with a pious little Jew like you, I could be wrong."

Kefira simmered. "You must have learned your manners from Mār," she grumbled.

"Or did he learn his manners from me?" The man laughed, undaunted by the insult. "That beast hasn't ten years yet, and I am more than dozen years his senior. I'm sure even you can figure the mathematics."

Kefira couldn't, but did not say so. "How much farther until the mess hall?" she asked lamely, surveying the now unrecognizable passageway.

"It's just down the corridor, that door to the left, right there."

"Thank you for helping me find it," she said simply, before picking up the pace of her steps and putting him to her back. He was laughing for some reason, and she wondered if he had smoked himself some alalega that morning.

There were words written above the broad door, she could not read them, but knew they denoted the significance of the open portico before her. She found herself still before she reached it. Rakhshan was in there, she guessed, and she heard voices.

"Did they see where you were headed?" The gravelly voice of Arsham.

"They saw that we were going south." A sigh from Rakhshan.

"Heh, after all that work I did to keep you anonymous, too. Well, yours were novice mistakes, but they're coming here anyway, so you're not to blame. Though I was *sure* I'd taught you better than that." A laugh.

Her eavesdropping was interrupted by Tahmour, who had caught up to her now. "Go on in, Kefira," he said loudly.

She stepped inside, tentative but hasty, into the near-dark of the mess hall. There were hasps for torches, but only one was lit on the far end of the room, where one of the many disheveled tables was illuminated, along with the two figures that sat at it. Arsham and Rakhshan straightened in their seats, conversation quelled by Tahmour's announcement. Rakhshan stood up from his seat, upon seeing her as she was led to the table. Her legs almost buckled. She knew it — her dream was written on her face, and he was reading it right now. If only the dimness of the room could hide her flush.

"Good morning," he said. And she replied in kind, before sitting on the bench, as far from everyone as possible without going out of reach of the food. Her eyes did not rise from the table, as she pretended to look and then with refreshed hunger gazed upon the meal's spread. There were loaves of bread, a jar of oil, a bowl of figs, bowls of wine, a basket of pistachios. Pistachios. They peaked from their shells like shy green pearls. Her mouth watered.

When her fist was in the basket and Tahmour had taken his seat, Arsham said, as he dipped a piece of bread in oil, "So, Kefira, I hear that you're afraid of Parudrauga."

The comment took her aback. She held the pistachios cupped in her hands closely, staring at the blatant speaker, as he took a bite of his bread.

"Oh, that's a good way to start," Rakhshan intoned dryly. "I thought you to be more tactful, teacher."

"I – I am not afraid of this place," she answered belatedly. She shot a look at Rakhshan – had he told him of her misgivings? "It is nice enough," she added without conviction. She cracked open a nut and chewed upon it vengefully.

"That's not what you said earlier," said Tahmour in sardonic singsong.

"I said nothing about being afraid," she shot to him crossly, sliding herself a bowl of wine before smelling it with suspicion, glaring at him as she did.

Arsham interrupted the squabble. "It's quite alright – your worries are not undue." He smiled behind the curls of his silver-streaked beard. His dark brown eyes glinted as he said, "This is certainly not a place for the weak."

"Are you truly hazing her on her first day here?" asked Rakhshan, before she had time to express her indignity. "She has nothing in the way of the might of body, but she's got the heart of a little lioness."

Kefira stopped biting the rim of wine bowl. "Why are you all talking about me? Is this not the sort of conversation usually reserved for when the subject's back is turned?"

"But how can we ever test a little lion's strength if she's not taken out of her cage?" intoned Tahmour to Rakhshan, ignoring her.

"What is *that* supposed to mean, Tahmour?" Rakhshan asked, as he shot a look at the other man.

The courier shrugged defensively, before picking up, "I mean *maybe* we ought to show her around the city. If she's going to live here, she's got to know that not every building is a brothel and not every man is a brigand or smoker of alalega."

"Leave talk of business to a bunch of children, and this is what you get," sighed Arsham, pinning both of them with a wry look. "Save this sightseeing talk for later. We must confer about the lady's dragon."

"Living here – me? My dragon..." Kefira was lost. She looked at Arsham. "What do you want to talk about? Feeding him, yes?"

"Yes. Regimented feeding is important for any young dragon,

especially considering the size he will get." And the man briefed her on his plan for Yonatan's diet, loosely based on what he had fed Mehrnaz when she was growing. "Though I adjusted his diet to this Kashrut that Rakhshan informed me of."

Kefira blushed. "Just as long as he gets fed," she said shortly; the figures and arithmetic of his adjustments didn't concern her. Though she hoped he did not resent the extra complication. "Thank you for the board, on both our behalves," she said, standing up to dismiss herself from the table.

And she departed. Outside the door, she stopped. It occurred to her that she had no destination.

Yonatan was not here to keep her company, and she was not travelling now, or fleeing guards. Or stealing bread. What was there to do here, but watch Yonatan eat and grow? She reveled in the thought of him growing to such magnificent size, but what would she do when he was fully grown? Would these people keep on feeding him? And, this silly notion of her living in Parudrauga notwithstanding, what were she and Yonatan to do? What did a dragon and rider do in Persia, aside from join the ranks of the Asman Kāra?

She walked into the garden and sat upon a bench, an unpruned rosebush clutching her back before she turned around to push away its branches. Maybe now she could rest. She was not being chased and running anymore. Perhaps she could just sleep a little longer. Why did she feel something like peace, here, in such a place? It was as though the ground beneath her had stopped moving, and she could finally stand still with it. "I ought not stay here," she told God quietly.

"Kefira, do you want to go with me and Tahmour into the city?" Kefira kicked herself for becoming lost in thought – for there was Rakhshan, halfway to her from the mess hall door. She stood up, arms folded in front of her.

"I thought you two were only jesting about that," she said, averting her gaze as he approached.

"No – well, I think you should see it, too. It's not all bad." Rakhshan had closed the gap between them and was standing a few feet away. It was impossible not to look at him now, without looking completely willful about it. "Do you want to come?"

"No," she replied reflexively. And then, before she could see the flicker of dejection on his face, she added, "Well, I do not want to, but I don't suppose that it would hurt anything to go."

He smiled. "I'm glad you are making concession for this one occasion."

"Yes, well…" She forced a smile. "When are we going?"

"Some time soon." Rakhshan seated himself on the bench, and winced as his sleeve snagged the rosebush. He pulled his jerkin loose from the thorns and said, "We leave as soon as Tahmour's done *freshening up*."

Kefira felt as though she should not stand in front of him as he sat, and so placed herself on the far side of the bench. "Why is he doing that?"

Rakhshan frowned. "He's just going to meet someone."

She nodded, glad that he would not be there to antagonize her for very long, then.

The Persian broke the silence, speaking in an undertone. "Let me know if he ever bothers you."

Kefira looked at him, abashed. "Oh. Very well." His change of mood surprised her. She shuffled her feet in the grass growing up from the cracks in the courtyard tile. "I had thought you two were friends."

"We are. He is merely less of a gentleman than I," Rakhshan said with a smirk.

Tahmour met them in the courtyard soon enough, black hair glossy as though he'd just bathed. They left the barracks, and Kefira saw that the dragons were not yet back from wherever they'd gone. She bit her lip. "When will the dragons return?" she asked Rakhshan.

"There's no saying. A few hours, probably," answered Tahmour.

Rakhshan said, "It is alright – Arsham will tell them where we went."

Kefira reluctantly followed them out of the dragon yard, growing more and more uneasy as the buildings bordering the barracks grew closer and closer. The town was just beginning to wake up, and people were about – women walking in groups to and from the wells, with urns on their heads. Merchants were opening shop, beginning to hawk their wares to passersby. A boy herding a few goats came down the lane. Nothing overtly evil. In fact, to Kefira, it reminded her of Hangmatana – just another city. Though there was the blue smoke of alalega puffing from the pipes of a good many people, she saw no one being murdered or prostitution being engaged in the streets.

But they passed a man on the street, hunched on the steps of a building, sharpening the blade of a long falchion. He was looking at her beneath cavernous brows.

She shrank to Rakhshan's side, and pretended she hadn't noticed the man, looking straight ahead. Rakhshan noticed her plight and laughed. "Just keep close to me and you should stay out of trouble."

"No offense to you, but I hardly think a large man with a great sword would be overly daunted by your presence," said she, causing Tahmour to laugh.

Rakhshan smiled bitterly. "Of course not. But we are, Arsham, Tahmour, and I, not unknown around the city. The fact that we keep the company of dragon deters most trouble. Just stay close."

Kefira didn't disobey. She even allowed herself to walk closer than arm's reach to him, and Tahmour fell into step beside her. "Feel safer, yet?" he asked.

Kefira just gave him a dry smile.

The city of Parudrauga was a rough-hewn blanket thrown halfway upside a mount. The spider-webbing streets gradually inclined upwards as they walked, and when looking behind her, Kefira could see that there were buildings below them now, in the low distance. Her thin legs began to ache. "Are we going to get there soon?" she asked – and then realized that she did not even know their destination. "Where are we going, exactly? What did you want to show me?"

"Have patience," said Tahmour, as their trio skirted a hollow-faced group of people, who appeared to be nursing headaches, faces in hands. Kefira stared a little at them, remembering her own morning after. She looked sidelong at Rakhshan. Then her eyes returned greyly to the street. Perhaps when they reached this mountain city's peak, Yonatan could find her and fly her back down.

A rouged, veiled woman leaned out of the second story of a building, to their right. She was calling out to them. Kefira balked. She waved to Tahmour, and just as quickly disappeared inside, after casting a red veil to drape over the window. "Oh my," she averted her gaze to Rakhshan. "Let us move on quickly, please."

"Actually, this is our first stop," he replied.

Kefira gaped at him, and Tahmour stepped forward as the women opened the door to her house and leaned on the jamb. Her eyes were accentuated with dark kohl, white teeth framed with smiling, berry-red lips. Draping over her shoulders was straight, raven black hair and huge beaded earrings. Through her shadowy outfit showed much of her brown skin.

"Who is she?" Kefira asked uneasily.

Tahmour encircled the woman's waist with an arm and said, "My lady, Ravan."

"Tahmour," she giggled at his embrace. Her voice was warm, deep, and silky. "And Rakhshan." She opened her arms in welcome. "It has been too long a time. Who is this desert flower?" Her almond eyes found Kefira.

"Just a little Jewish ankle-biter," Tahmour shrugged, before planting a kiss upon the woman, who in turn giggled again, and batted him away. "She's the rider of the new dragon."

Kefira stared at her feet, the scene before her making her palms wet. Her eyes jumped up to Ravan when she said, "You're the

Israelite, Kefira, then! I have heard so much about you!"

The girl pressed her lips together. "Me?" she asked, bewildered, as the woman loosed herself from Tahmour and stepped forward to take up her hands in her own. Kefira's fingers twitched.

"Yes, you," Ravan replied. Voice playfully conspiratorial, "You're the only Jew in the city, and you've a dragon like no other."

"Word travels that fast, then?" Kefira chuckled, although not feeling particularly happy.

"Come on, Ravan," Tahmour leaned against her house, jerking his thumb to the door.

The woman turned to him imploringly. "Cannot they drink some chai with us, first?"

"I've never had chai before," Kefira said slowly. When she was particularly hungry, she'd boil leaves in water as a sort of soup, but that could not be compared to chai.

"Ah, I think they'd rather be alone," Tahmour said.

"But they can be alone – I have more than one room."

Kefira felt Rakhshan fidget beside her, and she glanced at him to see that his face was growing red. "That's alright, Ravan; we're going up to the orchard."

"Very well," the woman yielded. "You two enjoy the city, but visit when you care to. I've missed your company. It was nice to meet you, Kefira." After a smile, the woman followed Tahmour into the house.

Kefira turned to Rakhshan. His face was still red. "What just happened?"

He cleared his throat, face returning to its normal hue. "Let us keep walking," he said, and began pulling her along by the wrist.

Kefira faltered, not knowing whether she wanted to pull her hand from his. They were alone now. "What about Tahmour?" she murmured. "We're leaving him behind?"

"Well, yes," Rakhshan said, voice low. "Ravan is a prostitute."

Kefira blanched, and looked behind them incredulously. "Oh. Right." The red drape. "I'd forgotten – she seemed so kind."

"Prostitutes *are* kind. It's sort of their job." The man led her adroitly through the crowd.

She watched him as they moved. There was a suspicion tugging at her, now, as she looked at him. Had he ever been with a harlot? Certainly he had, he was a man and grew up in Parudrauga. Ravan had acted *very* familiar with him, anyway. She studied him. He'd successfully kept his face devoid of telling emotion.

Should she ask? No, she shouldn't – that would be very nosy – not to mention, bringing up such a personal topic would be mortifying for the both of them. So what if he had been with Ravan? Kefira did not care. She had no reason to care.

Suddenly, Rakhshan spoke, meeting her eyes. "My mother was one."

Kefira blinked.

"Oh," was all she could manage.

He continued, eyes ahead. "Her friends told her to go to the shaman so that he might kill me while I was still in the womb. Or perhaps," he added, a mirthless light in his eyes, "offer me to Molech. But the gods do not care for a bastard child, for sacrifice or mercy; my mother did none of the things her friends suggested, and perished giving birth to me."

Kefira stared at him. "I – I'm so sorry," she breathed. She stopped walking, halting him along with her in the middle of the street.

Rakhshan didn't look at her. His lips were tight, as though he'd not meant to speak in the first place. "It is alright," he said. "Come on, let us go."

Kefira felt her cheeks grow hot as she looked at him, his face averted as he continued walking. Without thinking, she looped her arm into his. He turned his face to her, stunned.

The girl paled. This was humiliating. Her arm tingled. "Um, where are we going?" she asked, before he could recover his breath to comment on her movement. She met his eyes fleetingly, and pushed a tress of hair back under her shawl.

A pleasant smile touched his lips – unlike all the other mischievous expressions he'd flashed before. "Oh, a place," he said. "I think you will like it." And his arm secured hers at his side.

Kefira walked as though in a dream, arm locked to his like a link in a silver chain, and followed as he led.

Rakhshan took her to the orchard. It was the highest point of the mountain that was Parudrauga. Many huge trees, branches stretching to the sky. Their bark was scale-like and mottled grey, round green leaves hanging like an untamed mane from the trees' crown of branches. The noonday sun fell in spots upon the ground, and the air was cool beneath the canopy, as an ocean breeze jostled the boughs.

Kefira self-consciously unhooked her arm from Rakhshan's, reaching out to feel one of the leaves in her hand as she looked up into the branches. The trees bore beige nuts in clusters, a shade of scarlet fading at each tip. These were pistachio trees! She turned to Rakhshan eagerly. "May we eat these?"

"Yes, indeed. It is a community orchard; no one's owned it since the empire was run out," he said with a shrug, leaning against one of the trees.

Kefira frowned. The fact that the King had no presence here disturbed her. The lack of guards – not that she particularly enjoyed guards – but the general lawlessness that sprung up from their absence was disconcerting. Though she enjoyed the free pistachios as much as the other residents of Parudrauga, she, at least, did not smoke alalega, or prostitute herself, or threaten other people with daggers. "Why were they run out?" she asked Rakhshan. She noticed that he was watching her, and then tried not to notice. Holding her tongue from chastising him, she instead leaned against an adjacent tree to listen to his reply.

"Because of the taxes on the shipments, mostly. The cargo Parudrauga sent up the coast wasn't cheap. And the black market was too restricted for their taste."

"So," Kefira quipped with a dry smile, "They are free men, like you?"

Rakhshan cocked an eyebrow. "Not in my sense. They still let themselves be whipped by their deities." He smiled a little.

"I guess they do…" Kefira muttered. Revulsion for Molech and the Baals rose within her once more.

"What makes your god different?" Rakhshan asked suddenly. But when she looked at him, she could tell that he was earnest. "How do you know that *he* is not false, as you claim the others are."

"Oh." Kefira was caught off guard. She glanced away and then back at him. Looking at a tree, she murmured a silent prayer. "Well," she said finally, meeting his eyes. "It is sort of a feeling I have." But, upon voicing it, she knew that this was a weak explanation at best; she tried to muster a smile, and then kicked a pebble at her feet.

And then with a burst of inspiration, she said, "You know of the Jordan River, do you not?"

Rakhshan shook his head.

"Well, it is the great river my people crossed to get to the Promised Land, Israel, many centuries ago," she explained. "It was very deep when they were at it, flooded from snowmelt, and it was impossible to cross."

"I thought you said they crossed it?"

"They did!" She found herself smiling. "The Lord stopped the water upstream, so that they could cross the river bed." She paused a moment to recollect the story. "And once everyone got across, the Lord told them to take twelve large stones, that is one for each of the Tribes, I think, from the center of the river and put them in a pile onto the shore. It was a symbol that the Lord brought them through the river!" she ended triumphantly. "I remember my village's rabbi telling me that story."

Rakhshan nodded when she finished. And then he said, "You will have to show me that place, some time," looking amused.

Kefira turned to him, agape. "You don't think I'm lying, do you?"

"I just said I wanted to see it, nothing about not believing you," Rakhshan laughed.

Kefira relaxed a little, but she felt winded. He was not taking her seriously. She doubted Jehovah was yet any different in his eyes next to Ishtar and Ahura Mazda. He was looking off into the distance, past the trees to the blue plain of Al-Khaleej. Having lost her conversational momentum, she absently foraged for what ripe pistachios were within her reach and nibbled upon them.

"When is the day of your birth, Kefira?"

He was facing her again, and she quickly swallowed what she was eating and replied, "I turn ten and six years old at the beginning of the next year."

"Frawardin?" That is less than a month away, you know," he said pensively. "The new year, Resha d'Sheta, is soon."

"It is?" she murmured. She could not very well keep track of months. The only way she had been able to tell the transition of one year to another was seeing its festivities as she travelled. She could only guess the day of her birth from there. On whichever day she deemed appropriate, she just made a little extra effort to wrangle food – fare more festive than table-scraps – and sang to herself. She could hardly have any real celebration for lack of company.

And then she realized that, in her pondering, she'd been staring stupidly at Rakhshan. She recovered with a hasty question. "Why do you want to know?"

He shrugged and said obliquely. "Well, it is an important date. Ten and six is a good age."

He was absurd. She laughed a little. "What makes it any better than sixty?"

A smile crept onto his face. "Persian law states that a girl is eligible to be married at that age."

Kefira stared at him, face heating. "You're bringing that up again?" she asked, aghast. She folded her arms, turning her face to recover. "The law is meaningless in Parudrauga. Your claim is meaningless." Her shawl flickered in the corner of her vision, and she remembered the chuppah.

He tossed a pistachio at her. "And *your* own claim just defeated you."

The nut fell between her feet, and she blushed. He was right. If law was indeed meaningless in Parudrauga, her age would not matter for marriage, one way or the other. She looked up at Rakhshan, biting her lip.

"Forgive me – I guess that this is an unpleasant subject for you," said the man. "But, remember, it is never out of the question. Or have you forgotten the eight hundred shekels?" he smiled roguishly.

Kefira shivered, the reminder like a cold silver spear. How could she *ever* repay him, yet how could she ever live with herself if she jilted him of his due, and left? Marrying him was not an option, but she could not think of any other way to make amends, if that was truly all he would take in exchange for forgiving her debt.

"I shouldn't have goaded you. I'm sorry." He must have seen the expression of despair on her face.

"It is alright," she replied quietly.

Rakhshan blinked. And then he jostled her with an elbow. "You mean you're not going to rebuke me? Or rant about my wickedness?"

The girl stared at him for a moment, and then said, "No," with a melodramatic sigh. "I've learned by now how thick you are. Lecturing you only makes you worse."

"I'm not thick," said Rakhshan. "Call it stubbornness. *You,* on the other hand..."

"What? I'm not thick!" she said indignantly.

He ruffled her shawl over her hair and said, "Are you kidding? You are as blind as a bat."

Kefira stepped away, setting her shawl back straight. "You confound me."

"A simple person like me, confounding you. That only proves it."

"You know what they say about birds of a feather..." She glared at him pointedly.

"Now we are back to me again. I'm not as much a fool as you are."

"Then prove it," she challenged him.

"Then lecture me," he replied readily, standing squarely in front of her, hands on his hips. He raised an equally challenging eyebrow. "Just see if a lowly vagrant like me can fathom what you opine."

"Alright." She found herself laughing. "Of what should I speak?"

"About how *wholly inadequate* you would be as a wife, just like you used to say."

"When did I say that?" Kefira asked, frowning at the return of the subject.

"The first time I suggested the notion. You said that marrying you would avail me nothing."

"That is true, but that's not the same as calling myself *inadequate*," she amended. And then she hugged her elbows. "And why are you goading me again? I do not want to lecture you about this. I always thought you did not like my rants."

Rakhshan shrugged, and looked away, to return his gaze to hers with a smile. "Contrary to what anyone else may think, you're not the *only* one who likes to here you talk."

Kefira blushed, and then grew indignant. "What? I do not sound that way, do I?"

Rakhshan laughed, hands up as though preparing to deflect a strike. "Do not worry, I was only joking."

"Forget being a mercenary," Kefira huffed. "You should petition to become the king's jester, for all the joking you do."

"And I'd end up hanging from a pike for accidentally insulting him." Rakhshan leaned against the tree beside her. "You're just trying to get rid of me, I see."

"Where would I get help raising Yonatan, if not you? Dragons are not easily tacked and fed for free, you know."

"Oh, you would miss more than my money." Rakhshan tilted his head, smiling jauntily. "Every day of my absence after my execution, you'd pine away over me, and every night dream of having me back."

Kefira felt as though she'd just been struck in the stomach, breathless, the memory of her dream coming back to her like a fist. "Do not flatter yourself, Rakhshan." As she spoke, her voice faltered a little more than she'd have liked it to. She folded her arms across her chest.

"Don't flatter myself? If I do not, then who will?" the Persian cracked a smile. "You will not, certainly. You're always so reticent."

The girl looked him askance with mock-disdain. "Well, I was taught that, when I haven't anything kind to say, to not speak at all."

"Oh, that's a clever rule, for a child." Rakhshan cracked a smile. "I prefer to be a little more reckless, and say and do whatever comes to mind. It suits me just fine. Although," he paused, and watching her appraisingly, said, "I do have to watch myself around you."

"Really? I cannot imagine how you would act without those inhibitions, if this is how you behave *with* them." She hardly dared to ask what he was withholding.

Rakhshan looked off regretfully, smiling a little.

"What is it?" she asked, growing uneasy.

His amber eyes glinted, in an almost defiant boldness, even as his lips pursed in uncertainty. "Well – right now, I would rather like to kiss you." He paused. "But knowing that you would strike me for it keeps me in check."

Kefira's breath halted. Her gaze held his, unable to leave it. Had he truly said what she just heard? The way he was looking down upon her, the flicker in his eyes – he was looking at her lips. Hot shivers ran rampant down her spine. He was close to her.

Close. Too close. He settled his hands on her arms, bringing her closer, and she smelled warm cardamom. Why wasn't she resisting? She felt her face, her lips flood with heat, a heat not born of anger – as she felt his presence draw near, face stooped to hers.

Yonatan was her saving grace. Before she had a mind to shut

her eyes and not reject the embrace of the man before her, she saw the dragon and his companions, as small as sparrows, winging back the barracks far away.

Kefira flinched, as though coming out of a trance; a little too loudly, she said, "Oh – there, the dragons have returned. Yonatan's going to wonder where I am."

"Oh, right." Rakhshan stepped back just as quickly, abashed, eyes flitting to the ground. "We do not want him to tear up the city looking for you."

Kefira held her hands in a knot behind her back. "That would make a bad first impression."

"Come on, I will walk you back." And then Rakhshan winced, realizing the redundancy of his words. He offered her his arm.

The girl hesitated, and then took it. They made their way back, conversation at a happy minimum. She glanced at him from time to time, when he was not glancing at her, and saw his face was flushed with crimson.

She kept her eyes open for a bathhouse as they walked. Her underarms were as hot and sweaty as ever.

Chapter IX
Rain Comes

Kefira didn't know where flowers came from, in the dry lands of Gedrosia, but somehow there were gaudy bushels over every door in the city, petals of crimson and yellow and violet bringing life to the bleached-bone adobe houses of Parudrauga. These were the first ripples of the Resha d'Sheta celebration. The blooms began to gird the streets a week after they had reached the port city. The most innocent of Parudrauga's celebratory throes, Rakhshan had told her. Soon to come, he warned, would be dancing and feasting that would eventually mount into riotous carousing and drinking and prostitution – or more than what was usual. In short, Kefira was very glad that her station was in the barracks, the dragons surrounding keeping them all quite safe from anything that got out of hand. Though the window of her room was regrettably proficient at carrying the sound of the nightly revelry to her ears.

The day before he left with Sorushe to scout the countryside – looking for late pursuers of the Hardlā Thieves – Tahmour had Ravan over to the barracks, to fill one of the many otherwise vacant seats in the mess hall. Kefira was a little unnerved by her company, though she seemed to be a very agreeable woman, despite her disreputable station. She cooked well, anyway, and so rather than the raw nuts and fruit which had been the normal fare, Ravan had roasted for them twin rabbits in the abandoned kitchens. She'd marinated them for a day, prior to, in shallots and spices and the juice of lemons, as well as a sort of white paste – yoghurt – which she'd smugly attested was imported all the way from Greece. Kefira did not know precisely where that was, but apparently the distance was to be marveled at.

In any case, the rabbits were not Kashrut. Kefira fumbled with a polite refusal, although she did have a taste of the yoghurt. It was sour, and otherwise rather tasteless. Ravan said that it'd been made of milk, but Kefira remembered what milk tasted like, and this was not the same flavor. She wondered how it could be as fine as the woman said it was. Incidentally, Kefira had spent that meal trying not to watch everyone else enjoy it as she ate her loaves and pistachios.

Yonatan was enjoying eating more than she was. Since they had gotten to Parudrauga, he'd finally gotten beyond Mār's shoulders in height. Unlike the stocky, lizard-like physique of the Persian dragons, he had the sleek body of an Egyptian racing hound. His chassis was long, he had a narrow waist and barrel-chest, with elegant legs. Yet more unlike the Persian beasts, his neck was very long, enough to double back upon itself, in contrast to their shorter stalks, and his long tail was carried off the ground with an air of pride. His muzzle was smooth, no unsightly teeth jutting from his lips, contrary to the vicious snout of the Azhi Dahaki and Gandarewa. The Persian dragons' faces were thorny, with studded brows and crude horns down their chin and spine; there was a smooth horn above Yonatan's nostrils, and across his cheekbones, and a pair of antlers that crowned his head like a red buck's – sharp, regal. His face was clean, imperial, a beautiful ferocity. And Kefira knew why the Hardlā was the pride of Israel.

"But you are still quite skinny. Here, eat." Mehrnaz nudged a goat to Yonatan. Mār snorted disdainfully as the Hardlā wolfed down the creature whole.

Arsham seemed pleased with Yonatan's growth. "Though it seems as if the quantity of his prey cannot keep up with how much he grows. Perhaps we should see if someone with cattle would oblige us to sponsor him."

"Is that where you are getting the livestock?" Kefira asked him, bewildered. She couldn't imagine anyone in the city giving away their beasts to feed her dragon.

"Indeed, yes. Your Yonatan is something like a community project, here. Men are happy to sell their animals at a lower price to the dragon riders." His words of this altruism were unthinkable to her, but she had no time to absorb them when he asked, "Mehrnaz did not grow like this after she was out of the egg. In no time he'll dwarf her." And his dragon did not seem jealous at the prospect. Mār, on the other hand, did his fair share of griping – mostly under the guise of pious disdain for the youngling's gluttony.

Arsham, Mehrnaz, and Yonatan seemed to be the only relaxed ones in the barracks. As soon as Tahmour left with his dragon, however, tension had seemed to dissipate in Rakhshan, a tension she hadn't noticed until it left. But a day prior to the Barids' expected return, the thin lines in his brow reappeared.

He was ever confounding her. Whenever she thought of him now, it was either guilty reminiscence of her dream, or mortification of how they'd almost kissed in the orchard. Half of the time, during these moments of internal duress, she convinced herself that it had been just one of the awkward pauses of conversation that occurred, and nothing more. But when she remembered the way he was looking at her, or at the way his hands told her that he was about to embrace her – she was yet unconvinced. Whatever the case, she could not decide whether or not she regretted having drawn attention to Yonatan's appearance, there in the orchard. But some questions were better left unanswered.

Kefira gazed out her window. Beyond the glittering rise-and-fall of dragon flanks she could see past the side of the barracks, into the city streets. There were dancers, in dresses as thin and scanty as spider webs, but with bright colors that now outdid the fading glory of the drying flowers. The women spun in circles or swayed like snakes through the air, with dizzying rhythm, weaving their bodies to the muted cadence of pipes and lyres. They moved with a provocative slowness, like dripping honey, hypnotizing men as they trod by. Kefira stopped watching.

Ravan came to the barracks that afternoon, in anticipation of Tahmour's arrival. Kefira had seen her coming after she'd finished a prayer with Yonatan, and was departing the dragon-yard. Upon noticing her approach, she'd half a mind to pick up the pace and slip into the barracks before the woman called out to her. But she suppressed that urge. Arsham and Rakhshan had isolated themselves again, and were busy talking somewhere, so hesitantly Kefira decided to take up the mantle of hospitality. "Good afternoon," she offered her a pleasantry.

"And to you." The woman's rouged lips parted in a smile. "Where are the men?"

"Talking about politics inside." Kefira folded her arms. Whenever the men went off to confer, Rakhshan never told her what they'd discussed. He had used to be so expository, when they were travelling before. "Tahmour has not yet returned."

"What a shame," the woman sighed. "Well, I suppose I would see Sorushe, if he was." Ravan cast about the courtyard, and then as the gap in their conversation grew wider, she looked an uneasy Kefira up and down with appraisal. The girl stood awkwardly, now regretting her attempt at congeniality. "I know what we should to do pass the time. And anyway, you do need a bath."

Kefira's feet grew cold, upon finding the reason for her scrutiny. Could the woman simply read her desire for one, or did she smell? "Oh," was all she said. What was this *we* business, again? The girl would not like to bathe with anyone. "Do you know of a place?" she still found herself asking. She hoped the woman would not answer with a public bathhouse.

Ravan cocked her head. "Don't you? There is a room underground here, fed by a hot spring." She grabbed Kefira by the wrist. "Come along, I will show you. It's a wonder none of the men took you to it before! That is the first place Tahmour brought me."

Kefira submitted to being led down the halls by the half-stranger, for nothing if not the desire for warm water and a way to be clean. Ravan seemed to navigate as though she had herself a map, invisible in her mind. How often had she been here?

In one hall they passed, Kefira heard voices from a room. Rakhshan and Arsham. "Not in there," Ravan giggled when Kefira paused to try and listen to them. "But we can bring Rakhshan, if you like."

Kefira almost tripped as she was tugged along. "What?" And when she looked at the woman, she saw her expression was earnest. She cleared her throat, and replied faintly, "No, no, thank you."

Soon Ravan found a stone staircase that lead down to the dark mouth of some sort of room. "Oh, we'll have to get a lamp, I suppose, what a bother."

"There is always a lit torch in the mess hall. I will fetch it," Kefira offered.

"I will go get it," Ravan laughed. "Tahmour told me about how you'd gotten yourself lost."

Kefira smiled with embarrassment. "Very well," and she didn't argue further, as the woman was already receding. The echo of her footsteps dissolved into silence.

Alone, the girl stood at the staircase, looking into the darkness below. Tentatively, she stepped down, sandals slapping on each stone step. A gust of warm, wet air buffeted her face and then she was at the bottom, staring around the dark mouth. A faint shaft of light cut by her shadow was all the illumination there was inside, the tiled floor glistening with warm dew.

It was very hot. Kefira glanced behind her, looking up the stairs and removing her shawl — trying not to imagine someone up there, watching. Certainly Rakhshan could not have heard of their talk of bathing. No, he would not be so dishonorable as to watch, she hoped. One could not see much of anything inside from the top of the stairs anyway.

She could not tell whether it was the steam or sweat that was sticking to her skin, but it was too hot there. She stepped out of sight of the door shaft and reluctantly shucked her outer garments, standing in her underclothes in the darkness. Disrobing now would be better than doing so when Ravan returned, anyway.

The room was illuminated by a sudden burst of orange light — Kefira jumped, before remembering it was Ravan. "Ah, I see you've found your way in." She put the torch into a socket in the wall. "Is this place not beautiful?"

Pillars held up the domed ceiling, and in the center of the room there was a steaming pool, a spring harnessed in rock and tiles for the pleasure of the military's favored ones. The walls were inscribed with a stone relief of dueling dragons. One of them Kefira recognized as a Gandarewa – it had eyespots on its wings – and it was fending off other beasts. Descending from storm clouds, there was a heavily built dragon with a ring in its nose, and from rising waters a leviathan reared from a waterspout. From a cyclone of fire reared a dragon with three heads.

"Do you recognize any of those beasts? I think you'd be better at it than I," said Ravan absently. "I know what Sorushe is, and Tahmour told me that the three-headed dragon there is a Greek beast, but I know nothing beyond that." Kefira saw with no small amount of dismay that she was disrobing too, tossing her clothes on the stone face of a lion statue.

Feeling incredibly out of place, Kefira folded her arms across her chest. "I do not recognize any of those except for the Gandarewa. I did not realize such a dragon existed – the three-headed one," she replied, frightened at the concept. She'd heard that once a lamb had been born with two heads, but it had died soon after its bearing.

"I've heard stories of their Sky Army. They have some very queer dragons, indeed. Now that I recall, that one is called a Cerberus," she said, pointing to it. "Its kind guards the gates to the Underworld."

"Dragons do?" She could not imagine Sheol in the way of the heathens. Would not angels, the messengers of the Lord, be the ones assigned to the task? She tried to ponder this, as she averted her eyes from the unflawed figure of Ravan entering the water.

"Who can say? That is what the Greeks believe, anyway." Ravan dismissed the discussion with a wave of her hand. "What are you waiting for? Come on."

Kefira colored with embarrassment – she would look like a child compared to her. But in the end, she was glad to remove herself from her dirty clothing; they smelled salty-sweet, dry sweat. She folded the garments and set them on the lion's lap.

"You've the hips of a child-bearer," Ravan observed aloud when Kefira bashfully turned to the pool.

Before speaking, Kefira promptly slid into the water. Eyes blank and incredulous, face reddening at the observation, she looked up at the woman across the pool. "Is that a good thing?" she replied uneasily. The heat of the water did not assuage her blushing.

"That is what a man looks for, if he wants heirs. Though you are a little skinny. You've a good face on you, though."

Kefira stared at the woman, and wondered what resided between her ears. "Why do you say such things?"

"Young women like you are awkward, like newborn lambs you stumble about. You cannot walk on feet you do not acknowledge." As she opined, the woman was very casually washing her hair.

"What do you mean?"

Ravan giggled. "Oh, you. Rakhshan told me you do not have a mother. I am only saying what she would say, if she saw you now." Kefira was taken aback. She didn't know whether she should take her words as kind or pretentious.

"I – I'm not used to being spoken to with such forthrightness," said she, confounded.

"Then let me stop speaking." Ravan turned around and reached into the mouth of one of the lions, where a shiny dish was kept. "Look into this mirror – see why Rakhshan delights in you."

Kefira almost dropped the mirror into the pool, when it was handed to her. "What?" she breathed.

"Just look into the mirror, silly girl."

It was a little disc of copper; Kefira looked at it hesitantly and then back to Ravan. It was a mirror. She'd never seen one before. In it, people were supposed to see their faces. She did not know what she looked like, beyond patch-working an appearance from what she gathered from her parents, and what distorted visages she saw in water.

But what would she truly see? Fear made her fingertips thrum around the flat instrument, but she did not hesitate for long. She brought it to her face. Too close – she could only see a nose – so she removed it to arm's length and saw her reflection.

Her face was like a tanned goat's hide – no, not so rough – perhaps it was bronze. She wasn't fair, with the white complexion of an opal, yet not wholly unlovely. Her eyes were large and dark, and between them there was a nose that arced softly from her face. Her eyebrows were dark, unkempt, but not too unbecoming. The best of her features were her lips; they were chapped of course, but had a full shape. Kefira touched them unthinkingly. This was her. This is what people saw when they looked at her.

"You said that... he... delights in me?" Kefira asked quietly.

She could see Ravan's incredulous smile past the mirror. "You mean you cannot tell?"

The girl flushed, setting aside the mirror. How could she tell? The man acted so forward with everyone. She was certainly not receiving any special treatment. But her silence only proved the fool Ravan thought she was. "I guess that he has talked about..." she trailed off. "Um, marriage, a little."

"He wants you to be his *wife*?" Ravan exclaimed, astonishment plain in her voice. But Kefira decided not to take offense to her bafflement at the prospect.

"He just said that it would be a fair trade," Kefira said quickly. "Because I owe him money."

"Oh? What did you do?"

Kefira was reluctant to retell the story. "Instead of taking the bounty for retrieving Yonatan's egg, he broke me from prison."

"He had not told us of that part!" cried Ravan. "Kefira, why do you not take his offer? That would be a splendid arrangement for the both of you!"

Kefira sank lower into the pool, swirling her arms slowly around in the water. "It is not that easy..."

"What do you mean? Do you find him objectionable?"

"We are just – friends," Kefira stammered, hunching her shoulders. Friends – were they even friends? He was *Rakhshan*, he was a *pagan*, after all. She remembered the night at the inn. 'Friend' was truly too kind a word.

Ravan wrinkled her brow, growing stern. "Kefira, how long have you traveled with Rakhshan?"

"We flew for about a month, I think," Kefira replied, a little disconcerted by her change of mood.

"And still you cannot see with whom you travelled?" Ravan waved her hands through the water. "Are you blind?"

"Well, he is handsome," Kefira confessed. "But I'm not to marry a man according to what he looks like," she ended firmly.

"Oh, I know *that*," Ravan snorted. "I mean blind with your heart! He is a kind and clever man, and strong. And he likes you as you are, without jewelry or kohl."

If you like him so much, why do you not marry him? Kefira almost asked. But then she realized that she did not want that. "I guess you're right," she found herself admitting.

"Then why do you insist upon friendship when he wants to marry you? Friendship will not keep you housed and fed for very long. And anyway, you *must* marry some time, unless you want to undertake *my* profession. How old are you?"

Kefira rounded down. "I have ten and five years."

"And he is ten and nine, or twenty, now, I do not recall – anyway, that is not so horrid a gap in years, and besides, would you give your *friend* the dishonor of reaching his twentieth year and being without a wife?"

"Well, he does not have to marry *me*," the girl defended.

"Kefira," Ravan sighed. "You know what Empire we live in, yes?"

"Yes. Persia."

"And men have their way in Persia. Yes, I know that women here may work independent of them, earn wages for themselves, own property, and even go into the military – which drives the Greeks across the sea absolutely mad. But – know this. Despite it all, men have their way."

Kefira listened.

"Persia is an empire where men have their way with women," Ravan continued. "The King, may he live forever, may take any woman that pleases his eye into his harem, with no questions asked." She looked at Kefira with earnestness. "With your face, your everything, they will get their way with you, if you are not careful."

The girl was beginning to wonder if Ravan was speaking from the bottom of a wineskin. She was growing unnerved by her words. "What do you mean?"

Ravan's voice was solemn, words oblique. "It is on your terms: either through their coin purse or a head thick with wine or a dark alleyway – a man will have his way."

Kefira shivered, despite the heat of the room. She looked away, remembering the inn and the village and waking up alone.

"But Rakhshan is a good man. He is not like Tahmour, or a drunkard, or a sick jackal. He wants to marry you. But if you don't let him, you will not be protected! Kefira, if you do not let him have his way, have your hand, then some other man will; and he may not be like Rakhshan."

Kefira was silent.

"I am still waiting for Tahmour to want to marry me – though of course, I am not a virgin." Ravan's voice was softer, rolling over the water. "The – the men that we keep company with, these lawless men, you are fortunate that there's an honorable one among them that wants you to be his wife."

Kefira held herself tight. Her words were small and flat. "You're right."

"I am." Ravan nodded and smiled softly. "So, you should oblige him."

"I will think about it," replied Kefira.

Ravan looked up at her from the water, where makeup left her face in black tears. But this time she seemed to shrug off Kefira's lackluster reply and continue in washing.

Kefira was quiet as the scrubbed her scalp with her fingernails. Her hair floated around her like a dark, arm-length halo. She combed her hands through it. "Yonatan would not be happy to know what we are discussing."

"Oh, the beasts would certainly be a problem. Jealous creatures, they are."

"Yes, indeed," replied Kefira absently. She wondered if Mār knew the thoughts of his rider, about her. Certainly, he would not withhold any caustic remarks about it, if he did, so she guessed he was in the dark. She loathed what he might do if he knew that an annoying Jewish brat enamored his rider. Yonatan himself would not be pleased by her even *considering* the brigand Persian's offer.

Ravan stepped out of the water and began to dry off with her discarded garments. Kefira rested her head on her arms on the rim of the pool, pondering. "I cannot marry, not with Yonatan," she announced. "He is protection enough, besides."

The argument gave Ravan pause; she looked contemplatively upon the stubborn mule that was Kefira. And then she said, "What about when you are old and grey? Dragons stay young for a long while, and Yonatan will need a companion, and certainly he will not take just anyone. Marry Rakhshan, have a child – or better, many children – for Yonatan and Mār, both! It is a perfect arrangement."

"Ought we be naming these children now, too?" Kefira grit her teeth, perturbed by the destruction of her argument. "I think you are getting a little carried away."

"You mayn't know this about me yet, little sparrow, but I happen to be the match-maker on my street. I cannot help but do these things," she purred. And then she looked at her disheveled garments. "Oh, curses – I never brought any fresh linens." She held her clothes with dismay. "You do not happen to have extra, do you?"

"I have none at all," Kefira said; as a matter of fact, that pile at the lion's feet was all the clothing she had. "Can we wash our clothes in this pool?"

"That probably breaches decorum somewhere, but I will not tell anyone that you did it," replied the woman. She looked at the water suspiciously. "Although I do not know if this dye would stand for it." She glared at her many-colored fabrics.

"Well, I haven't anything fancy." Kefira reached and dragged her clothing into the water, and dunked it with a vengeance. Well, there were the garments that Rakhshan had given her in Hangmatana, but those were well-worn by now. Fine clothes did not retain their fineness after being dragonback very long.

"Nothing fancy? That is a pity. I should let you borrow some of my things. Though I have already given my old, small things to my niece; I will have to look for something your size."

Kefira glanced at the woman's clothing. She wondered if it was linen; she could see no tassels on it. She ought not wear it – she remembered some fabrics were reviled by Jehovah. Certainly, He would not want her dressed in revealing, translucent veils, anyway. "Thank you," she said anyway, hoping to dismiss the subject.

"It would be my pleasure," Ravan replied absently, still scrutinizing her clothes. "This is fresh enough, anyway. I can re-wear it until I return home, at least."

Kefira pressed her lips together, to keep from smiling – her pettiness amused her. She just finished rinsing her clothes and wrung them out, to wrap herself into the clingy, warm garments, infinitely heavier. Before leaving, she thought about looking at the mirror again, maybe taking it to her room, but Ravan was using it to reapply her makeup.

"Thank you for talking to me," Kefira said, standing in the pale square of light that was the door. "And for showing me this place. I'm going to… freshen up in my room." She fidgeted.

"Very well." Ravan smiled, looking at her past the mirror. "I'm glad I could straighten you up. Be sure to remember what I said."

Kefira clenched her hands behind her back. "Oh, yes, I shall be sure to, thank you. Good bye."

When Kefira emerged into the corridor, there was a strange twilight quality to the world. It couldn't be dark – it could only yet be midafternoon. She walked into the courtyard and looked up into the sky. Clouds like lumpy, curdled milk were beginning to cover the blue. She sniffed. The air smelled cool and metallic, like rain. It hadn't rained in a long time. The farmers here would no doubt be pleased.

She just hoped the ceiling in her room would not leak.

Eventually, she found her room, and shut the creaking door behind her. It was lit only dimly through the window, floating dust catching the struggling light.

Her rags had lost all their warmth, and were clinging to her like cold, wet cobwebs. Making sure that her door was shut tightly and dragging a cot in front of it out of precaution, she stripped to her undergarments and hung the rags upon some of the empty cots to drip and dry.

Then she fell into bed, cuddling up into the blankets to watch the ceiling again. She did not care if she missed the midday meal. She was too vexed to eat. Maybe if she stared at that singular crack for long enough, though, the vexation would leave her and she could cease to think. That would be nice.

But the girl's thoughts persisted, and she began to bite her fingernails. She did not like the talk that she and Ravan had. What was that nonsense, about him liking her? She was only Kefira – she did not have any capital or connections, or the coy eyes of a doe, or the body of Ravan, or any domestic talent. It did not stand to reason that she should at all be able to satisfy her suitor, let alone be proper recompense for her immense debt to him. Ravan had been given over to delusion, making that assumption. Marriage – that he actually *wanted* to.

In any case, it was wrong. She couldn't even think about marrying Rakhshan, unless the miraculous occurred and he decided that he fancied the God of Israel. She could not be yoked unequally.

There were no exceptions.

Ruth, one of the ancestors of Israel's greatest king, David, had been a Moabite and a widow. She wasn't of Israeli blood, but she followed God's statutes, saying to her Jewish mother-in-law Naomi, 'your God is my God.' And she married a Jew: Boaz. They had begotten the father of David's father. They were the ancestors of kings, and they hadn't known it.

She scrutinized the distant crack. She could not imagine a stubborn man like Rakhshan, let alone one so put up against the gods, sincerely taking it upon himself to accept her Lord. It was a useless pursuit even thinking about it.

No, stop thinking. Look at the crack, that little broken line.

And then the sight of the crack dimmed significantly. Darkness. The sky was now fully enveloped in clouds.

A sunless chill crept upon her. She pulled the blankets tighter, rough wool against her skin.

Then a hiss, low and steady slithered to her ears from the window. She looked; it wasn't a crooning Yonatan, but grey sheets of rain, falling, falling down to hard-packed earth. Suddenly she was aware of a sharp, cold wetness on her nose. She looked up at the crack. It was leaking.

"Leagues. Mere *leagues* from us." Tahmour's clipped words.

"They have come too soon. This was not the appointed time!" Arsham's voice was just as frustrated, echoing up to Kefira from where she was leaning on the corridor railing on the second floor.

"When word came of your defection and Rakhshan's arrival, I imagine they indeed hastened themselves, but I did not expect this so soon."

When Kefira had heard the flutter of small wings through the rain's din, she knew that Sorushe had landed. Anxious to hear any news of their pursuit, she had quickly dressed and was about to shut the door behind her when she heard them speaking.

She left her door open. It would make noise if it shut, and she didn't want the men to halt their discussion. Maybe she would finally be able to listen in on one of their conferences, now that there was no one around to stop her.

But what she heard next was not what she expected.

"I admit that seeing that army has caused me to lose faith." Tahmour speaking wryly to the man. "You still believe that having him will deter them?"

"Yonatan's value is not even to be questioned. Not a drop of his blood can be spilled. The king would let no harm come to him."

Kefira's stomach dropped to the soles of her feet, suffusing her with burning liquid fear. They could not mean it. She could not be hearing correctly.

"Rakhshan had said that the Hardlā was an isolated matter, though; only the Median satrap knew about him. Who's to say the rest of Persia will recognize his breed?"

Their voices faded as they passed, echoes of words and footsteps melting into the monotonous hiss of rain.

Kefira stood still, trying to puzzle things out, a familiar knot growing inside her. Dread.

No, it couldn't be. Not again. He'd said he was sorry. Her stomach burned. Her eyes burned.

She ran down the hallway.

Rakhshan's door burst open. He had been sitting on his cot in the glow of lamplight, looking at a piece of fabric in his hand, when Kefira lurched into the room.

He stood, casting the shawl away behind him hurriedly. "Kefira," he said, bafflement in his expression.

The girl stalked right up to him, steps rigid and sharp. He glanced behind himself and then back at her as she approached, finding her hard gaze with his eyes. "Why am I here?" she asked.

He stared, and she waited for an answer. For a stuttering moment, he searched her face. "What do you mean?" he finally managed.

"I thought you were - " the girl stammered, fists balling. "I thought you had changed! I thought you were never going to sell out me and Yonatan again!"

"What are you talking about?" Rakhshan insisted, feverish. But she knew that that was comprehension dawning in his eyes – she saw it.

"You tell me." She set her jaw, as though that might steady her voice, even as her eyes bloomed with heat, his face blurring. She blinked away the stupid tears, and his face was lucid once more. "What is this army? Why did you want to bring Yonatan to Parudrauga? I know now it is not because you cared for his safety," she spat.

His jaw moved mutely, his gaze faltering; she pinned him down with her own. At first she thought he would ignore her as he stood in silence – but he finally spoke, meeting her eyes. "Would you – sit down?"

She looked at his cot. "No."

He ran a hand through his hair and straightened, lips pressed together in a tight line. "You *were* brought here so that Yonatan could be safe."

"I know that is a lie." She spoke the words like they were thorns in her mouth. Vengefully, she wiped more emerging tears from her face.

"It is not." He looked at her squarely, hands on her quaking shoulders. She shrugged them off, and he folded his arms. "But," he said quieter. "That's not all you were brought here for."

She shivered, and clenched her trembling jaw. "Go on."

He exhaled, exasperated. "Would you sit down? You look like you're ready to fight."

Kefira reluctantly crouched on the edge of the cot opposite to him. He sat on his, and leaned forward, elbows on his knees. "Well," he finally continued. "Parudrauga is a tick on Persia's back, since it got rid of the Empire's hand in it – not half a dozen years ago. Mostly, it went rogue to evade shipment taxes, and so now it collects money from foreign ships and cargo, coin that originally would go into the Empire's purse. Ships from south and east and west all must pass by Parudrauga if they want a port to house them before they leave the gulf, and so this place was much prized by the Empire. So they want it back."

"That explains the army." Kefira frowned. "What about Yonatan?"

Rakhshan's face fell. "They'll not spare the rebels. We have dragons, five counting the two priests, without Yonatan. They'll bring many more than that."

"Well, I dare say *six* dragons could stand against them, even with Yonatan's size!" Kefira shot. "And I would not put him in harm's way for the sake of this place!"

"It is not about him fighting. The king wouldn't risk letting any harm come to him, so…"

"So Parudrauga would be safe?" Her lips twisted bitterly, and the room became blurry again. She pressed her palms to her face, and when she looked up again, her eyes were clear enough to glare at Rakhshan.

"Kefira," he began, getting to his feet.

Her fingernails dug into her arms. "Everything is a lie, then. You did not even bother to tell us of your next great plot, even as it brewed in your mind." Her voice was strained, like silk with an axe pressed against it. She burst, "Tell me – did you come up with this plan *after* you rescued us from Hangmatana, or was it devised even before, and getting me locked up and Yonatan taken away by Deioces all a part of the trick from the beginning?"

"No, it wasn't a trick," Rakhshan insisted, roused. "I - "

Kefira cut him off. "It *wasn't* a trick? Then what was it? You lied to me – again!"

"I'm sorry," he said, and she heard anger rising in his voice. "But I did what I had to do. I knew that I could not tell you, or else you would react exactly like *this*."

Kefira was almost at a loss for words. She stood herself now.

"How else could I act? I may be an urchin, a thief, but I condone this wayward place's punishment from the empire. If you think that I would act any different a week from now than I would a month ago, finding all this out – you're wholly wrong," she seethed, whirling away from him, her stupid eyes like hot springs. "Using Yonatan, me…" She turned to him again, savagely. "When *were* you going to tell me of your deceit? Were you going to wait until before or *after* we were married?"

Rakhshan had no reply, face flushed, eyes like embers.

"That was all a part of your ploy, too." She sniffed, forcing ferocity into her words to smother the sorrow. "Because if I was your wife, you would always have me here – Yonatan would never leave Parudrauga, and every thief and harlot here would be able to live the rest of their days in merry bliss, for all their ill-gotten freedom and riches!"

She blinked, her vision cleared, and she saw that his eyes were glistening.

"I did not lie about that." His voice was low, almost a whisper.

Kefira stared, fury boiling down, leaving her limbs to feel leaden, immobile. How could he so deceitfully use Kefira and Yonatan – yet at the same time feel as he did about her? No answers came to her, and she stood in silence. Again, she blinked the blurriness away, hot streams trickling down her cheeks. Then cool hands cupped her face, and her breathing stopped.

Her eyes widened. Rakhshan was covering her lips with his own.

Terrified, the girl braced her hands against his chest, shoving out of his embrace and away. "Stay away from me!" she cried, and raced to the door, crashing out of it, and staggering in the puddled hallway outside. Her heart pealed like the thunder that rippled the sky, frenzied breath hissing as her feet carried her to the dark of her room. She slammed the door behind her and ran to the window. "Yonatan!" she called. Rustling sounds outside. He was coming.

Running to her cot, she snatched up her few belongings and rolled them into her blankets.

"Kefira!" Rakhshan's dim voice, causing her heart to leap as his fist rapped outside the door.

The girl shot a look at the doorway, tying the bedroll off. She grabbed the little clay lamp, too, and the nuts and raisins she had stashed away, and shoved them into the roll. Yonatan was at the window, golden eye looking in. He crooned.

"We are leaving," she breathed to him.

And Rakhshan came through the door. His eyes found her all packed up, roll under her arms and leg poised to climb out the window. "Kefira, I'm sorry," he said, approaching her, and the girl stared at him like he was a jackal. She made to propel herself from the window, but the man caught her first, with an arm hooked around her waist. "Let go of me!" she cried, as she fell backwards into him.

"Wait!" he snapped, pulling her terrifyingly close; fear shot through her like lightning, feeling him all too real against her. "Stop struggling!" Without another word, he thrust his hand into her clothes, hand running sharply over her skin. Horrified, Kefira tried to arc her body away from him, limbs stiffening like rods. Her fingers were frozen on his arm as it roved.

After a catatonic moment, she cried out in disbelief.

Yonatan heard, and snarled viciously, snapping the tip of his muzzle through the window. His head recoiled, and then claws entered, thrusting through the narrow opening. He tore outward, mortar crackling, stones grinding – and the better part of the bunkroom wall was torn open. Rain hissed inside, until he stuck his head into the gap, tongue lashing as he hissed, formidable teeth borne, glaring with inflamed orange eyes at Rakhshan.

The man released her immediately, backing away with his hands up. She staggered upon being dropped, falling to her hands and knees. She stared at the floor for a moment, panting, and saliva fell from her lips. She turned her head to stare at him after what seemed like an eternity, and felt her body drain of conviction.

He.

He – Rakhshan.

The man gazed back at her with desolate eyes. He looked at Yonatan, at her. And he turned away, shoving past the door and into the night, heavy footfalls fading to echoes.

A deep sound from Yonatan's throat resounded through the floor, shaking Kefira to the bone. She scrambled to regroup her things on the ground, straightened up her disheveled clothes, and scuttled onto his back. The new cloth rigging they had bought was soaked through, the fabric dark grey in the rain. She looped herself into its heavy confines, and leaned forward onto his neck. Hot streaks mingled with rain and ran down her face. "Fly." Her voice was just high enough to be audible. She could feel Yonatan's muscles shiver beneath his scales, a silent response.

"What was that for?" Mār's voice growled through the rain. "Tearing up the builting like that!"

Kefira's heart stopped beating. Sheets of water pelted down, a grey haze all around them, but she could still make out the three other dragons, all awake, eyes fixed on them.

The upheaval of the room seemed to draw more attention from inside. Kefira could see smaller movement from the mouth of the barracks. "What's going on, here? You do not mean to go flying in this monsoon?" Arsham.

"Fly!" Kefira urged Yonatan.

"Wait, hold on – where are you going?" Tahmour's exclamation. "Keep them down, Mehrnaz!"

Yonatan reared, to avoid an attack, but no motion was forthcoming. Kefira craned her neck to see past his shoulder, heart pounding, but saw no golden movement coming towards them, just the blink of storm-blue eyes. Yonatan beat his wings, not quite lifting off, but looming upright above all of them, hissing.

"Rakhshan – there you are! What is going on?" Mār's urgent growl. "Where are they going?"

Kefira's heart stuttered. They wouldn't chase them. They couldn't. How could they, after this? "You aren't going to keep us here against our will, are you?" she cried down cuttingly.

"No – no, let them go." Rakhshan's words.

What?

"Are you out of your mind, boy?"

"Rakhshan – what did you tell them?"

Yonatan hesitated no more. With the urgent pressure of her legs, he launched into the air, and put Parudrauga far beneath them. Rain pelted her face all the harder, now, stinging, biting her skin, and she huddled in the crook of his neck, face down. A dragon uttered with distress beneath them, and wing beats aside from Yonatan's pulsed in her ears.

"No, I said let them be!"

Kefira looked up to catch glimpses of two riderless dragons; Mār was a green streak to the left of them, and Sorushe almost blended into the rain ahead. Already he had cut them off.

But he didn't make to attack Yonatan, but spoke, flying circles around his head, Kefira cringing at his proximity. "Where are you going?" he piped. "Don't you know there's bad people? Outside the city just west of us! You don't want to leave!" Yonatan snorted, shaking his head to deter the smaller dragon.

There was more shouting from the ground, and the two dragons deferred. Sorushe halted in his haranguing and hovered, to disappear below Yonatan and behind them.

But the Azhi Dahaki tore forward. Kefira looked behind them, heart in her throat, as she saw the eyes of the swift beast just past Yonatan's wing. He wheeled to the side, and Kefira thought he was lunging for them, but instead, he pulled up short with a roaring snarl. "If you ever have the guts to come back," he growled, "know that you woult not be welcome here!" Lightening illuminated the fury in his eyes, and she saw acid running with water down his neck.

Yonatan lashed his tail in the older dragon's face and growled gutturally, voice reverberating in his cavernous lungs like a second thunder in the storm. He stretched his wings farther to scoop the air, and pushed away from him. It was with a vindictive screech that

Mār let himself fade into the darkness.

Then the only sounds that remained were the rattle of the rain against Yonatan's wings and the hiss of his frustrated, toiling breath. Kefira found the courage to look behind them. Through the near-black, the orange glow of Parudrauga seemed already leagues away, with curtains of rain between them. She saw no dragons.

Kefira rested her head upon Yonatan's neck once more, and the tears returned. She slipped an icy hand into her clothing. What had she done?

Her fingers felt the soft leather of a scroll inside, and she knew nothing anymore.

II
- Persian Empire, 541 BC -

"How can I give you up, Israel?
How can I let you go?
How can I destroy you like Admah,
Or demolish you like Zeboiim?
My heart is torn within Me;
All My compassion is aroused.
I will not carry out My fierce anger,
Nor will I turn and devastate Israel.
For I am God, and not man –
The Holy One among you.
I will not come in wrath.

They will follow the lord;
He will roar like a lion.
When He roars, His children will come trembling
from the west.
They will come trembling,
Like birds from Egypt,
Like doves from Assyria.
I will settle them in their homes,"
declares the Lord.

- Hosea 11:8-11

Chapter X
Jackals

The rain continued to fall throughout the night. Water pooled on the hard ground, and the white earth did not take it in. Kefira could feel the puddles gathering in the darkness, cool pressure against her hands as she roused from sleep. Higher upon Yonatan she clambered, dragging her sodden things with her. The dragon was awake now, too, blinking a sleepy eye. He recognized the increasing turbulence of their dwelling place, a flat plane, reduced to mud beneath the pounding water from the sky.

Despite the cover of his wing, water was getting everywhere, flying sideways in the wind to pervade them. Kefira felt the trickle of water running cold between her skin and soaked clothing. Never before had she felt such chill, never had she been in such a storm. The lightning and thunder had moved on some time earlier in the night, but the rain remained with all of its fury. Yonatan had never experienced rain before in his life, and she could feel him shuddering as it invaded beneath his scales.

She watched through squinted eyes as he craned his head towards the fading rumble of the ocean. The cliffs had diminished in the land behind them, and now they were level with the waters of Al-Khaleej. Yonatan took in a breath, and his head lowered down to her, to where she was nestled between his foreleg and wing. In a moment, half her clothing and the blankets she was wrapped in were caught between his teeth, and he raised her an alarming height into the air. "What is it?" she cried to him past the rain.

He snorted, and his tongue flicked above her head. She found herself leaning back to see where it had pointed, and in the darkness through the pall, she could just make out the ocean. It was a dark, flat mass, blurred against the pale mass of the land; it didn't lap against the shore, its darkness merely mingled with the pale, in swelling ebb and flow. It occurred to her now that there was no shore at all. There was only water, torrential rain water flowing from the land into the sea. The storm had reduced the earth to lakes and rivers, to send them crashing into the ocean.

Yonatan shuddered, looking down, causing Kefira to sway in his grip. After scrabbling to clutch his face with her hands, she looked down herself to see the mire the ground had been reduced to, the clay turned to mud sucking upon the dragon's talons. He'd long since clambered to his feet, and was puzzling over the way the earth gripped him, even as the water level was rising upon his ankles, rushing with the waves, and pulling at him. "Yonatan!" she said uneasily. "You – we ought to get off the ground!"

He snapped open his wings, and they were tugged upon by the wind, rain clattering clamorously against them; and he seemed to hesitate only a moment before taking the girl up into his jaws.

If a deeper darkness could be imagined than the surrounding night, this surpassed it. At first Kefira was too taken aback to grasp her location – dark, hot – she could be at the bath again save for the raw-smelling air that hissed through the teeth that surrounded her. Kefira put her hand against the serrated bars, shocked. Before she could gather her bearings, a primal fear began coursing through her, shivering her hands.

And then she was flattened as he took off, the forces of flight keeping her from lifting her head. His body quivered as it was struck by gusts of wind, and she jostled in the cage he held her in. He dipped his head downward, and she fell against his incisors. A wet thud – her body against his teeth. She could hardly believe it. Yonatan carried her in his mouth.

She blinked, blinked repeatedly, but not a wink of light touched her eyes. She could not see, only feel. Feel hot air, hard teeth, and sodden flesh. Did Yonatan know what he was doing?

Time's passage could only be told by the cadence of her breath. Minutes passed with insufferable slowness, and for every one that elapsed, she had to remind herself not to panic. Was this how prey felt? Trapped, hot, scared beyond reason? But she was not prey –

Yonatan was just bearing her away from the storm.

Even so, she had never been afraid of him before. As her heart regained a tame pace, she reflected. She'd seen him kill the crocodiles, and carry dead antelope, but never until now had she feared him. She knew her fear was irrational, but as she could only see darkness and hear his labored breath, it settled like a heavy stone in her stomach. Her eyes could not help but gape at the canal of wind and deeper darkness on the far end of his mouth. How is it he seemed so much larger from the inside?

Suddenly, his voice emanated from his throat, sounding strange, unmuffled, like wind. It was his same "Khhh..." of inquiry, only it was resonant as though spoken in an antechamber, and infinitely louder.

Kefira cleared her throat. "I am alright," she affirmed, and her voice cracked mid-sentence. They were buffeted by another burst of wind, and she heard the leathery beating of his wings as though from a distance. He seemed to recover from whatever torrent afflicted him, and then crooned, a reverberant purr from his throat.

The girl confined herself deeper in her rain-soaked blankets. She could feel against her stomach the surface of the scroll. She did not know where it'd come from and she could only guess what exactly it was, but knew that it could not be ruined. She was not going to get any dryer, yet.

She shut her eyes, and she let a silent prayer pass her lips – for safety. Then she told Yonatan, "I'm going to try to rest." She did not believe this would be an easy task, given her precarious situation of surrounding storm and confinement in the mouth of a dragon. Yet, hunched in a ball and swaddled in black heat, she was surprised with how easily she passed into sleep, with the lullaby of Yonatan's swaying head as he carried on through the rain.

For all the water there had been earlier, it didn't stand to reason that there should be so little, now. The land had been emptied and filled like a bucket, the days passing hot and windless, despite the tempest that had swept in earlier. The only sign that the water had ever existed, to so desolate the landscape, was the steam that rose from the ground in the mornings.

Kefira was too weary to consider where they were going. West they had flown, ocean to their left and far away, since Yonatan discovered with illness that its salty waters were not fit for drinking. There was nothing, it seemed, fit for drinking anywhere.

The morning after the storm, Kefira had gotten out the scroll. It was a map. And upon recognizing what it was, she knew where it had come from. It was Rakhshan's. And folded in its confines was a cloth – a shawl, of black, white, purple, and turquoise, tasseled on the corners.

She could only guess as to how she'd gotten them, hardly willing to comprehend that these things had been yielded of the Persian's assault. Yet she had them: Rakhshan's map, and a masterwork shawl. Upon their discovery, she'd been more than distraught. To know now that he may very well have not wished her ill, not wholly, while she was yet in the desert, did not please her. What now, did their flight mean? Ought they return to Parudrauga? Ought they return to the north?

From what she could tell, she and Yonatan were two fingers' breadths west of Parudrauga, the dot she recognized as the port town on the coast of the Great Gulf. She remembered each day's travel on dragon back being the breadth of a single finger. Of course, her fingers were smaller than Rakhshan's, but she guessed that still put them out of Gedrosia into the nether parts of Carmania. Mountains were near them, and before that, desert.

She rolled up the map and put it uncomfortably back into her sweat-dampened clothing, disconsolate upon Yonatan's back as he lumbered over the ground. White-washed desert glared around them. Only a few times a day did she allow herself to look at the map – that was as far as she would indulge her worry. Worrying, thinking – she tried to do as little of that as possible. Any attempt to sort out her tangled feelings of anger and confusion, and puzzle through what had happened, would only bring her more anger and confusion. That man.

She had lost her old shawl some time during the storm. Her head felt naked, despite the tangled mane that fell down her back. But she would not put on the shawl. Why had Rakhshan given her a shawl, anyway? Perhaps it was Ravan's, and it had gotten mixed up in her clothing after they bathed. That was what she wished. But she knew that none of Ravan's clothing was of this color, and she did not deign to wear shawls, so that could not be so. Certainly, it had been given by the man.

The girl tried not to look at it much more than she had to – only twice for a very extensive period of time – firstly to observe its vibrant stripes in daylight, and secondly to figure out where to imprison it. Finally, she decided to use it to tie up the scroll, so that it would stay raveled tightly in her blankets.

It was the third day of their drifting, and cicadas moaned under the heavy heat. The only signs of the storm that remained were the striations in the clay that the water had carved, and scattered dead vegetation. There were even some drowned animals, and Yonatan sniffed at these as he walked, dirt-caked nostrils flaring. He was hungry. She was hungry. Her provisions stowed from Parudrauga had not lasted even the first day of wandering, and she went as she had for so long before – with empty stomach and swollen tongue.

She shifted her dry lips. She wanted to speak, to ask him where they were going. Many times before had she talked to him of her vexation, her disinclination to go onward, yet her disinclination to go back to the city. He at least seemed to be intent upon some destination. Every morning he was more attentive and ready to get up and go than she was. West, west, he insisted, and every day, that was where they went. Of course, they were not very fast, reduced to moving on foot, now. After the first day, he'd stopped flying.

She watched a weed struggling in the dirt quiver in sync with Yonatan's footfalls. He'd had nothing but a frail, mud-caked goat to eat, and hadn't grown a cubit since they left. She worried for him, for his thirst and his hunger – he needed the sustenance, he was still so very large, much larger now, than Mār ever was.

And then her mind halted, shoving the thought of the infernal dragon away, even as his hostile words in the storm echoed in her mind. *If you return, you will not be welcome.*

There was a bitter taste in her mouth, from the thought those vexing mercenaries, their betrayers, and for thirst. In the northern lands, water was not nearly so scarce. She wished she had a wineskin, anything to sustain her. She could only imagine how much worse Yonatan felt. There was salt caked around his eyes. Water. They needed to find water. The cicadas seemed to share this sentiment, for their maddening hum grew with the day's heat, as her mouth turned into a desert.

"Certainly we will not perish out here," said she, to the wilderness, to God, and to Yonatan. "Our people had manna and quail in the desert. Why ought we have nothing? The last dragon of Israel will not perish of thirst."

But upon these words, no manna fell and no quail came to them. Yonatan looked back at her, jaws parted in a pant, his red tongue flickering out. His eye glinted, a dull lens flicking back to reveal bright yellow once more. He stopped in his tracks.

"What's the matter?" She leaned against his neck and squinted up at his face.

The dragon let out a breathy pant, and looked down at her.

She was too tired to try and read a meaning in his expression. "Is there trouble?" she asked, looking around before he shook his head in answer. She sighed in relief, dry bitter breath. He lowered his muzzle to her side and tugged on the bedraggled rigging that surrounded her.

Puzzled, Kefira looped herself into it. "You're not going to fly, are you? You ought not, you must conserve your strength," she told him. Despite her feeble protest, when she was strapped in, he took off. It was hard for her to maintain herself, flying was so dizzying now, and Yonatan was weak himself. She kept her face to his scales, hugging close to his neck so that she could not see the bright wasteland wheeling away below.

She felt the interval between every wingbeat, the hollow strain of his flight, and felt his wings quivering. But before she could muster herself to make him set down and stop the flying already, his wings mantled and they landed. There was a burst of glistening white as his forelegs hit the earth. Over his shoulder, her eyes fell upon the ripple of a stream.

The girl almost tumbled off his back as she clambered down. The robes up to her ankles were saturated as soon as she found her footing. "Oh, praise the Lord!" she cried, laughing up at Yonatan. He plunged the tip of his muzzle into the shallow waters and began to guzzle it down in great, audible gulps. She drank her fill as well, and did not care that her hair fell into the water. And then she collapsed to sit in the shade of Yonatan, against a tree. "How did you find this place?" she asked him breathlessly.

He flicked his tongue out in answer, and he rolled onto his side beside her, flanks rising and falling at a pace that no longer spoke of fever.

Kefira let out a breath through her soothed throat. Her mouth no longer felt as though it would crack and bleed. Her eyes stretched over the expanse of the waters – it flowed to the sea, far away, she could tell, and flowed from the mountains in the distance. Trees were not scant here, and there was grass; it did not look wholly like a desert along the strip of water. She looked up into the spider-webbed branches of the tree where leaves fragmented the blue of the sky. She then tried not to notice the tree further; it was the same sort that she and Rakhshan had sat under the first night he suggested taking her hand for her debt. She rubbed her knuckles in disconsolate reverie. The peace brought on by the stream did not last very long.

She spoke to Yonatan, voice small. "You did not think that we made a mistake – in leaving – do you?"

He seemed not to have an opinion on the matter, as he stared at her. She heard his tail rasp over the grass.

"I do not know, either," she replied unhappily. She frayed a piece of tree bark in her fingers and tossed it behind her. "Where are you taking us?" she asked him. "Was it here, did you know this place would be here?"

The dragon blinked, looking at her, eyelid flicking another translucent lens to pass over his eye. He lowered his head and stretched slowly, forelegs reaching forward, almost over the water, to face the pale palms of his talons upwards.

Was he shrugging? No, with the bowed head and supplicating talons – it looked rather like a posture for prayer. Kefira cocked her head as she looked at him. She almost didn't understand. "You mean that you prayed and…"

Yonatan shifted his wings abashedly as she trailed off. Kefira smiled, growing in incredulity and pleasure. "You mean that you feel you're being led?"

The dragon bobbed his head.

Kefira looked at him in wonder. Why did it seem so strange to her, the striving Jewess of Persia, that the Lord should be a guide, should move her dragon? It was not manna or quail, but it seemed just as unbelievable and wonderful. She looked at the stream fondly. "And so He has provided us with water."

The rustle of earth and grass against scales met her ears as Yonatan stood. She watched him lower his muzzled to the ground, tongue flicking in and out. "What is it?" she asked him, and his head went up to scan the surrounding lands. In answer to her query, she heard his belly rumble.

She got up and examined the ground where he'd sniffed it. In a patch of dry mud, there were animal prints, marks of a cloven-hoofed beast, as well as a pile of droppings. She looked around; there were no antelope to be seen, of course, but she guessed that her dragon sensed them near. "You must be ravenous, go on and hunt, love," she told him. "You must eat."

He lowered his head down to her eye-level, and then shifted his forelegs uneasily. "It's alright, do not worry about me," the girl urged him. "Go on, catch yourself a whole heard of antelope. You must eat, and grow to be as large as Mount Sinai."

In reply, he breathed an if-you-insist sort of hiss, making to pick her up. She held up her hands emphatically. "No, it's alright – if I go flying with you before I've refreshed myself, I shall faint," she laughed. "I will just be here to find some food of my own; do not worry, I've been alone before."

Yet displeased, he gave her a long look as though he couldn't imagine her existence before his. By way of waylaying his opposition, she kissed him on the nose. "Go on, love," she encouraged him. And with no more resistance, he turned away. She was a little surprised that that was all it took, but glad to know that he would soon be able to fill his belly.

She had not eaten very much, either, in the past few days. Tempted had she been to consume some of the leather of her sandals, even, before now. But here there would be things for her to eat. She crouched by the stream and began to rifle through the water plants to find suitable tubers.

It occurred to her, midway through digging up a plant, that Yonatan had not yet departed. She turned her head to see his progress.

And just as quickly, she looked away. He'd been standing a little ways distant beyond the tree of her repose, with his leg hiked and tail arched.

When they travelled, the dragons had always relieved themselves downstream of wherever they had camped, or in the very least outside of eyeshot, when there was no water available. Mār had said that leaving one's scent in water would make them difficult to track by scent, and so they had gone accordingly. She could not fathom, by any stretch of her imagination, as to why Yonatan was choosing to go on the plain. If they were being followed at all by the beasts of Parudrauga, he ought to be going in the water to mask his scent.

As a matter of fact, he was acting in a way that suggested he very much wanted to be detected. Indeed, he was scent-marking a circumference about her.

"What – what are you doing?" Kefira stammered to him, when her incomprehension could no longer be maintained.

Yonatan turned his head to her, and dropped his leg. With the shifting of his eyes, he for a moment looked rather embarrassed, before recovering with the flick of his tongue. He ruffled his wings, placing them like a shroud about his head. When he saw that she didn't understand, he beckoned her closer and drew a rudimentary circle in a patch of dirt with a claw. He pointed at it, and then pointed to himself many times before drawing a smaller circle inside and pointing to her.

Kefira's mind went to a dog that she had seen in Parudrauga, when it had hiked its leg on an urn, after which another dog came chasing after it, aggravated. "You are marking your territory?" Indeed, it was a pungent banner of ownership, his marking. She covered her nose with a sleeve. "That is wise," she said. "No sane creature would come anywhere near your scent." She laughed a little, dubiously glancing at the circle he'd made in the earth. "There, I am safe," she told him. "Shall you go and eat, now?"

Grudgingly, he nodded, looking down at her. He licked the air again, as though to be sure of his scent-marking's validity, and then backed up to take a running start into the sky. The grass flattened in the wake of his pumping wings, and Kefira caught another whiff of his sentry.

The girl watched his form disappear into the blue, the sudden uneasiness of his absence only just staved off by his safeguard. She cast about to take in her surroundings once more, before going back to root around in the water.

She had grown lazy, with all of Rakhshan's provision, she realized as she foraged. Had it been almost two months since she last had to scavenge for her meals? She washed off an uprooted tuber in the water, before biting into it. Its taste was sharp and bitter, and she spit it out, wiping off her tongue and rinsing out her mouth. Perhaps this was a sort not to be eaten – she was not familiar with the plants of the south. She glared at the remainder of the root like the betrayer that it was and threw it into the water, whence it floated off.

She continued in her endeavor for food off the shore; it seemed as though most of the plants around the waters were of that bitter sort, and so she moved to the trees – or intended to, before something caught her eye.

On the bank of the opposite shore. There were prints in the mud. They were not small.

Tentatively, she pulled up her skirts around her knees and walked across the creek to look at them.

Her heart sunk into her stomach. They were unmistakably dragon prints. In the soft earth by the water, a set was distinguishable. But they were not like Yonatan's raptor talons; there were three broad toes to be seen, no thumb apparent, and the innermost toes were abnormally large of claw.

Kefira was no huntress, but she knew that the maker of the prints had to have been here recently: the prints lay in mud, fresh enough not to have been washed away by the storm. A few days, at most.

She cast about warily, her heart beginning to race. And she wasted no more time – to the tree she went and pulled herself into its branches. Her breath was ragged in her throat – the tree would not waylay a dragon. She should call Yonatan! But no, even if he could hear her, so might the beast. She had to wait until his return, and stay hidden until then. Certainly that would not take too long. After all, Yonatan was only getting a quick meal. He would come back very soon.

Despite these reassurances she repeated to herself, her hands were shaking, and she clutched the tree as though it were a rope in the ocean. Her eyes went to the far bank. Of course there was no movement there – she'd be able to detect anything near to her. The trees did not number many, and the grass was not tall. And whatever beast was here would certainly be repelled by the scent of Yonatan.

But there was motion. Not from the sky, from Yonatan, but from the ground, in the distance, from upriver and through the trees. Kefira's heart stopped, her breathing stopped, and her hands went still. Bark pressed to her face, she watched as the movement took shape.

It was a little dragon – or little, as dragons went. It was mottled with brown and yellow, almost donkey-like in size and manner, with its long, muscled legs and thick neck, but the resemblance stopped there. It had a face like the crocodiles, but short and mashed, with twisted horns protruding from its brow. Its short tail whisked over the grass, and its ugly head rose to lick the air. It licked the ground. It stopped moving. Flick, flick, flick, went its forked tongue, and Kefira knew it could smell Yonatan.

The creature brayed – no, it was a second creature that did. Kefira whipped her head around, neck burning, to see the creature on the other side of the brook. The first beast cackled back to it, rustling its tiny, useless wings.

A third joined the cadence. And a fourth. There were more beasts, all cackling and grunting and snorting outside of the scent-marked ring. Though all their lengths in a line could not span Yonatan, they each of them were sizeable enough to pull her out of the tree, if they saw her and so desired.

Kefira hardly dared to breathe. It was only a matter of time, she realized.

Cold sweat broke out upon her skin as she stared at the tree and began to pray.

It was the bravest of the beasts that stepped across the border, snarling at his fellows with scorn. This one had a hide the color of dry bones, bleached and sallow. Tentatively, his companions trudged after him and joined him inside the border. They were all sniffing the air, tongues lashing in and out, casting about – but as no great contender appeared to vanquish them from the marked territory, they appeared to relax, and grow bolder.

One of them chittered to the pale one, and Kefira could see its throat bob, its small wings twitch. The leader's lips writhed over his teeth, and he raked the other's flank with the jab of a hind-talon, and his opposition was silenced to mewling. He raised his head and looked at his companions with a tyrannical eye, and they turned their blunt faces away with all the servility of jackals.

Before Kefira could hope they'd break into a fight and thusly be distracted from discovering her, the leader's tongue lashed, and his orange eyes glinted. She could see his nostrils flare and watched as he slowly sauntered to the tree – her tree. Every step he took was a moment her heart skipped a beat, and as soon as his grey nose touched one of the outlying branches, her body was frozen hot with fear.

His compatriots followed his lead and she was hopelessly surrounded. Had they seen her? Or could they smell her? Were they of poor eyesight? Either way, she did not dare to breathe, let alone to risk climbing higher. Her eyes squeezed tight, and her head hurt with the silent exhalation of prayers.

A victorious snarl and a tug, branches snapping, and she was spinning towards the earth. Kefira landed with a yelp and a thud onto the ground, in-between the talons of the white Shaghāl. He recoiled his head from her, looking down loftily at his prize and around at his companions, who at once made to lunge for her – stinging claws batted her as they reached, grazed her, until they were halted by the leader, who took one of them by the neck and flung him to the earth squalling. He got them all back into order with a barked command, and promptly began to nose into Kefira, until his teeth found a handhold in the front of her clothes. "Let go of me!" she cried, knowing with bitter certainty that these were not creatures to be reasoned with – not like Yonatan or Mār – these were just as evil and stupid as the crocodiles. A brute's shrewdness was in the dragon's baleful eyes, and she knew her words would not give him pause. She cried out as he jerked her savagely, and heard her garments tear. With a rush of adrenaline, her hands were thrown forward, and she clawed the soft flesh around his eyes, kicked his muscle-knotted chest.

He hissed at her, foul meaty breath burning her nostrils as he drooled over her in a moment of speculation. He was otherwise undaunted by her attack, and she set her jaw as he re-secured his grip on her. A horrible shadow fell over her, and she knew it was the rest of the pack closing in.

Suddenly, a deeper cry than could by produced by any of the other beasts shook the air, the earth rippled, and then the leader was no longer there. She was wrenched free, and hit the ground, opening her eyes to see if Yonatan had finally come, for certainly the Shaghāl was being shaken in the jaws of a great dragon. The captured beast wailed high-pitched and his voice split into a scream as the jaws of his oppressor burst with orange flames, his cry grating off into a moan as his charred-black body was tossed away in a bubbling heap.

Before Kefira could so much as register the carnage that had just ensued, and realize that this new beast was indeed not Yonatan, pain wrenched into her shoulder and she cried out as one of the Shaghāls had picked her up and was fleeing, the rest of the pack scattering behind it. With every gallop of its gangly legs, the pain tore further into her and she cried at every jolt. Heat was spreading over her arm, and she looked in a daze at the mottled face of her captor, the grey indifference in its eyes.

And then it squalled, dropping her as suddenly as he'd gotten her, leaving her to fall to the earth. Panting, she turned her head to see that the beast had been tackled by a second dragon that outsized it three times, the color of dry, cracked mud. It sank its teeth into the Shaghāl's throat, finishing it off – and just as quickly leaping high into the air again, wings spread to fall onto another of the fleeing beasts, offing it and leaping after the next, and the next, with bugling cries of battle fervor.

And so the skirmish diminished, descent punctuated with the

jackal dragons' death cries. When only the heavy breathing of the newcomers filled the air, she found strength to scramble to her knees and gape at them.

The one who had burnt to death the leader was indeed not Yonatan, for though he was shot with red and about his size, his scales looked as blackened meat did, and purple tinged them. It was a Thu'ban, certainly. And the other was a breed she recognized from Hangmatana – a stony-scaled warrior, an Abraxas.

Rippling against their hides were streamers of scarlet; both of them were rigged in cloth. They both had riders.

Kefira clutched her torn clothes to herself, quick enough to pain her shoulder. She looked at it and saw red on her skin and staining her robes, hot on her hand as she touched the wound. Her breath slowed in her throat, and her head pounded. She moved her shoulder, or tried to, but it would not respond. She felt flesh sliding unbidden beneath her skin, noncompliant, and there was an ache that felt as though it came from her bones. And the amount of blood – it was incredible – she had never seen so much of it coming from a person, sparkling and exposed in the sunlight, staining the alabaster ground.

She breathed, eyes sliding sightlessly to the dragons, and they came slowly closer to her, as though through heavy mist. She heard a voice calling out, one of the men, perhaps, and the smaller dragon repeated the inquiry. Kefira looked at him faintly, and then her eyes returned to the wound on her shoulder. And she saw nothing else before descending into unconsciousness.

Chapter XI
Stone and Stitches

Upon Mār's back, his rider sat quite motionless, offering no pats of affirmation, nor even tightening his legs against the dragon's neck as he dove and turned. The Azhi Dahaki feared his rider might actually allow himself to fall off his back. Mār pushed off from the wall gently, after setting down the stones to be rolled away by the waiting warriors for its reinforcement. As he caught the wind with his wings, his head craned back to look at Rakhshan, and he tautened the cloth that held him against his neck with a talon. "Really, Rakhshan, you ought not be so careless – you're as limp as a doll," he finally chastised him.

"I'm not going to fall off," Rakhshan replied, no small amount of irritation in his voice. He gave the hand-strap a quite unnecessary yank for emphasis.

"Then I suggest you make like it," Mār snapped back. It was not his intention to sound so caustic to his own brother, but everyone in Parudrauga had become ill-humored since last week's ordeal. The means of defense against their annexation now lost with the departure of the foolish Israeli beast, the unexpected preparation for a siege put everyone to scramble, causing tempers to flare. And *Mār's* time of it would certainly not improve if his rider fell off his back amidst the discord.

Despite his insufferable melancholy, however, Rakhshan seemed to be the only person who was not actively lashing out and angry; rather he had isolated himself in his own den of self-pity, Mār judged. Worrying over the Jewess, no doubt. But certainly that was not the only thing biting away at him – worry and wanting shouldn't be reasons a person would stay in their room for whole days and not come out to see anyone, even his own dragon. Certainly he'd turned himself into a recluse for the purpose of avoiding those who blamed him for the departure of Parudrauga's ransom.

The Azhi Dahaki landed in the little quarry he and Mehrnaz had dug in the foothills, to spit upon and scrape up more rocks. The humans had the idea that fortifying the gates with boulders would not permit soldiers entry, short of dragonback. A decent idea, for a backup plan. It would diminish the effectiveness of battering rams, certainly, but there were still the numerous Asman Kāra dragons to worry about.

Pebbles quavered on the ground beside him as Mehrnaz landed and stooped to collect more rocks. She muttered a greeting past a boulder in her jaws and took off again, clutching great chunks of earth in her talons. Mār followed her, making his way to the western gate once more. He'd learned not to let it bother him that she could carry more than twice as much as he could; but in his youth, he'd not permitted their great difference in size to excuse his comparative weakness. Of course quarreling with her had done nothing to prove himself her equal either, so he'd learned to tolerate her superseding him in this area. She did not gloat over him either, and at least he was stronger than Sorushe, and so was content with his lot of comrades. Though, he thought in an almost sadistic resignation, put in the light of contest against antagonist beasts of an asmanaba, they all three paled in comparison. Even the aid of Kashayar Atash and the other priest would not do much to turn the tide of impending battle, if they were as sorely outnumbered as Sorushe said.

It hadn't been in the plan that they were going to fight. It hadn't been in the plan of course, that the upstart Hardlā and his rider would leave. While Mār never minded a little bloodshed, he knew that the humans had their laws and killing was uncouth; Rakhshan was especially displeased with this outcome. Spilling the blood of one of the King's soldiers was an offense punishable by death – treasonous. The men hoped that it wouldn't come to that – but what did they expect, now? It was their hope that once the soldiers tried to breach and couldn't, and the dragons contested against one another, that it would become a draw, and they might be able to negotiate for Parudrauga's freedom. But Mār was no fool, and his pride was not so great that he was blind to their acute disadvantage, in the arena of aerial combat. If Yonatan had stayed, they could have stood a chance, for the King's men would not want to risk harm to him; and even if they did not care or know of his breed, his size would benefit them greatly in battle. Of course, all this circumspection was useless now that the impudent hatchling had deserted them, so Mār was content to be sullen.

He could have very easily put Parudrauga to his back, and leave it behind in all of its self-inflicted vexation. He could get along without this place or any other city. It was for the sake of Rakhshan and his human kith who were so leashed to society that he fought. When they weren't off making mischief elsewhere, this was where they dwelled – a haven of safe, crowded revelry.

In short, this place did not beguile him, but Rakhshan seemed to be partial towards it, so there.

Bitterness welled up inside him. It will be lost. Because of the flight of cowards. It should be lost already, judging by Sorushe and Tahmour's estimate, only apparently the soldiers were taking their time, or halted altogether. Probably strategizing, just as he hoped the humans here were doing more of. More strategizing.

Rakhshan seemed to grow fainter and fainter on his back, as though he were gradually diminishing into a pile of feathers. Mār turned his head to him. "Rakhshan," he said with the utmost patience. "Please holt on as though you mean to stay on my back."

The manling seemed to stir out of a stupor and wrapped his arms in the hand-straps. He looked so very tired, though not tired enough to pass the opportunity to look at his dragon with a sardonic eye.

Mār found more purchase upon the rocks he held and said to him, "Why don't I let you off at the barracks. You look like you want to sleep."

And after he left the boulders at the gate, he winged back to the barracks and dropped Rakhshan off. "This is your room, yes?" he inquired, already putting him through the window with a talon.

Rakhshan nodded in reply and thanked him. The dragon bobbed his head and gave a half-hearted chuckle before departing. "If you do not wake up for it, be sure that I shall come and get you *after* I fight off the Asman Kāra." And, in retrospect, he rather hoped that his words were not prophetic.

Rakhshan didn't stay in his room.

No, with everyone else gone to work on preparing for a siege, he would take this moment of seclusion, not to sleep, but to pace restlessly.

Arsham and Tahmour had made some sort of unspoken agreement with each other to treat Rakhshan as a sloth when it came to the preparations. After, of course, Arsham had hazed him, asked him why on earth he'd told her, why he'd let them go! Then he had just folded his hands and excused the traitor that he was from all duties previously assigned him. He'd wished it was only discipline from the elder, but he knew there was pity in his actions as well. Even Tahmour seemed to tiptoe around him. They took care not to mention anything of Kefira, only their lost Hardlā. Of course, they were more worried now about Parudrauga's precarious position, now without the leverage that was the truant dragon. Tahmour went right off to go recruiting in nearby villages with Sorushe, and Arsham had gone directly back to conferencing with the heads of the city. They had things to do.

And apparently they thought they were doing him good by depriving him of that, or perhaps it was small vengeance – pity or spite, he did not know which was worse.

Rakhshan had long stopped pacing, and he realized that his feet had carried him to Kefira's empty room. The giant hole in the wall that Yonatan had made was covered in a sheet, quivering in the wind. He looked around the barren room. Then, without further hesitation, stepped inside.

There was a creak as he sat in the cot across from her bed, and his mind was silent for a long time. His eyes rested on the place, the cot, where she should have been, taking an afternoon nap, or calling out to Yonatan, or chastising the wicked, wicked man sitting across from her.

Despite the late day humidity, a cool breeze trickled past the billowing curtain, and chilled Rakhshan to the heart.

He had betrayed her, yet again. There was no excuse.

Fool, fool, fool, he growled to himself. Her anger was all justified, everything she'd said that night was true, save for the reason behind his impulsive stolen kiss. He regretted that sorely. *Should* he have pursued her to her room? He'd looked to make right, to make sure that she wasn't going off to do anything foolish. In his gut he knew that she would leave. So he'd brought the map and the shawl to give to her, praying to whatever god that cared that she would see them and understand. Well, the map had not yet brought her back to him, and she would not take the shawl for the token that it was, and if she did, she would revile it anyway.

For how could she not? The manner in which he'd given them to her was hardly to be taken as a kindness. His jaw clenched as he looked at the rumpled cot, stomach burning. When he'd saw her going out the window, he'd been so afraid that she'd leave before he could give them to her, that he'd moved as quickly as possible, not recognizing the violence of the action.

The fear, the disbelief in her eyes when she had fallen to the ground before him, it stabbed him through the heart. She was so young. So young. What would she think? What could she think of him, now?

Certainly she would not see the shawl and take it for the regard it stood for. Her last memory of him would be an ill, contorted one.

Heat hummed in his legs, filled his feet, and arched throughout him. He stood up again and paced.

He could not tolerate not seeing her again. He wanted to apologize, a thousand times, to make up for his wrong. But where could he find her? Where could they have taken it up in their naïve heads to go? They very well could have gotten lost in the storm. He wanted to search them out, to make sure that they were safe, that Kefira was finding things to eat well enough, that they weren't getting assailed by crocodiles. But of course Mār was averse to go looking. He would have to help prepare for the siege, anyway. The army was close.

Rakhshan froze.

The army. The realization stunned him — unless they had changed their westerly direction, they would head right into it.

His eyes pored over the cracks in the ground. What did that mean? What would be done with them? It was not to be determined. They certainly would not be harmed, certainly not Yonatan — and Kefira would be safe for the sake of his restraint. But what after? Would they arrest her? Confiscate Yonatan? Rakhshan imagined that the resultant anger from the both of them would be enough to rend the world from corner to corner.

He sighed, trying to cool down. The worst the Empire could do would not be death for either party, he reasoned. Yonatan would be safe, and if any harm came to Kefira, certainly they would anticipate his reaction. They were both untouchable, if their captors were rational.

What then? What would the army, the King, do to the rarest dragon in the empire, and his illegitimate rider? Rakhshan could no more determine that than he could map the stars on a cloudy night.

He rubbed the stubble on his chin and finally sat down again, feeling suddenly very tired. He found himself on Kefira's cot, now. She should be there, and the pang of her absence made him shut his eyes. He pressed his fists into his forehead and opened his eyes to stare at the floor.

Another breeze ruffled the curtain, lifting its hem to impart view of the gap; Rakhshan remembered once more her cry of disbelief — and then, disjointed, the old image of her in the dark of the inn, dropping her cup, sprawled on the bed — *guilty, guilty*. He remembered Yonatan's burning fury, tearing, crumbling the wall away to reach in and punish him. He swallowed.

"God of Israel and Kefira." His quiet words struck the air as he let them drop. "If you can do anything..." And he trailed off, not knowing what else to say. He turned his head to see the curtain billow, his words leaving the room, and wished now more than ever that he had never taken her within a hundred leagues of Parudrauga.

When her eyes returned to focus, Kefira saw there was a ceiling of dark cloth above her, that she was in a tent. When her ears stopped pounding, she heard voices – men, many of them, the skitter of hooves and the rattle of metal. More immediately, she noticed that she was on a mat, and not alone. There was someone sitting beside her on the ground, dabbing something cold on her shoulder. Her head jerked to see them, and sighed when she saw that it was only an old woman. Face haggard and unsmiling, the eyes in the caverns beneath her brow did not meet hers. They were fixed on the wound on her shoulder, dabbing, dabbing.

Kefira opened her mouth to speak with a hoarse voice. "Where am I?"

The woman's eyes found her face and she replied in an equally gravelly voice, "War camp, Hazarabam of the King Cyrus."

Memory came flooding back to her. The army. A host of a thousand men. "The King is here?" she sat up, frightened, before the woman pushed her back down with a wiry arm.

"Of course not, little fool," and she began to pat her wound again.

Kefira's eyes found her shoulder, and pain hit her like a wave. She grit her teeth and looked away, tears flooding to her eyes. It had been sutured with thread, and the woman was applying balm to it that did nothing in aiding the pain. "Where is my dragon?" Kefira beseeched through clenched jaw, when she could speak again.

The woman began to tightly wind a cloth around her shoulder.

"You were found with four dragons, Shaghāls, all of them killed."

Kefira pressed, "None of those were - "

"Perhaps you mean the dragon that flew in last night."

"Yes, yes, I do," she said, hoping that she meant Yonatan. "Was he very large?"

"Yes. Raised hell before he was stopped." The woman knotted the cloth fast to her arm, too tight, and Kefira winced.

"Raised – stopped – what happened? Is he safe?" Kefira felt her heartbeat race in her shoulder. She tried to get up again, but the woman, with surprising strength, pushed her back down.

"Stay down or you'll faint."

Kefira looked at her imploringly. "Please, I must see him – is he safe?" Once again, she tried to get up, and the woman crossed her arms, face wrinkling with resign. But she didn't push her back down. So Kefira made for the tent flap, anxious to see Yonatan. Her head swam as her hand clutched the fabric, opening it to dizzying sunlight. She saw a man, he himself making his way into the tent.

He wore red and white robes, and she could make out leather armor beneath. His dark beard was short, and hair pulled back in the out-of-the-way fashion of a rider, but his bearing was regal, and he looked down at her from imposing height, eyes imperious. The word *'king'* came to her mind.

She stood agape at him, hand still clutching the doorway.

"You are not allowed to see the beast," she heard him say, and his words fell like stones.

"My – milord," Kefira breathed, almost not comprehending. "I must – is he - "

"He is fine," the man said. "But you are not permitted to visit him."

Kefira felt her eyes begin to burn and she spat, "Who are you? What gives you the right?" even as she dreaded the answer. "I am his rider, you cannot - "

"I am Siamak, General of this Hazarabam of King Cyrus, and you are a thief," said he. "A thief of the rarest beast in the empire." He inclined his head to her. "Now, sit down."

The girl's fists balled up, but as she held his steely gaze, she swallowed her will and stiffly returned to the mat beside the old woman.

Siamak stood looking down at her.

"I did not steal him," Kefira said, voice faltering.

"More than a dozen soldiers and a satrap in Media attest otherwise."

"I just found him, and they took him away – but then he chose me, once he hatched, and..." she could not manage more. "I did not steal him, I promise."

Siamak looked as though his patience was wearing already, his eyes narrowing. "Enough, girl. I am not your judge on this account."

The brief moment of pause before his next words seemed like an eternity as Kefira listened.

"You are going to Pasargadae. The King has chosen to decide your fate himself."

Chapter XII
Young City

Hues of blue, fuchsia, black, and white rippled in the corners of Kefira's vision. The shawl imparted by Rakhshan had been donned. As soon as she was forced to leave her tent, she had no choice but to use it – the camp was teeming with men, and her reservation had gotten the better of her willpower.

She was aback a soot-colored Zarek dragon with Siamak himself. They, or Yonatan, rather, were being escorted by a flight of beasts, four of the six dragons that had been brought to take Parudrauga. Half the party consisted of the Thu'ban and Abraxas that had rescued her from the Shaghāls.

Yonatan was forced to fly close to the ground, almost out of sight, and in-between him and his rider were many other dragons. Even given his growth from the provision at the war camp, he was still no match for the force of veteran dragons, despite the fact that none of them could best him in a contest of size. But Yonatan reviled the disadvantage, and in defiance of it had tried to reach Kefira almost a dozen times in the duration of their travel. But those attempts were in vain, all ending with him pressed to the earth at the bottom of a pile of senior beasts.

Every time it was a blow to her heart. Siamak had irritably ordered her, on pain of cutting her throat, to stop her infernal cries, by the third instance. She could only watch now, in silent agony, as Yonatan dashed himself against his captors. She knew he had to be wondering why she was not returning to him; when there was not fury in his eyes, she saw sorrow, directed upon her.

After a few days of recuperating her shoulder in the hazarabam, she was deemed fit enough to travel, and so travel they did, with the dispatch of dragons and their riders. The next two days consisted of flying from dawn until dusk, quickly supping, acquiring a restless sleep, and repeating. Siamak was severe. When she found courage to speak to him, to ask him the reason for their speed, it took much prying to acquire a response. "We can neither defend from nor attack the rogue city without these beasts spent to guard the Hardlā. The defenseless soldiers back in Gedrosia would thank us to make haste in our errand."

She thought of Parudrauga now, and her hands tightened to the cloth that held her to the Zarek's back. The place wouldn't stand a chance when a fire-breather and the other beasts in the army returned. Her mind went to Rakhshan, and the shawl brushed her face. He had to see their madness, the lunacy of holding out against Persia. He was a thief and a liar, but he was not a fool.

It was with the utmost reluctance and dubiousness that she prayed for his safety. And then, upon reflection of the act of petition, she did not know why she had done it in the first place. It seemed unlikely that anything would be done on Jehovah's part for the pagan man, even without her own indifference towards him. Her heart panged.

Past the Zarek's shoulder, she searched for her dragon, and saw a hint of Yonatan's golden-wine wingtip. Her stomach sank. If this was punishment, was it not just? She thought of the goat, of the many goats she yet owed to God for her past prodigal years, let alone the ones she ought to give for her questionable obtainment of Yonatan. Certainly, she was now being punished for it. God had shown her what a fool she was in choosing friends – with Rakhshan and Mār – and was reproving her for stealing the egg now, with Yonatan's oppression.

Siamak had told her. Her dragon would very soon belong to someone else.

For the hundredth time that day, her feet went cold and she shut her eyes. The wind was streaking in icy rivers the tears she couldn't keep in, and she stared fixedly at Siamak's tied-back hair, until she could regain control of her weeping.

"Tomorrow we will be in Pasargadae." Siamak's words to her before she was escorted to her tent, after the day's flying.

Kefira peered at a distant rise, where indistinct shapes were shifting – the dragons that had herded Yonatan all day, enclosing him beyond the hill. Tomorrow.

She looked at her guards; they had been dispatched from the army's caravan guards, she knew, to keep an eye on her. They had lean, soft faces, not as weathered or rough-hewn as the rest of the men. "Will I be able to see him before we – will I see him again at all?" she couldn't help but ask.

He seemed surprised by her sudden words – she had not been disposed to speak to anyone at all, save for when provoked by Siamak. The man blinked, and after exchanging a glance with his companion, opened his mouth as though making to reply. Then he just shut his mouth and his hand rose to usher her into the tent of her confinement. She tried to turn around and face them, to implore for an answer, her fingers clenching the cloth wall. A hot provocation was on her tongue, but before she could utter it, the man spoke. "Have more faith in your King," were his words, and Kefira felt all the heat inside melt away.

"Your supper will be brought in shortly," the other man said, and the flaps were shut.

There was a mat waiting to be sat upon in the small interior, but she didn't go to it right away. She was still piqued by the man's words. Why she ought to trust a king she did not know, who was not hers at all, was beyond her.

The knotted mass of yarn in the corner of her mat was still there, waiting to be plucked at again. For four consecutive nights she'd been unweaving the fibers late into the night, until her emotions stopped running around in her head and she was permitted sleep. At first she had considered unraveling the shawl in such a manner; but of course she was not yet sure how she felt about it or him. Betrayal, regret, anger, and desire all writhed together like a stirred vipers' nest inside her, and they were not to be separated or understood. And so she tried to ignore them altogether. As of yet, it was best not to worry about the shawl. Who knew, it may be taken from her just as the map had been. She ought not grow too attached to it.

She folded up the fabric and placed it in the corner of the tent, away from her. Her hair was left to hang now, and she ran her fingers through its unkempt length with nervous jerks. But this wore upon her shoulder, so eventually she was reduced to stillness, waiting for the tent flap before her to move. Despite her mood, she yet had an appetite. Maybe she might talk to the guard again, when he brought her bread. Both men, both of her guards, did not seem very unkind – perhaps, she thought fancifully, they might let her sneak out at night to see Yonatan.

Kefira loosed another row of threads, the twine rough against her fingertips. She knew she was only kidding herself. The guard would do no such thing.

Then she heard Yonatan in the distance, a keen cutting through the rabble of the camp. She halted, listening, as though to the lamentation of a death procession.

A sudden heat churned inside of her, as her spirit unwound and she lay back on the mat. Her eyes were fixed upon the ceiling as though she might by some miracle see him through it.

Tomorrow. They would be in Pasargadae.

The capitol city of the whole Empire of Persia. And there a king was waiting for her.

She did not pray that night.

The shouted orders of one of Siamak's officers awoke her and the rest of the camp before sunrise the next morning. Kefira rubbed the sleep from her eyes and sat up, seeing the silhouettes of two lumps outside her tent. Perhaps the guards hadn't managed to stay awake that night. She ought to have snuck out.

Before she could kick herself, she heard commotion of the morning meal outside: foodstuffs being unloaded from a dragon's harness, soldiers tossing the fruit and loaves to one another and calling out to each other like it was a game. There was creaking and rattling as leather and scale armor was donned. There was also a voice at her tent. "Break your fast. We fly soon."

She was given scarcely five minutes to consume the small portion given to her before her tent was taken apart and packed up around her, servants doing them away. Before long it was time to mount behind Siamak upon his beast once more, for a final time. The company set off, half an hour hardly passing sunup before they were in the air.

Kefira could tell by the torpid rowing of Yonatan's wings the diminishment of his spirits. She was feeling no better than he.

"It is as disadvantageous for you as it is inconvenient for your handlers, your ignorance of the situation in which you shall soon find yourself," Siamak spoke, loud over the wind.

Kefira started from her stupor, straightening at his words. He did not look at her as he continued, "When at the capitol, you will see the king." And her heart very nearly stopped, before he then said, "After a couple fortnights of training, under Mahasti of the Harem and advisor Tobias Ben-Seraiah, you will have his audience."

Kefira had felt as though she had been struck twice. What was her business with a woman of the harem, and who was this Tobias? He had a Jewish name! "What?" she gasped.

"Oh, I suppose you do not know. One of your kind shares the king's ear. Understandably he is the son of one of your old priests."

Kefira was speechless.

"And you will be staying with the harem, in the quarters of the king's wives and concubines. You will be... polished there, as you are by no means to be presented to him in your current state," he explained with enough distaste to make her blush.

"Very well," was forced from her lips, even as a chill swept through her. She cleared her throat. "How much longer until we get there?"

"It is in that valley."

There were blue mountains ahead; she stretched her sight. Therein laid her prison.

"You should know how to tell time by distance, by now, for all of your romping about the countryside," he said. "Tell me, how long until we reach the valley?"

Kefira fidgeted, taken aback by the question, and peered past his shoulder, careful not to touch him. 'Not long,' she was about to very stupidly blurt, before she caught herself and ventured, "Have we until noon?"

Siamak slouched, and she could almost feel him roll his eyes. He straightened. "Wishful thinking ought not have any influence upon your calculations, girl. We will arrive sooner than that. You are poor even at guesswork." She felt the flesh and hide beneath them reverberate as his dragon snickered.

Despairingly, Kefira searched past the flashes of multicolored wings beneath them, but she could no longer make out Yonatan. There was not scrap of golden red hide to be seen above the rippling landscape below, only their slithering shadows. He must have been flying directly beneath them, out of sight beneath the Zarek's flashing scales.

Try as she might to deny its passage, time wore on, minutes turning into hours. The earth below grew gradually less ragged, the sweep of the storm long behind them. The dirt and sand soon became covered in shrubbery, a thin tree here and there. Ahead the mountains were getting closer, tighter, like a rope around her neck. She could make out a thin forest on their rugged slopes; and through a gap in their peaks, the green valley and a glistening river therein.

She was reminded of the breath of the Shaghāls, the dread she felt as she awaited the death in their maws. But the fear that coursed through her now overthrew even that. She stared, gaze empty.

They did not stop for anything, no water break to refresh the dragons, no time for anyone to relieve themselves, nothing to give Kefira an opportunity to pace out her anxiety. So she just traced the scars on her knuckles, and emitted an almost audible whine as soon as the mountains were below them. Siamak tersely glanced at her over his shoulder.

She didn't notice. Her eyes were all for the land beneath.

Canals and roads both flowed radially around the city, orchards and estates rumpled up together in the spread of the basin. Such splendor she had never seen before – yet it was infinitely smaller than she imagined it being, somehow, not half the size of Hangmatana.

Still, her dread gave way wonder as she took it in. It was not a spread of monolithic buildings of judgment as that northern city was, but rather it looked like a giant garden, an oasis in the desert. Even upon the cold wind she smelled its fragrance; figs, flowers, grapes, a whole manner of flora. The buildings themselves looked very new, shining and incomplete, many yet girded by scaffoldings. Outnumbering those structures she saw temporary residences built up in the form of fine tents and bivouacs. She squinted to the far mountains and confirmed her suspicion with the vague sight of quarries.

Pasargadae was under construction.

She blinked. Amongst all the green was a huge walled-off court with a canal running through it, and surrounded by sections of garden she saw about half a dozen colossal buildings residing in the grounds. Only two caught her eye and held it, however. Both were in the process of being made, but already she could tell they were the grandest buildings of them all. Their stone bases and skeletons were borne to the sky past layers of tile and block and cedar, with workers on ladders attending to them. They were being embossed in paints of red and blue and white – but beyond those colors gleamed gold. Workers were putting it on in pounded sheets, glittering in the sunlight like scales.

"The palace," Siamak didn't need to say.

Her heart sank and stomach jumped as the dragon banked, moth grey wings tilting to land. Then from below came a cry of defiance, grating against the sky. She felt both the dragon and

Siamak tense before her, and he jerked to a halt in the sky, hovering. Kefira scrambled to look over the beast's shoulder. Distracted and sedated by the civilization Yonatan's sentry had become, and this time his strength and fury proved too much for him – for there he was, ascending among their ranks like an angry serpent – she heard men on dragonback shouting – men on the ground calling. Her dragon sent the Abraxas sprawling with a pummeling wingbeat, and past a vicious snarl, she saw that his eyes were fixed upon her.

The Thu'ban whirled, confused, but mouth already smoldering. Yonatan vaulted his wings, pounding forward in a lunge, and Kefira heard herself scream as Yonatan looked, and then a shadow from the ground sprang upwards, a mass of glittering black. She blinked, and then her dragon was out of sight. "Yonatan!" she cried.

Siamak was livid. He thrust her back with a rigid hand and said, "Enough! Do not fret, that is Kia, and he will not hurt the fool."

Kefira twisted to face behind them, looking down the Zarek's tail. She could see that the great black dragon had launched into Yonatan – they were already a hopeless distance away, grappling in a field – and had just missed landing amongst the construction. Yonatan was outsized, writhing beneath the beast, both of them thrashing like rabid hounds. Tears flooded her sight and she could no longer perceive them save for the distant sound of snarls.

The other dragons below were flustered, but seemed otherwise relaxed, as though everything had returned to normal. She felt the Zarek look over his shoulder at the scene she stared at, but they all began to land and the sight was quickly removed from view. She heard a cry from Yonatan, but it was not a sound of victory. And a wall rose to blot out all sight.

Her breathing had not started up again, as she wiped her eyes, shaking. The world shuddered as they landed; then another quake, and another, as the other beasts returned to ground. She stared at Siamak's back, his hair tie. He turned around; they were getting off. She did not move – she could not breathe again, wind stopped in her lungs – and had to be bodily transferred off of the dragon's back as a corpse.

She faltered and stood, pitiably, clutching her arms above her head as she tried to stave off hyperventilation. The only sound to be heard now was the blood coursing through her ears, but she could see men's lips moving as they milled about, unpacking their dragons, conferring with one another, new faces, servants, runners, guards assuring that the situation with the new beast was under control, porcelain-skinned people in colorful clothing coming out to see the spectacle of new arrivals. Then, the man, Siamak. He was talking to her.

"What?" she managed to stammer, looking up at him with a start.

He grunted in irritation. "Follow me."

She didn't make to, instead whirling to the direction of the fight, but two familiar-looking guards were promptly there to enforce his words.

So reluctantly she obeyed. But too much anxiety buzzed through her head for her to think clearly as to where she was being taken; she hadn't even the energy to absorb her new surroundings. Splendorous painted walls and jeweled tiles and gilded pillars passed unnoticed as her vision blurred hotly, and heart struggled to stay beating at a reasonable pace; and even though she was the target of many curious glances from richly adorned people, she returned none of them. Her eyes were for her feet or the back of Siamak's head.

And then Kefira bumped into his red-white cloaked back, as they drew to a stop. She averted her face when he turned around. "The quarters of Tobias Ben-Seraiah." He pointed down a half-constructed hallway – and indeed there was a half-constructed room to accompany it, temporarily retrofitted with a white and blue tent within. "Go with the eunuchs to see him, and then you will be taken to your quarters."

Her guards' smooth faces were stolid and unexpressive, even as she glanced up at them with recognition of their title. Then, head low, she looked up at Siamak, and back to the tent. She didn't dare to ask what was going to happen therein.

"Go on, then," he said. "And do your best not to make a fool of yourself," he added as he turned away.

That did nothing to hearten Kefira. She pressed her lips together bitterly – but had no time to assemble the uprising indignation into words before the eunuchs were already at her shoulders, prodding her on with mere force of their silent presence. And so, past tinkering laborers and a harried servant, she went, her feet echoing with staccato tak-taks down the hall. Punctuated by golden spears, there were guards dressed in purple and yellow stationed at the tent's entrance; their emotionless faces contrasted against the bright colors they bore. They did not look at her, but were staring at some point beyond the hall.

She, with the same intensity, avoided looking at them. As her eyes moved slowly past the gold of their weapons, they fell upon the looming tent. The room, half-illuminated by a gap in the ceiling, surrounded it; apparently the tent was a temporary measure until the building was fully tiled. Sunlight cast deep shadows upon the entrance flap; her insides boiled beneath a sheen of cold sweat as every step she took mercilessly brought her closer, until finally her legs wouldn't move. She turned to one of the eunuchs. "I am not to just go in, am I?" she begged him, hoping he would bring up some sort of protocol that might stall her arrival.

"A runner was already sent ahead. You are expected."

What terrible words. Kefira's jaw clenched so tight that it hurt. And then she turned on her heal, every nerve burning in revolt as she forced herself forward. Fabric billowed behind her. She was inside.

The room was not as large as it had appeared from the outside. The fabric ceiling practically glowed from the shaft of sunlight coming in through the roof, and lamps glowed in the interior. There was a bald, grey-eyed man sitting upon a pile of cushions on the far side of the room. She stared at him in silence, in the twilight of the room, waiting for him to speak.

His eyes did not even meet her own. He was old – did he know she was here? Beside him a silky-haired hound lounged, turning its tawny face to look at her. There was a boy sitting next to the old man, who gazed upon her with equal indifference. They knew she was here, at least.

Then she was almost startled when the old man's voice arose, like dew dripping off a leaf. "Hami, I believe our guest has arrived. Fetch the basin, if you please." And then the old man stood up, legs rickety tent-poles, and the boy, Hami, helped him up before moving away.

Kefira stood on legs as uncertain as the elder's. She straightened her posture as her eyes remained wide, looking over the old man; he began to speak again, white beard shuffling. "You are the young Kefira, no?" he inquired of her.

She nodded slowly. And then jumped as she felt a finger on her shoulder. One of the eunuchs. He pointed emphatically at his eyes. With a start, she looked back at the old man, realizing that his eyes were not upon her; they did not seem to be looking at anything, glazed.

"I am, my lord," she affirmed him quickly. She glanced at the eunuch again.

The servant boy stepped up to her with a bowl in his arms; he nodded to a stool and she sat hesitantly upon it. She looked back at the old man as he said, "My name is Tobias, as you may already know." The tassels on his robes shifted as he trundled his feet to stand a span from where she sat.

"Yes, my lord," she said – and then looked down with surprise at the boy. He'd very deftly removed her sandals, and put a cloth to her feet, washing them in the basin. She gaped. No one had ever washed her feet before. And here was a boy, tenfold her worth no doubt, doing just that for her.

She was about to object, to stop him, but before a word could leave her mouth, he looked up at her with dark brown eyes, silencing her with a glance. She shut her mouth, returning her gaze to Tobias, as though he might notice her discomfort.

"How was your journey, child?" came his next words. He gave her a smile, weathered, wrinkled skin scrunched around shining grey eyes.

"Very long, my lord," she replied diffidently; she did not know of which of her journeys he spoke. Her mind was not in the conversation; she was taking in his raiment; he wore the same shawl and headband as had her village rabbi, and the same robes; yet these were all of much finer make, clothes of black and white and yellow – or was that golden threat? Her eyes consumed the sight. The king had kept this man in finery!

"It is the longest journeys that tend to have the most worthwhile ends; otherwise they would not be taken, no?"

Kefira couldn't answer – she would have rather liked to point out that it had not been her decision to come to Pasargadae at all, but held her tongue, looking away to the dirtied basin at her feet. Hami straightened and carried the water away.

Tobias spoke absently. "Of course, you probably do not find this place to your liking, despite its magnificence. How could you, under the circumstances?" he inquired, as though talking to himself. Then, "Please, does your dragon fare well?"

"I'm sure he does not," replied she, before she could check herself. "I do not know how he is," she stammered, before picking up in rising urgency, "He was fighting a dragon called Kia – do you know of him? When we got to here, he tried to fly to me, but this great black beast stopped him – and I do not know if he's hurt!"

The old man put his reed-like hands upon her shoulders. "I am blind child, not deaf – you need not shout."

Her voice had been rising. "Oh," she said, much quieter. "I am sorry."

He dropped his hands and gave a sympathetic smile. "Do not worry about Kia. He is not a cruel dragon, and you may be sure that your gift from God has not been harmed."

"How do you – you know his name?"

"Yes, indeed. You underestimate the ears of the King. We have picked up a lot of information on you and your travelling companions. Informants – they're an underhanded sort of method to acquiring information, but it is more favorable than other means." He must have heard her go quite still, for he added, "But there is not much beyond names known, save for a few reports of your miscreant actions," and he actually chuckled.

Kefira's head stooped. "My lord – I – I have been trying to find someone – a priest, to make up for these things, but I have not found any other Jew, let alone Levite, for many years."

The old man's face softened. "Do not worry yourself, child. You have had difficult past months. I did not mean to spite you." He turned, dog pressing its flank against his leg. "Please, sit upon a mat. We must talk."

And so Hami helped him to sit back on his cushions, and the dog flopped down beside him, and Kefira removed herself to a mat.

Tobias knit his weathered fingers together and said, "Were you born in Babylon, Kefira?"

She shook her head and said, "No, my lord. My great-grandparents fled Israel before the Temple was destroyed."

"I was one of those who left, as well. Where did you live?"

"Western Hyrcania, that was where my village was; it was small. It burned up." She successfully kept her voice devoid of emotion. "One day when I returned from our flocks, I found it destroyed."

She was staring fixedly at her newly-cleaned feet. Then she looked over across the floor, to her sandals, and dragged them back to try and tie them back on. She looked back at the old man while she worked. "Rabbi, may I see my dragon soon?"

Tobias's sightless eyes were full of regret. "I will see to it that you can meet with him as soon as possible. Would you tell me where you found him? That is important to me."

Kefira nodded, recalling. "Um, west of the Atrak River, in

Hyrcania. A small house was there." She caught herself before she mentioned the dead man. She glanced back up at Tobias, and returned her eyes to her sandals; she was doing a poor job at retying them, and Hami seemed to notice.

"Was there someone in that house?" asked the old man.

She glanced guiltily at the boy as she admitted, "Sir, there was an elder there." Her eyes went to Tobias as his expression changed. "He had fallen asleep," she said, voice small.

The old man's brows knit, wrinkles deepening in anguish. The dog licked his hand, and Hami looked at her before standing and leaving.

She felt as though she had done something dreadfully wrong.

"Sir?" she ventured, stomach dropping.

"Lemuel," the name came out hoarse. "I believe you found my brother."

Her heart wilted. "I'm so sorry – I did not mean to - " she stammered, staring at him amazement. She bit her lip, pausing. "I – I gave him a proper burial, my lord." As proper a one as he could hope to get, at least, she remembered guiltily.

He did not say anything for a while before he nodded and said, "It is well. My brother was received with our fathers."

Hami was back. He was carrying a tray of fruit and bread and honey, simultaneously balancing an urn on his head. He placed the foods on a tray between the two Israelites, and poured the contents of the urn – milk – into fine ceramic cups.

She accepted the liquid wondrously. Never since she left home had she seen any but curds or sour cream, and this was the sweetest milk she'd ever had. And then there was honey, a delicacy she rarely came across. Her eyes devoured the veritable feast, before she gathered enough courage to partake of it. It was like eating gold.

They did not need to speak during the meal. Hami filled Tobias's plate as the old man fished around with his fingers for morsels. It was like watching a grey heron sift his beak through a pool.

So methodical and repetitious was the fashion with which he ate, that she was surprised when the pattern was interrupted and he said, "I ought not keep you in the dark, Kefira, for I know of what you fret." She looked up, eager to hear his words, relieved she need not ask further. "You shall see Yonatan soon enough, I will make sure of it. I may not have as much authority as Siamak or any of the other generals, but the King would indulge me, I think."

"Thank you, lord," she bowed her head, forgetting his impairment. Was he truly in familiar terms with the King? She glanced at Hami, then the dog.

"Of course." He grew graver. "What you heard is true. The King means to judge you and your dragon himself. But do not fear — the King is not one who would punish unjustly, and he is most understanding. You will have an audience with him soon, but you will not be alone in your appeal. You have friends here."

Kefira nodded doubtfully.

"I will be your counselor amidst this, if you would permit me. I would like to assist you in growing acquainted with the quirks of Persian royalty and customs of the court, as well as vouch on your behalf before the King; I can tell you are a girl worthy of your burden, and should God give you the strength, I see you will overcome it."

The sincere words rang hollow within her, as she remembered the ball of unraveled yarn from her mat. Weak as a crushed sprout. She still felt the limpness in her heart, not aroused by his words. But she recognized his intention and replied, "I would appreciate your help, my lord."

"I would be glad to aid you." His eyes disappeared again as he smiled. But the expression soon faded. "I am not happy to disclose, however, that there is a cosmetic sort of preparation that must be instilled as well. I have no doubt of your own beauty, but a woman named Mahasti shall prepare you in the fashion of a maiden of the King. She is head mistress of his wives. All I can with assurance say is that you shall be well taken care of."

Kefira was not so sure. "Siamak said that I would stay in the women's quarters with the harem?" The last word was uttered with distaste.

"You have a small private room in the women's quarters, yes, but you will not be a part of the harem as far as can be helped. Though you will be treated there."

"What will happen to me?"

"You will be washed and polished and painted, as I understand it," he replied dryly. "It is probably better than prison though, where many think you ought to be. The food shall at least be better."

Kefira suppressed a groan. Her fingers traced the little hairs on her arm. "Very well," she said resignedly. "When shall I see Yonatan?"

"I will have a specific appointment for you when we meet tomorrow. I am sorry that does not sound very soon, but it is the best that can be done."

"When is my meeting with the King?"

"Two fortnights from tomorrow, I believe."

Had she been a child with a month to wait for her coming-of-age celebration, two fortnights would have sounded like an eternity. But with an object of dread at the timespan's end, it was as frightful as though the meeting was set for tomorrow. The bread grew dry in her mouth.

Hami moved to press his fingers against Tobias's hand, and the old man nodded. "Our time is at a close, Kefira," he said. "But before you go, we must thank God, that there are two Jews in the world who ate a meal together outside of bondage."

And so they prayed together: he spoke to God, after which she abashedly stumbled over a few verses of a prayer.

She thanked Tobias and said goodbye, before being led away again by the eunuchs, who seemed to be on a schedule. "We go to the women's quarters, now," one said.

"Very well," she replied, voice a ghost.

Chapter XIII
Serpent's Promise

"Do not knit your brows. You shall wrinkle further," the songbird voice of Mahasti ordered.

The last thing Kefira cared about was wrinkles. She was boiled-red, naked, sitting on a longchair, and was surrounded by a ravening pack of handmaidens, armed with razors, brushes, sugar strips, and ointments. Hardly had she woken up from her massive bed before she was stripped and shoved into a scalding bath and subject to their cosmetic instruments of torment.

Tobias couldn't have warned her enough. Never in her life had she been so assaulted. After a brief and rather degrading physical evaluation by the lady Mahasti the previous evening, as well as supping upon lean, fresh meat and fruit, she had been put to sleep in the biggest bed she had ever seen with a room to match; understandably, they were small by palace standards, but she could still lie down in the middle of the floor without being in arm's reach of any of the walls, and the ceiling echoed when she spoke. But hardly had she grasped the awe of her new quarters before she was put to the tweezers of her hostesses.

"Calm yourself, girl," Mahasti said, as Kefira was ushered shaking from the tub, and mercifully covered in a towel.

Her skin felt raw – they'd scrubbed it with porous stones, despite her protests, and pinched her face to no end, before releasing her from the hot water. She quavered, looking at her flesh. "Am I supposed to be the color of a pomegranate?"

"Red is an improvement upon that primeval tan," her captor quipped. Her own skin, past the powdered blush was creamy white and without flaw, as was that of the rest of the maids. Before Kefira had always envied the porcelain skin of rich ladies, but up close it only appeared sallow. She bit back a retort on this account, as she was made to sit and lie upon her back on the chair. She was like a roasted antelope, set upon a table for a feast, the surrounding maids pretty and brightly-colored vultures.

Kefira smelled something sweet as they unwound strips of cloth and removed a paste from a jar to put upon the linens. Her fists loosened; this new bout did not look like the wiry brushes and the razors they'd used to tame her fingernails, at least.

"What is this for?" she began, trying to find Mahasti's face past the servants. But before the woman misunderstood she added, "Why are you going to such pains to make me look like a - " and her words ended abruptly with a yelp as her right arm exploded with fire. She looked on in horror, to see that her skin had been entirely rent of hair. Flesh burning, she tried to sit up, but then was set down again.

"Please lay down," chirped a girl younger than she. "Sugaring hurts at first, but it will only take a minute and you will like how you look much better."

Kefira implored, "You're going to rip out all my hair?" And then she grit her teeth as her other arm was stripped. Her eyes flooded.

"I will not have you prancing about in the King's court as hairy as a mountain goat," sniffed Mahasti with a pert eye at her as the girl's face was covered in the paste-covered strips.

Kefira cried out with dismay as they ripped hair from around her eyebrows, from off her face. "This is stupid!"

Her reasoning did nothing to sway them, and just as she was ready to throw punches, turquoise nails flashed, Mahasti putting her hands up to halt the merciless surgeons. "Kimiya, you must relax now if you want - "

"It is Kefira, and I did not want this," she retorted, voice as defiant as she dared – but her voice was reduced to a whimper as they ripped the last hairs from her last leg. She licked her lips nervously; her face tasted sweet from the treatment – were they truly using so much *sugar* to remove her hair?

"Well, it is what the King wants, and I hardly think you should like to defy him, in your position."

Kefira was stalled, jaw set. The King: torturing her beyond bearing before making the verdict to take her dragon away. She gaped at her raw, pink limbs, entirely riven of their dark, fine hairs — the humiliation of a shorn lamb.

Her arms were raised by soft cool hands, and she winced, turning to watch her stitched shoulder. The young handmaiden looked at it too, as she held her arm gingerly in waiflike fingers.

"Did a dragon do this to you?" she asked.

Kefira nodded.

"I hope the stitches come out in time for your skin treatment."

"This is not the skin treatment?" Kefira asked incredulously, paling.

"No, although you shall find it much more pleasant, do not fret."

Kefira shut her eyes, not believing her for a moment. They rent her underarms of their adornment, and her skin burned. She felt her pounding heart throughout her entire body, beating through her skin. They finally had to be done. She crossed her legs before they put them flat again to rub them in an oil. It hurt at first, but then the sensation tingled away. Laying her head back, she clenched her eyes tight with the relief. And then her teeth snapped over her tongue as she stifled a scream.

She coiled up on herself, limbs crossing tight as she hugged her knees to her chest, the pain of uprooting burning low. "Are you mad? Are you Egyptians?" she cried, unable to contain her fury. "Must you shear my head, too?" Her beaten-animal eyes found Mahasti, and she could hardly keep from cursing at her. "Why?"

The woman's cool blue eyes sparked as she offered the heartless explanation: "To petition the King, one must either be a man or a maiden — not somewhere in-between."

Kefira seethed inside, deciding that Mahasti was a slender, painted version of Siamak. But at least this general of cosmetics did not object to the relief of being slathered in cooling lotions. Relief flooded her as the woman had her girls put out the fire on her skin.

A girl even approached her with a sliced vegetable, attempting to put them upon her eyes. "What are those for?" Kefira asked, recoiling, wondering if the girl had so mistaken her eyes for her mouth.

"They will help your eyes grow brighter, and remove the dark circles."

Kefira submitted to the treatment reluctantly, after peeking to make sure they were not going to sneak up on her with more sugaring while she was blinded.

Soon there was dull pain rising in her feet; they were grinding away at it with stones. "Why must you bother my feet?" she asked, and it took all her willpower not to jerk her legs away as she reclined.

"Your feet are as padded as a hound's. The extra skin must be removed."

"Why, pray tell, does the King care about my feet?"

"I care about your feet, and that is what matters now. If you defy me, I shall make sure yours is a strict diet of cucumber and sour cream from now on."

"I'm used to having no food at all, so that should still be an improvement." And Kefira permitted herself a smile. She could not see the expression of indignation past her eye coverings, but knew she'd struck well.

All conversation now was left to be carried by the maids, and Kefira did not listen to them overmuch. Even though she'd been wearing sandals in the past months, the callouses on her feet had hardly diminished. She felt with no small amount of lamentation as the protective pads, which had defended her soles from hot sand, ridged scales, and spiky burs all her life were worn away.

She was going to be as fragile as a leaf when they were done.

"When will you finish?" she asked. "When can I see Tobias?"

"This afternoon."

"This afternoon? You will not be done until then?"

"Young lady, we are fitting a year-long treatment into the span of two fortnights. You are lucky to have *this* stage done sooner than next month."

Am I? She brooded beneath her ailing skin, falling onto her back again, already weary, despite the early hour. Her eyes fixed onto the ceiling as they worked, and she clutched her arms together to recapture whatever modesty she might. But her fingers braised her skin with even the lightest touch, even past the oily remedy the girls had rubbed on it.

They were soon finished with their sanding, finally. They had her sit up again, removed the vegetables from her eyes and washed her feet. Just when she thought that was it, however, they began brushing and combing and pulling on her hair. "You are not *truly* going to pull that out, too, are you?" she asked uncertainly.

"Not unless you should like to wear a wig," Mahasti replied.

Kefira shuddered at the prospect, but couldn't tell whether or not her opaque tone was sarcastic, so she assured her, "No, please," and without further complaint, submitted to having her wet hair reanimated.

She passed time nibbling on a fingertip until Mahasti told her not to. Then, as they combed and pulled her mane, she noted with concern that she could not smell anything. Nothing besides the stony aura of the room, and the fragrances of the women around her. She herself lacked any scent, any aroma, now. Her whole body; there was no more earthy-salt-scent to accompany her flesh – she, in fact, smelled like nothing.

It was supernatural. It made her uneasy. "Must we reconvene after today?" she asked the woman. "Can I not be ready after this treatment?"

"Oh, the naivety of youth..." Mahasti sniffed. "I thought I had explained well enough – no, every day for a fortnight you shall be under preparation, is that clear? You are clay for my molding."

Kefira flushed at the chastisement; she'd hoped she could have gotten around it somehow. She should not like to see or smell these girls and Mahasti again at all, not after this. Never had she been uncovered before anyone besides her own mother, and that when she was a girl, and never on such abrupt or intrusive terms! Their scouring and polishing was as offensive as it was irrational. She felt like a tent cloth, being taken down and off of its poles and away from its old stakes to be none-too-gently changed to fit a different frame. After her hair was taken care of, her face was pinched and poked again for what felt like an eternity.

But eventually, arduously, it was done. Hours had passed before Mahasti relented with a yielding breath. "There, your first month is done in a day. You are to meet Tobias in half of an hour."

Kefira's heart leapt, and she managed a smile through the hot towels on her face. She laid her head back in a relief, even as her body tingled with residual ache. Before she shut her eyes, however, she remembered her state and asked, "May I put on my clothes again?"

"Prepare yourself for disappointment, if you expect us to drape you with those old rags. You shall have fresh raiment." She signaled to a pair of maidens. "Clothe her."

"No, I want to do it myself," Kefira protested, quickly taking up the fabrics upon the women's arms. The cloth was brightly colored and soft. She took no more time in admiring them before quickly swaddling herself in the shift. But before she could wrap herself in the robe, she noticed one of them doing away with her old clothes; Rakhshan's shawl caught her eye. "Oh, no – please, mayn't I keep these?" she cried out, taking up the shawl and throwing it over her head. "They've been mine since I was a child."

"It would do no harm, if you have a sentimental attachment to them." Mahasti conceded. "They certainly smell as though you've had them a long time. They shall be washed."

A handmaiden moved to pluck Kefira's shawl off, but she held it taut to her head. "No, please, this one isn't dirty, I want to wear it." Only because it preserved what dignity she had left.

They reapplied linen to her stitched shoulder. An ichor that made the girls cringe was coming from it, and Kefira wished it would heal to preserve her from more of their distaste. But finally she was dressed and the wound was hidden, with more clothes than she had ever worn in her life – the girls insisted upon adding more and more layers, helping her with articles that were alien to her, until at last a blue stole was draped over her shoulders. Before she could balk at the unaccustomed weight of the raiment, she checked herself, remembering that this was a significantly better fashion than that of the scanty sort she'd seen some of the other women traipsing about the quarters. Her stomach sank at the hems of her garments trailing on the ground, without tassels, but her protest for kosher was swallowed.

Her shoulder began to ache.

She was engulfed in a sparkling hill, topaz, ruby, and agate all shimmering around her with the musky scent of dry leaves, as she was embraced by Yonatan, coiling and re-coiling about her in a possessive earthquake. He rumbled and purred and whined as she clung to his foreleg. His yellow eyes were almost manic. Upon seeing him she'd cried many a "Yonatan!" and "Thank God," before her throat had constricted and she became as mute as he was.

Tobias had taken her immediately to him as soon as they convened. "The King had given Siamak a good thrashing when he found out that you'd been so kept apart," he'd said with a chuckle, explaining the promptness of the unexpected reunion, as they'd walked, or she half-ran, to reach the garden of Yonatan's captivity.

Now Tobias said nothing at all, standing beside Hami, as he blindly watched the great beast that had been his brother's charge.

"Oh, Yonatan," she hugged his cheek, bony ridges and great burgundy scales pressed against her face. "How are you? Are you well? Oh, I wish you had not lunged for me!" He thrummed, and she amended for the chastisement with, "You were not hurt, were you?"

His eyelids narrowed bitterly, and she knew he was recalling his bout with the dragon. Then he shook his head, scales ruffling. The gold in his eyes glimmered with concern as he looked intensely at her, and breathed in at her, tongue flicking. "No, do not worry, I am alright, too," she assured him. "They've just been cleaning me, that is why I have no smell."

His tongue tapped her shoulder and he crooned, eyes anxious as his teeth flashed – he'd caught aroma of the sanguine wound.

"One of the little Shaghāls bit me, it is alright, now." She dare not show him the wound, however. Seeing it would not much smooth down his nerves.

He brayed, mournfully, and she stroked his nose. "No, no, it is all very well." She leaned on him, staring into his great, sad eye. "It is not your fault at all. None of this is your fault, my love." His breath hissed through his nostrils, in and out, but soon his jaws drooped and his breathing slowed. "It is alright. We're – I have you again, I'm here, you need not worry any longer."

An orange flash twinkled in his weary eye, a residual, melancholy anger, but it glimmered away as he blinked. His breath rustled through his throat and he nuzzled Kefira. She could feel everything about him was tired; she stroked beneath his eye.

"Yoni, I should introduce you to someone," she said quietly, after a while. She did not want to ignore Tobias. "He is an elder – an elder of our people," she continued, and instantly, Yonatan perked. "His name is Tobias," she said, and her dragon was already turning his head to see the old man.

She said louder, "Tobias, this is Yonatan," feeling a little redundant in pointing it out; could he tell the dragon was there? Certainly he could, even if he was blind, feel his breath, know he was looking at him.

He did, she saw with relief, and his eyes disappeared in a broad smile of wonder. "Yonatan," he said quietly. And then he bowed, stooping over his cane. "It is the highest of honors to meet you, my friend."

Yonatan cocked his head, lowered it to his eye level and hummed his pleasure, eyes wide.

Kefira did not know how to further introduce them — did Yonatan recognize this man as his keeper's brother? Or could he? How ought she tell him, or would Tobias introduce himself accordingly?

But then she had no time to worry about the issue, for suddenly, Yonatan's head raised, and she saw his pupils dilate. She looked past his folded wing to see the new object of his interest, and her heart skipped a beat.

A kingly figure was approaching, mere steps away, and her feet turned to ice.

He was surrounded by a dispatch of guards, and was garbed in robes of deep purple and scarlet, laced in threads of gold. Older than twenty but no more than thirty, she determined; he was angular of face, with an orange cast to his skin, eyebrows cocked in a perpetual state of disdain. Who was this? Why hadn't Tobias told her someone else would be joining them? Who was this?

His hard, dark eyes fell upon Yonatan.

Who was this?

"I see the beast has grown," he said, words terse. The dragon's head dipped to him, with an inexplicable friendliness that astonished Kefira; she was frozen.

Was this the King?

Tobias seemed to recognize the new arrival, and she exhaled when he spoke, introducing them inversely: "Kefira, Yonatan, this is the Babylonian Ambassador, awilu Shaza'eil."

"Thank you, Ben-Seraiah," the man said, through a gritted smile.

Kefira gaped openly at Shaza'eil. Hangmatana! He was the man who had bought — wanted to buy — Yonatan! He was here? Why in all of Creation was he here?

Yonatan sniffed him, tongue flickering, as though he somehow found no wrong in him. She tried to catch his eye, but the dragon was staring at the Babylonian as though enamored. Of all the times not to be hostile to a newcomer — why was he being so friendly?

"Sir," she remembered to acknowledge, as polite as she could possibly bear – and she dipped her head. "I did not expect to see you again," she said, the plainest civility she could manage, as she otherwise looked at him like he was an asp.

"That is funny," he said, stepping up to her. "I've never seen you before in my life. You must be mistaking me for someone else."

Yonatan blinked and did not hamper the man as he secured her by the arm and directed her away with a civil, "A moment, if you please, Ben-Seraiah." And he steered her away from them to a bench on the outskirts of the garden; and to her surprise, she let him, heavy-footed as she stared over her shoulder at a motionless Yonatan. The man made her sit down, and her eyes felt huge as she stared up at him.

He stood, arms folded, rings glinting in the high sun, as he surveyed Yonatan, who was sniffing something on the ground. "The beast has grown," he repeated his first statement, words hardened.

She had nothing to say in response. Her hands clutched the stone bench, knuckles whitening, as she glanced after her dragon. Why was he not stepping on this man? Before, he would have snarled at Rakhshan for much less!

"How long has it been since his coming of age?" the Babylonian asked abruptly, facing her square.

"What?"

His lips twisted scornfully beneath his coiffed beard. "You mean you do not know when your own dragon is mature?" he asked. "Let me educate you, girl – he has not reached his full growth by any means, but he is very much a bull. His horns are no longer bare, they grow prongs; they and his brows are crowned in the red plates of maturity, in the way of Israeli beasts, and the spikes in his cheekbones are grown and plated," he explained, as though giving a diagnosis. "His scales have lost their luster and his skin flakes of the first molt."

Kefira blinked, reexamining Yonatan as he described the changes, realizing he was right. Her mouth hung open stupidly.

"Tell me, do you know anything of your dragon at all?"

She glared up at him, standing. "Did you take me over here just to criticize me?"

He only looked amused by her outburst. "You need not act like a slighted wardu, girl, I was simply asking a question. But perhaps I was too brash, and a civility would suit you better: may I inquire after the health of your husband?"

Kefira paled. "What are you talking about? I have no - " and then she stopped. She'd been under that foolish guise in Hangmatana, at Yonatan's hatching.

A crooked smile. "I guessed as much."

Kefira's hands were in fists, and she growled, "But I thought you said that you'd never seen me before! You're not trying to hide anything yourself, are you?" she needled.

"That is what I wanted to speak to you of," he said coolly.

"Oh? I take it, then, that the people around here don't know about your escapades in Media?" Kefira asked, smiling a little herself now. "It would not be good for you then, for them to know that you were looking to steal the Hardlā from a man of Israel?"

"Israel," he said, "is but straw beneath my feet. I was only searching for what was rightfully mine."

It was all Kefira could do to keep from striking him in the face. Suddenly his hand was on her shoulder, strong, ungentle hand forcing her back, and she felt his fingers in proximity of her throat. He grinned balefully and spoke slowly, as though carving his words in stone. "You are not going to tell *anyone* about Hangmatana."

A grim, equally angry smile touched her lips. "Then it is a secret?" she inquired with feigned naivety.

His smile broadened, darkening his expression further, and Kefira believed that he was about to strangle her.

"Kefira?"

It was not the Babylonian who spoke, but Tobias, shuffling into view. "You've been allotted two hours of time with Yonatan until you return to treatment; and if you've been away from one another for half as long as Siamak boasts, I guess you'd not want to waste a moment of it."

Hami was beside him, looking at Shaza'eil's hand. Kefira breathed as the man removed his grasp, stepped back, and said, "Of course; Kefira, go and enjoy an afternoon with the dragon. I'll see that we may meet again soon." And he smiled in a way that made her feel that he would make sure of it.

Chapter XIV
Two Tales

Queen Cassandanē. Daughter of Pharnaspes, mother of two sons and two daughters, and most beloved wife of King Cyrus.

Kefira had seen glimpses of her in passing a few times; past a column, or a curtain, or through a procession of guards. Understandably, she was a sickly woman, the sort of pale that was not desirable among the harem girls, yet she maintained her renown and esteem, if not by her station than by her gentle temperament. Kefira had even been acknowledged by her once, aloofly, though not rudely. A passing nod and measuring look, as though the queen were touching a pool with a toe to find its temperature. It wasn't any of the dumb curiosity or disdainful looks that she'd grown to expect from the nobles, but rather one of enigmatic appraisal. Kefira did not know why this was.

Nor did she trouble herself in wondering. The previous night after her visit with Yonatan had been engulfed by yet another bath and a restless sleep, as she had been practically embalmed by aromatic oils and lotions; when her mind permitted her to think of anything but the overwhelming smell, it was upon Yonatan's apathy and Shaza'eil's threat. Of course, Rakhshan could probably find some way to explain it all away and dismiss her fears, but he was not there. She would have to figure out how to deal with the Babylonian and figure out her dragon's quizzical behavior herself. Doubtless she would never hear from him or his advice ever again.

She'd been awoken bright and early, was made to eat a breakfast fashioned to a "special diet" for the reason of "fleshing out" her "positively skeletal" figure. Well, she was happy simply to be getting free meals – let alone free meals in such number – a blessing which disarmed her against all their thoughtless insults concerning her body. Morning, noon, and night she was to be fed, a quantity of supping she was not used to. Very soon indeed she would be fleshed out, she supposed, and too much so if the ladies continued in such a fashion. No, the meals did not bother her, but the meticulous, almost neurotic grooming quite had her at wit's end. "I shall do it myself, please," she said finally, reaching her threshold of exasperation for the invasive handmaidens in charge of her scrubbing. What the silly maids thought they were achieving in bathing her after she'd been cleaned twice not a day prior she had no idea. But they insisted upon it; and if Mahasti would ever be swayed by the Kefira's protestations, then she had sorely misjudged her stubbornness.

And woe unto any hair that grew out of the boundaries of her scalp – everything that had been plucked was re-plucked, like weeds in a flowerbed. The only hairs besides her mane that were suffered to persist were those in the narrowed borders of her eyebrows. The pain of the tweezing irons was almost equal to that of the sugaring the other day, as one by one each trespassing hair was mercilessly removed from her skin. A flawless complexion, the Persians called it, but she only saw mourning red skin.

Once her hide recovered from their persecutions and the ointments they applied were well soaked in, they even put on her cosmetics. Never in her life had Kefira ever been made-up, but nonetheless, she grudgingly submitted to the application. It felt slimy and bizarre as they smeared and smoothed a sort of oil over her face. Not until she looked in a mirror did she realize it was intended to make her skin look fair; indeed, it only succeeded in making her look like a pale ghost. She pointed this out in horror, the dubious handmaidens glanced at each other, and condescended to agree that the look did not work. Even Mahasti expressed her resignation on the subject. "One ought not trim a mule to look like a mare, but give a mule golden tack. There's nothing to be done about your skin," she opined abstrusely. Kefira did not know whether to be offended or grateful. In any case, the infernal cream was removed from her face, but before the girl could allow herself relief, she was then subject to eye and lip paints.

It was torture, watching the black-tipped brush descend to her eyes, having to resist twitching and blinking, and endure a scolding when she could not. Finally the girl with the brush said, "You may shut your eye – I don't need it open for the upper lid."

"Why didn't you tell me earlier?"

"I thought you might want your eyes open, but when you started looking towards the door it occurred to me that you may find this unpleasant."

Kefira could not comprehend the obtuseness of these people. She tried to fathom it, as she shut her eyes and her lids were painted, yet no explanation came forth. "Please, now you must open your eyes for the bottom lids – I won't poke you, I promise," the horrific words came. Kefira squinted open. "A little more, please," and she relented, quaking.

The lips were not so bad. They just dabbed a stain upon them; that trifle, when compared to her eyes, she did not find overwhelming. The stuff they were putting on certainly tasted bad, however.

"Do not lick it," Mahasti cried. "It is made of gemstone!"

Kefira balked. "Why in all Creation – do you make it out of gemstone?" she exclaimed, and was promptly chastised by the girl applying the stuff.

"You disdain the expense? Perhaps you might rather go down to Egypt and have smeared upon your petulant mouth crushed beetles."

These words silenced her, and she remained still as the stain was applied. Gemstones – truly. Why were they treating her, deemed nothing more than a thief, to such invaluable things? She had spent the last night in a balm of myrrh – *myrrh* of all things – stuff so precious that she had never so much as caught a whiff of it before in her entire life! And now they were covering her lips in gemstones, even as she chewed on cloves? Certainly it could not have been the King's idea. But then again, she couldn't imagine Mahasti stooping so low as to have to put up with her backwards, street-rat charge if someone without higher power had not ordered her to.

She looked into the mirror again once they were finished. And, after absorbing the shock of her fine appearance, could only with good conscience conclude that she looked different.

The girls fawned about how far she had come in two days.

"Sit back down again, Kefira," Mahasti ordered. "Your ears are going to be pierced."

Kefira gaped, but hardly had strength to argue

Needles went in, filling her with alarming pain; they'd given her a piece of fabric wadding to bite down upon for the duration, yet she'd underestimated the duress she now felt. Reflexively, she'd tried to bat the surgeons away, but the needles came out just as quickly. Her hands flew to her ears, and returned before her eyes with spots of blood.

Oh, Adonai, have I sinned? Her mind scrambled frantically through her memory – were body piercings not a heathen practice?

Before she could say a word about it, they washed her ears in wine and put silver rings in them. They put up her hair, combing out the strands and pinning them in a bun, curly tresses cascading like a captured waterfall down her neck. They'd stated many times how much they admired her hair, and asked her how it came so thick, but she could only answer with ignorance. Into the mirror again. She looked older by many years. Her fingers went to her earlobes once more, silently horrified at their beautifying mutilation. What would Tobias think, if he could see them? Maybe she ought to ask him if God would be angry.

That day she was not allowed to wear her shawl, despite her protestations. They robed her in an orange terracotta color, with adornments of red and white, before sending her off to another meeting with Tobias.

As they led her, her two eunuch guards, whom she'd now come to know as Navid and Remus, seemed to passively notice the change in her appearance, as one would notice a change in weather. But to her horror, when they'd emerged from the women's quarters to those of the staff and advisors, where the sentries were not eunuchs, she noticed that this remodeled lower-than-a-servant street-rat did not go unnoticed; that, indeed, she was looked upon with even a small amount of pleasure. It was all she could do not to wipe off her face and remove the jewelry then and there.

Tobias, thankfully, did not notice a difference. After both partook of a temperate bowl of spiced wine, he went to the task of educating her on Persian propriety and customs.

He imparted that, when conversing, it was significantly more important to listen than to talk, and when speaking one should not act overly eager to do so. And she ought not whisper to one person in the presence of others, lest they think the worse of what she says. There were many other trivial and rather ridiculous strictures, such as abstaining from coughing and sneezing in the presence of anyone greater than a servant and, that when speaking to a person of such a high station, she must cover her mouth with a hand or kerchief, as nobles were sensitive to the smell of breath. He reminded her, "The decorum is rather silly, but this place is much different than the world outside." With that Kefira could not argue. After another string of idiosyncratic social rules, he said, "And, I know you need not know this yet, but keep this in mind. You may not be seeing the King on the level of court, but in such an occasion you are to kiss the ground before him upon approaching. You speak only when spoken to, and when you do, begin each address with, 'may you live forever.' And when you are bidden leave, do not turn your back on the King until you've left the hall."

Kefira was taken aback. "Does — does that mean I'm to walk *backwards*?" she asked incredulously.

Tobias nodded and then chuckled, "If I can do it, I am confident in your ability to oblige the court."

The girl laughed a little, though uneasily. It would be impossible remembering all this decorum, though she would try, for his sake.

Remnants

But the subject wearied her. "My lord," she began. "I know I must know how to conduct myself here, but I am not going to see the King for more than a week yet; I know of Persia, tell me of *our* people."

"What would you like me to tell?"

"I've always desired," she began, rather self-consciously, taken aback by her own words, "that if I were to meet another Jew – let alone so revered a Levite – I would – I want to know more of our history." And then she realized that her words were not going where she intended, and so stated plainly, "What happened – what of our fall? I was not told of it very much when I was a girl."

"I'm heartened that you've maintained an interest of your people." He did not seem displeased by the change of subject. "I shall tell you then, of the times of old. I'm sure you're familiar with some of it."

She nodded, keen on what he was about to impart. "Thank you."

"Four hundred years ago, when Israel was still a young nation, the country was split by a rebellion, after King Solomon died. Two new leaders came forward from the riven land: Jeroboam of the tribe of Ephraim, who took the Northern Kingdom, Samaria, and Solomon's son, Rehoboam, who took the southern, Judah. You know that Samaria did not last for long after that, besieged by Assyria and other hostile neighbors. Hoshea the Vile, the ten-and-ninth, and last king of the North was killed in the sixth year of his reign, wasted away in an Assyrian prison. Judah, sister-nation, lasted longer; the South went on for centuries, but the evil of the kings that made up its lineage grew, even as the nation thrived. It was not long, however, until Babylon, having lately taken Assyria into its empire, turned its eye to us."

He was slow and deliberate in his words, like dropping pebbles in a clear pond, and waiting for them to hit the bottom. Kefira had time to interject. She already knew most of this, and wondered at the *why* of it all. "Why did it all collapse, then?" she implored. "Why did Israel fall?" Her words were so sudden that she surprised herself. But she continued with growing vehemence, words like fists against a tree. "He promised us that He would make us a great nation."

Tobias's response was slow. "And He did."

Kefira felt her heart begin to quicken. "My lord," she said, realizing she hadn't adequate words to go on with, but could not but continue. She remembered Shaza'eil, and anger began to fill her. *Trampled under our boots.* "I've heard stories – horrid stories – women – women who hadn't already eaten their babies from starvation, had them torn from their bellies with the sword. Children were left to die in the streets with no charity, dragons devoured the prisoners – and those that survived were left to serve the very murderers of their kin!"

And she caught herself up short, at a loss as to what had come out of her. She held her breath and stared at her feet. Tobias's voice was melancholy as he said, "I know. I know, child. Firsthand."

Kefira was wracked with shame. "I'm sorry, my lord," she said quietly. Silent tears were blinked away, as she made herself say, quieter, "Why did it all happen?"

"Zion ran away from her Father," he began simply. "Peasants and Kings alike defiled themselves with the prostitutes of false gods. And, even before infanticide was induced by war and hunger, they burned their children on alters to evil spirits like our pagan neighbors." He said this all somberly, softly; she did not think he was going to say anything more before, "Just as one who is in deep sleep must be shaken to be roused, so were we."

She waited for him to continue this time, gravely, and he did, quoting something familiar to her.

"So it shall be, when all of these things have come upon you, the blessing and the curse which I have set before you, that you will call them to mind in all the nations where the Lord your God has banished you. And when you return to the Lord your God and obey Him with all your heart and soul, according to all that I command you today, then the Lord your God will restore you from captivity and have compassion on you, and will gather you again from all the nations where He has scattered you."

The words of Moses, she recalled, prophetic almost a thousand years before its time.

"Even if you have been banished to the most distant land under the heavens," continued he, "from there the Lord your God will gather you and bring you back. He will bring you to the land that belonged to your fathers and make you more prosperous and numerous than even they were. He will circumcise your hearts and the hearts of your descendants, so that you may love Him with all your heart and with all your soul. And live."

Kefira's hands were clutching one another tightly, and she felt heat in her eyes. "That is – that is His promise," said she, almost a question.

"It is."

"Shall it ever be fulfilled?" And then she caught the blasphemy in her words, and added, "In my lifetime?"

"That remains to be seen, young one, but I pray it is so."

Kefira spoke no more, and Hami shifted in the silence. The grey eyes of Tobias soon came upward again, and he arose from reverie. "Now, I will tell you your history – that of your dragon, and my brother and I."

Yonatan's father was slain by a horror of machinery, a siege weapon, late in the losing war for Jerusalem. Unable to be bested by the great Tiamats and fire-breathing Khumbabas of Babylon, the bloody and scarred Hardlā was finally brought low by a catapult, chest penetrated by a boulder, even as he had been wreaking havoc on the front lines of the Babylonian army. In that same battle, Lemuel and his younger brother, Tobias, who was a child at the time, were smuggled from the ailing capitol city with the last egg of the Hardlā. No one else could be spared to rescue the precious creature; everyone able to wield a weapon was a soldier, or else helping those that were.

On the back of a donkey, by a miracle of the Lord, they made it past the battle through back roads, through their dying nation, into the very belly of Babylon and out of it, and finally, into the safety of the empire of Persia. It was a journey full of starvation and fear and silence and restless nights of travel, that Tobias expressed he did not like to recollect. In short, they reached the Eastern Empire, and for quiet, biding years they stayed in a small shack of a house on a creek, out of danger but forever looking over their shoulder.

Their absence, in Babylon's death toll for the Israelis, went unnoticed. What loss were they to them? The Chief Priest Seraiah had many sons, and two missing ones were of no note; certainly, it was decided, that they were merely among the number of corpses that had been left unrecognizable on the roadside, and so were overlooked, even as their family and father were executed by the Babylonians. Just as quickly the rest of Israel fell.

Those who survived were dragged back to Babylon in fetters. Those very few that escaped looked on from their hiding places in fear as Israel's ghost evaporated before their glassy eyes.

Kefira listened to his story intently. "Were any of Yonatan's kin taken captive? Or have all of them perished as well?" she asked somberly.

"Babylon could take none of them captive, try as they might, so instead took solace in killing them. But there are two who are not recorded to have perished," Tobias recalled. "His mother, in fact, and a cousin. Even as Israel declined in virtue, so did the strength of the Hardlās. They began to fall, even in the smaller wars that led up to Israel's death. They had not been numerous to begin with, but when they started dying – from battle and plague – only a few were spared. Yonatan's father had stayed with Israel to his bitter end, but before that, the two females, Yonatan's kin, left for the wilderness. No one knows where they went, or if they yet survive."

"Would Persia, perhaps, have record?"

"Persia knows almost nothing of our nation's hallowed beasts. They had very little interest in us at the time."

"How then did you ever come to be an advisor to their King?"

Tobias said that he'd never intended to take up such an office from the start. Dozens of years after he and his brother settled in the wilderness, Tobias left his brother to travel to the old palace that was yet in Elam. It was a journey induced solely by a prodding spirit, otherwise unexplained, but his brother urged him to follow it. Tobias implored that he should come as well, but Lemuel insisted that the sanctity of the egg required him to remain thither. It was with the utmost reluctance that Tobias said goodbye to his brother and followed the pull of his spirit.

Cambyses the Elder, Cyrus's father, was king then, lord of a smaller Persia. He was a reticent and mild man, for his station; so, when Tobias came stumbling onto his doorstep in Elam, he was not brushed away for the lowly refugee that he was. When informed that the wanderer was an Israelite, Cambyses's interest was piqued. After much-needed food and a bath, Tobias was presented to the King. Cambyses had been troubled in the past years, as he witnessed the unity of the empires of the world begin to crumble: Media and Lydia warred, Babylon smote Egypt, and a diminishing Assyria was marauded by its neighbors. He wondered if Persia would soon be forced to engage in the warfare that seized her fellows, and the apprehension ate at him.

After the once-great nation of Israel had been ransacked by Babylon, the Jewish population that survived had been reduced to grim sects of prisoners and refugees, the latter of which flooded into Persia, the only nation that, in recent history, had never held malice for their people.

"Tell me, Levite," the old King had addressed him. "What would you have me do with these remnants of your people? Uninvited they eat from Persia's table; covered in ashes and sackcloth they steal into her hills and into her valleys and villages without so much as a by-your-leave."

Not prepared for the question, and prepared for audience with the King much less, Tobias uttered a prayer and answered the King.

"If I may offer my opinion, my king, I believe that Persia has no obligation to accept the wretches of a defeated nation. Nor does she have obligation to feed or clothe them. She might turn us all out of her dwelling place and not be in the wrong for it."

The King nodded, and then asked, "Is that what you desire?"

"No, my king."

"What is it that you desire, then?"

Tobias prayed again, and took a tentative deep breath, and replied, "I would want to ask for your merciful pardon on those weary ones who take advantage of your land, my king. I would want to request of you mercy."

The King mulled over his words, and Tobias's fear grew every second with the silence. The King then asked, "That is what you desire, wise man of Israel?"

"Yes, my king. If you find any impudence on my tongue, you may cut it off."

Another long pause. Tobias told her that he *had* expected his tongue to be cut off, or in the very least to be denied his request, but instead the King said, with a voice of good humor, "I like too much the words of your tongue to have it removed, Levite. If but half your kinsmen share a fraction of your wisdom, then Persia will be the better for it."

And so the remnants of Israel found welcome in Persia. And so Tobias was promoted from rugged pilgrim to advisor of the King, and thence the King's son.

"That is incredible," Kefira said, when he finished. "How fortuitous it turned out – for Israel, and the King. Did you get to see your brother very often?"

"My station did not permit me many excursions," he answered, voice losing its vigor. "I am sure if they knew of my brother," and he cleared his throat, trailing off. "I have not seen him since."

"Oh, I'm sorry," Kefira murmured, astonished. She wondered what Lemuel thought, in his latter days, without his brother. She pressed her lips together, desirous to move on to a less painful subject for the old man. "Did they – how did they, did people ever know about Yonatan's egg? You told no one of it, so how was there such an arousal when I found it?"

"From what we know, Babylon recovered information of it; in Israel, in the Archives, they found a scroll, the written genealogy of the Hardlā dragons, Yonatan's lineage, that noticed each dragons' unions, offspring, and dated their life. The egg of Raisa was not accounted for, as the other remaining beasts were, you know – his sire deceased, and the yet living Raisa and other female, Atara. So the Babylonians intended to find the egg, a dragon of such rarity, and find him soon, that he might be secured from the shell." He paused, recalling with sobriety, "So, of those they did not kill, they withdrew information. In time, they learned that the existence of Yonatan's egg was certain, that it had been entrusted with two escapees in the nation's last days. Though the land that the Babylonians had to search for us was broad, it seemed only a matter of time before their spies found us in Persia."

"And did they?"

"No – you found him first, of course." The old man smiled. "Which," he continued, "makes you the champion of a hundred-year race that you did not even know you ran in."

Kefira smiled, thinking fondly of her dragon. She could not imagine him in the hands of a wretched Babylonian, and grew ever more grateful that he'd been given to her. But her expression soon diminished to a frown, for she remembered Rakhshan quite suddenly. He'd been sent to look over the countryside by those who'd hired him in Hangmatana. He found the house, too, mere hours after she did. Kefira wondered; no – and just as quickly discarded the thought. He may have been a deceiver and a mercenary, but he could not have been a Babylonian spy, of all things. She could not stand for him to have a deeper trench of blame in her heart; no, her mind turned to Deioces, his employer – he was a Persian Satrap, not a spy. Yet he'd certainly be willing to be paid by Babylon to let their spies rove, she was sure – paid by

Shaza'eil, no doubt.

Navid had a message for her, when she left the tent. "A runner arrived while you were disposed," he said. "You have an appointment with the Babylonian ambassador."

Kefira felt all blood drain from her face, her feet. "What?" she gaped, voice pallid. No – no, this was much sooner than she'd expected. Much sooner.

"He desires audience with you. He would have you in half of an hour, at the Ambassador Commons."

Kefira's breath came shallow and sharp. Even as her shoulders tautened, Remus assured her, "Worry not, Kefira. We shall go there with you."

Her legs thawed only marginally, as they began to walk back to the women's quarters. Kefira asked faintly, "Why? Why does he want to see me?"

"A conference. The runner did not say what it concerned," said Navid.

"Though I can very well guess," added Remus dryly.

Kefira's heart began to stall with dread, like wagon wheels churning through mud. What could he say to her that he hadn't already said? Was he going to further haze her, mock her of Israel's servitude to his people, gloat over how little she knew of her own dragon?

Then another thought came to her. It was fanciful, improbable, horrible, but still, it clutched her heart. Did he mean to kill her? To finish what his hand told her he wanted to do in the garden?

Then they reached her room. The eunuchs told her that she had only a few minutes to herself before they left to get to the meeting on time. She didn't want to get there on time, not at all, but complied with her guards.

The maids were gone by now, but she managed before leaving to find the mirror without their help. She was afraid of wiping off her makeup, for fear of only smearing it around and not succeeding in removing it at all. So instead, to regain her innocence, she pulled the pins from her hair to let it fall, and gingerly removed her earrings, much to her ailing lobes' protest. Then she rummaged through the sheets on her bed to find where she'd stowed the shawl. She put it on and looked in the mirror.

Now she looked less like a piece of meat. More modest. Still, the makeup worked torturous wonders to make her look more comely. Alas, she did not want anyone in the palace to find her comely, least of all the man with whom she was about to meet, so it was with the utmost apprehension that she left her room with Navid and Remus.

There were quarters for the ambassadors with a mutual commons linking each chamber. There was a courtyard, rimmed with flowering hedges and a half-built fountain, bronze tube insides bared as two workers tinkered with it.

When reaching the portico of this place, peering in with fear at the sundrenched courtyard, she halted, jaw trembling as she managed a prayer. A sincere one for the first time in a number of days.

Dear God, I cannot do this.

She looked at her guards. "Must I go? Would it be wrong not to?"

"There is no one for you to fear in the palace," Navid said to her.

"If you believe in the words of your prophets," said Remus.

Kefira's mind reeled, and she stood woodenly at their peculiar reassurances. "Very well, then," she replied, before she found herself stepping into the courtyard.

There were stone benches throughout the circumference of the place. Upon one of them reclined Shaza'eil, fanned by a manservant with harried eyes. Four guards stood stolidly behind him – two of them were Persian she knew, but the other pair was armored differently, with pointed helms and square faces and black corkscrew hair; Babylonians, she knew instinctively. Other than that party, the courtyard was devoid of people.

Shaza'eil noticed her, of course. And if Navid and Remus had not been behind her, the girl would have turned around and left then and there.

"There you are, Kefira," the dignitary said. She hated the sound of her name spoken by him. But unlike yesterday, his voice was quite devoid of malevolence. This caught her wholly off-guard. As did his next words: "Come, sit down."

She was glad of the brownness of her skin, as it hid reddening well. Face hot, she sat stiffly on a bench crossways from him, a safe span away, she figured. She felt the air behind her bolster, and knew that her guards were there, as well.

"You wanted to see me?" she asked shortly, glad to practice Tobias's statute of reticence, but happily ignored addressing Shaza'eil with any sort of appropriate title. This man was not worthy of a subservient *my lord*.

"Yes," Shaza'eil confirmed, voice languid, as though he were a lounging Egyptian house-cat. His expression was accordingly aloof, but did not hold the disdain of yesterday, rather a sort of interest.

And so it occurred to her how different she must have looked. Less red from the skin-treatment, and with the addition of makeup, certainly more like the females he was akin to seeing. Her stomach grew more unsettled, and she avoided eye-contact, fearing what she might see.

He finally spoke. "I believe we got off on the wrong foot yesterday, and for that I am ever regretful." His voice was filled with earnestness that Kefira guessed was wholly affected. "I beseech you now, for forgiveness, and a chance to explain my previous ill-temper."

Kefira finally looked at him, surprised – was this the same person who'd put his fingers on her throat just the day before? She masked her disbelief, evening her expression into indifference and replied, "Very well."

He tugged a corner of the scarlet fabric that cloaked his head. "Come here and sit – I do not want to have to shout over at you."

She hated it, as she did not disobey, and now the sole barrier between them was a tray of food held by a servant. She hated it, as her posture was as meek as a lamb's, hands folded and face avoidant. If only he might say something very stupid — that she could muster the rage and insolence of the previous day!

She was offered a dainty from the tray, but refused; her stomach would not hold it if she consented. "What do you want to tell me?" she asked, voice hardening.

"Well, I thought that we might both tell one another things," he said, eyes narrowing as though to measure her response.

"Very well," she replied absently; she found herself quite distracted by the fact that, he too, was wearing makeup. Lining his eyes was the same dark khol that accentuated her own. A newfound revulsion for Babylon rose within her, even as he spoke.

"Kefira, where were you born?"

"Uh," she said, recollecting herself. "A small village in Hyrcania, the north," she answered. "Where were you?" she did not ask out of interest.

"I was born in the city of Teima, twenty and nine years ago. How many years have you?"

"Ten and six." She did not look at him.

"Have you family?"

"No, they are dead."

"And that is why you are set to the streets?"

"Indeed it is."

He seemed to take her short replies with all the thoughtfulness they merited, now falling quiet briefly before speaking once more. Before Kefira thought the conversation could grow more contrived, he was saying, "A tragedy, your life seems. We, our stories, are quite opposite. Like the god and goddess Anu and Antu." He looked up at those who attended them, then. "Leave us," he ordered, waving a gilded hand.

Kefira straightened and faced the fountain, as she saw the guards move to line a nearby wall. Navid and Remus did not move, however. She looked at them. It seemed as though the ambassador might have something secret to say, though she could not imagine what; it may be that he just wanted her alone, that he might kill her with more ease. But before she could fully measure the risks, she found herself signaling her two guards away. Oh, but had she authority to direct them?

Whether she did or not, they moved away, faces taciturn.

Shaza'eil turned and faced her squarely. "Opposites, as I grew up with plenty, only ever touching the streets on a litter," he continued, to what arrogant point she did not know. "Opposites, because as soon as your life took a turn for the better in finding the Hardlā's egg, mine became acutely worse."

It was all Kefira could do not to state quite plainly that she did not care. "I'm sorry." She wasn't.

Shaza'eil looked at her appraisingly. "Do you know what I have spent my life training for?" he asked.

"I hardly think I would know," she replied.

He smiled patiently. "Well, I will have you know that my entire upbringing has been devoted to refining myself into the rider of the Hardlā."

Kefira felt as though something was about to be made sense of. She asked, "What do you mean?"

"Babylon knew of the Hardlā's egg for many years. It had been only a matter of time until it was found, as it had been those months ago, and so a designated rider was always needed in anticipation of claiming him.

"So I was trained in the tongue of Ugaritic and Hebrew, beyond my own native language, as well as how to hit a target a hundred cubits distant with a spear on dragonback, among other entailed skills. My lineage had been chosen by my King to undertake this task; my father and his father before me waited all their lives for such an occasion as I had this last year," he ruminated. "So, you must understand and excuse my previous anger."

Kefira clutched her elbows and did not respond for a moment.

And then, noncommittally, she nodded.

His expression brightened, angular eyes gleaming like onyx. His next words were of a different subject, and quite unforeseen. "Kefira, are you afraid of seeing the King?"

"I would be a fool not to be, I think," she answered, surprised.

"Indeed you would, and you would be all the wiser to worry."

Kefira blanched, dour. "Have you advice beyond worrying, my lord?" she recovered.

He smiled wryly. "Indeed – if you would have it, a warning."

She wondered if he intended to threaten her again, and subconsciously tautened her shawl, eyes moving to the men on the walls.

"King Cyrus, may the gods bestow upon him eternal life," began the man extravagantly, "has intentions for you, my dear girl. Intentions preordained before you even are to meet him."

Kefira did not understand, and resented his address. "Please – what do you mean?" she asked shortly.

"Think, Kefira, I'm sure you know."

"I might better know if you tell me."

The man tilted his head. "Consider your magnificent dowry."

And suddenly she felt as though she'd been struck.

That had never occurred to her. Yonatan.

She had nothing to bring to a union – nothing except for the allegiance of her dragon, who was worth more than any herd, any estate, any gold that any other dowry would be comprised of.

All the heat that remained in her body was banished by uprising fear, whence it just as quickly rebounded to her face. Her ankles crossed, hands folding into her lap.

"I take it now that you understand."

She did not believe him. He was trying to scare her.

"You do not favor the King's design?" he inquired.

Her voice was brittle. "Why do you tell me all of this?"

He looked off into the garden. "I thought, after a window to my past, you might appreciate one to your future."

"You mean to taunt me," she accused him. "Have you any proof of your words?"

The Babylonian's expression was veiled. "He has taken wives for less reason than to obtain the most powerful dragon in the world."

Her fists trembled, as a hundred thoughts rushed into her mind at once, a thousand worries. No, it could not be.

So she stood. Was she supposed to be bidden leave? She did not care. She turned her back to him and walked away.

Leather sandals on stone – he'd gotten up, too. Her spine tingled as suddenly she anticipated some sort of attack – but none came, even as she refused to look back. Her eyes went to Navid and Remus, who were already detaching from the wall and moving to flank her. Thankfully, they did not object to her abrupt and impudent adjourning of the meeting, but faithfully led her back to the women's quarters and her room.

She fell onto the bed, one of the eunuchs said something vague about Mahasti's dinner plans for her, and then they left to keep sentry outside.

Only when they had gone did she allow herself time to weep.

Chapter XV
The Night

When Kefira woke up, she was hastily stripped of her cocoon of lotion and myrrh, and then, as usual, shoved into the hot bath. They were so fervent this time, however, that she was not allowed to wash herself and had to submit to a degrading scrub at their thorough hands. Afterwards, she was subjected to more plucking and a face-massage, once Mahasti said, "My dear girl," not a term of endearment, "Your eyes are all over in wrinkles – were you crying last night?"

"No," Kefira defended, not looking at her, as an older woman did something with her shoulder, and other maids polished her skin, or combed her hair, or honed her nails, or dyed them, or a thousand other things at once. Mahasti shoved beads of pomegranate into her mouth. They tasted delicious, but their savor did not keep Kefira from complaining, "Please, why are you all going so hastily today?"

Mahasti put in her mouth salty curds of goats milk, and fumed, "The King, may he live forever," and she did not sound as though she wanted him to, "has decided to move the date of your appointment. You will see him tomorrow night."

"What?" Kefira choked, sitting bolt upright in horror. She spat out her food and cried, "No, no, why would he do that?"

"Lay back down and lower your voice," commanded the woman infuriatingly. "Touca is going to remove your stitches." And a woman put a glass to Kefira's lips.

She smelled alcohol, and refused it. "No." She wanted to feel the pain. It would give her an excuse to cry in front of these harpies.

Mahasti had to be lying. She was only making a false excuse to whip her into ladyship with more compliance – and Kefira gasped as twine began to slide from her flesh. She stopped breathing; she was asleep, she was in a dream, in a nightmare – she really had a week left until her appointment. The threads hissed like firebrands in her shoulder. No, no, no. The King had no reason, no reason whatsoever, to bring up the date. Pain numbed her mind, and hot tears cut through the ointment on her face.

Tomorrow. Tomorrow she was going to lose Yonatan, or else keep him and marry against her will. Searing pain, flashing through her soul and body as they revolted with the fear.

She wanted to see Yonatan.

"I want to see Yonatan," she said aloud, and knew she sounded like a mewling child. "When will you be done?"

"Not until late this evening. You are going to get an hour with him, and then we will resume."

Very well, she could see him, this relieved her a little, until the open prospect now permitted her to think of what she would do when she did join him. What could she tell him? *Goodbye, I may never see you again.* Or, *I'm going to get married, that we may keep each other.* Either way, his fury and grief could not be mitigated. He would steal her away, if he didn't do all he could to destroy the palace first.

She began to scribble out the possibilities in her mind – she wanted him to take her away.

Then they would go off into the wilderness, and never have to worry again. There would be no one to tell them what to do, to keep them apart, ever. No one to pull out her hair or paint her, or bind his wings. They would be free.

But free to do what? Forever they would have to hide from the law. They would be without allies. They would be as hopeless as Parudrauga. And maybe just as cowardly.

She reviled the thought.

If they would not run away, if that was not a good thing to do – what could be done? Mahasti's commands may be ignored for a while, but Kefira could not but be cowed by soldiers, and Yonatan by Kia. They were not in any position to rebel. But what was she to do? Lie down and let it all happen? That was out of the question. She could not face the King.

The King! The king of the most powerful empire in the world! The king who could kill her twice as easily as bless her. She could not stand in his presence. Her legs would fail her. She would fall on her face before him. She could not look at him, his eyes would foretell his intentions, intentions she did not even want to think about, because she could hardly change them. So how was she going to speak with him on behalf of her and Yonatan? And, if she could open her mouth to do more than gasp, how could words from the likes of her even change his mind?

Certainly he was going to take Yonatan, or else her and thence both – and she did not know which was worse. Dear God! Her life was collapsing!

"Stop crying, Kefira," Mahasti ordered her, but her voice had diminished in its hardness. Again she put the goblet to her lips. "Drink. It is for your own good."

Kefira looked at the glimmering liquid mournfully, remembering another time with a clay cup in a darker room, before submitting to her mercy. She was left to spend the better part of the day in a haze. Around her she could feel the handmaidens doing vague, probably beautifying, things – and only perceived the fierce anxieties that surrounded her like one would observe a thunderstorm from a cave. She knew they were there, but they were grey and far away, and so she regarded them only dimly.

Sleep came, she did not know exactly when, or even remember the act of falling asleep. When she woke, though, it was with a fright and a headache – was it already the next day? No, it was just the afternoon of the previous, she was to go see Yonatan, now. After they coated her with more makeup, of course.

So Navid and Remus took her to him.

He was in the same courtyard, alone, save for a few grey Zarek dragons stationed watchfully nearby. No, he was not alone, beside him, and half-obscured by his bulk was a comparatively small yellow shape.

Yonatan lifted his head, and eagerly got to his feet. With two steps his head was above her and he casually nudged away her guards. With a croon, he nuzzled her into his embrace as he lay back down again.

She rested her head against his breast, weary, and was as mute as he was. The scales on his face glimmered like jewels, glimmering as though he'd been rubbed in oil. Yellow shifted beside her, and she realized the odd shape was a husk. It was shed skin from his face and the better part of his neck. The rest of his body seemed loose and flaky. He was indeed in the middle of shedding his skin, and the new scales beneath were glossier than she ever thought was possible.

Kefira rubbed his nose, feeling the metal-like plates. He hummed. She wished to forget some of her sorrow in their mutual silence, and even managed to misremember herself a little, looking at his face. Still, it was a false peace, and tears welled up in her eyes, as she realized again that this was all going to be lost to her.

She caressed the lid above his eye, the diameter of which now exceeded the width of her shoulders. It was as orange as flaming gold, as glorious as a great gem, and in his pupil she saw her reflection.

The fire in his eyes was kindled warmly as she said, "I love you." He looked at the ground and began scratching with a claw. Lines, triangles, and lines, and after a few moments his work was finished.

He'd been getting lessons in writing from one of his guards, a grizzled Zarek lounging on a nearby parapet, named Farzan. And now, great words of proclamation looked up at her from the dirt. She could guess enough of cuneiform to see he'd responded to her in kind. A joy welled up within her, as she took in his words. His words. The words of her mute dragon.

He began to write again, but this time she could not guess as to its meaning. She looked between him and what he was writing, a little embarrassed. But before he could notice her inability to properly read it, her eyes were caught by Remus, standing a ways off, who'd been watching the large characters form on the ground.

He came forward a little ways, and Yonatan looked up with suspicion. Kefira glanced nervously at the man, who took a step back and said, "He asks you, 'When will they let us leave?'" And then the eunuch pursed his lips, as though discomfited.

"Oh – thank you," Kefira said with self-conscious brevity, as the man's gaze mingled upon Yonatan before he returned to the hedge with Navid. Was that pity in his eyes?

Kefira looked after him for a moment before returning her attention to Yonatan. Her hand was frozen on his foreleg. He looked down at her, so painfully naïve, as if to repeat the question. After a moment, she let out a breath. "I do not know," she said. Wearied, he lowered his head beside her and let out a deep sigh, ruffling the flowers a few paces beyond.

She brushed away the despondency and tried to make conversation. "Has the dragon Kia bothered you again?" He shook his head. "Have you been eating well?" And he gave her a vigorous nod, which gave her pleasure. "So you are not being treated poorly?" And he nodded again. Then he lowered his head once more, flicking out his tongue, eyes mournful to gaze at her, to reflect the question. *What about you?*

Terrible. But she couldn't tell him that. She set to petting his face again. "I do quite well."

A scent must have found his nose before it did hers, for he straightened to look up, and then she began to smell cooked meat. Servants carried a roasted something on a spit. He looked away, back to her.

"It is alright, you may eat," she assured him. "You will not bother me." She would have rather liked to taste some of the meat herself. It smelled as though basted in lime and garlic, and made her stomach growl. Perhaps she could take a sliver of the meat for herself before Yonatan ate it up.

She was reaching out to put a finger in the steaming roast – she'd never seen so much cooked meat in her life in one place, on this – was it an ox? Yonatan was watching her with pleasure, seemingly delighted to impart upon her some of his meal – when she noticed that the guards were moving.

Her hand froze, and she stared at Navid and Remus as they, for once with hesitancy, came forward. Her eyes were upon them with fear, disbelief. No, no, the hour was not done already – it could not be, could it? And as though answering her silent question, Navid nodded, a slight tilt of his beardless chin.

Give me time, she pleaded, forming the silent words with her mouth.

They did.

She stood, ox ignored, gaining Yonatan's attention even as horror began to crawl up her legs, a feeling of the surreal leavening her head. Blood rushed through her, chills. Yet she managed to keep her voice calm. "I need to go now," she heard herself say, slow and quiet. He crooned, but she knew he did not know the gravity of her words. "I will let you eat in peace." He seemed a little disappointed. His tongue flicked to the ox. *Were you going to have some?*

Kefira smiled a little, a bitter expression. She looked at him in silence for a moment, before moving her eyes to his dinner. "If it would make you feel better," she murmured. He nodded with an air of pleased indulgence.

The flesh of the beast was hot, but she did not feel it beneath her shaky fingers, as she raised a sliver of the meat to her lips. She was looking at Yonatan – no, she ought not look at him – she could already feel the tears coming on. How could she possibly say goodbye? She put the meat in her mouth, and began to chew for him, and her dragon looked pleased, even as she avoided his gaze.

Time was slipping away; she could not taste the meat. Her heart was pounding. Time was slipping away – Yonatan was slipping away. Already his eyes were turning to his meal.

Despairing, Kefira leaned on his muzzle, wrapping her arms about what girth she might. She didn't want to let go, ever. "I love you, Yonatan" she repeated.

He nuzzled into her, warm scales against her face. And she held on as though it was her final dying act, face growing pale. "You are a gift from God, Yonatan, one I am glad to have been blessed with. I've never had a greater friend or a closer brother," she said. "Thank you for watching over me, my love." He hummed, pleasurably, sadly, eyes closed.

"Enjoy – enjoy your dinner," she wished him. "Have a restful night." Joints stilted and hot-cold, she got up on the tips of her toes and kissed his brow, and then his eyelid. "I will see you again soon," she lied, the words trickling to almost silence as her throat constricted. "I love you."

And she walked away.

The eunuchs bordered her shoulders. Close support. Their boots hid the sound of her sniffling, as she with some success stifled her tears. Remus passed to her a kerchief, which she gratefully used to blot at her eyes.

She did not look behind her, and she did not swallow the meat, even as it turned to mud inside her mouth.

Her head was hurting. She didn't even notice they had reached her apartment until she was able to collapse on the bed. But the handmaidens returned soon after, and she was molded and painted and cleaned up further, until it was late, late in the night, and an exhausted Mahasti told her to get some sleep, as she would need it. The lamps were blown out and they left.

Alone, woefully, dreadfully alone, Kefira stared at the blanket over her face. In the darkness, her breathing inevitably quickened, and the tears came.

Yonatan. Did he know she'd just said goodbye to him forever? No, the fact that the buildings around her were still standing was proof of that. But he would know soon. He would know a few days from now, when she did not come back. He would know when he caught wind of her blood, searched for her, to find her body impaled upon a spike in the middle of the city, the proper execution of a thief. He would know.

She hated it more than anything, that she had lied to him. *I will see you again soon.* She most certainly would not.

The heat of misery flooded her face. But she couldn't allow herself to make a sound; any cries she uttered would leave through the window and be a testament of her cowardice to all who heard. So she held her breath to the point that she shook, keeping the imminent sobs at bay with teeth clenched over a knuckle. She took a slow, controlled gasp every minute.

What would have happened if she'd never walked into Lemuel's hut? What would've happened if she'd never picked up Yonatan's egg? Would she be where she'd always intended to be? To disappear in the coastal cities of the Mazandaran? Eating stolen bread and sleeping, without this pain, beneath a palm tree?

Oh, Adonai, she could not regret that now, of all times. Of course these things happened for some sort of reason, though she could not see it. At least she'd been able to share in his friendship for a time, however brief. But as she considered it, she knew that she was not satisfied. She was not satisfied with only that brief time. She could not go on the same. She could not go on happy, not any more. Almost, she thought that she'd rather have not come across his egg at all, than taste this Promised Land of his friendship, only to have it torn away. Dear God, what did You do? What did You do? Why are You doing this to me?

For such a time as this.

For such a time as what? Dismay roiled within her. She did not see how any of this was hopeful, or even what it could amount to, if anything. She was going to be tortured by the very presence of the King, and then lose her dragon. And that would be the end of their story, the end of what joy she'd had in life. Even if she wasn't killed for her thieving, her life would be reduced to only breathing and taking water without Yonatan. She would be alone again, with no one, with no love.

Unless.

What Shaza'eil said was true.

Her breath caught short. He could have been telling the truth. What if the King – did – intend to marry her?

It was unimaginable, unbelievable, unbearable. Yet it was possible. What better way could a man secure for himself a dragon that was not his? To be united with the person the dragon held dear as its rider. Her fingers clenched the fabric of her blankets, a mounting horror blossoming cruelly in her chest. That made sense now, the way she was being made up and cleaned. It was not only for the purpose of not repulsing the King.

Tomorrow was not their wedding night, was it?

The thought appalled her, and her eyes went dim. If Shaza'eil's words were true, she was as hopeless as one cast into the pits of Sheol. Her hands clenched her scalp, trembling. Standing, speaking, seeing the King were all impossible, horrifying feats. But – becoming one of his wives was absolutely unfathomable. Unthinkable. She could not have found will to give herself to a mercenary, much less a King.

And she had never known a man. She had never been educated on the subject, had never even given thought to it, never known that she would. So how could she tomorrow night? She would have to be merry with wine for him to get any sport beyond screams from her. Would he let her sleep? Could she sleep through it?

No, such dreadful thoughts could not be borne. She would have to inquire of Mahasti, and twist her arm if she did not deign to tell. She could not go into the night without knowing what she was getting into. Certainly the woman would agree that ignorance was not helpful in this case!

Once this resolution was made up in her mind, the tide of her thoughts was given over to woe. Her mind went over in merciless detail the possibilities of tomorrow's despairs and the misery of today's goodbye.

The girl hugged her knees in bed, open eyes staring into the darkness of the covers. She would not be alone, the next night. She held her breath, as tremors wracked her body. Her mouth wanted to burst forth with cries, and eyes with tears. But she successfully maintained her silence, even as her head pounded, floated, ached for air. Even as her mind screamed as loud as a sandstorm.

Kefira eventually fell asleep. It came unexpectedly – as she'd wanted to stay up as late as possible to stave off the waking that meant the next day. But eventually, as the moon climbed the sky, her mind slowed, slowed, hushed, and thoughts began to come milder, more distant. Softly, she let a breath escape her lips, softly. It was as though an angel was drawing her breath for her, before it gingerly enfolded her in the darkling wings of sleep.

The only thing she could remember from her dreams of the last night was the sound of wind-chimes. She thought of Rakhshan. She'd woken up earlier than usual, and the maids were not yet there, she looked up, and wearily mused as her exhausted lungs ached.

If she'd stayed with him, would she be safe?

Army and King and harm deterred by Yonatan, would she have been safe in Parudrauga? She certainly would not have her dragon taken from her, she would not have to be anyone's wife. Things would have been so much different. But she did not care to think of it; she would not have been able to manage staying after such betrayal, anyway, and neither would Yonatan have stood for it.

Yonatan. She peeled herself from the bed and her moisturizing wrappings, soft skin gleaming. To the window she went, and knelt to rest her chin on the sill. Her view was into a steaming courtyard surrounded by half-made buildings, the cloistered lounge of the harem. She had no way to look out and find in the distance where Yonatan lay.

Her door opened, and the maids were there, a little surprised to see her up. A few carried the tub of hot water, and the girl compliantly stood. She submitted to the bath, eyes nigh shut, until Mahasti cried, "Kefira, did you retch last night?"

Kefira straightened, blushed. That's right – she had. "I'm sorry," she stammered. "I was – I've been feeling – badly." And she winced as a few of the poor girls were ordered to clean it up. "I'm sorry," she repeated.

Mahasti knelt to her, and put a legion of cloves into her mouth. "Chew, chew, chew! My dear girl, it's natural to feel as you do before such a momentous occasion, and we're all doing our best to make sure you do not make a fool of yourself, but you need to help us as well!"

"I – I'm doing the best that I can," Kefira protested, wincing around the pungent sweetness of the cloves, and cringing as the maids invaded her with the sapo once more. "But – how am I – I don't even know what I'm going to do, what I'm supposed to do, or even exactly what is going on."

"Tonight, you are going to the King. Upon seeing you, he will decide what to do about you and your dragon, and if you are lucky, grace you by taking your own opinion into account."

This was certainly a better verdict than the doom the Babylonian heralded, but she needed to know if his theory was valid as well. Fearful of the answer, however, she could not bring herself to ask the woman. If his impression was a true possibility, then today may very well be her last day of freedom.

She was lathered in lotions, wiped down and smeared again, until she gleamed like one of Yonatan's scales. Her hair was combed to flawlessness and hot ceramics were set to put her hair to curls. Different fabrics were set against her eyes and skin to see which colors would best complement, and glimmering jewels sparkled in and out of view. Words were said about their work on her, her figure, and corrections that needed to be made.

"I think turquoise and teal, maybe with a few orange highlights would be best."

"No, those are too many cool colors, they convey unfriendliness, and the gods know that she needs no more of that."

"Warm colors, an inciting gold and red-mauve like her dragon, would be more appropriate and most inviting."

"I still see her bones – look at those ribs, those hips, so angular; oh, how I wish you hadn't thrown up your dinner!"

"Her cheek bones are nice, but I wish she had a proper year to wait – those melancholy little breasts!"

Kefira hugged herself indignantly.

"Is your breath better? Oh, yes, I can smell the spice from here. Have some water."

"Don't you think we ought to use smoky topaz and darker colored clothes? Her skin might appear paler that way – the trick of contrast, I learned that from my matron."

"Where are the thrice-dratted priests? They should be here by now to make Ishtar's blessing."

Kefira was put off in particular by this last comment. "No, wait, why do I need a blessing? I don't like Ishtar, or Asherah, for that matter - "

"Well," Mahasti cut in. "It is customary that," she searched for the right words, for the first time appearing to have a difficulty finding them. "If the King should choose to obtain - "

"Yonatan by marrying me?" Kefira finished bitterly. And her blood began to heat. "And so I should be blessed with fertility by the Divine *Harlots*?"

"And neither should you have a problem with it, you irreverent girl," Mahasti retorted with finality. "By hapless chance you have been bestowed the possibility of a great blessing - "

"I – I do not want it, though! I cannot, and would not for all the blessing in the world, if not to save – to keep Yonatan." Conversation elsewhere stopped, and Mahasti's face blurred as Kefira's eyes grew hot. "I am so afraid."

Silence.

"What if he gives me the choice of keeping myself and losing Yonatan, or giving myself and keeping him?" her breath caught, and she continued woefully, "What if I choose to lose him?" She cried, "I'd sooner be killed for the thief that I am than betray him in such a way!"

No one spoke for a long time. There was a scrubbing-sound on the ground next to the bed, but that died away too. Then, Mahasti said, "Forget the priests. Roksana, send word for the Levite."

Kefira was dressed by gentler hands. It took what felt like years for them to decide on the fabrics, the colors, the jewelry, but they finally agreed.

A dress of lavender, deep blue caftan, with a sash tied about of orange and white, that was to be her trappings. There were great turquoise gemstones set in gold for her ears, with a necklace and golden bangles to match. Mahasti stated that she had once had grand intentions for her hair, but instead had it straightened, to simply fall down her back like a black sheet, and cascade from her shoulders like the mane of a mare. And then, to Kefira's surprise, there was also her shawl, freshly washed, to drape over her head. "It seems to be an item of comfort for you, so by all means have it – I pray that it will keep you from fainting." Then she admitted, "It is a rather fine piece of fabric. I do not know how you ever came by it."

Kefira did not shed any light upon the subject. She was half-way through being dressed, and much distracted by the raiment and ornaments with which she was being adorned. She was in a new pair of underclothes that were thin and smooth, the handmaidens fawning over it by the name of silk. Kefira was not so amused; yes, they were comfortable and very soft and elaborate, but their make was as provocative as they were beautiful, and she pondered if, judging by the outfits of some of the other women she'd seen, they were originally meant to be worn on the outside.

Mahasti inexplicably took her, before she was finished being clothed, and sat her upon the bed to look down on her. "Now, Kefira," she began, "It's merely a matter of possibility, you know, a possibility you might wed. No, do not cringe, you act as though we're talking about a barbarian-lord of old Assyria. Listen to me: you are a young woman, but you are not so young that your ignorance may be justified. No, listen. You are worrying as though we ask you to jump of a cliff, but no, this is a perfectly natural thing, and is truly quite exquisite, and you shall certainly laugh about it in the morning, *should* it even happen."

"What about the meantime, when I am not laughing?" Kefira interjected. "May I not have any wine beforehand?" she surprised herself by asking.

Mahasti gaped at her, horrified. "No, you may not be *drunk!* That would be most insulting, as though you were one going to be tossed to the lions!" She rubbed her temples, exasperated. "Kefira," she repeated again. "You must act your age. Your anxieties are understandable, but everyone marries at some point in their life. So clear your mind of your fretting and think: if your chief anxiety *does* come to pass, which it may not, but if it *does*, then nothing else will go wrong. Ever. You realize – if he does deign to bless you by taking you in marriage, you will be the safest and most powerful girl in the world. Even if you do not have his full devotion, as her majesty Queen Cassandanē, you would have his protection, as well as maintenance of the dragon that could have for supper any other beast in all the empires. Does that sound like a nightmare? I thought not – you must keep things in perspective. Just one night of discomfort and you will be able to keep your friend and never again suffer a disturbance from anyone else for the rest of your life. Just permit yourself to think."

The wave of words washed over Kefira, and she did think. And could almost agree. "But what am I to do in the meantime? What if he does marry me?" The words felt bitter on her tongue. "How – what do I do?"

Mahasti took her shoulders in her fine hands and steered her back to the maids. "Oh, you will know when the time comes," she replied with an unhelpful degree of flippancy. Then, quieter, she added in a darkening voice, "What it is *I* would be worrying about instead, if I were you, would not be if he *does* marry you, but what will happen if he does not."

She was fully dressed and made-up when Tobias and Hami were bidden enter. Self-consciously, she made an effort to render her clothes more modest as they went to a pair of couches therein to confer – the Levite and his assistant on one, and Kefira on the other. Many of the maids still surrounded her, still modifying, primping, painting her. Finishing touches still had to be made.

Kefira offered words to Tobias that she did not believe. "Good afternoon, my lord."

Tobias's head dipped. "You needn't feign happiness for my sake, Kefira. I know by your voice that you are anything but."

The girl smiled wanly. "You've more insight than those who can see." She paused as color was applied to her lips, and then frowned. "I just wish you'd have told me – of what might happen tonight."

His expression became somber. "Child," he said, voice as gentle as leaves. "I did not tell you, not to harm you, but because nothing could be done about it. Nothing but worry, and that is an arrow that can only splinter in the bow of its wielder."

Kefira nodded, hands shifting. Her shoulders tightened. "But what if Shaza'eil hadn't told me? What if I'd have found out too late?"

"I would not have sent you to your lot unprepared; it was not my intention to keep you in the dark." He paused. "You said that the ambassador told you?"

"Yes, he did."

"Hmmm…" his face scrunched ponderingly. "Has he tried to contact you since?"

"I do not think so." Half of her wish he had, and possibly given her more understanding of the situation.

Tobias nodded, and then shut his grey eyes as he shook his head. "Well," he said finally. "That sounds like him."

Kefira looked at him sidelong, wondering what he meant. And then she was told to look up, as the kohl that lined her eyes was adjusted. She tried not to blink, and in-between spasms she said, "What do you think of – how am I supposed to - " the words came out with diffidence. "If he does mean to – I mean," and then she began to whisper, "He, the King, is not a man of Jehovah, and I am Jewish – is that not impermissible?"

He was silent for a thoughtful while. Certainly he knew as she did that an Israeli's marriage to a pagan was not at all good. How then could she do it? Perhaps Mahasti would see this and let the King know, and the arrangement might be called off.

"In our history," Tobias began, "Such unions had contributed to our downfall. A man takes a pagan wife or the other way around, and so might be persuaded by apathy or seduction into their idol worship. King Solomon fell prey to this, taking wives of many nations, and he was not the last king or man to do so."

He seemed to pause, looking through the floor, and Kefira wondered with hope if that was his final verdict, but no, he continued.

"So it is a very valid and wise statute, not intermarrying. However," he said, cutting off the prospect of his prohibition, "Ruth the Moabite woman married Boaz the Israelite, and nothing but goodness came out of that – namely, nine generations later, the King David." And his recollection ended; he let out a sigh, sounding like the wind through a tired tree. "It is in God's hands," he nodded. "I trust your faithfulness."

Oh, if only he knew how unfaithful she felt. She made herself nod. "Please pray for me," she said.

And he did, they did together, and the only thing that kept tears from her eyes was the dread of having to redo her kohl. When they finished, Tobias offered her some less spiritual encouragement as well, with a small smile. "You needn't worry about his temperament, either; he just defeated the dissentious sheiks of the east. Like fleas they've been to him, until recently, since he's routed them, and so is in merry spirits."

Kefira thanked the Lord silently. "That is good to know," she sighed. For another few minutes as Kefira was attended to cosmetically, a small but exquisite lunch was served to them. Kefira had none of it, and only had enough water to wet her throat.

Eventually the dreaded time arrived for Tobias to leave; he stood, and held Kefira's hands in his own. "Kefira," he said, even as fear of his departure swelled within her. "Do not give up hope. Do not think that Jehovah has brought you all the way here only to leave you stranded and alone."

Kefira's hands began to tremble, and she could not directly reply. "Will this be the last time I see you?"

"Certainly not," he said with a small chuckle. "This will not be the last time we meet. It may appear otherwise, but you do not go to your death tonight." His voice grew tender. "If it were so, my daughter, I would do my all to prevent it."

Her head dipped, and she stared at the ground between her feet, as the name she'd not heard in years was invoked. She held his warm, wicker hands all the tighter, unable to speak.

"Remember what I taught you," he reminded her. "But most importantly, know that you are not alone. The Lord goes with you, and he knows your heart and your path."

And so he departed. Kefira wished she could have left with the old man and his servant. Instead she returned to the maids with a sigh, who were armed with perfumes and more lotion and more chastisements, "You must not sigh!" With half a will, she submitted herself to them once more.

And then someone else was at the door.

Kefira looked up from her fingernails as they were being dyed. One of the maids said, "I don't know that we are expecting anyone else."

Mahasti said, "It must be the priests; I guess no one told them they were not needed." She glared pointedly at Kefira before saying, "answer it, please."

Kefira's heart sank. What words could she use to refuse them, and still be polite? She watched mournfully as the girl answered the door. "Oh, Ambassador – you were not expected."

"Like the sun on a summer day, I wasn't," was a short dismissal.

"May I come in?"

"I - "

"You've not been notified of my appointment? I am advising the girl, too, as Ben-Seraiah had been. May I come in?"

"Well - " the girl looked back into the room for Mahasti's approval.

The woman stood up, arms folded crossly. "Yes, let him in, that I may tell him off."

Without another word, the maid opened the door wide, revealing the Babylonian. Kefira knew not whether to feel dismay or relief. Then her view of him was quickly blocked by Mahasti. She was smaller than the man, but twice as formidable. "What gives you permission to go past the eunuchs, lord?"

"What allowed the Levite through? And who is higher than the eunuchs?" he retorted.

Mahasti replied, "I can certainly arrange for you to be *equal* to them, if you so desire a promotion." Astonished by the words, Kefira pressed a knuckle to her teeth to keep from laughing.

"Your wit is sharp but your blade is not," he said tersely. "Let me through, please, or else I'll have nothing better to do than report your disrespect."

Kefira could almost feel how badly Mahasti wanted to clench her teeth and snarl, but saw that her lady-like strictures won the battle. "Of course, ambassador." She turned. "Kefira, back to the couch. Please, sit, ambassador."

Sullenly, Kefira found herself obedient. Two maids sat on both sides of her, thankfully, cosmetic sentinels, and took to rubbing her hands in oil; one was on the floor and rubbing her feet, as well. Tentatively, self-consciously, she looked across to Shaza'eil. "Hello? What did you want?"

"To give you a lesson in Hebrew," he said, resting his regally-coiffed head on a hand. "You know *some*, I assume?" he asked, in the very language, this time.

Kefira looked around, wondering if any of the maids

understood. "Um, not well," she replied haltingly in the same language – she hadn't used it in a long time. It was a language used only for reading holy scrolls, or speaking on holy days, back in her village.

"That is better than not at all," the Babylonian replied. Then he straightened and said, "The Head Mistress of Maids is a painted, big-headed mule with no sense of fashion." And he laughed.

Kefira balked, anticipating an explosion from Mahasti. But they were merely looked at quizzically, with a little concern by the servants; and the Head Mistress of Maids carried on, lips flat, as though she had no irritation beyond the verbal-combat undergone at the door. Kefira looked back at Shaza'eil, mouth agape.

He laughed again.

She was a little abashed by his rashness, and his skill with the words; he knew the language and spoke it much more eloquently than she did, when she should have been native to it. "What is it you wanted to tell me?" Kefira asked finally.

Shaza'eil inclined his head. "What is it that you want to tell *me?* I know of your anguish; the gods goaded me to help you, and here I am, an ear."

Kefira looked at him, sidling. If she were a cat, her ears would have gone back. "Well, my *anguish* is for the doom that you foretold, as you must already know. Your words have caused me many anxious nights." She looked down as the maids finished with her extremities. A second layer of dye was being added to her nails, the pungent scent of henna filling her nose.

"I am ever regretful," he said, voice as smooth and leisurely as a whetstone, "for having caused you so much grief, for having occupied your nights in such an insubstantial way." Kefira looked at him as he spoke, and saw with no small amount of despair that his eyes were following the maids' hands as they refined her. He continued, voice quite languid as he met her gaze once more, "but do know that I had your welfare in mind, and I have no intention of leaving you with only my words."

"What do you mean." She could not manage a quizzical lilt in her voice. She just kept his gaze locked with her eyes, uncaring of how intense an expression this might make on her face.

He smiled; not the baleful sort he'd riven when he was angry, but neither was it a very pleasant counterpart. "I can help you keep Yonatan."

Kefira balked, astonished. "But I thought you wanted him? Are you not desperate to have him?"

His expression was one of patience. "Of course; but that was before I had seen your devotion to him. It warms my heart."

Kefira had no care for his heart. "But how can I keep Yonatan?" she persisted. "What authority have you – how?"

He laughed again. "You shall need to be more eloquent than that stuttering if you're going to speak to the King," he said. "Did the Levite not give you lessons on oration?"

"He taught me as well as anyone. I'm just not very articulate to begin with." She was distracted mid-sentence as a second necklace was draped over her neck, adornment a sachet of fine-smelling spices. Before his eyes went to the low-hanging amulet, she quickly diverted his attention and said, "But I can hardly worry about speaking if I cannot even bear his presence," even as she wondered why the maids were dressing her like a prostitute.

He pursed his lips remorsefully, as his eyes mingled with hers. "It pains me to see that you must bear so much fear, so much anguish for a cause that is already nigh lost." He looked at the door. "And it pains me further that the help I desire to offer you will likely be held at arm's length and then shirked as the coils of a viper..."

Kefira leaned forward, "Wait – you haven't even told me what you mean to do, yet! I want to know."

Mahasti interrupted in common tongue, and their conversation halted. "You have two *hours* left, Kefira. Make this gratuitous lesson *quick*. We still have some finishing touches to make."

Kefira absorbed this information grimly, and felt fear as it began to boil within her. Her eyes went back to Shaza'eil. "Well?" she asked, back in Hebrew. "You must tell me!" She began to tremble.

The man grew more solemn. "Listen to what I say, and I will tell you what to do," he said.

"Yes, yes, I'm listening."

"Very good. Abscond from this place, under cover of lie or fleet foot, I do not care which; do it tonight, instead of going to the King. Go to the courtyard where Yonatan lies, and I will be there as well. Two Babylonian dragons will be nearby, those of my men, inconspicuous under the premise of going out to hunt. They are more than twice as large as any of the Immortal dragons, and can easily defend your escape with Yonatan."

"Escape?" Kefira almost whispered.

"It's a wonder to me that you did not do so before." He smiled. "But then, you did not have my protection. Yes, you will escape. And thence you will be safely escorted out of Persia's reaches, never to be trifled with again. And you will keep your beloved Yonatan."

Kefira could not believe what she was hearing. She stared, incredulous, and he looked as though he enjoyed her surprise. "Free?"

"Free of Persia, and all its tyranny," he replied. "Free to be with Yonatan to the end of your happy days."

"What would I owe you in return?"

"Nothing but willing heart and grateful smile."

Kefira did not quite believe him, and said nothing for a while, hands clenched beneath her chin. "I will think about it," she gave him. "You will have my answer if you see me in the courtyard."

"I will tell Yonatan he shall see you shortly, then." And Shaza'eil stood up.

Kefira was only restrained by standing as well by the hands of the girls. She looked up at him. "No, do not tell him – I do not want him to get up his hopes; we already said goodbye," she trailed off. But then she finished, "Please, do not tell him, my lord. He shall know when I meet him."

The Babylonian's kohl-lined eyes narrowed, but he nodded.

"Very good. It is in my prayers that you take this offered freedom, Kefira." And then he shifted into common language, and said, "This was a good lesson. May it serve you well when you meet the eternal King. Goodnight, my lady." And then he, too, was gone.

Kefira sighed, to the chagrin of the handmaidens, as they finished their work. Her eyes watched Mahasti, fearfully, as though the woman had heard every word of their conversation and was just waiting for the right moment to strike her disapproval and send a servant to report the plot to the King. But in her heart Kefira knew that she was the only one who heard. And as her body was polished and fabricated to be as beautiful as the palace itself, her mind was reduced to a battlefield.

Before she knew it, a mirror was thrust into her face. "Here, please look at yourself," Mahasti did not sound pleased, but Kefira herself saw nothing that should shame the woman. For she looked beautiful. She looked divine, hardly like herself.

"It is as good as we can do," Mahasti's expression was one of despair as she spoke, "in so *wretched* little time."

"Do you think I look incomplete?" Kefira asked.

"Only by more than eleven months," the woman lamented. "But it will have to do; *he* was the one to reset the date of your due, in any case."

"I do not look *bad*, do I?" Kefira questioned, growing fearful.

"No, no, he'll probably be surprised that you were ever a street-child in the first place. But by the standards of decent society..."

"I think you look absolutely lovely," a young maid encouraged defiantly, looking with a smile at Mahasti. "You are too hard on yourself, mistress."

"It is what makes me so good at what I do – *usually*," Mahasti surrendered with a wave. "Just – add the final perfumes. And another layer of lip-stain – her talking wore much away."

Kefira's body was by far readier than the rest of her, and nausea began to fill her, as things happened too quickly to grasp. Soon, Mahasti said, "You're as about as unconventional a potential-bride ever to shame a King, but he will have to deal with it." Then she gave her a quiet blessing: "Do our work proud, and see if you can keep your dragon while you are at it." And after one or two of the girls kissed Kefira on the forehead in parting, she was handed over to Remus and Navid. And she was shaking like a flower in sudden storm.

She stood outside the door with the eunuchs beside her. Waiting. She hardly looked at them, trying to fight the demand to retch. If she had eaten anything that day, she would have been sick despite it all.

"Kefira, let us get walking," Remus said, voice prodding but gentle.

She took a step, and through halting breaths she asked, quite stupidly, "Is it night already? Am I already going to see the King?"

"Yes," Navid's warm hand was guiding her by the elbow. "We go there now."

"Really?" the girl asked faintly; inside she was wholly abashed by the losing of her nerves. She was almost frozen still in the vice-grip of panic. And she realized she was looking down the hall, the opposite way her guards were trying to direct her. She stood, looking down the passage, orange in the dusk; a lone lamp-lighter was bringing fire to the torches. She heard the giggles of the harem in the distance.

The way to Yonatan. The way to freedom. Where the Babylonian's promises lay.

"Kefira?"

She straightened, looking at the eunuchs with something like fear.

One of them asked, "Kefira, are you coming?"

Kefira felt as though someone else with her voice had said "Yes," in reply. But before she knew it, her feet were following them. Away from Yonatan, and to the King of Persia.

Pillars, pillars, pillars, pillars. She didn't count them as she passed, but noticed every one of them just the same, taking them unthinkingly in down to intimate detail. Each one marked ten more steps closer to her doom. How she wished that those golden giants would relent in holding up the ceiling and drop it upon her.

Lining the aisle were what seemed like hundreds of motionless sentinels, in robes of many colors – red, blue, white – that hid gleams of polished leather scale-mail beneath; gauntlet-braced hands held gilded spears erect, shafts gleaming in torchlight. No sound but her footsteps, and those of the eunuchs. Only heard by her was the sound of her breathing, and her pounding, pounding heart.

There were eyes of dragons in the dark, Zareks, dragons of the Immortal guard – grey scales glittered with inlaid gems. And gold glittered ahead. But there was no one on the throne.

Navid and Remus did not lead her there. Instead, another path was taken in the gilded darkness. Torches were passed, and she wondered how many more lay between her and – but before she could continue the thought, her mind revolted and she made fists.

At many points throughout their seemingly endless walk, Kefira had halted, legs refusing to budge. It took some coaxing, but the men always got her walking again. When more guards and another great hall materialized before her, she stopped once more. "We are close, now, come on." Remus didn't need to say.

And so she moved. And they walked. There was a large door, ornaments of gold and silver girding it, along with enigmatic veils of silk like a forebodingly beautiful web. Surrounding, black shards of onyx glimmered in the darkness. This wall had deep blue eyes, staring, and the pupils narrowed as they seemed to calculate her. Kia. She shivered and tore her gaze away.

The only other place to look was back at the door. She knew who was behind it.

Many guards stood stolidly by, as though the great black Gandarewa wasn't sentry enough. They looked as though they were ready to open the doors – but were otherwise impassive.

Kefira didn't take another step. She grabbed one of the eunuchs, did not know which, by the hem of his sleeve, as she stared at the golden teeth before her. A calloused hand covered her own, and his dark eyes met hers. "Do not fear."

She held his arm tighter. "I cannot."

Gingerly, he lifted his hand from hers. "Then have more faith in your King."

With a silence that belied their size, the doors glided open, gold-plated cedar maw spreading wide.

No, no, it was too soon! She did not even have time to pray! Though bidden enter, she did not, could not move — until she felt Navid and Remus at her shoulders. They kept her on. On, into the vast, red-lit room, moving forward despite herself, eyes unable to rise from the floor.

The hands on her shoulders disappeared. And then the eunuchs disappeared. The doors closed. And she was alone. Almost.

There was a tall man. He wore no crown, but his robes were fine raiment of scarlet, white, and indigo, inlaid with gold like a tapestry. He was unlike anyone she'd ever beheld, she knew, upon just a second of seeing him. And when he spoke, she could not bear the sound. Soft, rough, roiling, was his voice. "Kefira." He said her name. "Daughter of the wandering remnants." Voice like a lion's whisper.

She exhaled, staring at his sandaled feet. And then she remembered. She knelt, bowed, no — fell onto her face — "My lord," she breathed. She shut her eyes, tight, already ashamed. She was in a cage with a lion. Who was she? Just a stuck lamb, marinated in myrrh, spiced in perfume, dressed in lavender. She was dead.

"You've been a fugitive for two months, yet you have been running, on your feet your whole life. Wings have only been a recent promotion. Is anything I have said incorrect?"

Her fingers were cold on the floor. "No," she said — and added quickly, "eternal King — may you live forever." She shut her eyes, knowing that her stupidity was as tangible a presence in the room as all its gold and finery. She was just a jester in his court. A soft, fragrant, and foolish blossom for him to crush in his hand.

There was a chuckle from above. "My vanity is appeased, girl. You may stand, if you can manage."

Her arms were clenched close, but she loosed her hands to slowly push herself from the floor. She felt the adrenaline tingle throughout her limbs, as her eyes looked for a window.

"And you may look at me, too. You are going to be here for a while yet, and you might as well recognize the one who is in contest for your dragon."

Upon those words, her vision became blurry, her face flooding with heat and her mind with panic. *Do not shed a tear.*

She didn't. And when her eyes cleared, she saw the King's face. She blinked.

The man did not look young, but neither did he look old – as though he had not been turned by the years, but caused the years to turn, himself. His hair and beard were black and curly, coiffed nicely, but still somewhat wild; like a great stallion only half-tamed. His face seemed to have been chiseled out of the ocher stone zargun. Beneath his dark eyebrows glimmered amber eyes, which she hardly dared to look at. Those dark pools would tell her future.

She blinked, looked away, even as his lion's eyes did not waver on her. His voice was lower. "Are you prepared to plead your cause to me? To tell me why you should keep the great beast you stole?"

Kefira could not put any words together.

"Speak the truth."

"I am not."

"And why is that."

"I did not have enough – " and she stopped. *Do not accuse the King!* she could almost hear Mahasti shouting at her. She amended, "One cannot be prepared enough for such a time as this. My king."

She heard him smile, and she knew that he saw every thought behind every word she said. There was a moment's merciful silence. And then, "Do you know who I am?"

Kefira froze, blood draining from her face. Like a fool, she was about to reply, *the King*, but knew he wanted another answer. She stared at his feet again, feeling another fit of weakness coming on. Swallowing, she shifted her weight; but the gap after his question was growing long – she must respond, whatever unsuitable answer she might throw together. Hating herself even as she did so, she answered, "You are Cyrus, the King of Persia, son of Cambyses – may you live forever." And she almost winced, anticipating a rebuke.

He tilted his head, in a way that painfully reminded her of Rakhshan. "Now, who are you?"

Breathing through her nose, knowing that she was giving the wrong answer again, she almost whispered, "Kefira, daughter of Kelub." What did he want her to say?

"To your title you did not add, 'rider of Yonatan.'" The King's response. "How do you expect to plead your cause when you already believe it lost?"

She was failing – utterly. Shaking her head softly, she took in a breath to stifle a whimper. "I – I do not know."

He began to pace, with slow, meaningful steps, looking at her as calculating as Kia had; dread began to fill her – but then he said, "Then I shall help you along."

More than a little surprised, she haltingly met his gaze. And waited for him to speak again.

"Why did you take the egg of the Hardlā?" His voice sounded more curious than accusatory.

Still, she replied cautiously. "I – I found a house, and inside – "

"Yes, I have been told the circumstances, the when and where, but I would now like to know why, with your own words."

"Well," she began again, slowly, "I saw it and did not really know what it was – it was a small egg, nothing like another dragon's, yet it was red," oh, that was redundant! Her face flushed; she could not disclose to him that for a while she'd only considered its market value, upon first finding it. She found another thread of words that suited his question better. The words were true, now. "Well, I feel like it came to me. Not the other way around – that is, me coming to it." She stopped, realizing how foolish her words sounded. "And – I felt that it was precious, even before I knew exactly who and what he was. I hoped – being – having been alone for a very long time," she said, voice softening, remembering the hatchling that had rolled from the egg, "I thought I could find a friend in him, I suppose."

His lips were touched with a rueful smile. "Then your ties are sentimental. That is the rope toughest to cut."

Suddenly fearful and ashamed, she looked away.

"What are your feelings for him, then?"

She bit her lip before replying. "My lord – he is my only family; my feelings for him surpass…" how could she put it to words? "I love him," she fumbled. "Like he is my own child, and my father, all in one."

The King stopped, looked at her. "That is a sort of affection unable to be severed by gold. Am I wrong?"

"Gold?" she asked, hardly grasping what he was saying.

"If I were to give you his weight in gold, an estate, security, capital. Would you exchange him for such fortune?"

A vision, a vast panorama of milk and honey, boundless wealth opened before her, horrifically like a Shaghāl's gaping jaws. Brows knitting, she recovered from the stunning offer. "No," she breathed. "I would not trade – anything for him."

The lines on the King's face slackened, and he began to walk again, surveying her. "There are thousands of men I can think of that would easily have made that trade. Your obstinacy, loyalty, it intrigues me."

She looked down at her feet, warily accepting the compliment.

But his next words brought her back to dread. "You realize the only option aside from a separation."

Her breath came in sharp, and the floor seemed to whirl about her. No.

No. This wasn't really happening now, Shaza'eil was not right. Not what she'd dreaded. It did not lie before her, already. It could not. Still, her breath did not slow.

Her eyes darted to a window. If she could jump out – could she make it to the ground and still run to the courtyard where he and Yonatan waited? Could she make it? Her chin trembled.

No, no, she was showing fear to the king – that was undesirable; a fool he might tolerate, but a cowardly fool was insufferable. She steadied herself again, eyes on his feet, but slowly they rose to meet his gaze.

An image of Yonatan's affectionate golden eyes flickered before her. It – would be for Yonatan, yes, it would. She felt her legs tremble. But she did not collapse. Even when the King said, "Disrobe for me."

The girl flashed hot and cold, feeling as though she were in a trance, a distant but unstoppable nightmare. Feebly, she tried to imagine Yonatan was there to protect her, as, slowly, she raised her hands, fingers working to unwrap the first garment. Yonatan, please stop me. God, help me. She had to do it. But her hands froze on the first tie.

She could not. She could not move.

Frozen.

Her mind reeled in slow motion as she grasped the realization: no, she could not do this. Her jaw clenched – it was for Yonatan, but no, he had to stop her. He would not want this. But would he want to lose her, instead?

She had to do it. Eyes tight shut, she conjured up the image of Rakhshan, and loosed her outer robe.

A hand was on her shoulder; a strong, weathered hand. She shivered. He was already behind her. In a subdued panic, she quickly tried to imagine that it was her mother, and she was eight again, and she was just going to give her a bath. She shut her eyes, breath hissing through her nostrils. That was what it was like, wasn't it? Couldn't it be just like that?

Cyrus's hand gently took the shucked sleeve of her garment. She stopped breathing. But – he spread the cloth back over her, rendering her decent once more.

Kefira exhaled, opened her eyes, quivering but not daring to move; she stared at the opposite wall as he walked back into her view. His expression was unreadable.

Without rising in volume, his voice hardened, and she was still trembling when he spoke. "I can take both you and your dragon, you know, and no one will protest."

His lion's gaze was steady on her, solemn and condemning. "A king may take any dragon that he finds suitable into his army," he said, "any woman that pleases him into his bed, and have anyone who he deems a criminal stoned, and no one can so much as bat an eye…"

Face flushing, Kefira's eyes fixed on the floor, fighting back tears. She was condemned. She was condemned.

Unable to contain herself any longer, she brought her hands up to cover her mouth, clenching a knuckle between her teeth. A sob escaped, and she had never hated herself more for it in her life. She shut her eyes, praying that he would kill her, then and there.

Then he was right before her - but he was raising her head with a hand beneath her chin. His golden face was lined with sympathy, and his soft voice finished, "but I am neither a tyrant nor a man ruled by his appetites."

She stared up at him, astonished by the change.

"You have no reason to fear, Kefira, daughter of Kelub."

Her eyes searched his face, overwhelmed. Was he tricking her? Was this a ploy? No, there was no malice in his eyes.

He continued. "Do not worry about what I've said, girl. My advisors always suggest I haze my guests before indulging them, so that they know who is in command. But I see you are a young woman of virtue: you do not intend to use Yonatan for material gain. Neither do you intend to seduce me that you might keep him; but you are willing to sacrifice yourself for your love."

There was a silence; Kefira could not even begin to find words to return with. She just stared, trying to decide if she was hearing him correctly.

As though to confirm what she doubted, he murmured, "Such virtue, such a willingness to sacrifice, that is uncommon." Pause. "If Israel had half as much character before its fall, it might yet be standing today. And then you would not have grown up as an orphan, a street-child, one begotten of a generation of sorrow."

His words, they were striking, but she did not understand why he spoke them.

"But then Yonatan would never have had the opportunity to come to you," he observed. Small smile returning, he said, "It is funny, how symbiotic you realize time and choices and fate are, when you ponder these things."

Kefira nodded, not understanding a word he said. And then he shook his head, as though to clear it. "But I have yet to decide your fate, child. I have seen more than I expected in you, and that is enough to make me less decisive in my verdict." He paused. "Tomorrow is the feast of Sizda Be-dar. We will have another meeting then, and discuss this further."

It was about to be over, she realized, a flood of incredulity sweeping through her. He was about to dismiss her.

He approached her again and rearranged her robe and her shawl, so that all was in order once more. All the while she gaped at him. "I hope I did not give you too terrible a fright, earlier," he said, and then pursed his lips. "For what nightmares you may have of angry kings in the future, I apologize."

Dumbstruck, she stared – and then nodded. "Th-thank you."

He smiled. "Now you may go. Get yourself some rest for tomorrow."

She was leaving unscathed. The girl woodenly turned around. And she noticed for the first time that there were guards inside the room, too, next to the doors. They made to open these, but she halted, and turned back around to face the King. "Sir – my lord," she stammered, "May I inquire – ?"

"Yes."

"If you can forgive my boldness in asking, well – I was wondering – if you knew that I was not ready for this – with only four, five days of preparation – why did you bring up the date?"

His amber eyes glinted. He said simply, "I did not want you to be ready."

Confused, Kefira thanked him again and left – leaving his chambers, and remembering to walk backwards this time, upon recollection of her manners. It seemed so abrupt, so surreal when the doors finally shut, and she was left standing with Navid and Remus outside, surrounding Immortals stationed stolidly the same as before, Kia still watching.

Then she turned and looked at her companions. They said nothing, but Remus gave her half-smile as if to say, *I told you so.*

There was a great stretch in-between there and her blessed, blessed bed, and she felt as though she could hardly move another step. But she did. When she reached her room, she surprised herself by embracing both the eunuchs before they took their posts at her door. It was unlikely that there was protocol for handling the throes of a desperately grateful girl who had just been to death and back; but they handled the unforeseen event well enough – awkwardly, shortly hugging her back before sending her to bed.

There was no one in her room. The maids hadn't expected her to return so soon. That was alright – now she could be very alone on the bed, and laugh and cry in peace as she thought of the King, and the next day, and what they held for her.

Chapter XVI
Bride Price

The heat was enough that it should have turned the sand to glass. Mār's mouth was dry, the roiling saliva that was his pride reduced to a sticky, tiresome morass in his panting maw. Even the wing he hung loosely out as shade for Rakhshan provided no reprieve – the sweltering waves radiated from the very ground.

Still, the oppressive sun did not sway the dancing girls, who celebrated the day of Sizda Be-dar as they spent every day – only this time with a thin excuse. Not as thin as their clothes, however, which were scanty – appropriate for the heat – and flowed behind them like rainbows as their shiny bangles glistened in the sunlight.

It was only the colors that Mār coveted, and the gleaming things that they wore, unlike many of the human cads who would slow their pace for other reasons as they walked by. Silly stags, they were, driven by their dim eyes. But it was what they liked, and to each their own. Besides, if everyone thought as he did, he'd have too much competition for what really mattered. His eyes locked and fixed on a girl's gleaming bracelet, as he tried to determine from his great distance whether or not it was real gold.

It was this he watched, instead of the horizon where Rakhshan stared. They were supposed to be the eastern watchmen of that hour, but on that day, everyone shirked at least a few of their duties. For example, while the dancing girls would have been more helpful sowing in the fields with the plain and less stupid women, they were not; but none of the men complained.

"I do not enjoy this gauty show of flesh, so Rakhshan, why do you not survey them insteat, and *I* will watch for the army," he offered, very courteously, his wet-wool dejected human.

"I'm fine, thank you," Rakhshan replied, voice not holding any of the gratitude his dragon thought it merited.

"Very well," Mār conceded, very patient with his rider. "Then we shall both sullenly stare into the wastes, if that is a pastime you favor more," he grumped. "When will someone replace us? I woult rather like to fint some shate."

"When the sun is a quarter before its apex our shift will be over."

Mār half-lidded his eyes and squinted at the sun and its trajectory. Disheartened, he sighed and lowered his head. "Why must we be on watch? Nothing is happening, nothing *has* happent. I'm beginning to think all our preparations have been in vain."

"Not for long, or so Tahmour thinks."

"Please elaborate – neetless enigma is something only little girls fint charming."

"When he went back to spy on the camp, remember, he saw many of them; half of the dragons left with - "

"The Israeli whelp, yes, now I recall." Mār had been trying to forget. "Speak of it no more."

But still Rakhshan continued, voice lowered to a hiss. "I still don't know why you wouldn't take me, or at least let me go – there is nothing for me here, not anymore."

"Fah!" Mār snorted. "I woult not let you follow them because such an enteavor is foolish ant impossible! Even on the back of a horse, you woult never catch up to them."

Rakhshan returned his gaze contemptuously. "That is why I beseeched use of *your* back! But you would not even do that for me."

Mār put back his ruff, the parapet's stone girders grinding beneath a talon. "That is no way to talk," he said, in an attempt to be placating. "Ant anyway, I am not a camel to take you wherever your heart drags you to go."

"When have I ever treated you like a camel?"

"Well, you have – many times, I'm sure - " the Azhi Dahaki broke off, and, upon finding his error, came to no conclusion at all.

"There you have it," Rakhshan topped him. He looked away again. "I just thought – that you would be more willing to help me –

and them."

Mār craned his neck to him, shifting his claws. "Rakhshan – I woult have taken you, of course! But – you're a fugitive of the law, ant it is not worth the risk."

Rakhshan's gaze fell upon him. "What if I had thought the same thing, six years ago?"

Mār blinked his jade eyes, and searched his rider's face. "What?"

"What if, as a boy, I had not thought it a worthy risk to save your egg?"

The scales on Mār's face itched. He looked away, comprehending. "Oh," he said.

When he was still in the shell, an egg left by its bearer to hatch alone, a Shaghāl had found the foxhole it had been buried in. Not too far away from this very city. Little Rakhshan, nothing more than a wandering urchin at the time, had been in the area, hunting for his supper in the wilderness, as no bread was spared for a bastard like him. He came across the place of Mār's egg unwittingly, seeing his egg only as it was dug out by the jackal-dragon. He'd almost run away – a boy like him would have been a quick and blissful meal for the beast, but instead he hid in brambles nearby, knocked his makeshift bow and watched.

The Shaghāl had intended to eat his egg, thusly eliminating a future predator and competition. But before it could crush it in its jaws, Rakhshan, by some miracle, put an arrow in its eye.

"Yes..." Mār trailed, feeling a bit guilty. "Well – I am sorry. Truly, I am. Ant I am sorry that you ant the Jewish – um, Kefira – dit not – well, but, there is nothing for it, now."

Rakhshan half-turned his face to look at him, the sad ghost of a smile on his face. He looked back to the wastes. "Do you think they are in Pasargadae?"

"If the King is as clever as his heralts attest, then they probably are." To what end, he would not give a goat's hoof, if not for Rakhshan. He glanced up. "Oh, look – the sun is a bit higher now."

Rakhshan did not look, and Mār snorted. "When we are done, only *I* will go to the meeting with the others concerning the attack-siege-thing everyone is so anxious about, do you hear? I want you to go ant do something besites moping. I can almost hear your spirit wither!"

Rakhshan waved a dismissive hand. "Mār, I am going to the meeting, just like everyone else, now stop worrying. You are like a great hen."

"Only if a hen were a formitable and hantsome beast," Mār snapped back. "But no. I will botily prevent you from going to the meeting. I will sit on you, if I must."

"Oh, no."

"Oh, yes! You will not go within a huntret paces of the barracks, I will make sure."

Rakhshan looked at him sidelong. "And what ought I do instead?"

Mār looked at the dancing girls. "Do not tell me you can't fint occupation in this city. Just enjoy yourself, for once."

Rakhshan did not reply, so he persisted, tail swishing as it dangled off the wall. "I know how happy you were with the Hartlā's girl; why don't you be happy with..." he glanced at a pleasing-looking woman below. "Look at her! Her hair is nice, long, and shiny, very shiny. Maybe she is a woman like Ravan."

Rakhshan hunched forward, shooting Mār an unhappy look, for some incomprehensible reason. "Kefira was the only woman *unlike* Ravan in this city."

"What does that even mean?" Mār said, shaking his head, tired of the riddles. "No," he began again. "Any man of mine is as high as the King – ant even the King's men have a goot many women, you know this. Console yourself then, why don't you? If you *do* ever see Kefira again, I am quite sure she woult well understant that your actions were only taken because of your pining away for *her*."

Rakhshan stood, and for the first time the dragon noticed how much he looked like a dam, pent up against a pressing tide of waters. He did not look pleased, despite his encouragement. "I will help in the fields," he said. "It's been a while since I've done some honest work."

Mār huffed. "Fine – take your day off to work, then, if you so desire."

"Tell me about the meeting, once you're done," Rakhshan said.

"That was not in the agreement," the dragon replied, watching as he descended the steps back to the streets. "Ant why are you going now?" he asked, looking up at the sky. "Our shift is not over!"

"Parameters of time for my day off were not in the agreement, either, therefore I shall deduce that I have all day at my disposal. You have fun, Mār."

Flowers Kefira had never seen before flourished in the garden. There were roses the colors of sunset, and little red, purple, green Hosn-e-Yusuf leaves growing underfoot. White and orange lilies pointed to the sky, violet-petalled spires beside them, pure white Roses of Sharon looming like bright trees of stars, and there were so many more. They were like radiant jewels amongst verdant green gold. The King's Fourfold Garden.

There were places in the park that quiet gardeners still worked, where black soil laid empty, waiting for more exotic seeds or other young plants imported from distant lands. Despite that, it still looked like the Garden of Eden, and she now fully grasped why the Persians were renowned for their horticulture. The peaceful sound of the wind in the tall cypress trees and the gurgling babble of the canal almost made her forget that this place was her prison today.

Understandably, the table arrangement of this gathering was not usual, Mahasti had critically pointed out before she arrived. The King and the royal family, she'd told Kefira, should rightly sit at a separate table from the invited guests – say, advisors, contemporaries, and her. But everyone was at one table, for this feast, and nervous Kefira was seated in-between Tobias and Mahasti. She had no objection whatsoever to their company, but could not get over the terrible feeling that she did not belong. Had she really been invited here? Or had she heard the King wrong, had Mahasti misinterpreted the order that morning?

Because, of course, next to Mahasti, was none other than the royal family. Or families, rather. And at the head of the table, the King. At his left, his second wife, regal Shokouh, and her young daughter Artystone, as well as another wife, lapis-eyed Amitis. To his right, the spectrally pale but beautiful Queen Cassandanē sat, and beside her were her four children – two daughters, Atossa and Leily, both younger than Kefira herself, the latter of which's chin hardly topped the table. Then there were the sons – lanky Bardiya with tousled hair, and the eldest child – who was actually a little older than her – named Cambyses after his grandfather. He looked like a more youthful replica of the King, only his eyes were dark brown pools, like his mother's. He wore a white tunic over green raiment, and Kefira conceded, despite her inhibitions, that he was rather handsome. There was young stubble on his face reminiscent of Rakhshan's, and she heard herself sigh.

Mahasti glared wrathfully at her before regaining her serene composure. "Remember your manners, Kefira," she said quietly through a smile.

Kefira hunched sheepishly, and then remembered not to slouch, and squared her shoulders.

To her left, aside from the royal family's half of the table, were the guests. Among them there were a great number of people she'd never seen before. Dignitaries, advisors, she saw – and among them she distinguished Siamak, sitting importantly beside another military leader, clad in red. Fearful that he would notice her, her surreptitious gaze swept across the faces – and, lo and behold, she saw Shaza'eil.

What was he doing here? She saw no other ambassadors!

He met her gaze, and she jerked her eyes from his with a gasp – this sound causing another silent rebuke to shoot from Mahasti's eyes.

Nervously, she tried to make eye-contact with Tobias – remembered that was not possible – and then prayed silently that the feast would begin soon.

The last of the rich people arrived with fervent apologies, finally, and the King stood to speak, words concerning his pleasure that they all could spend this beautiful Sizda Be-dar together coming forth; then words heralding the impending delicacies of the feast, that white-robed servants now swooped in to bring. Then he sat, having fulfilled his role as a host. Kefira couldn't believe how different he sounded, shouting jovially to a multitude in the afternoon, compared to last night's quiet, somber conversation.

Another person, grey-bearded, clad in a white and black robe and a turban, took his place in speaking. The orator he was, with the appearance of some sort of priest; he began to speak about Sizda Be-dar. The tale he narrated, Kefira figured, could only be meant for the entertainment the King's young daughters – it was pagan lore that she did not pay much attention to, distracted as she was by her acute discomfort. Her mind attended a bowl of pistachios set before her, rather than the story that was unfolding.

Sizda Be-dar, the thirteenth day of the first month Frawardin, commemorated the day the Demon of Draught was smote. Smote by the Angel of Goodness, who was empowered by the purity and joy of the people of Persia, and the throwing away of bad thoughts, and a good many sacrifices to the gods. By these things seeds would be sown, and cracked, dry earth would vanish between abundant crops. Those loyal to Ahura Mazda would usher in a new year with pure hearts, to ensure the prevailing of the Angel and the year's harvest, against the great demon Angra Mainyu.

Kefira thought this was all nonsense, and could tell by Tobias's quiet abidance that he did too; but she was too anxious to express any of the resignation she felt. She truly shouldn't have been at that feast, she should rightly be sitting in her room and eating curds. Why disgrace Mahasti and Tobias further by her presence here? Aside from that thorn rankling in her side, she once more became conscious of the fact that Shaza'eil was there. There, at the feast. He must be furious with her for not joining him. She tried not to look in his direction, all the time wondering why in all Creation had the King invited him.

After years of stewing in her worries, trays of the main course were set out on golden platters. Upon them there were what seemed like hundreds of bristling sticks, arranged in artful, absurd fashions, cubes of roasted meat and vegetables were impaled on every one. She took in a deep, appreciative smell – lamb kebabs. Like jewels on necklaces, shallots and garlic girded the lamb, and her stomach growled, and at the same time she thanked God that it was kosher.

Thankfully Mahasti stopped her before her she grabbed a skewer with one hand and dived into the pistachio bowl with the other. Before she could raise her hands above the table, the woman had caught her by the wrist. Kefira blushed, abashed, and waited for the servants to attend the royal family's plates. She couldn't watch without leaning past the woman, and so just listened to the gurgle as wine was poured. The cupbearer tasted the drink, and after patient minutes did not keel over, and so the feast began.

Her hand jangled in the bowl of nuts, but still this resulted in wrath from Mahasti. "Wait to be served." And she rolled her eyes to Tobias, as though she thought he had trained a performing monkey rather than a lady.

Kefira recoiled her hand, hoping, hoping no one else had noticed, and heard Tobias chuckle softly beside her. She let herself smile a bit and began to surreptitiously crack open the shells in her lap, as the servants descended upon the gathering.

Young Hami served both she and Tobias. He seemed to fill the elder's plate by memory, with a familiar number of dates and raisins, bread, greens, and a kebab, unskewering the meat onto his plate.

Then Hami helped her. Dubiously, she looked around. No one was serving themselves. "Do I just ask you what I…?"

His eyebrows raised and he nodded, as though addressing a small child — even though he was years younger than she. She pursed her lips. "Oh — may I have some pistachios, then?" But his hand was already bringing some to her plate, expression smug.

She smiled self-consciously. "Thank you — and, well, I do not know many of these names... How about — may I have a kebab?" Her eyes scanned the rest of the vast and colorful array. She'd never seen so much exotic food in her life, and never had her nose been witness to such decadence — scents of hot turmeric, sweet saffron, and nutmeg flitted in the air like benevolent spirits. "Um, that, please," she pointed to a braided, puffy loaf of bread — sheerval, it was — and then cringed at the reddish morass beside it. "What is that?"

"Jellied grape," Mahasti intoned, and then said quieter, "Enough meat and bread — have some fruit, or cabbage dolma, like Tobias."

Then, as soon as the words were said, the woman promptly proceeded to order her things for her, and Kefira blushed like a chastised child, as candied radishes and capers were spooned onto her plate. She couldn't help but notice that the actual children at the table were getting all that they wished — except for when young Bardiya received his fourth fried bamieh ball — his mother promptly making that his final as he licked honey from his fingers.

"May I eat, now?" Kefira asked Mahasti, returning her gaze to her own plate.

"Yes, please do — you do not want to appear dissatisfied with the fare."

Kefira popped the previously-snatched pistachios into her mouth, and brushed away the shells, anxiety giving way to the pleasure of the meal before her. Her eyes pored over it. This meal was probably worth more than all the food she'd ever eaten her entire life. Her mind went back to the humble jerky and flatbread she'd shared with Rakhshan but a week ago. Had only one week passed? It felt like a lifetime away.

Indeed, it was a lifetime away — she'd like to think that she was a completely different person now, less a fool, perhaps. Still, she glanced from time to time at his shawl, draped over her head in the corners of her vision.

Before her mind continued to think of so consternating a subject as Rakhshan, she picked up the kebab and – after a glance around to make sure she ate it right, she removed a piece of meat with her teeth. And with one bite, she knew that she'd never tasted anything so delicious. She shut her eyes, relishing its savor – and couldn't believe how many other such delicacies she had at her disposal. Whatever else could be said about the King, he certainly had a generous table.

The first throe of the feast and celebration was concluded with clinking glasses, and exultant cries of, "to health!" and, "to tossing the Thirteenth!" Kefira joined mid-chew in the besalamati draught – and listened with half an ear as the tongues loosened by wine began to prattle. Accompanying the rising voices, the King also bid the minstrels to play, and Kefira began to wonder, not for the first time, if she was really there.

Mahasti continually brought her back to reality, however, in-between conversation with the queens and other important women, turning on occasion to tell her to *chew with your mouth closed*, or *stop shoveling food into your face*, or *please sit erect – you're not invisible, you know*.

Kefira did all of these, looking down at her lap even as she saw Shokouh's tartly amused face.

"Pray, let her eat in peace, dear Mahasti," Kefira heard a soft and silvery voice – and was dually stunned. Once, at *anyone* calling Mahasti *dear*, and also because she'd just been indirectly addressed by a queen. Cassandanē's depthless eyes gazed at her from across the table.

It took Kefira a moment to realize that she was not being mocked. She gawked back, eyes wide, dipped her head, blushing vehemently all the while. And distracted herself with a bunch of grapes – praying that the feast would end soon. When would the meeting the King had promised occur? Soon, please, soon. She couldn't stand this terrible wait, no matter what would be decided when it was over.

Of course, nothing happened soon around here, save for the dreaded exception of her previous night with the King. During this feast, she was doomed to wait, and despite her desperate wishes, she could not go unnoticed, and many times she felt eyes on her – not all hostile, but none particularly friendly, either. Was there a plaque in front of her plate – somewhere she couldn't quite see – that identified her? Could they all see the words, "I am the dragon thief," carved before her? Did they all know?

She tentatively put her cup to her lips, silver goblet and purple wine flashing below her eyes. Her gaze darted from face to face. Everyone was conversing, or else just eating, but some had seemed to have moved their eyes away upon making contact with hers.

Cambyses did not look away, however. Like a startled doe, her gaze froze on him. He smiled a little. She blinked, face warming, and quickly occupied herself with a pistachio.

When her eyes ventured up again, another gaze drew her, like a moth to a flame. Her breath caught as she met Shaza'eil's flat, dark eyes. A small, unhappy smile curled his lips and he raised his cup. She saw him mouth the word, "Shalom."

Fear-struck, she tore her gaze away, and stared at Tobias. She wished he could lean forward just a bit – then she would be out of the Babylonian's line of sight. Instead, she just pressed her back against her chair, regaining her posture, and became shrouded by her two borders. If this was a social misdemeanor, Mahasti did not remark. She was currently addressing Artystone and Atossa concerning what color scheme would suit them best when they were old enough to dress up and wear cosmetics.

Listening to this conversation bored her, as she picked at her radishes. She was reminded of how much she hated radishes, and turned her head to find Hami. "Excuse me? May you hand me some bamieh?" With a knowing smile, he did, and she indulged in the delicious little pastries – thankfully Mahasti did not notice; she'd once been afraid that woman was omniscient. Hot dough and drizzled honey filled the next few minutes, until she was finished, the exultance past, and quickly grew skittish again.

Gathering her courage, she asked Tobias, "When will this be over? I am weary already."

The old man's hand paused over his plate and he said quietly under his beard, "I regret I must tell you – a feast is not a short ordeal."

Kefira's heart fell, but he spoke again. "But it may be cut short, to accommodate the meeting."

Her hands knit in her lap. "May you tell me a little about what will happen then?" she asked, and glanced at Mahasti. "I'm afraid I was not well-informed."

Tobias replied, "The feast will end, a good portion of these people will leave – to join other festivities and competitions of strength and skill about the fairgrounds. Some advisors, such as I, and a few other involved parties will stay, as will you of course, and so Yonatan's situation will be discussed."

Kefira was glad to be enlightened, but at the mention of her dragon's name, her heart fell. "I wish he was here."

"As do I – he would make a most pleasant companion – but worry not; he is in the company of other dragons in their own celebratory meal, not terribly lonely."

"Other dragons? Is Kia with him?"

"Yes, but do not fret – they've gone along quite nicely for a pair of bulls who sparred at their first meeting. Kia is an honorable beast, and respects Yonatan."

Kefira found that hard to believe. She wished that the people might eat with the dragons, as she had eaten with Yonatan and Rakhshan and Mār, all as a group. She could speak much easier, with more confidence and grace, somehow, with Yonatan beside her. She bit her lip. "Will it be like a council?" she wondered uncertainly, "The meeting, I mean – it won't be like a trial will it?"

Tobias smiled wryly. "That depends on whoever is speaking at the time. But the King is a fair man – everyone shall have a moment of his ear and you will also, and if someone does speak ill of you, I do not think he would allow it for long."

Kefira tried to find some semblance of solace in those words, and swirled her radishes around her dish, looking around the table for something else to eat. Upon her request, Hami gave her a divine, ruby-cluster pomegranate and more of the fluffy bread. She ate until she could not hold any more, thankful that Mahasti did not notice. The strict mouthfuls she'd received at the harem did not compare. But when she became conscious of the sum she'd consumed and the disdainful looks she was receiving, she took a drink of wine and stopped eating, eyes avoidant of all faces.

Soon the wine made her head too unclear for her liking, and she set that down, too. Hands folding anxiously in her lap, she looked around and saw that most of the table was empty, now – plates and platters bare of food, and conversation was winding down as scraps were tossed to the simpering mastiffs. How long had it been going? The sun had crested what felt like hours ago, and was slowly descending on the western hills.

Kefira's heartbeat quickened, and she wished then that she hadn't eaten so much. Now the feast was coming to a close, and from here everything would only happen all too quickly - the meeting was surely about to pounce upon her. Her throat was in a knot as white appeared over every shoulder, the servants clearing the dishes of everyone, save for the most avid and portly of those still cleaning up their plates. She watched Hami fearfully as he lined his arm with platters, a balancing act like so many arrows being strung on a bow.

The interrogation would begin soon.

She tried to remind herself of the King's lack of malevolence the previous night. She had nothing to worry about, truly.

Her eyes opened before she realized she'd shut them - and there was another dish before her. Surprised, she noted that everyone else had received this round cup as well, and her fingers touched the dish. Orange glistened inside, and strange, cold moisture stuck to the outside of the cup as well. It was the coldest thing she'd felt in her life, colder than winter frosts and the rains of the flashflood and the lakes of Hamûn.

Her hands withdrew without Mahasti's order. But the woman was holding her own cup of the stuff, smiling at her naïve little charge. "It is sharbat of oranges, Kefira, not of tigers – you may try it without losing a finger."

Kefira thought she heard the princesses giggling, and a queen's laugh, like the trickle of a brook. She blushed, but upon glancing up at the fair faces, she let herself spread a self-effacing smile when she concluded that they were indeed not mocking her.

Sharbat. She returned her attention to the anomaly, picking up the cup. Was it a drink? She smelled it, patted it with the spoon, and determined that it was not – not quite, anyway, but neither was it solid. It was in a class entirely of its own, and that was confirmed when she tasted it.

She'd never had anything so refreshing, so primly sweet, so startlingly tangy. She gazed at it, wide eyed. "How ever is it made?" she asked stupidly. "How do you turn the juice into this cold, creamy – stuff?"

"The artisans keep their methods under a lock and key," Queen Amitis said secretively, "All they tell is that the orange fruit and blossom it is made of are imported from the orchards of northeastern Margiana, where the trees grow like scrub acacias, and the ice is brought even further from the Pāmīr Mountains in the far north of Persia."

Kefira looked at the sharbat again. She was eating the stuff of lands she'd never see. She wondered how much of the rest of the feast had traveled such a distance to the table. To her distress, the remainder of the sharbat very soon thawed, but she was reassured that if she drank it then it would be just as well; it yet tasted like nectar. The peace, derived from its consumption, however, soon dissolved again, as the orator began to describe the oncoming festival, events that would take place on the fairgrounds – he spoke of contests in archery, sparring, as well as the ball and mallet game of chōwgān – a tournament on horseback and another variant for the riders of dragons. He rattled off many names she did not know – all contestants in varying arenas, apparently renowned for their skill, would be playing that evening. To punctuate the night would be a pair of Thu'bans and a flight of torch-bearing dragons in a display of whirling light – a show not to be missed. The list of events and attractions went on, but Kefira stopped listening, resolve having melted with the sharbat.

The meeting would start soon, and she no longer looked forward to it. These people were hearing where they would enjoy themselves next, and then they would leave, and then there would be the meeting. She wondered how many of the people around her would stay. A dozen? Half? Maybe only the children would leave and she would still have a giant congregation to pierce her with their words and eyes as they dashed whatever she might utter to the ground.

The time she dreaded did come. The King stood, everyone stood. There was a general exchange of valedictions – the people thanking and extolling him for such a lovely feast, the King blessing them and bidding they enjoy the rest of the Sizda Be-dar festival. The exchange was almost mute in her ears, as she supported herself with a steadying hand on the back of her chair. She watched as the table vanished at the hands of the servants, carried off in pieces along with chairs. The queens – apparently they were staying – were saying goodbye to their children and handing them to the care of handmaidens and guards, to go and enjoy the festival. Kefira watched as they and others took their leave, as mats were being spread onto the bare ground by servants.

The girl shifted from foot to foot, taking note of who was staying. She was thankful that Tobias was not leaving, and neither was Mahasti. She was speaking with Amitis, and the old man – to her chagrin – was in a conversation with Siamak, who did not so much as look at her, except once as though he were evaluating a firstborn calf.

She saw a few other men who looked rather like him – weathered faces, hair put-back, and red-garbed – military people; there were still others, sagely men like Tobias, other advisors, no doubt. She wondered how many of them wanted Yonatan. He would fill their hungry coin purses. She wondered how the King would manage them, if that indeed was even his intention.

Once the mats and cushions were laid out in a circle, everyone sat. Though stationed between Tobias and Mahasti, Kefira still felt alone and bare. She sat crisscross nervously, fiddling her hands until Mahasti corrected her with a murmur, as a general silence settled. *Ladies were supposed to sit with their legs closed, reclining on one hip, to preserve modesty.* Kefira flushed and obeyed.

The two dozen or so of them were all in a ring, now – everyone could see everyone else, and so Kefira glanced at the King. His dark hair was streaked silver in places, she could see now in the afternoon light, the regal gleam coupled with the golden crown on his head. He looked less imposing than he did in the lamp-lit chamber, but he still had an almost tangible air of power about him: the strength of his hands on his knees, the discernment in his brow, and those leonine eyes that she thanked God were not on her.

"I am sure you all know why we gather here this afternoon," he spoke. "And once this little ordeal has been resolved, you may yet return to the festivities." He smiled. "But until then, we shall discuss this matter of the great Hardlā found in Persia, by a young woman who is among us."

Silent mutters began to curdle in the following pause, and Kefira hotly managed to keep her eyes open. Was she supposed to say something?

The King held up a hand, and everyone was instantly quiet. "You have all been briefed on this matter: Kefira, daughter of Kelub, came across the egg in the satrapy of Hyrcania, in the keeping of

Tobias's late brother. Prudently," he continued to say, to her surprise, "she took it into her care when it hatched – prudently, I say, as, without her care, this priceless dragon would have hatched alone and condemned to the life of a Shaghāl."

It wouldn't have. She remembered Rakhshan's contract to take him in. To Shaza'eil, by Deioces. Did the King know? Any words he said further were silenced by the roar of blood in her ears when she met Shaza'eil's gaze. The steel in his eyes.

The King did not know.

She was brought back to the words at hand when the King finished, "and I would hear you all out on a method to secure the dragon, short of separating him and his rider."

Kefira released a breath, and looked at the King anew. His golden eyes met hers, and it felt as though her back were being washed with sharbat.

"If I may," Siamak readily intoned, after an affirming gesture from the King. Kefira's heart fell at the man's condemning tenor. "Short of separation, I do not see us ever securing the Hardlā, eternal King Cyrus. It is clear that his taming by the girl has not benefitted him. During our journey here, he indeed acted the part of a giant Shaghāl – he injured half a dathaba of men in his defiance, before we escorted him here; and upon arrival he would have done further damage if not for the interference of Kia, the hallowed dragon of Persia."

The blood drained from her face and she opened her mouth to object, but Mahasti silenced her with her eyes, and she conceded to draw her lips into a line.

"With all due respect, General Siamak, I must point out that the whole journey he was kept separate from Kefira – would not your Zarek have a similar fury if forced from you?" Tobias had spoken up; her heart leapt.

The words were mild, but were as hot coals to the other man. "Kamran has been disciplined and properly trained, and knows not to lash out on any men of the King, even when perceiving a slight," he countered brusquely. "Which is exactly my point. The Hardlā should be trained, properly, in the Asman Kāra. A girl cannot undertake such responsibility, let alone for a breed so exceptionally rare."

A churlish looking older man spoke in kind. "A woman has never been given a Gandarewa and Thu'ban for thus a reason – and how much more valuable is this beast? His very bloodline is gold."

It was all a matter of her gender? Indignant thoughts burst in her mind. And what was this talk of the Asman Kāra? Questions whirled within even as her body burned at their caustic words. She had never been discussed at such a scale; these words should have been hissed behind her back, not spouted off in front of her face. Her fingers were taut on the mat.

"She has never been educated," Siamak continued – he was on a warpath. "She knows nothing of riding, weaponry, draconic husbandry, or anything even a layman rider should."

"And of course she has never been in combat," said another. "She knows nothing of the blood and carnage of a battle on dragonback – in her first skirmish she would be ill."

More protests rose up, and Kefira recognized all the condemnation she'd expected – she'd expected it for weeks, now. And it made her feel as though she were melting.

Siamak honed the words of the other men and said, "In short, she is a wholly inadequate substitute for trained riders, that would have actually paid a substantial egg price for him, and have had skill to bring to a union. She proved her own ineptitude within the few fortnights she *did* have with the beast."

She felt Shaza'eil's fury should be mounting upon the words of Siamak, and did not look up. She wondered how many others would have paid – or killed – for Yonatan, and how they feel now that he is, for free, in the hands of a little girl. It felt like someone had set her back aflame. People were looking at her.

The King had been quietly watching the procession of protests until all fell to silence under his unchanging gaze. But it was not he who spoke next.

Cassandanē murmured softly, but with a voice as clear as the moon. "Siamak?" she began coolly, "is not Pantea Arteshbod a dragon rider? Is she not also your superior officer in the Immortals? She has a Zarek, herself. Do you challenge her legitimacy as a rider as well?"

Kefira was surprised by the defense. Her eyes went to the woman, but she was not looking at her.

Siamak seemed staggered by the rebuke. After taking a moment to find a polite way to retort, he said, "Forgive me if I have been offensive, my queen - you have a valid point, but the chief of the Immortals has had instilled since the age of seven the rigorous training and discipline required for her station, as all of the Imperial Guard have been. But – Kefira – she has a dragon considerably more valuable than our blessed Zareks, this value directly proportionate to her inadequacy. Besides that, Pantea's station is solidified by her marriage to General Aryasb, who is able to hold for her the value of her beast, whereas this girl has no solid capital or connections to stand upon in this way, without even an education upon which she can build. I must respectfully press that the Hardlā's current rider is unfit."

The King watched the discussion, but Kefira wished he would order one of his guards to run Siamak through. No such thing occurred, and Kefira's fingernail pierced through the threads of her mat, despondent in the man's words until Mahasti spoke.

"What is to say she cannot learn?"

The suggestion and its speaker surprised Kefira as much as it did everyone else. For once she looked up, and Mahasti's gem eyes clipped past her own.

An ancient sage replied. "She is – how old?"

"Six and ten years."

"That age is years past when a normal woman's schooling years end. You cannot be expected to learn the mathematics and dexterity and fighting skills and other attributes involved without the foundation that must be instilled as a child."

"Is no one else conscious of the fact that she is a thief?" A younger man spoke up. "She has no right to begin with to the dragon that she stole, she is a law-breaker."

"Am I not the law?" The King's voice was a sudden pillar amongst the whipping brambles. "Do I not decide the rights of a man, or woman? Now, reign yourselves in – I did not ask you for the problem, but for a solution."

Kefira shifted, rocked by the outburst. Did he intend to listen to them? Why didn't someone ask her what she thought about all this? She wanted to speak, to shout her outrage – though of course that would only be scoffed – just emotional drivel that further undermined her tenuous position.

"There is no way for her to manage the responsibility." Voices were quieter now, less audacious. "A woman is not fit to organize the breeding rights, the diet, let alone cohere to an Asmanaba. They must be separated, my King, may you live forever."

"I must respectfully concur with him, my eternal lord."

"Separation."

The words were tearing grains of sand as Kefira was engulfed in a maelstrom. Only Tobias and the voices of women stood up for her. *Persia is not like its neighbors – like Egypt, where you must wear a beard to have power, or like Greece where women are only valued if they are daughters of Zeus.* She only heard these protests from a distance, the Levite's words. But then she surfaced when new words cut her ears.

"I have a suggestion that would satisfy all parties."

It was Shaza'eil.

"Ambassador," Siamak almost spat out the title. "You can keep your forked tongue behind your fangs – I do not even know why you are here."

"If I may speak, general," the Babylonian pardoned himself, sitting straighter on his mat. "Some zealots of my people might consider Yomadan, by law of Nebuchadnezzar's Dominion over

Israel, property of Babylon – were I to be so audacious as to make such a claim – though I would never take such an insolent position on the matter. The Eternal King Cyrus had no qualms in inviting me to this momentous conference, and it is by his generosity that I am qualified to sit among you."

"What is your point?"

"The grounds I have just laid pertain in no way to my point – as I had just been validating myself to your indirect question as to my presence, here," he cracked a patient smile and continued to speak, as Kefira stared at him. He did not look at her, even as her eyes bored into him. Yomadan? What right over Israel? Did he think that because Babylon had the Jews as footstools that her dragon was then his?

His words began to pierce through her indignant thoughts, and his oiled-steel gaze finally met her own. Her mind pieced together the words, but they didn't make sense.

"...I suggest a marriage."

Something in Kefira snapped.

She didn't believe that the words were actually said until they were confirmed by Siamak's resulting outburst. "And I suppose you're the one to take up that mantle, too?" he bit out.

Shaza'eil leaned back and lifted his hands, as though he was quite indifferent. "It is merely a suggestion. But I believe it would placate all the current objections: the man might organize the dragon's affairs, be educated *for* the rider, and act as a surrogate rider in times of war. Also, with this joint ownership, her sentimental ties to the beast would not have to be severed."

A contemplative silence fell over the congregation, but Kefira screamed inside. No – no! It was last night all over again!

"But what would determine the husband?" someone asked with incredulity. "The depth of his pockets?"

"Like a regular Babylonian marriage market," another said with disgust.

Despite their words, though, no one appeared overly displeased by this suggestion. Fear rose in her throat like bile. Someone uttered a number, a large number – and someone else said a higher, until her mind's eye was blinded by mountains of golden ingots.

"Five hundred talents."

"I have six hundred!"

"I am willing to pay eight hundred."

They were naming bride prices.

Stunned, she looked at Mahasti, who appeared to be reaching her boiling point beneath her porcelain skin. Past her face, she saw another. Cambyses was looking at her, then at his taciturn father, mouth ajar, as though he were about to name a price.

"Two thousand talents of gold, and six estates south of the Tigris; a bride price, as she has no family, I humbly offer to the King."

Her eyes went from Cambyses to Shaza'eil. The speaker.

The Babylonian was offering a bride price for her.

"You are cunning, Babylonian," Siamak began cuttingly – even he had offered a handsome price for Kefira himself, only to be trumped by this. Her palms were wet, and she almost jumped when the King interrupted the dispute.

"Silence," he ordered, loud but controlled. "Here are my most honorable men, reduced to bickering like fishwives over a bolt of silk."

Kefira's hands cooled, and she breathed for the first time in an hour. Until:

"Truth be told, I concur with the Ambassador, Siamak."

Kefira saw the general flush red, and Shaza'eil's flat lips curled upward, even as her own heart sank.

"A marriage is the most viable option – it secures the dragon as well as his relationship with Kefira."

Her lungs filled with mud, breath thick and heavy. She was going to marry him. A man who'd wanted to kill her.

"But, I shall not be so covetous as to let gold determine the union," he said, and Kefira shut her eyes gratefully. When she opened them again, the King was looking at her, addressing her for the first time. "I will give you a week for suitors to make offers to you, and for you to decide with whom you will be united."

Sudden fear jumped and writhed in her like a living thing, as she stared at him. Seven days. All that would persecute her this week were looking at her.

She was the sole auction of a marriage market.

Mahasti was urging her with her eyes. She must say something. *Acknowledge him.*

She blinked slowly, painfully, in the silence, and a soft breeze teased her shawl, relieving for a moment the oppressive heat of the day. Incited by the wind, a chime tinkled somewhere. Her breath caught.

"My King," she stuttered. "I am betrothed."

"Next year at Sizdah Be-dar,
I hope to be my husband's star,
As a lady holding a baby!"

There were little girls playing in the fields, under a tree nearby, who did not relent in the recitation of that song. One of them smiled at Rakhshan; she was missing a tooth. Her friend was giving him cow-eyes as she wove grass strands together. Little girls.

He almost chuckled at their naivety, and continued working — helping an older man hook a pair of ornery oxen to an ard. After a bray and a shake of its horned head, the final beast let itself be harnessed to the yoke. Rakhshan let the man get the plough situated beneath them, and then slapped their flanks to get them moving.

The girls jumped up from their play, and followed the man with a basket of seeds, casting them into the groove the ard carved into the earth, and Rakhshan tried to ignore their demure looks as they passed him by.

He himself went back to his previous task — he'd been on the border of the peopled fields, looking out for predators, and more importantly, a military arm from the men camped on their doorstep, if the army intended to flank them during their sowing. He didn't think they would, but at least he was doing something.

Once again, he withdrew his bow and held it in his lap as he sat upon a hot boulder. The sun was low in the sky, now, and soon the workday would come to a close. He knocked the bow, fletching tickling his cheek as he leveled the arrow on a distant hare, hopping to its den for the evening. And then he lowered his arms. He could put a bolt through its eye, but he didn't want to eat it.

He hadn't eaten any meat in the last week. Certainly not because he did not like it, but rather for the painful reminder it bore. Eat a rabbit and be violating Kefira's statute of kashrut – eat a goat or a chicken according to kashrut and bear the painful reminder of Kefira. So he left meat behind completely. This new habit was one Mār found most dreadful.

As though summoned by his thoughts, a wind ruffled Rakhshan's hair and he turned to see the green streak coursing towards him from the city. He seemed undecided on his trajectory, but when his keen eyes singled him out, he banked and brought a gust of air with him.

"Rakhshan, there you are, come on," the dragon clipped upon landing, and then, "Oh," looked down at his left talon and snapped up the stamped rabbit.

"What's so urgent, all of the sudden? Did something happen at the meeting?" Rakhshan stood.

"You will see, you will see," Mār replied, hoping he did not appear too antsy. "Just get on." He helped his reluctant rider onto his back and tried to be patient as he looped on the rigging. When he was secure he leapt up without a wasted moment. Something had happened at the meeting – something grand was decided.

Of course, Mār resolved as the descending orange sun glared in his eyes, he would make sure that Rakhshan did not know until it was too late to protest.

By the look on Mahasti's face, that was the wrong thing to say.

"I see no betrothal ring!" Siamak was the first to scoff, incredulous.

Distantly, Kefira felt her fingers tug at the hem of her shawl. "This was given to me as a token, not a ring," she said to the grass.

"Kefira!" Mahasti balked. "Why did you not say so before?"

She had no answer, and felt a hotness begin to press against her face, her eyes.

"This is preposterous!"

"To whom?"

Kefira surprised herself by bringing her words higher than a whimper, to a point where her voice actually sounded confident. "To Rakhshan, rider of Mār."

A stunned silence filled the air until Shaza'eil burst, "The insurrectionist in Parudrauga?" His voice rose with his indignation. "The one who stole – that is a lie!"

She boldly met his eyes and wanted to retort, *and how do you know that?* But instead, "I see no grounds for your claim, that I am a liar, Ambassador, given you haven't been present in the past years of my life." She dared him to speak again. He couldn't deny a word without betraying his position in Media with Deioces.

Mahasti looked at Kefira sidelong, but reinforced her with, "Well, that does explain the richness of the fabric," she spoke of the shawl. "It must be the bride token. Never could she have paid for it herself."

Siamak had the visage of a slapped bear, exclaiming, "A scrap of cloth – a frivolity – exchanged for the greatest dragon in the empires?" He looked at the King. "Surely this cannot be consummated – for the Hardlā to belong to two brigands, no less! It cannot be done!"

The King was looking at her calculatingly. Kefira's stomach dropped. She knew that he saw her lie. As plain as a jackal among sheep.

He stood – and the disgruntled ring around him followed suit –

Kefira slowly, suddenly weary. "This discussion is over, friends," he announced, to many a man's dismay. All their uprising protests were squelched by a raised hand. The King was not jesting. "Enjoy yourselves now, at the fairgrounds, and be sure to watch my sons in the chōwgān tournament." He dismissed them all with a smile that did not look particularly happy – but it was Shaza'eil who's grin was venomous.

Kefira hugged herself tightly, waiting for Mahasti to hurry her back to the harem, even as she felt Tobias's bony hand rest on her shoulder. "I pray you know what you are doing, child," he murmured. "For I believe you may have just displeased some choice people."

Her face heated, even as Mahasti turned on her, and she saw a volley of impending scoldings waiting on her lips. But then she just as quickly rounded on Siamak, who was also approaching. And Kefira saw Shaza'eil's hard eyes behind him.

But then they all parted, as she heard the King's voice. "You may all leave, now." It wasn't a suggestion. "I am going to speak with Kefira alone."

Tobias patted her once, Mahasti cast her a concerned glance, and the rest left with varying degrees of concealed anger.

She was left standing in the garden, alone with the King again, save for the stolid guards.

He looked at her appraisingly, not saying anything, and she felt like a child. She pretended to study a purple flower at her feet until he spoke.

"Rakhshan, a mercenary?" he asked. "The rider of the feral Azhi Dahaki, deserter of the Asman Kāra?"

"That is he," she said, less certain, this time.

He looked at her with concern. "You understand that both the crimes of you and him are punishable by death?"

A knot in her throat began to strangle her. "Yes."

There was a long silence, but to her surprise, he exhaled a small chuckle, turning to look past the foliage to the aqueduct flowing by.

"If I did not know better, I would think you were bent on inciting my advisors to kill me – or you."

She grimaced, afraid to look at him. "Truly, I did not mean to be such an aggravation – ever."

"When did you become betrothed?"

She straightened at the sudden question. "Two months ago."

"That recently?"

"Yes," she said, a small frown forming on her face. "He somehow found me pleasing when we first met, and we had no families to turn away such an arrangement." She found she did not like saying these things.

"Did he know of Yonatan's egg, then?"

"Not until it hatched."

Kefira stood sheepishly as he considered her words, even as she felt his discernment lay a hand on her lie. "I must say – I was secretly hoping you would find my eldest appealing, a hope brought up short as soon as you enlightened me as to your current situation with the mercenary." He smiled dryly. "But I am a proponent for second chances. If you have made a prior arrangement," he continued, and his golden eyes pierced her, "I will see it honored."

Kefira almost fell to her knees, right then and there, her relief was so heavy. But the King added, "If he will."

Kefira's fingernail's tautened on her elbows. What? Rakhshan would, of course – certainly he would. He'd wanted it from the start. So he must now. She needed him to. And then her thoughts pulled up short – what was this? She actually desired it?

She looked at the grass. No, she did not.

The King's eyes lowered to her own. "The swiftest members of the Barid will be sent tonight to collect him from Parudrauga and bring him here, whence he will be further evaluated."

What did that mean? Kefira returned his gaze, wide-eyed. "Very well," she said, feeling as though she needed to respond.

He rubbed his bearded chin, looking at her like she was a heap of spilled mosaic tiles. "Go back to your quarters, now, and pray to the god you serve that you do not make further enemies here."

And it was over, like that. The King became girded by his sentinels once more, to whatever other celebratory throe he might choose, and Kefira turned back to the garden in the fading light, tottering on unsteady feet. Then she found herself almost running through the bushes, before, shrouded beneath a Rose of Sharon, she fell to her knees and vomited.

"We should have done it sooner," Tahmour explained to Rakhshan. "Much, much sooner. Given the fact that the army is left with only three Abraxas – I guess they hope that we wouldn't notice their absence – it is the perfect time to rout them."

It was early the next morning, and the sun hadn't yet risen, but Rakhshan could still see Mār bob his head with enthusiasm. Rakhshan gaped at his taller counterpart. "Rout them? The – the army, the one west of here?"

"Yes, my friend," Tahmour replied exhaustively, grinning like a fox. "*That* army. Without their fire-breather and the Immortal, their wings are headless! Even if our fighting men number half of theirs and haven't comparable equipment, our dragons are far superior in number and ability, and would make up for it."

Rakhshan shook his head, looking at the dark, still starry horizon. Minuscule smudges of orange campfires were all he could see of the camp. It didn't feel right, defending Parudrauga anymore.

"What does Arsham think?" he asked.

"Well you know, since his plan with the Hardlā fell," Tahmour explained, an air of bitterness in his tone, "He's not had his usual fervor, but he likes this idea, instead of just preparing for a siege, as will hit us when they get their dragons back."

"But is not Mehrnaz..." Rakhshan trailed off, glancing sideways at his dragon.

"Gestating?" Tahmour finished for him. Mār spread his bright ruff smugly.

"She told me that she could fight off *all three* Abraxas with clipped wings, even while carrying an egg," Sorushe insisted sincerely over his rider's shoulder.

"There you go," Tahmour said, bolstering a hand on Rakhshan's shoulder. "Her size coupled with Mār's spit and the priest's fire, and the Abraxas and men would not have a chance."

The men. The people on the horizon. Rakhshan looked at the city behind him. It slept, in the small hours of the morning, and he could see the smoke of old fires rising, and hear drunken sleep-sounds. Even if it was the place of his founding, this place wasn't worth taking another person's life over.

"Rakhshan?"

"When do we attack?" he asked lamely.

"Arsham and some of the footmen are determining our approach, but he said that it would start before dawn. Their asmanaba's reinforcements could come as soon as noonday, and we need their army to be scattered by then."

Rakhshan rubbed his chin, and looked back at the men on the horizon. "Are you sure we should be doing this?"

The insane question surprised him as much as it did Tahmour.

"What do you mean?" the man replied, and he saw the two dragons cock their heads. "The attack?"

Rakhshan arched his eyebrows wryly, and shook his head. "Never mind. When is Ravan bringing us breakfast?"

Tahmour gaped at him as though he had just upped and sprouted wings. And then he put a hand on Rakhshan's elbow. "Whoa, whoa, whoa – you aren't actually taking their side, are you?"

"No, not at all," he replied, taken aback; he retrieved his arm and stepped back a pace. "I – it just does not seem…"

"Right?" Tahmour asked. "What in all Creation are you talking about?"

Rakhshan was walking on tarpaulin. "If we send them off this time," he began slowly, "Will they not just come back with a bigger army?"

Mār looked as though he hadn't thought of that before, but Tahmour was not swayed. "No, they will see that we are not to be messed with, and leave us alone; we are just a rogue tribe to them, and it is no more than for the King's pride that they are here to take us back.

"While it would have worked better if we had the leverage of the Israeli beast to hold against them, they'll still realize, if slower, that we do not harm them in the long run, and they will treat us in kind. We just need to give them a gentle push away."

Sorushe nodded, head bobbing like a bird's.

"And we'd have Parudrauga," Rakhshan said, folding his arms.

"And we'd have Parudrauga."

Right now, Rakhshan was thinking that this place was nothing but a bladder of black bile. It was not populated by honest farmers and families and honorable men, but vagrants who would snuff out those decent sorts for a shekel of bronze. And there he was, ready to defend it.

"Do you hear that?" Sorushe tilted his head, his ruff twitching, as though to catch a sound.

"Duzahk!" Tahmour cursed, and ran to the edge of the wall, peering into the darkness.

There were shapes blotting out the light of the camp. Rakhshan's heart leapt to his throat, and he came alongside the other man. "What is it?" Of course it was a dragon – no it was more than one, he could see – each held a pair of fiery braziers.

"They're already coming!" Tahmour snapped, and whirled to hop onto his dragon's back. "I'm going to get Arsham and Mehrnaz, and the priests! You, be ready!"

Rakhshan felt his blood roar through his veins, as he darted to Mār. "Why are they trying to show themselves?"

"It must be a trap!" he hissed in reply. "Quick, let us go out to meet them!"

"You just said it was a trap!" Rakhshan jerked on his belts. "Curse it all – I do not even have the right arrows!"

"What do you want me to do about that? Let us stop them now, before they drop the braziers on the city!" And Mār launched off the parapet. "I dit not think we woult get to fight so early."

Rakhshan grimaced. It may be the last thing they ever did, if the Thu'ban had returned. He heard the horns in the city sound behind him – the people being alerted of the attack; though the dragons were still a long way off. There were horns being blown from their direction as well, quick bursts from what he perceived to be a winded sounder.

There were three dragons, he could now make out, each clutching lights in their front talons – and that gave him pause. If they intended to attack, the torches would not be in their foreclaws.

And soon Mār grew slower as well, and he risked turning his head to say, "Why, Rakhshan – those dragons are Siyutūrai, ant a Zarek. Only Barit, by their tack."

The approaching riders sounded their horns again, and Mār banked to one side of them, bloodlust turning into wary curiosity. The Zarek let out a grating call. Mār observed, stymied, "I do believe they want to speak with us, Rakhshan."

The Persian felt something turn inside him, as though his breath was leaving through the soles of his feet.

"You should land."

"What?"

"We should talk with them."

"What?"

"Mār, land!" Rakhshan said, exasperated.

His dragon tensed beneath him, and he felt his tail lash. "Have you gone mat?"

"Mār!"

With an irritated snarl, the dragon's wings curled and he began to descend. "It's you're hite," he growled, and let out a low cry upon landing, that the emissaries would meet them.

They were already spiraling to the ground, lights whirling about them; they were slow enough for Rakhshan to second guess himself a dozen times. Every muscle in the Azhi Dahaki's body was bowstring taut, wings half-mast and ready for flight. Rakhshan was twice as alert. "What do you want?" he called, when the dragons landed, and their riders rose wearily from their backs. The beasts were panting like racing hounds, and one of them had trouble standing. "What business do you have coming here with such haste?" He tried to sound challenging, assertive, but was really quite as drained as they looked to be.

The round-faced rider of the Zarek said, "I am Immortal Kavos, rider of Afsar, and we are on the King's business."

"Why do you not then sack the city and be done with it?" Mār asked cuttingly. "For I shoult like to see you try."

"You must be the Azhi Dahaki," the rider said. He did not look the least surprised – in fact, he sounded almost bored, past his exhaustion. He looked at Rakhshan and tugged his ample beard. "Then you are his rider, Rakhshan of Parudrauga?"

"Yes," Rakhshan replied slowly.

"Well, I suppose you would be, unless you were another brigand who killed him and somehow took his dragon," the man grumbled, as though to himself. He cleared his throat and shook his head. "Fancy you being the first one we meet – instead of having to dig for you in this slime hole."

One of the Barid tossed Kavos something, and he caught it. "Oh, yes. You have been summoned, by the King," he announced, without even looking up from the scroll. He said it as casually as though he were an instructor at an academy, telling a child that he was summoned to confer with the headmaster.

"What?" Rakhshan gasped, at the same time Mār did. The dragon put back his ruff and jerked to look back at his rider. "What does he mean?"

"Why – what..." Rakhshan shook his head, trying not to stutter. "What on earth for?" he asked the riders incredulously. Thoughts of execution loomed over his head, and he felt Mār come to the same coiled conclusion beneath him. Ready to run, or attack. He thought he heard wingbeats behind them. Sorushe and Mehrnaz and the others would be with them, soon.

Kavos looked at him sidelong and said, "To disentangle the matter of your marriage with your betrothed. Kefira, the rider of the Hardlā."

Rakhshan stared.

"What? What marriage? What betrotht? This is lunacy!" Mār exploded. He turned to one of the Siyudūrai. "You flew all this way just to give us this piece of matness? I woult have rather you attackt us!"

A thousand thoughts buzzed through Rakhshan's mind at once. It felt as though he had just stepped into a dream, a nightmare. Had he heard correctly?

There were voices behind him, now – a sharp blurt of surprise from Sorushe, and a cry from Arsham, "What do they want?" Tahmour, "Rakhshan, what are you doing with them?"

Mār hadn't attacked, thankfully – he no longer spoke at all. He was just staring at his rider, cat-eyes round, almost fearful. "Rakhshan?"

What could have possibly incited this message? Had someone cooked a bushel of alalega into dinner, and he was now experiencing a warped dream in result? No, the pain in his head was real. Marriage with your betrothed, Kefira. But something was sorely amiss. They were not betrothed.

Something was wrong.

Kefira – it had to have been Kefira – she'd lied about this, but why? What could possibly force her to such undesirable straights if he could not have done so with his own affections?

A bitter taste was in his mouth.

Say something – say something! He was a blind man crossing a river. What could he say? What was even happening?

He turned. Sorushe and Mehrnaz were closing in on them, and neither party of beasts knew if the other was going to be hostile, every scale was on end. He raised a hand. "It's alright," he called up to them, and they hesitantly slowed.

"Rakhshan!" someone exclaimed. "What is going on?"

He took in a breath, looked at Mār, and replied, "I am going to Pasargadae."

Chapter XVII
The Pact

The morning sun offered just enough heat for Yonatan to feel the shadows of his watchers on his back, as they circled the yellow sky above him. There were only enough of the gilded grey sentinels to cause him irritation, if he chose to deviate from their will – luckily for them, he currently had no real desire to do anything besides hunt. The gold-fingered men had become less stupid and more lenient with the strictures they held for him and his Love, Kefira; and since the festival in which there was much roasting of lamb, two days ago, they had allowed him to see fledging violet Love every day since – as though they really did have dominion to arrange such visits. He could see her any time he wished, and just as easily tear open a shiny-shingled half-made roof to do so – if he knew exactly where she lived. Heat flushed beneath his scales as he thought of their audacity to keep them apart in the first place. He did not understand why she had to sleep so far away, and why she was not happy even when she was with him, and why he was seen by bright-clothed men with curly black beards more often than her. They held her back, he knew, but they were nothing but upright-walking deer, without horns, and would not make the stupid rules or imagine them to be obeyed if they did not have greater beasts like Kia and Akhgar and Sepehr to enforce their stupid whims.

His tail had been lashing inadvertently, an action he only noticed when it snapped a scrubby tree; the plant's appearance like a split bone brought him back to the present and his hunger for a fresh kill. He glanced back up at the nuisance Zareks – well, Farzan at least could not be wholly classified as a nuisance – he'd taught him writing. But the rest were like flies – only considerably larger, and with teeth, and pretty gems embedded in their scales. Their shadows would probably frighten off what prey had actually dared to venture into a place so heavily-scented with dragon; he wished he could go outside of the valley, but he was only allowed to go so far as the hillocks surrounding – a border that he was pressing now.

He wanted his eagle-distance lilting guards to fly even higher; if one would come down to see him, he might write his will out for them, but that would be a great amount of work, so instead he stolidly harrumphed and pressed his nose to the ground. His tongue flicked, and between his talons he discovered a small trampled trail, thin churned ground dark beneath the crisscross of tree shadows; the hooves that made it were cloven. The dry, musty scent of old droppings discouraged him – nothing had been here recently, most likely. But if this was a regular passage, then it may lead to a watering hole, where certainly prey would be.

Yonatan loped onward, conscious of how his steps shook the brush. The budding leaves quavered on the ends of their stems, and the stalks and shoots of the new growth that he did not crush underfoot shook as though the earth itself were quaking. He was not stealthy. Nor could he even try to be, as the Zareks did not allow him to fly.

So if anything *did* roam these hills, he'd only be able to come upon it if it were lame or perhaps tied to a stake in the ground, he thought sullenly.

Beneath rumpled risings and fallings in the hills before him, he saw the trail recede, and a glimmering water shape appear. He slowed his steps, flicked his tongue, catching wind of a familiar, sweet smell. When on his long neck he could peer over the ridge that led to the pool, he recoiled and lowered his belly to brush the grass below. There was no animal there yet, but there would be soon enough, and perhaps it would be there long enough for him to fall upon it before it escaped. If it was perhaps quite decrepit and maybe caught its leg in a ditch.

He still resented the fact that he could not pursue prey on the wing – he could not be on them swiftly, and they would smell him much sooner than he could reach them. Just see how the Zareks would like circling over him for half the day until he finally *did* catch something in this stupid ground-stuck way.

There were a few trees that enclosed the ridge about him, sparse but adequate cover to dissuade a very dumb animal of his presence. He snapped off a large branch, that he might clutch it to his breast, and better camouflage himself, for what it was worth. As he did that, he caught wind of the scent again – the woody sweet soft smell that was not from the tree.

He'd smelled it elsewhere, on the bronze-skinned man with the tight-curled beard and glittering fingers, the one that made Kefira angry. Yonatan's eyes went to the pool, and everything in the world seemed to become more shiny and bright as the scent became stronger.

So he leapt off the outcropping he'd been hiding on, and dipped his foreclaws in the sparkling cold water. He flicked out his tongue – the smell was quite strong, though it was not from this. Before, it had emanated from a small root from the man. But he did not see any small roots, or the man.

There used to be emptiness behind his tail, but now he felt a presence, and stiffened, whirling about.

It was another dragon, unlike any he'd ever seen before. Her horns were not pale ivory, like the Persian dragons, but were like ebony thorns on her face and spine. Her color was like that of a yellow emerald, or an algaed log, with golden studs on her nose and in rings on her ears. She was large even curled up, and had been hidden beneath the ledge. She was not standing up or stiff-crouched, but rather lounged quite placidly over the earth, gazing at him. Her nose had touched his tail, and now she said, in a strange tongue, "*Allû, parpola rapsu.*"

He was alert, regarding her warily, but found that she was the originator of the smell. The scent striped her face and trailed down her neck. Made her grey eyes all the brighter.

He relaxed somewhat, and let out a cautious hiss of acknowledgement. He had not expected to find another dragon; did the Zareks see? Was this an overgrown wild beast? Hesitantly, he began to turn his face away, but she caught him, rubbing her head beneath his chin. "*Allû, mūru harāsu.*" He heard clicks as their horns clacked together.

Taken aback, he turned to face her – was this some sort of attack? He was used to simply being jumped upon with claws and teeth, but she was acting like a sleepy wildcat, only purring instead of growling. She looked intrigued by his movement, but did not get up, remaining ensconced in the fold of the ridge. Letting out a long breath, she looked up at the sky. With broken common, she said, "They not seeing. The birds."

Why would she tell him that? He began to wonder a good many things, until the smell washed over him again and diminished all his thoughts, and her brightening eyes darkened everything else around him. Dapples of tree-shade danced on her earth-colored scales. "*Mūru, parpola,*" she said again. "I am Sarpanitum."

It took him a moment to realize that she was indicating her name. For the sake of being civil, he would have offered his, but he guessed that she wouldn't know what he wrote.

She touched his nose with her tail. "Yomadan."

That word sounded disturbingly like what Kefira called him. His muzzle wrinkled, a question, but she did not offer explanation. By now he would have turned and left this creature who should not have been there, but the smell was like a collar of flowers around him. It made his heart quiver, his eyes slow. But now he saw something Love would not like in this mare's eyes. Reflexively, his nostrils sealed, an ability he'd acquired after getting water therein one too many times while drinking. Now the smell did not cloy at his face so much, but he took care not to flick out his tongue. He saw there was a red air in her pale eyes, sharp behind her dancing pupils.

It was then that he decided that he would leave. Leave this odd, thorny snake where she lay. But before he turned, he realized Sarpanitum had moved. The side of her neck was pressed against his, spikes turned away, and the spines along her back tickled his stomach. Her tail was swaying as though caught in a breeze beneath him, caressing, touching his legs and his tail and his legs.

He was too stunned to move. Was she going to claw into his stomach? Tear his throat? No, her voice was not a roar, but a crooning, *"Agana, salālu ramanī."* Her tail caressed his legs, and his hackles were overcome with throbbing.

Frightened, he leapt up back to the outcropping, or tried to – as he was gripped about his legs before he could get very far. Her talons were on his flanks, holding him with surprising strength, no longer friendly – and so he responded savagely. He whirled, twisted about, and landed his teeth on her muzzle with a snarl. She made no yelp or cry in response, to his chagrin, despite the blood that sprang up, but her strength failed and he managed to spring free. He scrabbled onto the ridge, hearing rock scratch away underfoot, dirt tumbling down, brush tangling away. Once he was back on flat earth, he whirled around, prepared for confrontation. The trees wavered, unhappy.

But there was no pursuit. He could still smell her, though.

Yonatan was hot all over, itching beneath the scales, and his legs ached from within, as though his very bones reviled him. What had just happened? Why had she attacked him? Why did she not attack him, now? She was not leaping over the rise at all, talons reaching – he did not even hear approaching feet.

But he dare not look over the edge to find her. He looked to the sky, instead. The crow-circling Zareks were not any closer. Had they thought he was just pretending to be a grasshopper, leaping about? Had he been startled by a rabbit, to recoil so? Thick grey beasts, probably thinking he himself was thick.

Hunger did not ail him any longer, not even the previous boredom of time spent without a hunt – he wanted to return to Kefira. They had a meeting that noon, yes? He would be fed, then, and he might try to explain what had occurred to her, that she might make sense of it.

He took another moment to peer where their encounter had

been, to make sure that she indeed was not creeping up on him. He saw nothing, and started loping in the opposite direction, towards the sparkling garden scaffold city in the bowl of the valley. He saw the dragons above tilt in course to accommodate his movement; and then he saw them begin to descend as he himself could not abstain any longer from taking to the air, even as his blood ran hot in his veins.

Kefira spent her morning in hot water and scrubbing hands and sapo, nose filled with the smell of lavender. Now that she was not being made to please the King, they were more lenient, letting her decide herself some detailing that would be done to her body. Upon being presented with a number of expensive spices – myrrh, cypress, orris root, saffron, calamus, and others, she'd dubiously requested lavender.

Then she was removed from the bath to be sugared again, after the lavender oils had saturated her hair and body. She was draped in a towel to be laid bare before them once more.

The smell of the oils soothed her, softened her mind to a sleep-like peace, but still she could not help but break it and think of what she'd done.

She had lied. She had lied to the King, and she had said that she was betrothed to marry Rakhshan. Rakhshan, the Persian who she'd met not even three months ago.

The thought had consumed her mind for the past few days, like a wolf overlooking a flock of sheep. It was temporarily ameliorated, of course, when she got to be with Yonatan, but that would not be a reprieve for long, as she would actually have to tell her dragon, soon. She could only imagine his response. Dismay, confusion, jealousy, anger – but she prayed he would not feel betrayed.

But certainly, he'd rather have her married, than not have her at all. Or he may just toss it all to the wind and take her away, himself.

She herself was tired of running.

Mahasti still had not let up about the revelation at the meeting. "Do you realize what an outrage it would have been if you'd have gone into the King as a woman betrothed to another – even if he is a nobody – political chaos! Mud on your already pitiful name, and shame to the King!"

"I never thought about it, before, I did not know – but I believe you've informed me sufficiently," Kefira replied.

The woman let out a sigh, fingers massaging her temples. "You are a shameless tempter of Fate, Kefira. First you come into the palace a thief, living upon mercy, and then you prove yourself deceitful, as well. You are fortunate not to have been hung on a stake a week ago!"

Kefira did not say anything in reply, and winced as her struggling hairs were yanked.

"I am truly surprised that your union is even being entertained as a *possibility*," she continued, and the flippant words pained Kefira. "I'm astonished that the offers, all that gold, were not taken, and *to the Pit* go your betrothed," Mahasti continued. "I have never witnessed such an upheaval of the norm in my entire life."

Neither had Kefira expected it. She hardly expected the arrangement to be upheld, even now. Even if the King was firm in his denial of the bride prices, and she would absurdly be allowed to marry Rakhshan, what if he had changed his mind?

What if he had changed his mind, and had found someone else? Or held a grudge against her for leaving? He could leave her be, to be ravaged by the court.

"Not twenty, a great sum in itself, not even two hundred, but two thousand talents of gold!" Mahasti marveled.

Kefira sulkily folded her arms. She was positive that most of the money Shaza'eil had was from the Temple's ransack, hoarded away by the Babylonians for just this purpose, if sneaking and conniving did not win them Yonatan – or Yomadan, or whatever he'd called him. She could only speculate as to the measure of Shaza'eil's rage, now that the gold did not work.

Her arms were separated so that the maids could work beneath them with the sugar and ointments. She reflected on how demeaning this was, instead of focusing on her other looming worries, and almost chuckled at the ridiculous way she was letting herself be treated. Even beyond the girls' less than conventional touching, she'd also had to get used to Navid or Remus barging in on occasion. They could only do this, of course, because they had been castrated, and therefore were generally disinterested in what would make a man of different situation blush. Despite her dubiousness of the arrangement, she had to laud them, as those blessed men never let their eyes stray from her face. Be it discipline or simply disinclination, that was a feat she'd never before thought possible.

There was a knock at the door.

Her mind went to Shaza'eil. Had he finally regained his head and his fake smile, that he might be here to bargain with her somehow?

No, the knock, she recognized, was Remus's. A girl opened the door and he came in. Kefira crossed her legs, trying to do so in the utmost nonchalance; this amused some of the girls, but their giggles quickly faded when the distress on the man's face became apparent. "Tobias Ben-Seraiah sends word."

"What does he want?" Mahasti asked. "We're not finished yet."

"He says something is wrong with Yonatan."

Kefira sat upright. "What?" she asked. "Is he sick?"

"No, my lady," Navid said. "But he is acting strange."

Kefira grabbed Mahasti's arm, imploring. "Please, this can wait – I must make sure he is alright!" Had Shaza'eil, upon realizing Yonatan would not be his, found a way to poison him?

After the girl waited painful moments for the woman's internal deliberation, Mahasti relented: "Fine. Get her dressed, swiftly now."

The rate at which they wrapped her and pulled up her hair was not sufficient for Kefira – but it wouldn't have been even if they went at the speed of Hermes. Five minutes later, she jumped out the door, and Navid and Remus and a put-out Mahasti kept pace.

Soon the hall dissolved into a veranda and courtyard, spilling sunlight, and Kefira saw the glimmer of Yonatan's hide. He wasn't inert on the ground in a stupor, she was thankful to see, but rather looked the opposite. He stood, legs straight like an offended cat, head wavering low to listen to Ben-Seraiah, who came up to the stature of his wrist. His tail lashed, wings half-furled. He was surrounded by a troop of four surly-looking Zareks, each a third his size but bristling with displeasure.

"What's the matter?" she cried. "Yonatan, are you alright?"

He'd been writing on the ground, but looked up at her now, and the relief on his face was visible. He crooned and stepped forward to embrace her, almost stepping on an Immortal in the process – the man had dismounted his dragon and had been inspecting Yonatan from the ground, even as his companions tried to decipher his manic scrawlings.

Kefira patted the dragon's face, staring into his large eye with concern. "Yoni, what is the matter?" She noticed the dilation in his pupil, an almond-shaped blackness surrounded in the gold of his iris. She felt his body was quivering, faintly. "What happened?"

He made an unhappy sound in his throat and began to write again. She was not the best at reading, but she could tell he hadn't advanced much in the way of constructing a coherent sentence, either. He'd scratched out his previous writing and began to scribble; Remus translated for her: "There was," and emphatically Yonatan underlined, "another dragon." He beckoned to grizzled Farzan, who looked expectant, as though he'd heard this before and was waiting for elaboration.

Yonatan let out an exasperated breath, and wrote, 'Face covered in horns and gold not Persian.'

"He may just have seen a shrine of Tiamat, then," one of the Immortals said. "The hills have many high places dedicated to gods. This one may just have been particularly scary." And there was a small smirk on his face that Kefira wanted to strike off with her hand.

Yonatan was twice as indignant at this affront, and snarled at the man; before it came to blows, another Immortal spoke up, a man with scars on his face. "No, let the dragon finish." His voice was insistent, but contained a sort of thoughtful distance that made Kefira want he himself to continue speaking.

Huffily, the Hardlā began to write again.

'She,' he underlined the first word, 'made like an attacker, and horns touched neck and belly.' He swiped away the previous words to make room in the dirt for another sentence. 'Smelled good and bad. Made as though to trip me, touched my legs with tail.'

The Immortal rubbed his chin as the last sentence was read aloud. Kefira saw the Zareks exchange knowing and disturbed glances. The man nodded, and said, "Judging by the flush of your skin," Kefira now noticed a redder quality in the flesh between Yonatan's scales, "and the swelling in your hindlegs," he paused, and looked at Kefira. "It seems he has encountered himself a Calypso."

"What? What is a Calypso?" Kefira asked, alarmed. Was it a malevolent sort of dragon?

Tobias's voice was grave. "A temptress in the Greek pantheon."

Kefira looked at Yonatan, who by now looked quite self-conscious, and had sat down. She did not know what they meant.

"Do not tell me those Greeks sent one of their three-headed abominations here to collect his blood!" an Immortal spat in disgust.

"No, the Greeks do not pierce their dragons – this one apparently had gold on her face," the scarred man replied. "Yonatan, describe to us what happened. Did she say anything to you?"

He carved the word Yomadan into the ground.

Before Kefira had time to be astonished, they were interrupted. Yonatan sprang to his feet, almost knocking her over. His neck craned upward, and he moved her beneath him with a talon. "What's the matter?" she cried.

Everyone followed his gaze. There was a dragon flying down from the mountains.

Kefira saw his lips curl. She heard his ribcage above her begin to reverberate with internal thunder.

"Is that her?"

"She must truly be a stupid beast to come flying here in pursuit!"

"Or else fiercely *in season*," one of the dragons added in bitter humor.

Three other dragons crested the rise behind it. "Yonatan," she asked, "were there other dragons with her?"

He shook his head slowly, eyes still fixed on the dragon, a snarl growing on his face.

"That is master Kavos," a rider said, "And flyers of Barid."

And it was then that she recognized the foremost dragon as Mār.

Kefira's insides became a void, even as she fell to the ground with the blow of a tempest, Yonatan taking to the air with a deafening roar. The sound echoed throughout the palace grounds, reverberating off of the golden rooftops like the clamor of a legion, and she heard curses spring up from the Immortals as the men scrambled up their exasperated dragons. With a weary sigh, Farzan leapt up after the Hardlā, the other Zareks with him.

Any cry of warning she could make to Yonatan was dead in her throat. She was still absorbing the shock.

They were here, already. And he did not even know why.

Mahasti pulled her to her feet. Both their hands were shaking.

"Who is it? Did he make to attack them?" Tobias asked, incredulous, unseeing face to the sky.

"He did!" Mahasti snapped indignantly, brushing the grit off of Kefira's palms. "It is the girl's betrothed, Ben-Seraiah. Kefira, whatever is Yonatan's relationship with your betrothed and his beast, that he should do this?"

Kefira could not respond, staring as Mār and the procession

around him pulled up short and veered to avoid a Zarek-covered Yonatan. Her dragon was bigger than the Azhi Dahaki and his escort combined, and he rippled like a snake in the sky after the green dragon, even as he was sparrowed by the immortals. She heard draconic voices of discord peal from the sky.

"He's not going to try and *kill* them, is he?" Mahasti gasped, and the question was answered when Yonatan suddenly relented. He slowed, as the distance grew between him and his swifter quarry. The Zareks squabbled with him, and herded him away, back to the ground and far out of sight. Mār and Rakhshan landed on the opposite side of Pasargadae.

They were here.

"Kefira, they have it under control. Back to your room – we must prepare." Mahasti held her by the elbow, looking doubtfully at the sky. "They will take care of Yonatan," she said. Woodenly, Kefira followed.

She found herself in her room again, naked save for a yoghurt and rosewater mask, and skin scrubbed in lemon and sugar. In any other situation she'd be licking herself, but her mouth was dry, eyes fixed upon the ceiling.

"Honestly, Kefira – you act just as nervous as though you were going to see anyone *besides* your betrothed." Mahasti watched a moment as the maids continued their treatment. She took in a solemn breath. "Did he – abuse you?"

"What?" Kefira exclaimed – she'd only been half-listening, but this question shook her back.

"It would explain your dragon's fury towards him, and your fear."

"No, no, he never beat me," Kefira assured her, still astonished at the very notion of it.

"Then grow up!" Mahasti replied, words jolting past her prior tenderness. "You should be dancing, girl! You needn't marry the Teiman, if all goes well!" Then she scoffed, "Sometimes you are so foolish, Kefira. Blind to your own interest even as you fight for it."

"W-what?" Kefira stammered – a heat of shame filling her face. Her own interest? She rubbed sugar between her fingers as she was rinsed off. It was for Yonatan that she did this – this was what was best for *him* – she was certain.

The girl spoke quietly. "When do we see each other?" She spoke of Rakhshan.

"Tomorrow, remember," Mahasti replied. "You must learn to keep your own schedule, Kefira. You won't long have me to be your calendar."

"What do you mean?"

"I am not your handmaiden." Mahasti smiled as though such a stupid notion amused her. "When you leave the Harem, you will no longer be in my jurisdiction."

"When I leave?"

"Of course. You will be united with someone who is not the King, therefore you will no longer exist in the Harem, where I preside."

Kefira looked dubiously at the ceiling. "Then where will I go?"

"To whatever quarters that the King deems suitable for you and your husband's station."

You and your husband. The words frightened her.

"Now, off with the mask," the woman ordered the girls, and Kefira's face was wiped clean.

It was impossible to sit still, what with the previous hour's momentum – every spare thought revolved either around her 'betrothed' or around Yonatan. He was being chastised again, no doubt – was Kia sent in to punish him? He still needed to be told why he could not attack those particular insurrectionists.

Kefira's heart skipped a beat. What if they were telling him right now? He could be informed as to her necessary union, and rage further. Would he feel betrayed by her? Would his anger against Rakhshan and Mār burn higher?

She should have told him immediately after, upon her meeting with him after Sizda Be-dar. Then he'd have time to understand why it needed to happen, he'd have time to simmer down and breathe. But given today's experience with the 'Calypso,' there would likely be no room for his blood to cool off about the arrival of her betrothed.

Once again, the degree of her regret reached new depths. "When, tomorrow?"

"You're going to have lunch together, and, if it is found that all lies well with him, reiterate your vows and sign the contract."

Lunch. Contract.

Kefira remembered the discolored spot on the rug beside the bed. Would she be able to eat? Probably not. How could she even face him again?

Her mind went back to their last night together. It was then, on that rainy night, that his deceit had been revealed to her. The way he'd touched her – she remembered it starkly – the fear in her, even after finding the shawl and the map. The map had been lost to her, but the shawl yet hung on her bedpost. Her mind delved further, and her lips throbbed at the memory of his forced kiss.

How could she ever look him in the face? A meeting, tomorrow? What good was a meeting when nothing could be said? Would she just hem and haw, and give the explanation of her lie, and hope he was willing to join in on her game? Hope that he still wanted to marry her?

What if he didn't?

He may have found someone he fancied more than she in Parudrauga. But why then would he come to Pasargadae? To gloat? No, even he would not do that. But perhaps Mār dragged him all this way for just that purpose. Mār would do that, and spit to the political ramifications for her and Yonatan.

She emerged from her thoughts with a plate of food in her face. "Eat," Mahasti said. "You are still skin and bones."

Goat cheese, and bread and oil, and fruit. She ate with half a will, as her digits were manicured once more. Her toenails were dyed in henna, and they waited to stain her fingers until she was finished eating. Then they positively saturated her hair with lavender perfume, that her tresses might absorb the aroma overnight.

"Will I be able to see Yonatan today?" Kefira needed to tell him.

"Probably not. I'd be surprised if they were finished reining him in, even now."

It had been hours since the incident.

"Where is Rakhshan?"

"No doubt speaking with chancellor Pashoutan and the others."

Was it now *he* who was being evaluated? Was he being tried for his hand in Parudrauga's insurrection, or were they only concerned with the marriage? Was his validity being affirmed or disputed? Were they interrogating him, trying to find a way to make his claim upon her illegitimate? Or was it going well, did they find him rightful and were they now agreeing to consummate him and his alleged betrothed?

Either way – she did not think that she would end the week very happy.

She was surprised to wake up.

The previous day had evaporated quickly. And now, here she lay on her bed, in the next morning's soft light.

Just as quickly as she woke up, she shut her eyes and waited for the maids to arrive. Her head throbbed, from the last night's anxiety as well as the smells of the beauty that embalmed her. Upon realizing that there was no getting back to sleep, she rubbed her eyes and face, still soft from yesterday's mask.

All the lines and spots on her complexion had disappeared under but a fortnight of treatment. Her whole body was soft, her own skin unlike any fabric she'd ever felt. Her hair was made to shine like a raven's wing. She was no longer emaciated, and now could be called pretty, even, and so the question came to her – would Rakhshan even recognize her?

But no; to him, she would still be the girl whose head just came up to his shoulder, the young Jewess with the arcing nose and the flushed lips pinched and ready to scold him. Past the fine clothing and earrings he would see her, certainly. Those things could not hide her from him, certainly.

But she would ask not to wear makeup today.

Remarkably, when they came with breakfast, the maids did not protest against her petition. Mahasti just looked at her wearily and made the appropriate amendments to the morning's treatments.

Steaming hot bath, cloves, a coating of honey on her lips that apparently was not a part of breakfast, lotions, oils, the milk of almonds in her hair, and the skin that had been rent of hair the previous day was soothed. When her body was finished, they moved onto her face. It was exfoliated and polished beyond Kefira's bearing; but it gleamed golden with almost the same luster of the mirror.

"Are you sure you would not like some eye makeup?" Mahasti asked her.

"I am very sure," Kefira replied. She just wanted to get this day over with, and to the sea with cosmetics. "And may I cover my head?" She added, "With the shawl?"

Mahasti pouted. "I suppose that would only be appropriate, as it is your bride token."

Kefira looked out the window. It had just reached midmorning. "Where am I going to meet him? Or will he come here?"

"There is a small conference room set aside for you."

Half of Kefira didn't want to leave her chamber. But it would be better than showing him what lavish luxury she'd been sleeping in since her desertion. Despite his deceit, she felt almost as though she'd betrayed him, by this.

Kefira was brought back to the present when she found her neck being rubbed in oils of lavender and orange; she was clothed before she realized it. She blushed. "May I choose what to wear?" The outfit offered too much of what little cleavage she had, and the girdle pulled her robes tight, making quite visible the curvature of her body. She could only guess as to what Rakhshan would say if he saw that this prim Israeli had turned to dress like an Assyrian courtesan.

Upon this request, half of the girls groaned, and Mahasti pressed her lips together.

"But don't you want to – impress him?" a young maid asked.

The comment wasn't intended to be a dart, Kefira knew, but still, it irked her. "I do not think so low of him as to believe he would feel at all gratified by my dressing in this way."

Mahasti waved the discussion away. "Fine, fine – dress her in the white one, then."

This one was just as beautiful, and thankfully, was considerably more modest. It was decorated with shiny pieces of shell and beads of turquoise, and would, she hoped, match just fine with the shawl. Or, should she wear the shawl? Would that be too forward? No, he'd never seen her without one, not that she could remember. Though it would still be awkward to wear the gift, that would be better than flaunting her shiny locks of hair. Hopefully. How shameful it would be to use any arts of allure against him, especially now; she couldn't imagine coming across as a temptress to him. For now it was possible that she could. For, if he was uncertain about going through with the union, it was not out of the realm of possibility to lure him into it.

But she pushed the thought away, instantly repulsed. Even if the idea was not wholly abominable to her, she was the last of all people to be able to accomplish such a mean.

She sighed, and then stopped quickly after a look from Mahasti. The woman inserted amethyst studs into her ears, and draped her neck with a band of turquoise and the purple stone. Then, without a word from Kefira, draped the shawl over her head, and situated each dark tress just so around her face.

"It is time to go, Kefira," the woman said, even as the Kefira herself recognized this fact, and swallowed.

Then the woman pointed a reproving finger at her. "Put away

your childish fear, now," she admonished. "Remember why you are doing this, and be strengthened." She cracked a wry smile, "It should not require too much of you. After all, there should not be anything overly difficult about breaking bread with your betrothed."

The room was small, and modestly furnished for a palatial chamber. The tiles were of fine mosaic and there was a cedar table covered in food, and soft cushions beside it; but aside from that, there was no other furniture. Kefira sat on one of these pillows, an anxious fire rancorous inside her. She was grateful that Navid and Remus were at her back, but even they could not stave off the revulsion of her nerves. Without them, she'd have climbed out the window by now.

Rakhshan. He would be there any minute. This unthinkable thought had her crushed inside an inescapable, rolling barrel.

Ever since she'd left her quarters to be brought here, she'd been trying to formulate some sort of greeting she might make – not overly welcoming, yet not repellently cold. What would be appropriate – *Hello, again – how are you?* Or offer a nod and maybe allow a small smile. Where do we begin? Where in all Creation do we begin? Would they greet each other like friends in the street? Or stare at the table until one of them broke the silence?

He was not there yet. Kefira stood, gladly forsaking the confines of the floor, and paced in front of the eunuchs. Hot chills went throughout her entire body. She could feel her lungs tauten; they could not get enough air. She went to the window, to emptily pore over the construction.

The breeze outside was cool, and the sun had not come over to face this side of the palace. She felt the building's blue shadow and it soothed her hot skin, the stone of the sill refreshing against her tense fingers. Maybe once he came in, she did not have to face him, and they might have a conversation this way, with her back safely to him. But the thought reminded her of how, in their last encounter – him, the window. Her teeth began to chatter

It was too soon for the door to open, but it did. She heard Navid and Remus straighten, and she felt stricken. The door shut. Footsteps, of soft leather shoes.

They halted.

Silence.

Kefira's eyes were stuck on a tree outside, fixed; he was behind her, wasn't he? She bit her lip — it still tasted residually sweet. Turn around, now. Don't be a coward. But she was frozen.

"Kefira?" That was Rakhshan's voice; soft, uncertain, but his.

He was really here.

Kefira folded her arms tight, hiding her hands as her fingernails bit into her palms. *Turn around, now.* She did, slowly.

She then saw the man, on the other side of the room, standing quietly. He was indeed Rakhshan. The ruddy olive tone of his face, his stubble, his disheveled, short ponytail of dark hair, this time unadorned by his usual linen scarf. Instead he wore fresh garments.

They silently regarded one another. The morose golden eyes met hers. Kefira looked away. "Hello," she managed, softly.

The quiet in the room was as thick as water, cold and unmoving. He shifted his weight, and crossed his arms, expression unreadable. He said, slowly, "You — look different."

Taken aback, Kefira smiled sadly. "Yes." Her blood was hot in her face; the only thing he may have recognized was the shawl she wore. He had not changed a bit, of course, save for his expression — it no longer held any mirth. It made her heart ache.

Kefira's eyes went down to her sandals. "Do you want to sit?"

Rakhshan had been eyeing the shawl upon her head, and appeared surprised by the offer, but they both took a spot on a cushion. Kefira was careful to sit in the ladylike position Mahasti had instructed her in. It took her mind, however briefly, off the one taking the seat across from her.

Silence enveloped them once more, as neither of them partook anything of the table before them. Kefira breathed painfully through her nose, and then heard Rakhshan clear his throat. She looked up at him, desperate for him to say something.

He did. "So – what happened, exactly, that you now come to this?" He looked at her, knuckles pressing against his temple.

Kefira lowered her head between her shoulders. "Where do I begin?"

"Why you left in the first - " Rakhshan began, but then waved a hand. "No, forget that. How did they take you here? Why hasn't Yonatan escaped with you yet?"

"We were tired – we could not find anything to eat during our wandering after the flood, and we were separated, and I was attacked by Shaghāls," Kefira explained – she felt like she was rambling, but the man's eyes held a concern past frustration. She continued to tell how she was rescued by dragons from the army, and how Siamak kept her separate from Yonatan all the way to Pasargadae, and then about her arrival there, and treatment after. "I was being prepared to go to the King," she admitted quietly.

Rakhshan sighed. "I figured as much." He leaned forward and scanned the plates with disinterest. "Why did he not take you?"

Kefira pressed her lips together. "I have no idea."

He knit his hands beneath his chin and said, "What I do not understand is why this is even *happening*. If things had gone normally, you would have no choice in this matter, and you and your dowry would go to the highest bidder, if not the King, himself." He shook his head, looking at her appraisingly. There was anger in his voice when he said, "And I understand *least* of all why you would then," he lowered his voice, "lie about *this*."

Kefira felt the color drain from her face. "I – I did..." she trailed off. "Well, as you said, I went to a council a few days ago – and they did very nearly bid on me and Yonatan," she explained quietly, abashed. "I was to be married to someone more capable of maintaining him; I know not why the King didn't..." she trailed off.

Rakhshan did not make to pick up for her, but remained quiet.

She looked down at her lap. "Do you remember Shaza'eil? The man from Hangmatana?"

"Yes," Rakhshan replied slowly, looking at her with wariness, as though predicting her next words.

"He offered – two thousand talents of gold."

Rakhshan was speechless.

Recovering, he said, "Such a sum is unheard of."

Kefira shivered and agreed, and continued, "He offered it to the King then and there, but then the King said that it would be," she paused, embarrassed by the words, "well – that I get to choose – my husband, that is. And so I did." She frowned. "It was the only thing I could think to do."

Rakhshan didn't say anything for a long time, and by this she was surprised; she'd hoped that it would not take very much for him to agree, given his previous sentiments. But much had changed.

"Rakhshan?" she ventured tentatively, after the silence had become too unbearable.

There was a solemnness on his face when he returned her gaze. He sighed, resignation apparent. "Mār would not be very pleased with this arrangement."

"And Yonatan is furious," Kefira admitted quietly. "And he doesn't even know, yet."

"Doesn't know?" Rakhshan exclaimed. "Kefira – mercy upon this city, once he finds out!"

Kefira hugged herself, ashamed.

Rakhshan put his fingers to his forehead, as though he had a headache, and then said, "And what is this *surrogate rider* nonsense? Did you not think your lie through? I cannot ride both him and Mār into battle! What would I do – have a leash on both of them to be dragged behind like a trolled fishing line?" The Persian halted in his outburst, and became taciturn once more, not looking at her. Kefira had never felt so wretched.

Rakhshan rubbed his eyes, and looked back up. There was a soft pain in his voice that tore at her heart, when he said, "I know you may not have considered this, but," he let out a breath. "This is not how I wanted you."

The words struck her. As his gold eyes were steady on her own, her gaze wavered. And he continued. "I do not want to be your last resort, nor do I want you forced into a union."

Kefira tried not to let tears form, distracting herself by pressing her fists beneath her chin as she stared at him. She swallowed dryly. "I – but it was my choice," she said.

"It wouldn't have been your choice a fortnight ago."

Kefira moved her hands to cover her mouth, as she stared at the table. The truth burned her inside.

Rakhshan was just a piece in her game for security.

She felt sick, and shut her eyes, and then opened them, lashes wet. She tried to keep her voice steady when she finally said, "So – you should leave, then." Her voice cracked midsentence, and she swallowed. "I never should have said anything; I'm sorry." *Whatever you do, do not cry in front of him.*

But she felt a tear trailing down her face, even so, and she cursed herself. Another tear spilled over, and she tried not to look at him, praying he did not see.

He reached over, to her surprise, and handed her a cloth napkin. His voice was low when he said, "I never said that I would not do it."

Linen pressed against her face, she stared at him.

"As much as - " he broke off, and then continued, "I could not see you with anyone else, not these fat, old, stupid men," he said with contempt, "not that Babylonian snake. I know that it would be hell, for you." His smile was small and sad. "But, then again, you may consider this hell, anyway."

"Thank you," Kefira gasped, but his last words sank in, and she grimaced, "I'm sorry – it's – it won't be hell." She bit her lip. "I did not think... I never mean to be so – the way I am – but – it is just that," she took a breath, "I am afraid."

Rakhshan seemed to accept this with a faint nod. He pretended not to notice as she wiped her face. "Of what?"

The girl did not reply for a while, looking down at the dampened napkin. Of what? Her throat ached. That was the question "This," she said. "Being – seen, being a problem, being - " she tried to explain, breath pent, "known, being known, and of people."

Kefira searched his gaze for understanding. His patient silence goaded her to continue. "I have always been alone," she murmured. "And I cannot see anything different, never thought it would change, never wanted it to change. But... I've found different, with Yonatan," she paused, "and you, I suppose..."

He looked away. But when his eyes returned to her, they held softness.

There was a brief silence, and Kefira suddenly found herself not wanting him to speak on her words. Still blushing, she said, "What of the dragons?"

Rakhshan blinked. "The dragons - "

Kefira looked down at her lap. "If we – if you help me, they will not be happy with..." she trailed off, avoiding his gaze. "With how we must go about things."

He appeared to grow as uncomfortable as she. "Marriage," he said carefully, "Mār has no concept of it in his head, let alone considered it for me, before this ordeal." He sighed. "And I don't even want to begin to think of how Yonatan will take it, when he finds out."

Kefira shrank guiltily. She was going to apologize again, but he continued speaking.

"But it must be done."

They looked at each other, realizing the gravity of his words. And her face heated. She looked down at the food, not hungry. After a period of quiet, she stood, legs shaky. "What do we do, now?"

Rakhshan stood as well. "Let things continue in the course you set them on." He held his arms behind his back. "Today, we are going to sign official... documents."

Kefira nodded, insides stirring. She glanced at him again, as though to confirm that this was actually happening. Their words seemed as insubstantial as the wind, surreal. They were going to marry. She met his eyes, and his gaze held a similar somberness. She was going to marry him. Not the King, not Shaza'eil. Him. The relief, an unexpected relief, almost brought her to her knees, before he stepped forward.

She froze, looking at his feet. "Thank you," she said quietly.

He let out his breath, slowly. "You are welcome." They were facing each other, wordless. She became aware of a keen thirst in his eyes, as the table no longer separated them. "Kefira." His arms raised, and her stomach dropped.

But he just placed a light hand on her shoulder. "Let us go to the scribe, now."

She nodded cringingly, conscious of the warmth of his hand until it left her. Bidden by the guards, they left the room and moved down the hall. Kefira did not know where they were supposed to go, but apparently Rakhshan did.

They walked apart. And they did not speak, either. Until Rakhshan glanced at her from the corner of his eye, slowing in pace. He said, "Kefira, before we get there, I must tell you of one condition."

Chapter XVIII
The Chuppah

"If a patrolling sentinel had not been there to catch him, he would have been severely injured, or worse."

These were the words Kefira had received upon waking that morning, from a young messenger who spoke with much less concern than his news merited. Mouth agape, she finally managed to gasp, "What happened?"

"A step was loose, and he lost his footing. Poor construction, no doubt," the lanky boy shrugged.

Her mind went to Rakhshan. It was only a day before their wedding, and this was the second time misfortune had befallen him. Last time he'd been bed-ridden for two days with an illness induced by something he'd eaten. Was God showing her His disapproval? Were these omens that she so blindly took as accidents? She could only observe these happenings from afar, therefore she did not know. She hadn't seen Rakhshan for a week. Since they left their marks on papyrus.

"But he is quite alright now," Mahasti interjected, moving past the young eunuch brusquely, "and is preparing for *tomorrow*, as you should be." She ushered Kefira out of the bed, even as she dismissed the messenger from the room.

Kefira crawled from the covers to obediently enter the awaiting bath. "I'm afraid he won't be alive by tomorrow."

"Then we would be blessed, in the forestalling of the impossible decision of your *dress*," Mahasti replied. She was rifling through garments presented to her by a maid. Most of them were red, the color of Persian matrimony.

Kefira swallowed a lump in her throat. "Are there any Hebrew dresses?" she asked stupidly.

Mahasti let out an exasperated breath, "Oh — I should have guessed — no, first you must ask yourself how many Hebrews there are in the palace, my dear. Of course there are not. But something according to your people might be fashioned, if you do not mind distressing a few of the imperial seamstresses in the process; and if you think your betrothed will not mind."

"Thank you." Kefira looked at the suds in the water, gnawing guilt rising. "Who will conduct the ceremony? Tobias, yes?"

"Yes. We came to a consensus that you would not complain about that, at least."

Kefira let out a sigh of relief. Then the anxiety jumped back: "How many people will be there?"

"Only enough to confirm the event even occurred. Any more and you'd probably faint upon being unveiled."

"Will you be there?"

"Who else will be there to make sure you do not trip over your own sandals?" The handmaidens giggled at this. Mahasti smiled pertly, and continued. "Now, we are going to remove your *fur* again today, and wash your hair and lotion you, all the while I explain to you what I gather of tomorrow's mongrel ceremonies."

Mongrel? Kefira flushed. She almost didn't want to know what she meant; let alone about the terrors that awaited her the next day. Her gaze went wistfully to the window. And then she remembered, heart skipping a beat. "Will I be able to see Yonatan today?"

"Kefira," the woman said incredulously, "It is the day *before your wedding.* There is too much to do for you to have time - "

"But he doesn't know this is all happening!" Kefira cried.

"We can send him a message."

"No, no, *I* must tell him – today, in person!"

"You mean you *should* have *yesterday.* You've had more than enough opportunities this week; I did not hear you make an effort to let him know, then. So for now, he must wait. And anyway, it would have not worked out, as he is busy today himself. You remember this, don't you?"

"What?"

"He is meeting Shoala again today."

Kefira's heart sank. The maids' fingers were rubbing sapo in her hair when she finally mustered words. "Is she..." then she shut her mouth.

There had been much debate in the recent days. As, now, the matter of the dragon's rider had been settled, the dragon himself needed to go in turn. It was determined that he was of sufficient age and maturity.

They had talked of pairing him with as many Gandarewas as possible, to bolster the ranks of Persia's breeding pool, and create a larger than ever before Persian beast. But Kefira couldn't bear the thought of him being studded off like a stallion in this way, and Tobias would not stand for it either, thankfully. "Polygamy..." he'd sighed. "Of men, King David had many wives, as did his son, though they did end up being his downfall. And of animals, sheep of the pasture practice likewise. But Yonatan is neither a man nor an animal."

The discord surrounding the issue was bitter, but polygamy was not settled upon. He would be 'married' to a young Gandarewa. All the young females of this breed, of eligible birth and pedigree, had since been flown to the capitol. The foremost of these candidates was a dragoness by the name of Shoala.

The whole idea of her Yonatan becoming united with another disconcerted Kefira; but who knew – maybe this was providence, and it would soften to him the blow of her own union. Maybe. Hopefully.

She remembered her last conversation with Tobias, concerning Yonatan's situation. "It is important that while he has young we preserve his bloodline. Although a foreign wife is not in the least desirable, there is no other option short of flushing out his female kindred from the wilderness." He paused. "And then, we'd be provoking our hosts to anger by depriving their nation of his fruit." She could tell this issue had been eating at him; even he, wise man of wise men, was perplexed.

Mahasti had only that morning been informed as to the idiosyncrasies of Jewish matrimony; and it was with this half-knowledge that she explained to Kefira the procedures of the wedding. In the way of Hebrew weddings, there would be a canopy and a veil, and, before the vows, there was to be a discomfiting custom in which she was to walk around Rakhshan three times, for what point Kefira did not see. Afterward, they would both partake of the same cup of wine, he would put a band on her finger, and the words of binding would be recited, which Mahasti helped Kefira memorize. And finally, following that, of course, would be their seclusion.

Kefira was wrong when she'd thought that hearing the proceedings would soothe her.

"Really, I'm *astonished* you're still so distressed by this," Mahasti sniffed. "You survived one night with the King, may he live forever, and are quite unscathed. And some might claim you are all the better for the experience; certainly *many* young women your age would have clawed past an army of Immortals for the chance."

Kefira's skin was icy despite the hot water she was immersed in. She spoke wincingly, protesting despite her better judgment. "But I did not know the king – but with Rakhshan - "

"The *opposite* was your qualm not a fortnight ago." Mahasti scorned. "You were afraid of being united with someone you did *not* know, which of course is a childish fear, but now, as I understand it, your feelings have reversed? If forever you think like this, Kefira, you will never be happy."

She didn't respond, knowing it was true. Either way, something uncomfortable needed to happen, and either way she'd wish the contrary. So, she finally cracked a smile. "Do you think Rakhshan will survive until tomorrow?"

"He took a fall, but he is still quite alive. I'm sure he'll be just fine."

Measuring cords were used to make a dress according to Kefira's proportions. The seamstresses involved came in and out in a fluster, in a way that suggested that they were just as put out by the wedding as Kefira was. *Could* a dress be made in a day?

"How long must I be about, tomorrow?" She imagined, with the added stress of the wedding, how sweaty she'd be by the end of the hot day.

"From the pageantries to the vows, I should think it shall be no more than half an hour." Mahasti smiled tersely. "It is because of those people who are looking out for you, that fear the multifarious opportunities for Rakhshan's *assassination,* that the affair is not spread over a month." She frowned and said with a wistful air, "There won't even be a feast, for fear of poison."

Rakhshan's assassination?

This concept had not occurred to her before.

"And then, after the ceremony," Mahasti continued without mercy, "will be what *your* people call Yichud, if I am not mistaken. That, of course, will take *more* than an hour," she purred.

"You have no sympathy," Kefira bent her head.

"I have no sympathy, my dear girl, because I know that which you fear ought not be feared in the first place."

Kefira sighed, leaning forward in the bath as the maids did more to her hair. She stared at her legs. Yichud. Why did *this* have to happen? It was a union *solely* for Yonatan's convenience, not out of free will or desire.

"It is only to show proof of your virginity; which, judging by your prudence, would stay with you till the day you died, if not for this union." Mahasti pulled her out of the water. "It is really only a formality."

Kefira shivered, even as a towel engulfed her. "Formalities are stupid."

She was thrust into a seat as her hair was brushed, excess removed, and nails filed and stained. Mahasti glared at her. "You need to stop fretting. It will give you more blemishes." She straightened. "We already went over this a week ago." She smiled with the utmost patience. "You will be alright."

Kefira sat upright. "I shall ignore myself, then," she stated, to no one in particular. It had occurred to her that all she had to do tomorrow was just ignore herself. That was the best thing to do. She would just let herself be guided by others, say what needed to be said, and do what needed to be done, without fear, or brooding about it. It was, after all, for Yonatan, certainly not for her own comfort.

But despite all this newfound resolve, it took her a special blend of chai and a soothing pomander to get to sleep that night.

The dress was white, in the plain Hebrew fashion. Although, liberty was taken, as it was hemmed and decorated with silver, and ornaments of sapphire and amethyst.

"It's so drab," Mahasti pouted, contrary to Kefira's high opinion of it. "But I suppose it cannot be helped, now." Anyway, it matched her shawl. Kefira imagined Rakhshan would like that.

It was fit onto her, and after a few adjustments, it was satisfactory to all.

"What should be done with her hair?"

"Kept down and left curly; the simplicity would match the dress well."

"Have it beneath the shawl, or rather, *badeken* veil – is that how you say it?"

"Should we place a circlet over?"

"One of silver would be beautiful."

Of course, Kefira wasn't paying attention. Her churning stomach felt as though it were trying to throw her out the window. She hadn't eaten at all that morning, but that did not stop the jittery moth's wings from fluttering inside her. Would that the whole day could just be over, everything said and done! Why did she have to experience it all, so agonizingly slow?

"Is it true that only two witnesses are needed to rightfully consummate a marriage?" she blurted.

Mahasti replied in the affirmative as she placed a band of silver over the shawl that would double as the veil.

"Then, that would be just you and one other person required to be there?" Kefira asked, and then said, "Can Navid and Remus be witnesses, too?"

This idea brought Mahasti up short. And then she frowned, "Kefira, we cannot just *call* off those who'd already been invited."

"But – I thought you said there would only be enough to prove that it happened. Does that mean – well – who else was invited?" Who else would *want* to *attend?* She was sure that the only reason anyone came to a wedding that did not directly relate to them would be for the festivities. But there would be virtually no festivities, here.

"Some people said they would attend from the start – of course, it was told to them that it was a private affair, as some of them might wish your betrothed ill; they were repelled; but there are those who are *not* malicious who were permitted to come," and as Mahasti explained, she trailed off. Finally, she sourly waved her hands. "Of course, if it will ensure that you do not faint – why *should* they come, *never mind* their positions of nobility!" She covered her face with a tense hand. "I thank the gods that none of them came from anywhere outside of the *valley*, lest they traveled a long distance for *nothing.*"

Kefira was astonished. "You mean – they – are you going to call them off?"

Mahasti let smooth steam escape her nostrils. "Of course. If only to assure that you do not plant your face into the ground during the procession."

Then, with that assurance, it felt as though Kefira's raiment weren't so tight.

But still she felt as though she was suffocating, on the walk to the small garden where the affair was to take place. It looked as though it had been ready to accommodate many more than their number, and the empty space did not help to console the chill in her feet.

Outside of the hedge surrounding the yard was where Mahasti dismissed the servants that had been following. Of course, the two eunuchs were allowed to stay, as against practice as the notion was. Kefira stood stiffly out of sight of the two men she knew would be waiting in the clearing. She stared at Mahasti, hopelessly.

"Remember all that I've told you," she simply advised. "You will do fine."

Pain throbbed in Kefira's head, but she nodded. She could hardly hear the woman through the pounding of blood in her ears. But she didn't need to, as she knew that the time was at hand after Navid and Remus had been sent ahead to sit down.

So she went, Mahasti at her back.

Rakhshan was dressed handsomely. Had they cleaned him up, too? She saw that the expression on his polished face was pent up with tension, but that faded upon seeing her step forward.

And then she stopped moving, as they regarded one another. The veil was on. He could not see her face. She was glad. She continued forward.

Traditionally, she would have been led to the canopy by her mother and Rakhshan's, and he their fathers. But they had no parents. So they were alone when she arrived at the canopy where Tobias waited, a white chuppah hanging above them. And she felt as though she were walking in sleep.

The bride blinked. Thankfully, Mahasti hadn't needed to shout a reminder to her – but she'd almost forgotten. Rakhshan wasn't moving, he'd remembered. She began to walk a circle around him. And she became aware of a pressure in the back of her throat as he watched her. His face was inscrutable, but she could tell the aloofness of their last meeting had left him.

Grass tickled her sandaled feet as she walked. She watched him as he searched for her face behind the veil he'd given her, whenever she rounded in front of him. Her face warmed. Had she gone around one too many times – miscounted? No, she stopped just as she ought; she'd been numbering her fingers as she went about, it was three. She found her place beside him.

Tobias spoke, softly as though not to break the silence. He could not see, so after he blessed the wine he simply held it before him to be received. "Blessed are You, Lord, our God, Sovereign of the Universe, Who creates the fruit of the vine." And Rakhshan took the offered cup.

The goblet was ornate, beautiful, but it was fashioned of unbroken silver, simple and humble compared to the other gilded and gem-encrusted wares of the palace. Kefira thought it fit the occasion well; or at least its participants. Rakhshan drank of the wine, and then stepped closer and held the cup before her lips from beneath the hem of the shawl. She raised a hand to steady the cup as she took a drink. Their hands were touching. Had she ever touched his hands before? Yes, the night when she'd hurt her fists, she recalled, fingers warm.

But the cup was not there to bind their hands any longer. It was removed and they faced one another. Relief flooded her. Were they already at the vows? The *vows* must be made, soon. And then unease shot through her once more. She was vowing herself to him.

She folded her hands before her, waiting for Rakhshan. He was to lift her veil now, she suspected. And that he did.

The verses of Tobias continued. "Blessed are You, Lord, our God, Sovereign of the Universe, Who created everything for His Glory.

"Blessed are You, Lord, our God, Sovereign of the Universe, Who creates Man."

The lucidity of Rakhshan's amber eyes soothed her. His face had softened since he could finally see her own. And she felt one of his fingers brush her cheek, after he lowered his hands from the shawl.

"Blessed are You, Lord, our God, Sovereign of the Universe, Who creates Man in Your image, fashioning perpetuated life. Blessed are You, Lord, Creator of Man."

It was only her and Rakhshan.

"May the barren one exult and be glad as her children are

joyfully gathered to her. Blessed are You, Lord, Who gladden Zion with her Children."

Children.

"Grant perfect joy to these loving companions," Tobias prayed, "as You did Your creations in the Garden of Eden. Blessed are You, Lord, Who grants the joy of husband and bride."

Husband and bride.

"Blessed are You, Lord, our God, Sovereign of the Universe, Who created joy and gladness, husband and bride, mirth, song, delight and rejoicing, love and harmony, and peace and companionship. Soon, Lord our God, may there ever be heard," Tobias murmured, and she felt sorrow in his voice as he continued to say, "in the cities of Judah and in the streets of Jerusalem," *though they are barren*, she thought, "voices of joy and gladness, voices of husband and bride, the jubilant voices of those joined in marriage under the chuppah, the voices of young people feasting and singing. Blessed are You, Lord, Who causes the husband to rejoice with his bride."

Kefira looked at Rakhshan again. Now there was a small sadness in his eyes, as well. She imagined there was in her own. Indeed, there were no voices of joy in Jerusalem. But its silence did not interrupt the proceedings. Rakhshan brought forth a silver band, which shone as though it were wrought of braided light. She silently halted in breathing as he took her hand in his – a weathered but warm palm – and put the ring on her finger. The metal had been warmed by his grip, and the touch lingered on her. He lifted her small hand before them.

"Behold, you are consecrated to me with this ring," Rakhshan said, "according to the Law of Moses and Israel."

Presented by him, these latter words surprised her. But this did not delay her in delivering her part. She gave him a ring, too, and slowly recited, "I am my beloved's. And my beloved is mine." She paused with uncertainty before she moved. Then her soft fingers traced his as she put on his ring. And before she knew it, Rakhshan took her abruptly by the arms and kissed her on the mouth.

Judging by the sound Mahasti made, this was a serious breach in decorum. Kefira even heard one of the eunuchs, as he could not stifle a laugh. But it was over as soon as it had occurred. Once more, the girl was standing beside a composed Rakhshan; the only things that betrayed the fact that he had kissed her were that familiar, mischievous smile, and the heat in her stomach.

It was hard to concentrate on the rest of the proceedings after that.

"Now, that was not so difficult, was it?" Mahasti asked, when they had finished the ceremony and reconvened in her room. Preparations were being made for that night.

Kefira was looking at the band she'd been given. "It is so strange to finally be over," she muttered distantly. It was truly finished. She was married. Yonatan was safe with her. He could no longer be taken away.

Though she had not been given the morning or noonday meal, it was brought to her attention that they were offering her food now. She was fed raw almonds; also, a dish of green things was thrust beneath her nose. She smelled the sharp scent of coriander, but the roughage consisted of more than that – spinach, leeks, and what looked like green scales – they called them artichokes. She ate; there was so much coriander it was hard to swallow; it was not as delicious as the normal royal fare. But that opinion changed when a maid began to spoon something spicy and sweet into her mouth. "What is this?" she asked.

"Honey, cumin, and pepper."

"That is a queer mixture." Although Kefira did not at all mind the taste. "What is all this for?"

"It will make you bear sons."

Kefira almost gagged. "Oh." It was not *all* over, she reminded herself now. She stared at her ring hand. "What am I to wear tonight?"

Mahasti smiled and unfurled another dress of white. But this one was decorated with red, in trim, in embroidery. "Scarlet," she said luxuriously. "The color of *passion*." And then she feigned disapproval. "Although, judging by that brash display of affection, you might wear an untreated goatskin, for all he cares." She shook her head, setting the dress aside. "He ought to do himself a favor and *try* not to let the barbarian within him show."

Kefira blushed for him. She still could not decide whether to feel violated or flattered by his action.

The treatment Kefira had undergone before her night with the King was repeated. Her body was saturated in sensuous oils and lotions that made her brown skin glow. Her lips were stained with the scarlet juice of berries, and softened with a coat of honey. Everything about her was beautiful, soft, and sweet, and it took her looking into a mirror of polished silver to realize what sort of vessel she was. She felt her flesh mutely. She looked and felt perfected. And as though part of herself had been polished away, along with so many layers of burnt skin and dust.

Had Eve, the bride of Adam, been created this way? Flawless and radiant? Or had she been sun-stained, hairy, with dirt beneath her unkempt fingernails? *Was* there dirt in the Garden of Eden?

Her thoughts were interrupted by Mahasti, putting cloves in her mouth. And as they polished her, they gave her sips of wine, and refined her until it was almost dusk. Then they put on the dress.

This was the last time she'd see this room. She was to reside in an apartment with Rakhshan from now on, chambers farther from the women's quarters and closer to the gardens where dragons dwelt. She had to go to that apartment, now. It was already time.

Kefira did not expect Mahasti's parting words, or that they were parting words at all. "As soon as the King did not choose you," she said, "I had no more obligation to you, Kefira."

What did that mean?

"And from now on, as you are leaving the parameters of the harem completely, you will no longer hear my voice telling you to sit up straight." Her bitter smile faded. "I do not know where you will live, once the whole affair with your dragon has blown over and it is time for you and Rakhshan to be settled out of the way. But wherever that is, my place is here."

As she spoke, Kefira was trying to decide if this was a permanent goodbye, and whether or not she would miss the woman. "But who will make sure I do not embarrass myself?" she quipped. Her heart surprised her when it panged with regret.

Mahasti smiled. "I was waiting for you to ask. Kefira, this is my niece, Leva." One of the youngest girls came forward at the woman's beckoning. This was the girl who did her nails, and had kissed her on the forehead before she went to the King. Her hair was raven black and eyes large. She could not have yet come of age.

Kefira found herself smiling a little.

Mahasti explained, "She has been assigned to nag you for me. She is a little young to be an attendant, but she is more than capable."

An attendant. Was she being given a servant? Kefira was incredulous.

"She will begin tending to you as soon as tomorrow afternoon," the woman finished. And Kefira wanted very badly to ask if she was serious.

"But enough of this," Mahasti took Kefira by the shoulders. "I am all for long, drawn-out goodbyes, but you mustn't keep your *husband* waiting. Navid and Remus will take you to your new chambers." But she did not shove Kefira out the door just yet. She looked as though she were deciding whether or not to say something, for once her gaze was fleeting, but in the end she just smiled. Not in her usual scornful way, but a little sadly. "Fare well."

And then Kefira was moved to the capable hands of her eunuchs outside. And she couldn't help but tentatively hold Navid's arm. When they dropped her off, would that be the last time she saw them, too? They'd been so good to her. What if they were being reassigned? As they walked, she found herself asking, "Are you two going to stay?"

Remus cocked his head at the question. "What do you mean?"

Kefira shrugged. "Stay with me, I guess – I was just wondering, as I just said goodbye to the Mistress of the Harem, if you would be leaving me, too."

"We were appointed to protect you, when your dragon cannot," Navid said.

Remus continued, "And that is a charge that we will hold to, until we go to the grave." He looked at her. "We will not leave you."

Her heart quavered at the tenderness in his almond eyes. They were both strong men and quite older than she, she observed, but they had young faces, without any facial hair, just smooth, weathered skin. She wondered for the first time if this boyish appearance was the result of their emasculation.

It struck her belatedly how much they had given up to become servants. She wondered if it had been their choice.

She realized she was staring, and looked at the tiles before them.

And then they stood by a door. The door. Remus entered. Kefira was about to follow suit, but Navid kept her back with him. Then after a few minutes, Remus returned and nodded to the other man. Then she was led inside. "Your husband will arrive shortly. We will be outside." And Kefira swallowed her fear as she was left in the chambers in solitude.

The apartment was bigger than her former quarters. At the door there was a small reception room. Past that, a larger room with a low table and mats, and a pair of longchairs – the drawing room. Attached to that, on the left, there was a room with a latrine and a wash basin, and a small, empty bedroom for servants beside it. On the other side if the drawing room was a portico that lead to another room; and there resided the bed of her and her husband.

She would be dancing out of joy for the incredible living space, if it weren't for the hitch in her lungs at the last discovery. The girl haltingly entered the bedroom. And did not move in the silence. She stared at the bed, as the sound of construction echoed in the distance. She stepped forward and felt the white and green fabric that was draped around the blanketed mattress. There was a white cloth upon it, reddened by the dusk light. She turned from the room.

It would be dark, soon. She lit a few lamps from a torch by the door, and illuminated the rooms. She set the last one at the bedroom window, and looked out upon the darkling city below.

Her head hurt. The fresh air did not help. She tucked the low collar of her dress close to her neck, and waited.

And she did not wait long. Because she heard the door open, and then shut. The sound of meandering footsteps. Then they stopped nearby, and she knew Rakhshan had found the bedroom.

She turned around to see him, realized that she had the lamp in her hand, and set it back on the window sill, where it flickered. "Hello," was all she could think of saying.

"Hello," he replied, taking a step into the room. He had something in his hand and placed it on the nearby tray.

She held her elbows, leaned against the wall. Say something. "What is in the bowl?"

Rakhshan appeared embarrassed, and shifted his weight. "It is – just honey." He shrugged. "A tradition," he began to explain, and then finished with, "Nothing, really."

They were still at opposite ends of the room. Kefira straightened, inquisitive. She made herself go across the room, but stayed a pace away from him. "I do not know if there is a pantry to put it in or not. Maybe in the servant's room." She felt weird saying such a thing.

Rakhshan shook his head a little. "No, no, it's alright."

Kefira shuffled her feet, looking sidelong. "Have – you seen the house?" she asked.

"Yes. I had no idea they'd give – us – more than a room." He watched her leave through the portico.

"Do you see?" Kefira stood beside the table in the other room, spinning about as though to display it. "It's very spacious." She added, desperate to fill the air with words, "I would never have seen a single room so large in my life, if this was the only room in the palace I'd been to."

Rakhshan looked amused, and nodded.

"You might keep the honey on this table. As night is falling, I doubt any insects would get to it." And then, feeling particularly restless in the silence, she went to the servant's room and found a shelf therein. "There's a place right here, too." After she heard no immediate reply, she leaned out the doorway and asked, "What is the honey for?"

Rakhshan was still standing by the table, the small dish in his hands. "It is just a – Persian tradition," he explained. "After two are married, they take the honey with their little fingers, and, well," he placed it on the table dismissively. "It's just another silly thing; like painted eggs and rosewater. Forget I said anything."

Though he smiled, she realized something. He had more than tolerated the Jewish wedding, without a single complaint. She had not thanked him.

So she stepped out of the servant's room, and knelt by the table. Hesitantly, she dipped her little finger in the honey, and it tingled warmly. She looked up at him inquiringly.

His smile was real this time, as he took the opposite side of the table and followed suit. Their little fingers spangled golden in the lamplight, even as their silver bands gleamed. Kefira watched as he brought his finger forward, close to her mouth. Before she could inquire, he said, abashed, "We are supposed to feed it to one another."

"Oh," Kefira blushed. No wonder he had been so diffident in showing her. This was an intimacy beyond the startling peck he'd given her earlier. But despite her misgivings, she cautiously parted her lips, and tasted the honey. Her lips flooded with heat, and she couldn't help but smile around his finger. Tentatively, she raised her own hand to Rakhshan's mouth, and did as he had. His cropped whiskers bristled against her hand, as he partook.

She looked down at the bowl, self-conscious, and they both withdrew their hands. Kefira held hers against herself. "Do we do the whole bowl?" she asked quietly, afraid to break the silence.

He laughed, "Only if you want to. But that might make us sick."

She nodded, smiling. The silence deepened. And presently, she stood. "Have you looked out the window, yet? The sunset can be seen from it," she told him.

He shook his head and stood as well. She cleared her throat, and made her legs move back to the window. She pretended to watch the orange sky fade to purple.

Rakhshan moved to her side, but he wasn't looking out the window. He leaned against the wall, and in the corner of her eye, she saw he was looking around the room, fidgety. She wondered if it was possible that he was feeling the same as she was, the same pressure in the back of the throat.

No, there was no dread on his face. She hoped he couldn't see hers. She'd run out of energy. She was too nervous. She rubbed the corner of her eye, and left a dark blotch of kohl on the tip of her finger. She wiped the stuff on the corner of her sleeve.

"I take it you are still not used to wearing makeup?" He raised his hand, and removed the smudge from beneath her eye.

"How can you tell?" Kefira smiled bitterly. She straightened a little, clutching her hands beneath her chin.

Rakhshan looked away, voice critical. "It is funny how attached to their mirrors the girls here are. They act mad, obsessive about it. But – you've never needed any of those things."

Her stomach stirred. "Oh, thank you," she replied, at the half-said compliment. The sun was gone, now, and her blush was hidden despite the lamplight; her face burned in the silence, and the depths of her ineptitude made her head swim.

He stepped forward, lifting her chin to look up at him. "Kefira." His eyes pored over her own. His next words were unexpected when he asked, "Are you… is this alright with you? Us, being alone?"

Her eyes fell to his feet. She turned away, went back to the table, and put the clay lid back onto the honey. "What... do you mean?"

"You know what I mean."

Kefira could not fool him; her stomach turned void. She did not look at him. She was not alright with it. But she had to be. This was all for Yonatan. So she nodded to him, slowly, a belated reply.

The man moved past the table now to where she was, and stopped with her before him, to look searchingly down upon her face. And then, the girl watched as his head dipped to hers after a time, and his lips touched her cheek, warm pressure. At that moment, the stone in her throat melted away, and she felt her pulse quicken like a spurred horse. She stared at his cheek, stunned.

He kissed her again, on the lips, and she could only hiss breath through her nose. Her eyes were open, upon his sealed lids as she watched his soft motions, and her feet throbbed as his hands moved upon her waist. She was frozen in the sudden warmth, astonished at the feel and the proximity, that it was actually happening. He was going to do it. She didn't have to worry. He was taking care of everything. He knew, he knew what he was doing. His lips met hers again and again, and she felt his hand on her chin. He was kissing her, she continued to recognize from a distance, and she was doing nothing about it. She was being kissed.

His eyes opened, and he was looking at her face. Kefira was staring at him. "Shall you kiss me back, or is that something you are yet disinclined to do?"

The girl blushed furiously, coming to. "Oh," she stammered. It had not quite occurred to her. But he smiled and kissed her again, whence she did her best to reciprocate. And she felt that she had failed utterly, though he seemed not to mind, even as he drew away. For he was smiling down at her, saying, "I have waited long for that."

One of his hands lifted to her shawl, and his eyes searched her own, as if to ask permission. She found herself nodding, and he lifted the silver circlet, letting it fall to the table, and drew the shawl away from her head. She followed him with her gaze as he ran a timid hand through her hair, and he smiled broader. "No wonder you've always been so avid about keeping your hair hidden. Kings might make war for a strand of it."

Kefira exhaled a laugh, and felt his hands trail through her hair, quavering inside, conscious of his every touch for the sparks it sent through her. She felt as though she were being unlocked. Never under any circumstance or by anyone had she ever wanted to be touched. She almost reviled his touch, but no. For some reason she was not moving away, or even pushing away his hand. Even as it moved down to her back, even as chill and heat ran up and down her legs.

And then she was in his embrace. She shut her eyes as Rakhshan kissed her again. His face was in her hair, she heard him breathe. Then she felt the warm air upon her neck as there he pressed his lips. Kefira's hands were motionless upon his sides as he advanced, and she wondered at him. The passion in his actions. She could feel his skin, the skin of another person, his lips.

Let him kiss me with the kisses of his mouth – for your love is more delightful than wine. Could this be what the words of the old king Solomon had meant? Wine indeed, for the exhilaration she felt made her mind feel loose and incoherent, as though what she was observing was very distant and not quite real.

Her legs were as weak as stalks of wheat, and immobile as pillars, but a compelling fire condensed within her, even as he pulled her closer. She could not move, but he did, skin thrumming with heat.

Step, step, he was moving forward, and suddenly the stone in her throat returned; she felt the bed against the back of her legs. She breathed out of her nose, feeling her heart shudder. Against her dissolving will her legs buckled, and she fell backwards amidst blankets and just as quickly bolted upright.

"Are you alright?" Rakhshan asked, quickly sitting at her side.

His face was flushed, and his hands held her own. He had never looked more embarrassed.

"I'm – it's alright, I just fell," she managed to stammer. She stared at the slippers on her feet, a little too fixedly. Rakhshan was no longer wearing his own sandals. Her legs thrummed. "I wish our room had a balcony," she blurted, and the word 'our' tasted funny upon saying it.

"Not so that you could throw yourself off of it, I hope," Rakhshan said, half-jesting. She looked over at him and saw that he was grimacing.

One of her fingers twitched against his palm, and she looked away without a word. Oh, she was acting so stupid!

"Kefira, what's the matter? You can tell me."

"I'm sorry, I just do not feel well," she replied, turning a little to face him. She removed her gaze from her feet to their interlocked hands.

"Do you want me to ask one of the eunuchs to bring us some chai?" Rakhshan tried earnestly. "That might help."

There was a white cloth lain over the bed, and its purpose was to catch the blood that would be proof of her virginity. No, chai would not help. Kefira looked at Rakhshan finally. "Only if you want some," she said. "I'm not thirsty."

"I don't like chai," he replied, just as resigned. Lamely, he asked, "Um, did they leave wine on the table?"

She shook her head, hiding a shiver. Of all things she wanted to be sober.

Rakhshan nodded, face coloring as the silence deepened. Their hands grew clammy and hot, even though Kefira felt as though her fingers were covered in hoarfrost. She released her hands, using the taming of a flyaway hair as an excuse to do so. They were sitting on the bed. *The bed*. Whenever she had been on such a thing, be it a mat or a bedroll, she'd always been alone.

Now she wasn't, and on such allegedly intimate terms. She wanted to stand up, to stretch her aching legs. But no, she couldn't.

Should she offer her hands again?

She glanced out the window. The sun's colored trail of light was gone. The only things holding away the darkness were the flickering lamps, shedding their golden light. Warm light. It was too hot. She wanted to stick her head out the window and suck in great lung-fulls of air. She hugged her elbows instead.

The silence was pierced then, by a distant sound, a low, mournful keen. Kefira recognized Yonatan's voice. It was despondent; a lament that chilled her to the core. Her mind flashed. Yonatan. Tears sprang to her eyes. "He doesn't know."

Rakhshan looked at her, stunned.

"He cannot know, now! But he sounds so sad," she cried. "Has someone told him?" She turned desperately to Rakhshan.

He shook his head. "I cannot say." And conciliatorily added, "But I do not think he would merely be keening if he knew."

Kefira pressed her fists into her eyes. It was true. He could not be helped, anyway. Her heart ached. "I'm sorry," she murmured.

He used his fingers to remove the smudges on her face. "It is quite alright."

She watched him as he did, and it occurred to her that she wanted to return to his embrace. Even where she was. Yet her body was immobile, noncompliant with her half-will. The white over the bed fought against her, even as she felt as though she was burning. She remembered a verse in a song of Solomon. *Love burns like a blazing fire, like a mighty flame.* Yes, fire burned within her, so hot that it hurt. But was it love? Did she *love* Rakhshan?

She did not, she did not think she did. Yet somehow she was not hindered in saying, "I think I feel better, now."

Rakhshan seemed to awaken from a thoughtful stupor of his own. His smile crooked wryly. "I wish you could have been quicker in recovery – for now I feel as you did."

"Well," she began sheepishly, "what usually provokes you into your usual manner of eloquence?" She decided to lean forward to punctuate the question, hoping the movement did not look too forced.

"Is it not obvious?" he asked, color returning to his face. "How many times must I romantically address you to get it through that thick mane of hair?"

She smiled, simply glad he was finally carrying the weight of the room and the bed and the words once more; he continued, "I'd always looked forward to this day. Now that it is here, that you are..." he trailed off, and did not continue speaking. Their eyes went to the window. They heard from afar two draconic voices now, a moonlight requiem, and listened. Did the dragons think, did they know the peril their riders were in that night? That they might lose both of them?

"I don't know what to feel," Kefira admitted, before she could stop herself. His eyes were a mirror of her own. "Mourn as they do? No, no; but still... Yonatan's sadness, or how sad he *will* be, once I must tell him – it breaks my heart."

"Our dragons, they are as brothers to us." Rakhshan nodded.

"It feels like more than that," Kefira said, mind unfolding. "Yonatan protects me as a father, loves me as a mother, and cares for me like a brother. And he is as my own child, to me." She flushed, at sharing these ridiculous thoughts.

But when she looked up, his eyes were not scoffing. His expression was warm. He looked out the window again. "They are blessings," he said. Blessings.

"How I wish they were not hurt so." She didn't add, *by this*.

"I know you are not comfortable," Rakhshan said slowly. And then he picked up with earnestness, "If there was another way for you to lawfully keep Yonatan, I would take you there." He looked away. "It pains me, the condition I had to take up on my end of the matter, but they would not have had it any other way. They would not have let me come." That was right. Her dowry was Yonatan, and his condition for the marriage had been the economic freedom of Parudrauga, the sinful port city; his conspirators had only allowed him to go to Pasargadae to help her on that condition. The King should have, by all rights, *not* accepted the exorbitant demand. Yet he had.

"It is alright," Kefira told him quietly. It felt as though she was sitting on a blanket woven of bone needles. She looked up at him, and then away. Despite herself, her legs yet shimmered with conflicting waves of warm and cool. Would that she could lie down and shut her eyes and let it all happen. She should, that's what she should do. That was what brides did.

But she didn't feel well. Her eyes fell onto the white sheet once more. She could almost envision it, marked red, the signet of her purity. What would happen to her purity after it painted the blanket? Would it have left with the stain? Or would it remain, leaving only a sign of her virtue? She wondered if it would hurt.

His warm hand reached out to her once more. "Are you sure you're alright?" He touched her arm.

"No," she replied, words brittle. "I do not think so."

"Are you sick? Is it nerves?"

Her emotions were as taut as the cords of a lute. "Yes, both." She watched guiltily as his face fell; voice small, she asked, "May we do this another time?" Oh, what a stupid thing to say! She regretted the words as soon as they left her stupid painted mouth.

Rakhshan's eyes flickered from her to around the room, uncomfortable. "Very well," he said slowly, "If that is what you wish." But then he seemed to catch himself, "Um, I mean – I'd like to oblige you," he forced himself to meet her gaze, "I – I hate to sound like a pig – but there will be people who want... you know..."

Oh, no – this would shame him, she realized. And the King. And Mahasti. And Yonatan. Without proof of her honor – or even proof that they had been properly wedded – her face burned with heat, and she felt her breath grow shallow. "I am truly sorry," she corrected herself. "Of course, forget that I said anything."

"Well, I can't really do that *now*," he said wryly. Pulling his legs up, he sat on his feet, looking at her sidelong.

"Wine?" she asked, a feeble attempt. Then she remembered

the clay cup and the inn, and flushed.

"No, no."

She felt as though they had been at a feast and she had sent everything splattering to the ground with a pull of the tablecloth. "I'm very sorry," she said again.

"It's alright." But apparently Rakhshan was still set on her previous statement. "Would you like me to go out and arrange for another time?" he asked, and she knew he was sincere. "You know how well I am with words. You can have food-poisoning, just as I had, or be struck with a sudden illness."

Lie to them? No. That would mean lying to Tobias and the King, and she could never go behind their backs after how good they'd been to her. "You needn't," she said, smiling weakly.

"Then what is to be done?"

Indeed. The young woman felt herself drain of energy. Well, there was nothing *to* do. Nothing to do about it. She would be anxious, afraid, even, but they must carry on, and prove the things that needed proving, and they would wake up the next morning.

But the dawn was still far off. She stared at the white linen. A small breath of duress escaped her mouth.

Rakhshan looked wretched. "I'm very sorry."

Kefira met his eyes, jewels of liquid amber, and she nodded uncertainly. "Um," she said, half to herself, and she floundered to the center of the bed. The cushions beneath dipped and pitched like waves below her. She sat down and glanced at Rakhshan, who was looking at her as though she'd just turned into a tortoise. "I – I am going to pray, for a minute," she stammered.

His brow knit, and arched. "Uh – Kefira..." he began dubiously, but did not say anything more when she knelt face down. She held her hands to her chest, brow to the cloth. The cushions shifted, and her heart faltered as she realized Rakhshan had gotten up.

After a weary moment, Kefira turned her mind to God. Adonai. And she paled at the thought of Him. Had it been so long since she'd prayed?

Yes, it had. A feeling of guilt washed over her. Only now, at her time of dire need, she called upon Him. Only now did she hope, or act like she hoped, that He could deliver her from her troubles. The more she thought about it, the more nauseous she felt, sick with dread. She'd been so terribly distant as of late, when her sapling faith was tested. In the drought, she hadn't even prayed for rain from the waiting clouds. But now, certainly the clouds would be gone. He would not help her, after she'd waited so long. That would be just.

Despite the misgivings, however, she whispered the ghost of a prayer in her mind, the silent words clinking out like wooden blocks. *Please, let me find a way out of this. I cannot do it. It doesn't feel right. Even if it was, I could not. I am too afraid.* She stayed silent a long time, repeating her doubt and fear and pleads in her mind, spinning like a wheel. From time to time, she heard Rakhshan fidget. She kept on. *I am afraid. I hate the fear, but I cannot do without it. Please remove it. I don't care if it will hurt me. Just remove it. Take everything I have, if only to remove my fear.*

But the fear was a part of her. To live without this fear was to live blind. *But I need it gone. Though I know You cannot remove it from me. I would know if You could. I would be able to see the way out.*

She was going deeper then she'd planned. She just needed His help, was all; she didn't need Him to play a harp to her soul. He needed to intervene. Part the Jordan River, the Red Sea. Would he not create a smaller miracle for her? A wave of disappointment flooded her, seeming to run down her face. Miracles were only for the Nation of Israel. Not for its little orphans. There was no way. She would disgrace Rakhshan. The realization filled her with hot shame.

Hardly before she could mutter an amen, Rakhshan exclaimed, shaking her up. "Your face – you're bleeding!"

"What?" she asked, startled, as he pressed the linen beneath her nose. She suddenly became aware of heat dripping down her face.

"Your nose is bleeding," he repeated, voice calming as the crimson was tamed. "How often do these occur?"

Confused, she didn't speak for a moment. "Never – none like this," she said, voice muffled past the cloth over her mouth.

"Well, it's over now, whatever it was. Maybe that is why you felt sick, an ill humor." He moved her aside and removed the white sheet, holding it up grimly.

And then they both stared at it a moment. A red stain. Rakhshan exchanged glances with her. And then their eyes stayed on the cloth for a long time.

And then he managed a smile. "Alright, then."

Kefira looked away, drawing her legs close as she rubbed beneath her nose; she watched as Rakhshan folded up the cloth and set it aside, whence it sat redly on the floor. She stared at it as her husband straightened, looking heavily around the room.

Her attention quickly returned to him when he beckoned her to the edge of the bed. "Come on."

She warily scooted up to him, and dangled her legs. He knelt. And then he lifted the hem of her robes above her calves. A chill ran through her as she remembered the window, Parudrauga, the inn, the cup – but his warm hands stayed below the ankles. Knuckles grazed her feet as he removed her sandals and set them on the floor.

And then he stood. Reflexively, she did the same, and he looked down at her, a half-smile on his lips. Then he promptly leaned over and drew up the blankets like a tent. He put a hand on her shoulder and ushered her inside. Her stomach knotted, and she didn't move for a second; she glanced at him, but he was looking into the darkness beneath the covers.

Biting the inside of her lip, she steeled herself and went inside. Sweat was beginning to bead on her temples. What did he mean by this? They had the proof already. Did that anger him?

As her mind raced, the girl found a place in the soft cloths and padding, and stiffly found herself lying on her back, legs crossing and uncrossing at the ankles. She slowly shrugged into one of the pillows, eyes fixed on the ceiling.

Despite her stillness, her heartbeat was loud and swift. He meant to do it anyway, she realized; her muscles seemed to turn into meek liquid inside of her. Why did she only now find herself obedient?

An eternity passed as the blankets billowed back down.

Then Kefira realized. Rakhshan hadn't followed after; he was still standing outside.

The man seemed taller as he regarded her. She inhaled as he leaned over, hands posting on either side of her. Apprehension froze her, and then indecisiveness him, as for another moment their gazes touched. Then he moved, hands tucking the blankets in about her. She watched the warm, lingering motions; he tucked the soft fabric up around her chin. His expression was soft but taught, as his eyes dipped to hers. She shifted her foot, apprehensive, but otherwise did not move. He lowered his head, and presently he spoke. "I hope you will not begrudge me this, at least." Then she blinked slowly as he kissed her on the nose.

Then he hovered over her a second, reaching past her to bunch a few pillows beneath his arm. Then he removed himself from the bed; but before he could turn away, she freed an arm and caught his wrist.

"Rakhshan." Her voice was thin. "Thank you – for ..." *For...* There was no right way to say it, so she found that she didn't say it at all.

But the man nodded anyway, seeming to understand. His neck appeared to hurt as he looked away, and walked out of sight.

The girl shut her eyes, feeling the heat slowly drain away. Her mind and heart felt numb as she listened for further movement. He must have picked up the purity cloth, for in the next room she heard the door open. He was hanging the signet outside. Kefira felt her face grow warm, energy seeping away from her, even as she heard words of approval – some dignitaries outside – accompanied by Rakhshan's stilted acknowledgements.

She exhaled slowly as she listened; soon Rakhshan shut the door and seemed to go to one of the longchairs in the drawing room; though she could tell by the cadence of his breath he did not sleep. Her own eyelids drooped, and her gaze was still on the ceiling. Dear God, whatever had occurred?

She could come to no conclusion, though she thought about it long, before her aching mind descended into slumber. In that time she had not shifted, and the blankets in which she'd been swaddled remained as her husband had put them.

Chapter XIX
The Wrath of Grief

Rakhshan was no longer in the apartment when morning came, though Kefira didn't realize it at first, upon waking. The recognition came with the stillness, and the silence. She had not needed to remove her eyes from the ceiling to realize that something was amiss.

She sighed, and with half a will, stiffly made herself get out of bed. She rubbed her face, as her sandals slipped half-way onto her feet, and she bent to crudely tie them off. Her nose felt dry, cracked. She licked a finger and made sure there was no dried blood left on her lips.

As she did this her mind was focused on the morning silence. There were birds singing, the sound of early activity from the servants and slaves employed outside. But no sound came from inside their rooms beside her footsteps. She checked the drawing room; nothing significant was there except the leftover dish of honey. All the other rooms were empty, too.

The certainty of his absence made a pit open up in her stomach. He was upset with her. More upset than his apparent kindness last night had made her surmise.

Yet somehow she was beyond feeling any despair about it. She stood by the table, holding her face in her hands, rubbing her nose, slowly. It hurt.

When she looked, the honor cloth was no longer in the bedroom. That was right – last night he'd presented it to the physicians, the sages concerned. Or maybe had she imagined that, and he'd actually tossed it out the window. Was he hurt by what occurred last night?

Whatever he felt, she found she did not regret it. *Thank you, God.* She had almost lain with an uncircumcised man, she realized. Is that what had stopped her?

No matter what it'd been, it stood to reason that she should at least find Rakhshan, and ameliorate what had passed between them. As they were married, she needed to make an effort to quench disputes before they grew. It was the least she could do, even she knew that. But where had he gone? Where *would* he go, after such a day as the last?

The girl knew suddenly that he had to be with Mār. Her heart sank. Was he so eager to shed to the dragon his review of the night? A feeling of shame enshrouded her; and then, the kindling of frail hope. Perhaps he was just resting in his dragon's company. Ought she visit Yonatan herself?

But this idea did not sit well in her stomach. She stood unsteadily, hand on the table for support. Did Yonatan know. That clear question rang in her mind. Did he know? She remembered his song last night. Was that his lamentation of her loss, or merely a cry of loneliness? Either was unbearable. But she could not see him — not without knowing what he knew.

Mār was lodged in a common garden, close to Rakhshan's old living space. Should she go there, instead? Her stomach churned. But how could she address Rakhshan in front of his scathing dragon? She had not seen the beast since their flight from Parudrauga. Who knew what he felt about her, given his scathing good-bye? She should just wait for Rakhshan to return to the apartment.

But what if he didn't?

The possibility smote her.

He might just as easily return to his old quarters, if they had not yet been turned over to someone else. And she did not know how to get there. If he went there before she could catch him at Mār, he would be lost to her. Now she could only hasten to where he was with Mār; or she would never find him at all.

She composed her appearance swiftly, flying to the powder room to wash her face in the basin, before moving to leave the apartment.

It occurred to her upon going through the door that she did not know what she would do when she found him. Her hand froze on the knob as she stood halfway in the hall. She would think of words, she reassured herself. She just needed to put some things to rest, and everything would be alright.

Remus and a guard she'd not seen before were standing outside; only half the contingent of guards was there, and Navid was not among them.

"Good morning," Remus greeted. Kefira nodded, moving self-consciously down the hall.

"Where are you going?" he persisted. He was already beside her.

She stopped, wishing he would not follow her. "For a walk. Down to the garden." Quickly, she added, "I will be back very soon. I just want to be alone," she forced an imploring smile, "if that is alright."

His face grew hard, and she knew that it wasn't.

She frowned, eyes beseeching him. She couldn't let him witness her shame. "I will be back in no time at all," she defended, "And I will never be out of sight of *any* sentries, you needn't worry; it is not as though I could get into trouble in the bright of daylight."

"The funny thing about trouble," Remus smiled bitterly, "Is that it oft does not care where the sun is." But she could tell by his expression he was letting her go. "Be sure to come back in time to break fast."

Kefira grew ill upon seeing Mār, curled up in the courtyard of a garden, a sight of gruesome splendor, just as when she first met him. His dusty scales glittered tan and green in the early sunlight. He was not facing her, sprawled away from the sight of the palace behind him. She could tell by the rhythm of his rising his chest that he was not sleeping.

There were other dragons in the vicinity, off-duty Zareks, mostly; a casually placed guard on the untrusted Parudraugan's beast. If not for these lazing witnesses, Kefira would have turned around and left. She just stopped, wondering which way to approach getting around Mār to Rakhshan without rousing the beast.

She made to step forward, and then halted again; her sandals scraped the pebbles on the pathway and she blanched.

Mār raised his head. "Brother?" he asked without turning. His voice had an unfamiliar, uncertain treble to it.

Kefira's feet went cold. She didn't say anything, realizing that she was waiting for Rakhshan's voice in reply.

It did not come. Mār's face turned slowly, and then he saw her. His pupils thinned to slits, even as her stomach felt as though it had plunged into a well. They regarded one another without speaking.

"I thought you were…" the Azhi Dahaki trailed off. "You smell of him." His voice was emotionless, wholly devoid of hatred, and altogether lacking the warmth of greeting. His forelegs folded against his chest, and she saw that the muscles in his wings were taut.

Kefira hugged her elbows, the scaly wall of the dragon before her. She looked at her feet. "He is not here, then," she said, stating what she already knew.

She forced herself to look at Mār when he audibly grimaced, teeth glimmering, a sanguine fire in his eyes. And then he smiled, unhappily. "Whatever gave you the notion that he woult be with me, little girl?" He rotated his body to face her, causing the nearby foliage to stir with the movement. He lowered his face to her eyelevel. "Why do you look for him? Oughtn't *you*, of *all* people, know where he is?"

Her mind went back many moons ago, when she first laid eyes on a dragon, this dragon, in person. She'd felt the fear of imminent doom at the claws of a beast, then. Now she only felt the dread of a less physical damage – not even to herself, but to who she was looking at.

But she had no desire to pity him. His snout was wrinkled in a half snarl, fangs dripping with his boiling spit, and she could tell by the look in his eyes that he had no desire for pity, either.

"I do not," she finally said. "Has he been to see you this morning?"

"I have not seen him since early yestertay," Mār bit out in response. "When have *you* last seen him? Certainly he coult not have wandert far from your den, unless particularly determint."

Kefira clenched her hands behind her back, feeling the pain of the repeated question. She was getting nowhere with this obstinate mule. "Goodbye, then," she said, turning away slowly and trying to keep her voice even. "I will look for him elsewhere." Even as she spoke, her mind was charging forward to locate Rakhshan, trying to forget the visage of his dragon.

But Mār made a clucking sound, and the movement of her legs was halted by the scaly mass of a tail put before her. "No, no, little sister," the voice above her chided. "I am not through."

Kefira turned to face him once more, resigned to whatever torture he had in mind.

He was lying on his belly, now, talons stationed on the ground on either side of her. He looked down at her from a lofty height, neck doubled back on itself so that he gazed down upon her from his blazoned chest; a grisly pharaoh. "What dit you mean by it, *lying* about your betrothal?" he asked.

The question was unexpected. She'd anticipated some form of barbed and disparaging words from him, of course – but none so grave in nature. To his credit, however, he spoke quietly, for a dragon, and when she could finally manage to glance about, she did not see that any of the beasts nearby had heard him.

His green gaze caught her once again. "That was a question intendet for an answer."

But as she looked up at him, her tongue was stuck in her mouth. No words could come. She blinked slowly, angry with herself and him. No matter what answer she gave him, she knew, he would not be satisfied.

But the question still merited a response. If she had one to give. But instead of mustering anything like an answer, she just said, "I am sorry."

Mār just stared at her. An unforgiving bead of saliva dripped from a spike along his jaw. After a moment of silence, he just shook his head and scoffed, voice low, "I'm *sorry*." His ruff quivered against his neck.

Both her heart and his head lowered, his neck craning like a serpent in the grass. He looked up at her, a cold light in his eyes. "I may not be happy, but I certainly hope that I am the *only* one in this arrangement who feels like putting leagues between himself and you." He looked at her sidelong, as though appraising the value of a bauble at a merchant's booth. "Wherever Rakhshan is. For his sake, I hope that he is not upset with his new mate." His tone had the mildest note of earnestness to it, but she did not know what to make of his words.

But before she could decide if they were even remotely good-natured, he spoke again, as though something were just occurring to him. "What dit you do, to make him a truant, I wonter?"

Her body flooded with a guilty heat. But she could not back away, his tail and forelegs fencing her before him.

He continued, not bothering to wait any longer for an answer. "I am no scholar concerning the matrimonial rites of men, but – if I may ask," he pardoned himself with feigned diffidence, "woult it be false to assume that you now carry an heir for my riter?" The mock-innocence in his voice was a blow to her. "Or maybe two – I am sure that woult please Yonatan, as well; once he fints out what you dit beneath his nose, it may make him think twice about destroying *all* of the shiny builtings in the city."

Kefira's face burned, and she felt as though she would be sick right then and there. She set her jaw, meeting Mār's challenging gaze. Once more, she had no words to speak. She wondered if he smelled the blood, if any remained on her face. If it was thus an invisible wound for him to pick at.

"If *that* you will not explain, at least intulge me this, as Rakhshan is not here to talk with me himself; how dit the ceremony fair? The night? Was he finally happy?" He breathed the last word with an air of wistfulness.

"Why do you keep on asking these things?" Kefira said.

He ceased his tirade, and gazed at her for a long time. And then he sighed acrimoniously, raising his head. "So you dit not." He let the droll words hang in the air.

She stared at him, hardly believing that the conversation was taking place, let alone with one so abominable as this dragon.

"You know, I am as displeast as apparently *you* are about this stupit union," he snapped, letting his veneer of naivety drop beneath self-righteousness anger, "but it doesn't make it any better to deprive my riter of the only benefit of the situation! You were *wholly using* him, I see now, to obtain the *legal rights* to your dragon," Mār harangued, "ant do not even have the decency to tie tails!"

The scales on his snout skinned her knuckles, and sent fire through her hand, but Kefira only had a mind to absorb the caustic barbs of the words. She stared at him, and her reddening fist.

He looked a little surprised that she had struck him; and he stopped talking. She clutched her hand to her chest, and saw layers of shredded skin. She looked down at her hand, eyes glossing over, not because of the pain.

"I never mean to hurt you. Or him," she said to Mār, voice low, as she fought to maintain control of it. "I have no excuse for such abuse of his... affections," she choked here, "but I can only say – that I believe you would have less a problem with it all if *Rakhshan* was the one who had been fighting to keep *you*."

She could tell that Mār finally had nothing to say. His eyes and expression were vacant again, as he gazed at her. And then he lowered his head, looking away. "When you fint Rakhshan," he said slowly, quietly, "let him know that I want to see him."

Kefira knew this was a dismissal. She stood there for a moment, trembling and feeling the hot throbbing of her hand. Then she turned away, leaving the beast and his lamentations behind her.

The bed was rumpled white and green and red, a pool of blankets and cushions, just as he'd left it – only Kefira was no longer there. Rakhshan felt the covers with a muted sense of alarm. They were still warm, recently occupied.

The voice of one of the eunuchs sounded behind him in the room. "It is my fault she is not here yet. I let her off not a few minutes ago. She said she wanted time alone."

"And you were foolish enough to indulge her? Did you not tell her of our errand?" Navid scoffed his companion with incredulity.

Rakhshan turned mutely out of the room, as the other man rejoindered, "I was under the impression that it was supposed to be a surprise."

Now the tray of delicacies he set on the table looked gaudy. He glared at them, the brightly colored fruits and cream-lathered pastries, and suddenly felt foolish. She was not even here. Why did she go out? He felt an ache of uneasiness creep into his throat. "Where did she say she was going?" he asked, staring at a clutch of amethystine grapes.

"A garden," the guard said, moving to stand a ways behind Rakhshan. "She did not specify which."

He heard Navid chastise Remus. "You did not even care to find out exactly where she was going? You're a novice, but I did not think you so foolish as to - "

Rakhshan wasn't listening to them. His eyes found the small jar of honey, left on the table from last night. And from there, the window. Then he remembered what they had heard outside, the object of Kefira's pain. Of course. He knew where she was.

"I am going to find her," he said, feeling his toes curl in his sandals as he stood.

"I will go with you," Remus volunteered.

"No, that is alright," Rakhshan turned to them. "I want you to be here in case she gets back before I reach her."

Navid cracked a wry smile. "I do not have a mind to lose both of you." He sighed, "But she cannot be in any danger, and I see that both of you have things that need to be resolved alone. Go on. We will wait."

Rakhshan nodded gratefully and left the apartment, the guards following to take their positions at the door with the rest of the contingent. The relief he felt at their absence was palpable, as though weights were lifted from his feet. Even if those particular eunuchs were agreeable enough, he knew that none of the guards anywhere in the palace trusted him, and he was never free of their eyes. But despite the fact that the halls themselves were lined with sentinels, the simple lack of an escort felt liberating. Now he could process his next actions without worry of their strictures. Because of course, his next actions were the most unpleasant a sort that a person could undertake. Yes; he knew where Kefira was. Yonatan was present in her mind all night, and she was with him now.

He pressed together his suddenly dry lips. Every fiber of his being revolted against going to see her in the shadow of the vengeful Hardlā, as he had seemed to have no qualms with attacking him and Mār when they first flew in. He felt a chill surge beneath his knees in recollection. Yonatan hadn't gotten a hundred cubits from them before he relented and was pulled down by the Immortals, but even from that distance Rakhshan had seen how much he had grown, and how much of a grudge he still held.

Would he go into Kefira's presence with this same beast, after he no doubt had been freshly informed of Rakhshan's new station?

A shiver ran down his spine. If Kefira was not there to deter him, going anywhere near Yonatan may very well be a death-sentence. He cracked a wry smile, discarding the thought immediately. Even that half-jested fear could not dissuade him. His steps did not falter.

For he needed to make sure that Kefira was not running away from him again.

Yonatan was tired. He had spent much of his recent days very much not lonely, in the company of many who were not Kefira. They were nice, good and golden she-dragons, there were many of them that he was acquainted with, now; a few were being brought to him each day. As though having so many companions might somehow be amusing to him or pleasing to him – as amusing him and pleasing seemed to be all the little men were intent upon doing; but it was all to no real purpose that he could see. The men must have had designs around it, for even when he was sleepy or just wanted to eat, they would keep him occupied with company.

He now had his own private garden, if a heavily guarded green square just outside of the green squares of other dragons could be called private. But most less-important beasts shared their squares with many others, whereas he was quite alone, outside of the company of the she-beasts and his guards. He could not ever decide how he liked the arrangement. He hardly had any time for thinking, anyway, except for night time, which was widely given over to sleep. His days were full of eating and the society of Gandarewas.

They had not brought him a lady yet, that morning, and now he just sprawled in his clearing, surrounded by his carpet of colored plants, waiting for them to bring him meat. He would have rather liked to get himself the meat, but they insisted, the men with their smiles and the dragons with teeth, that he be served. But at least they heated the not blood-fresh meat and flavored it with things, to make up for it. But despite it all, he sighed. He still would have rather liked to hunt for his meals, but they would not let him ever since the incident with the dragon with the nose-ring.

And despite all of the finery, he preferred the catching of small skinny things in the wilderness with Kefira, when the green spitting dragon was still larger than he, when he was just hatched. Those small things, the fish and the birds, they still had hearts. He missed Love.

And then he smelled her; faintly, as though from a very great distance. He raised his head, searching the ground for her small shape.

The voice that met him instead came to him like a leaf on the wind. It asked, "Is Kefira here?"

The speaker was nearby, somewhere on the side of his left wing. A searing incredulity rising in his veins, he craned his head to see; the voice was familiar.

The manling smelled of purple, of Love, and with the broadening of his pupils he could isolate the source of that smell, a small red stain on his sleeve. He did not need to look at his face to realize who it was. But he did anyway. He saw the creature's amber eyes, and saw the apprehension in them, as he bravely repeated his question.

Yonatan shook his head, unable to believe that he would dare ask such a thing, unable to believe that he was here. He had landed a week ago, without bidding, without reason. He and Mār had chased him and Kefira here. He was stating what he wanted, now. Why did he already smell of she that he searched for? Why was there blood on his sleeve?

Did he intend to finish what he had started in the city of his lies?

This time there was no longer a stone wall between them. He felt a growl reverberate slowly from his belly to the cavern of his throat.

"You mean that she is not here?" the deceiver of Kefira asked, as though he had not grasped the concept of his first answer. His stupidity silenced for a moment Yonatan's sound. The gold-fingered men had not appointed her to be here, and therefore she was not. This man should have known, so why did he ask? Frustration churned his gut – not for the first time – that he could not speak his fury at the man, and give questions to his questions. He could only write, and writing could not ever encapsulate what he wanted to say. *Did you lose her? Well, you had no business having her to lose in the first place! I did not even know you saw her at all since you came here! I did not know that you had not been killed for the wicked man that you are as soon as you landed.*

He seethed inside. It hurt his eyes to see this manling, this creature, that he did not understand and could not understand because it did not understand him. And he could not set his talon to writing any words, he was too furious, he could not write upon anything but flesh. But his claws scraped the ground just as readily. No words were formed.

He just stared at Rakhshan, and the man stared back, mouth stupid and open. What could be said when nothing could be said?

Yonatan ran his tongue sharply between his teeth in exasperation, and lowered his head to the level of the man. To his credit, he did not flinch, as though he himself remembered the days of kind and playful little Yonatan and his place on their shoulders. Yonatan remembered; and he also remembered not knowing how deceitful this man was.

The Hardlā gazed at him, soundlessly, head low, only half-paying attention to the mounting attentiveness of his guards at this point. He only had a mind for the creature before him. To derive understanding from him.

Why are you searching? he hoped the intensity of his eyes conveyed. *Why. Why do you come to me without explanation and ask about my beloved?*

Rakhshan blinked, and Yonatan saw that his skin glistened with the wet scales of discomfort. After a very long time, he said, with despair in his voice, "You do not know."

I do not know anything, because I cannot ask anything. Yonatan stared. *I cannot speak; I can only write enough words to be raised to the level of a barbarian in the eyes of the little. Tell me – what I do not know this time.*

The human looked as though he wanted to melt, but obstinate, bold bones held him upright. He looked past Yonatan then, as though searching. He was silently trying to come to a decision on something, mouth slightly open as though waiting for words to speak.

Yonatan flicked his tongue; he could taste the air that

surrounded the man – and the same salty scent that came from a fearful antelope was on him. He wanted to flee.

The dragon was irritated, but not yet ready to have him run of so; he withdrew his head a little and scanned his stunned-stag quiet form. It was difficult to tell from so up close, but he could make out no more blood than the small patch on his sleeve. He wore very fine clothing, a sort that was never his. Aside from the smell of Kefira, there was the faint scent of honey and fruits. That, and the blood, that most certainly belonged to his rider. His own blood curdled at this knowledge, but he forced himself to stay still. He needed an explanation. That was the only thing that kept him from flicking this man away into the rosebushes behind him, and stepping on him like a scarab.

Rakhshan could tell by the orange flex in Yonatan's golden irises that his patience was wearing. And he was just standing there dumbly, not answering the unspoken question. Then he noticed the dragon's eyes find something below his face. And so their gazes converged on his ring – the ring – could he possibly know what it meant? Rakhshan could keep silent no longer and sighed. "Yonatan, I am sorry. I know that you hate me, and for that I do not blame you, for I've done some things that were – not right."

The bitter humor in the dragon's eyes rang of his understatement.

Rakhshan tried to begin speaking again, aware of his shimmering reflection in the black pool of Yonatan's pupil, and the pallor of his face. What should he say? He had not come here to speak with Yonatan, but now that was unavoidable. To turn away now would be to admit whatever onus Yonatan found him guilty of. But he did not need to explain anything to him, nothing of their situation, at least; Kefira, would, in time. She might arrive any minute, now, to see her dragon, only to find him as well. She might be coming this very hour to enlighten Yonatan, and he did not need to say a word.

But he knew by the weight in his heart and ache in his stomach that that was not true.

Yonatan's guttural voice uttered a question, deep, low, and insistent. And Rakhshan knew that in Yonatan's eyes he had no right to ask for Kefira. He could not know what he was thinking, but he knew by the hard topaz of his gaze that nothing in his mind boded favorably for the human before him.

The dragon spoke again, unable to form words, just his increasingly frustrated question. Rakhshan heard his talons as they crushed the ground beneath them with the slow insistence of a mountain.

"Yonatan," Rakhshan tried, weary and conscious of a fear creeping up his spine; how could he answer a demand he could not grasp? He put forth a hand, palm damp, before the dragon, in a conciliatory gesture.

For an instant, Yonatan's expression was like sharp fragments of pottery, hidden by taut cloth, as though it took all his willpower not to thrash him, then and there.

Rakhshan took a step back, and noticed in the corner of his eye the Zareks suddenly become more aware of what was going on. But Yonatan did not move. He did not move for a long time, visibly swallowing his urge of violence, all the while glaring with scorn at the man before him.

He lifted a claw and brought it forward, watching with apparent satisfaction as Rakhshan tensed. But the claw came down again to the hard dirt of the path where Rakhshan stood.

An array of triangles and lines created two words; the first letters were neat enough, but then the characters slowly dissolved into angry scratch.

'Why what.'

Why was the traitorous Persian looking for his rider. What was wrong with her, and him, that she needed to be looked for.

Rakhshan should have known that this moment would come. How could he have expected to so callously betray him and Kefira, and not be reckoned with afterwards? And now he was an accomplice in Kefira's omission to the dragon, as without his knowing, he'd agreed to take his rider in marriage. The half of him that wasn't angry with himself was frustrated with Kefira. If she'd *said* something to Yonatan, he would not be in this position. He thought wryly, looking into the dragon's eyes, that death would perhaps have come swifter. These thoughts flashed in his mind in a moment, as he gazed back at Yonatan's command. He would not deceive him again, he realized as he opened his mouth to speak. Then he took a deep breath.

"To be able to keep you," Rakhshan began, voice quavering less than he'd imagined it would, "Kefira had to make a difficult decision."

Now Yonatan's gaze was captured by him, eyes wide and fearful and intense.

"It – it is not a bad thing," Rakhshan assured him, before he realized what he was saying. Then he added, dispassionately, "though none of those involved are very pleased with the arrangement."

Yonatan waited.

"It was decided by the King and his advisors," Rakhshan carried on slowly; he placed every word as though it were a footstep closer to his grave. "Kefira must be united with a man to maintain a dragon of your value."

He saw the dragon's pupils be reduced to papyrus-thin slits of horror, staring in stunned silence at him; then his eyes took on a remote sheen, fixed upon an unseen horizon.

"At first this man was going to be the King, but when it turned out that he did not – decide – that way, people started making offers," he continued, quiet as though ashamed of what he was speaking. Did Yonatan know of what he spoke? Did he know what marriage was? Rakhshan prayed that he would not have to explain it to him. "But then the King said that it was *hers* to decide, and would take no amount of money to change his mind…"

As he spoke, hoping that he'd come to a safe point for the dragon to come to his own conclusions, he looked up to appraise him. It looked as though Yonatan was watching Kefira die before his face, eyes glassy gold, pulsing orange. The grass beneath his muzzled did not stir. He was not breathing.

Fear for the dragon made him step forward. "Yonatan." Reflexively, unthinkingly, he finished, "It – it is me."

The dragon's eyes jerked to him, with an ire that suggested he'd known all along. Eyes flushing with newfound anger, Rakhshan was pinned against his gaze. Slowly, Yonatan's large head split with the snarling separation of his jaws.

Rakhshan became conscious of his proximity to the dragon, quite suddenly. Yonatan's face loomed just a few steps distant.

It was with shallow breath he spoke, louder, over a growing rumble before him: "You must understand – there were others that wanted her only for the prestige of owning you." His own words seemed to echo from far away – from Yonatan's mouth, he realized, as he stared at the vast grey opening menacingly slow before him.

Then there was no more reasoning. No more speaking. Rakhshan was transfixed with visceral awe by the space between the scalded orange of the dragon's eyes.

A willing horse could easily be stabled within Yonatan's maw, though by no means comfortably. Two rows of teeth would make sure of that. One set lined his jaws, and the second smaller set, narrow and curved as thorns, extended slowly from the flesh in the roof and floor of his mouth. Where teeth did not occupy his mouth, spotted grey-violet gums girded the ribbed cavern, speckled in wet light. A red, forked tongue stood still, inclining with gruesome grace upward to a place where the darkness converged, a place where the flesh of his mouth stretched around a black throat. His gums seemed to draw back from his teeth, the white spears extending perceptibly from his maw, gleaming like polished ivory.

From the back of the throat, a slow rumble grew, like an oncoming storm, a sound that entered Rakhshan's body and jarred his bones. This shook him from his trance, in time to recognize the sight before him. The spread of Yonatan's maw, the supreme display of bestial aggression.

Flashes of grey scales flickered above, and Yonatan staggered, suddenly, but stared with single-minded purpose at his frozen quarry. The last thing that Rakhshan could register was the sinking, sheathing of the second pair of inner teeth back into the grey. The insignificant function seized his eyes.

Then he was off his feet, the sky being jerked from sight as he felt a hard pain against his legs. After he realized he'd fallen forward, he then found that his feet rested against teeth, and his palms solid slickness. Only for a split second, however, for then his eyes were sealed as a sound that made his ears vibrate filled his mind, as he jerked forward and bone and flesh and heat battered him. Constricting flesh thrust him into darkness, and he heard his disappearing voice even as he felt wetness peel beneath his fingernails, as all light disappeared.

Though he was being accosted by the Zareks, the only sensations Yonatan allowed himself to feel at the moment were those of the throat. Still, he let himself be put to the ground by them, conscious only of the need to keep the arc in his neck. He heard the dismayed voices of men as they ran forward, and the commands of the other dragons as they swarmed him.

Vaguely, he recalled that he'd never before swallowed anything that still moved, and felt the knot as it ached a little inside. He too remembered his time at the lakes, the fishing, and the water that entered his nostrils. He wondered if Rakhshan could breathe.

His tail thrashed suddenly, at the sharp feeling of being bitten in the back of his shoulders. He heard Akhgar's voice, Farzan's – they were not happy, anxious, even. Disgruntled, Yonatan stood with a snarl, but otherwise ignored him. Though, as he kept his snout to the grass, he did recognize that now was the time to let the man go. He did not want to eat him.

He was bitten again, and breathed a roar of yielding. Of course they did not understand, so the men continued buzzing about him, and the Zareks to scramble atop him. They could not harm him seriously of course, so they just scrambled about with what dubious threats they could make. So instead of them, he concentrated on disgorging Rakhshan.

He felt the location of the man was somewhere between the apex and the base of his neck, and so then took the action of constricting the muscles in his gut, and let the hardened wave go through his chest to intercept his prisoner in a ripple of upwards motion. The ticklish feeling of a gag pressed the back of his throat, but he continued to work, all the while considering the foolishness of the guards. And much more, that of the dragons. Surely they should have recognized that if he truly wanted to eat the human, he could have done so irreversibly quick by raising his head very high and performing the normal jerking motions that would swifter receive him below. Of course, it was only because they were very alarmed that they did not realize, and that was acceptable. He himself would have been very astonished if he'd seen another dragon swallow a human, and probably would have taken action to prevent it, depending on the human they were swallowing; so he did not blame them.

But still, he was quietly smug when all of the noise died down when the human that had so concerned them reappeared in the grass, quite unharmed, save for bruises and unkempt body-cloths and mane. Even his chest still moved, Yonatan observed with satisfaction. He was not dead at all.

He noticed that men were coming forward to take up Rakhshan. But that would not do, yet. So he hovered his head above the body, to dissuade them. And then he promptly began to write.

When Rakhshan awoke, he was content not to get up. He just stared up at the scaled neck that hung above him, dimly aware that he was outside of it, now. Vaguely, he felt that various parts of his body were throbbing, even his lungs, as he concentrated on filling them with air.

Then the grass around him quavered, as grey shapes leapt off the golden hill above him, and cantered cautiously in and out of the dome of his vision. A small stream of red ran down the hill, and the Zareks spoke words of protest and growled their anger. He stopped the movements of his eyes, for it hurt.

He stared up again.

He was not dead.

He had been very certain that he was going to die, knew it so sickeningly clear in his heart, as the black snake constricted him.

His eyes fell shut once more, as he felt his galloping heart try to jerk to a slower pace. The adrenaline in his veins was sickening. His mouth tasted like sweet bile, and his bleeding fingertips trembled. He breathed with rasping throat.

The utter darkness. The nauseating lack of air. The press of unseen muscles, contracting heat on every side, squeezing him backward, as he cried out with a muted voice and futilely pressed his limbs against the walls of flesh that surrounded him. This was what he saw when he shut his eyes: a darkness deeper than that of closed eyelids.

Until he had felt the red light filtering through his tight eyelids, he did not believe that he could not die. He'd gone into his tomb. He wasn't supposed to leave.

Silently, he breathed, and watched the bobbing movement of the throat beneath the dragon's head.

Then, the head moved, and Rakhshan's heart lurched as Yonatan looked down at him. But his mouth was shut, and his eyes were devoid of anger, devoid of much of anything, like a freshly washed cloth.

A young soldier cried out as a talon was lowered to him – but Yonatan merely used it to turn him over, onto his belly. The sky and the ground switched places, and Rakhshan's stomach flipped. Blinking uncomprehendingly, he realized that before his eyes in the dirt was sharp cuneiform. A recognition. A pact. A promise. A threat.

In the ground read, 'You have my life. I have yours.'

Slowly, Rakhshan looked at the second sun above him that was the eye of Yonatan. And he felt himself nod.

The dragon stared at him for a moment, gaze unreadable. And then he withdrew, leaving the disgruntled Immortals to dubiously retake their stations or help Rakhshan up to his feet.

He did not know how he was able to return to the apartment.

Rakhshan walked through the door. He'd been heralded by the surprised and concerned voices of the men outside, and Kefira stiffened in her position at the table when she heard him enter. But he did not seem to notice her, for it was without a word that he dropped onto one of the longchairs.

She was too bewildered that he'd arrived for her to speak a word in greeting, and too abashed to want to. Before he came, she'd been looking at what he'd brought to the apartment. Remus and Navid said that he had wanted to get her something nice that morning, and though they insisted a servant fetch it for him, he'd gone to the kitchens himself.

When she saw him, she had no words to speak. She stood, astonished. And then he noticed her. He stood himself, unsteadily so. "Kefira," he exclaimed, equally surprised.

"Are you alright?" she asked, stepping forward, and dubiously grabbing his arm when he began to sway. "You look as though - " and then she could not come up with any explanation. As soon as he was steady, she pinned her arms behind her back. "Sit down," she pleaded. He did, and she did, across from him.

"I did not know that you returned." Rakhshan offered no explanation. "I'm sorry not to have been here when you awoke."

"It is fine." She shook her head, still incredulous. "Are you alright? Are you hurt?" Suddenly she recalled all of the sinister events that had befallen him in the past week. Had something else happened? "Did someone hurt you?"

"No, not really," he sighed. She saw him recline with difficulty over a pillow. His eyes had a distant look to them, as though he was not all there. His face and clothes were not clean, and she saw a purpling shadow on his neck.

A fear rose up within her that she tamped down. He would not answer her, so she would stop asking what had occurred. Instead, she got up and went to the washbasin in the other room, and dipped in a cloth. Ringing it out, she walked with speed back to Rakhshan and held it out to him.

He seemed not to notice, and so, after a moment's hesitation, she slowly wiped his face herself. It took a wince from him for her to realize that she went over a bruise along his jaw.

"I'm sorry," she said, and withdrew the cloth. "Do you just want to rest? I will leave you at peace."

He turned his head to look at the far wall. "It is alright," he said. "May you bring me some water from the table?" And then she realized how hoarse his voice was.

"Yes," and she stepped quickly to find a cup and the decanter from where they stood beside the fruit. She brought it to him swiftly. He took it and drank thirstily, and a small trickle departed unnoticed from his chin onto his jerkin.

She noted again, with displeasure, how unkempt all his clothes were, and that they clung to his body as an ill-fitting, second skin. And he smelled peculiar.

"Did they give you a wardrobe that you might change from?" Kefira asked. She had not looked yet to see if they already had raiment here. Certainly, they should have some form or another somewhere. Without waiting for an answer from him, she got up to search the rooms. Was there a chest of drawers or box somewhere that had yet gone unnoticed?

Indeed, there was a dresser behind a folding screen in the corner of the large bedroom. She opened the cedar doors to find two sets of clothing, one a woman's and the other a man's. There was nothing else in the accompanying drawers.

She roused him from where he'd dozed off and placed the garments on the divan beside him. "You ought to change." He looked up at her as though from a stupor, and did not seem to disagree. And then she realized that her request involved him undressing. Quickly, she half turned away and stammered, "There is a screen in there," and she indicated the bedroom with a finger.

He groaned loudly, and she recognized a hint of his melodramatic humor in the sound, though he did not smile. "Oh, I do not feel as though I can make it that far."

Kefira refused to entertain him, however, and left the room; though she was stifling a reluctant smile, she still was angry that he had not yet told her what had befallen him.

Ten minutes of silence must have passed and gave her over to worry about a whole manner of uncanny disasters that might be responsible for it; she waited for him to finish, as she nervously kept her wounded knuckles pressed to her lips in the bedroom. Finally she, impatient for an answer, peeked through the portico to the drawing room.

Rakhshan's old clothing was in a pile on the floor beside him, and he wore only half of what she'd brought him. He'd managed to put the fresh trousers on, but the tunic and vest were still half-folded beside him. He was asleep again.

Disturbed and confused, it was with shame that Kefira reentered the room. Though he was half-naked – had she ever seen him so before? – she could not help but look at him. She approached his form and saw a swathe of purple and yellow beneath his lower ribs. She noticed his hand in his lap, the pink-tipped fingers, and how a couple of his nails were torn, with old blood. She gasped quietly, and her eyes went to the clothing beside him, uncertainly, as she tried to distract herself from the opening pit of her stomach. What was he not telling her?

His face did not look serene. His hair was not dry. She saw beads of sweat on his skin. The bruised muscle of his chest, ruddy skin, with a scattering of dark hairs. She looked away quickly, abashed, and uncertain of what to do.

But she decided she would not wake him again. She refolded what he hadn't put on and set it neater beside him, and shuffled the old garments to a corner with her feet.

Then she returned to sit at the table, placing herself disconsolately upon a cushion; she would wait for him to wake up to pry from him answers concerning what had happened. In the meantime she lacked anything else to do but obey her hunger, so she began to pick at the pretty things on the platter.

Then she remembered. She freed one of the smaller dishes by dumping its occupants onto another, and fixed a plate for Rakhshan himself. She did not know what he liked, so filled it with the freshest looking fruits and sweetest pastries and, lacking a better place, set it beside him on the longchair. And then she moved away to quietly and uncomfortably attend to herself.

As he'd been the one to bring it, she felt guilty for eating without him. But the sun was already half way to noon, and so she nibbled anyway on the delicious things, though she did not wholly taste them. Her mind was occupied with how foolish she'd been to go looking for him, and how for her pains had been subject to Mār's scalding, only to know now that Rakhshan hadn't deserted her at all, and had been getting all these nice things before her.

When she'd returned to the apartment, they'd been waiting for her; but he was not there. Before she'd gotten back, he'd gone himself to look for her, Remus had said. Remus said that he'd supposed he knew where he was going, though now it was clear that he had not, she thought bitterly.

It was all very confusing, no more than a dumb misunderstanding that had sent both on wild chases. She felt stupid for running off to find him only to meet the wrath of his dragon; but then she realized she did not regret the conversation with Mār, though it had brought her no closer to finding his rider.

With a sigh, she recognized that she was married to someone she did not even know well enough to find after ten minute's absence. Though, how could she have known that he hadn't gone to see his dragon? Distantly, she wondered where he himself had gone to search her out.

And then it struck her. With disbelieving horror, her eyes strayed to the window, and then to Rakhshan; his bruises, the dim pain in his face. His reticence.

Then she stood, promptly, entered the bedroom, and wished there was a door she could shut behind herself. With wooden legs, she walked to the far side of the bed, and sat with her back in the corner, and there began to cry, teeth clenching her knee to keep the silence.

Chapter XX
Ransom of a Nation

The next days went by in stagnant procession. With no verbal acknowledgment needed, Rakhshan and Kefira consistently adhered to their separate sleeping quarters. They ate three meals a day in a silence that was not often broken, except for by the servant girl, Leva; Kefira had insisted she eat with them out of courtesy, though it seemed to discomfit Rakhshan, despite the girl's protests of decorum. Aside from Leva's prattling about Kefira's appearance, there was not much to speak of – or anything they desired to bring up, until Kefira finally pressed Rakhshan into telling her what had happened to him that day after. Eventually, he answered, with a confirmation that went beyond what she'd feared. And shame consumed her.

Leva had not finished brushing Kefira's hair when she insisted on going to see Yonatan at once. "But I'm not done," the girl protested behind her.

Kefira threw her shawl over her head. "It is alright, you can finish later. I must see him." And she could almost hear Rakhshan's thoughts: *You* should *have seen him weeks ago.*

"Just let me put a ribbon in what I've done thus far," Leva said, and held Kefira a moment longer to adjust wrinkles in her raiment. "Now you look nice enough." But her frown suggested she'd like to do about an hour more of primping before letting her go. Kefira put a swift, placating hand on her shoulder, before turning away.

She grasped Rakhshan tightly by the elbows. "I am so sorry. I had no idea he would do such a thing."

The man just shrugged a little bit, ambiguous as though the yellowing bruises on his skin were only from taking an accidental tumble, not from the gullet of a gargantuan dragon. "It is alright. I guess that was just his way of talking to me." His smile was brittle.

"Talking?" Kefira faced the door, incredulous. She shook her head. "He never meant to hurt you, though, I know it."

"Well, I wouldn't go *that* far," Rakhshan said, scratching his head.

She turned to look at him, silent for a moment. Then, repeated, "I am sorry. I never thought he would – well. For him I am sorry, too." When she noticed that Leva had surreptitiously begun to work on her hair again, sneaking up with her deft fingers, she straightened and said, "I am going to see him. Now. I don't know when I will be back, so do not wait on me for the midday meal."

Leva sighed much like her aunt would at the flightiness of her mistress. "I will check the kitchens for a fresh bowl of pistachios to accompany our next meal."

"Thank you, Leva," Kefira said absent-mindedly as she went out the door. Rakhshan heard her offer a brief explanation to the eunuchs, and heard few pairs of footsteps go down the hall.

But he was not about to be left here with the girl. He was glad he had not been given a servant, himself; he was appalled enough that *she* had to *live* with them. Not only that, but she'd had reached the stage of youth that filled her with words and questions and unyielding persistence to match. He left out the door a minute later, with a brief nod to her, before she could ask him why he hadn't combed his hair.

Kefira saw that Yonatan had detected her, even at the great distance where he was merely a golden hill rising from the garden. She heard him utter a keen as he lifted his head to gaze at her, a wounded sound, past the staccato of footsteps – Navid and Remus had to walk unceremoniously swift to keep up with her near-jog. She saw her dragon stand, and, heart sinking, wondered if he knew that it was she who should have taken Rakhshan's punishment instead.

But she knew he would not think that. There was only aggrieved love in Yonatan's eyes. His forlorn expression made her hesitate to embrace him, but she did, slowly, her head resting next to his eye.

"I am so sorry," she whispered, knowing that the words were not sufficient, and hating that she had to express her apology so inadequately. He blinked, slowly, in response, eyelids low. She kissed his brow, one of the red plates that spanned it. Her fingers rested against the ridge of a scale. She felt the thrumming of unheard croon beneath.

"I knew that I'd have to get married for a month now, and I never told you," she confessed, giving herself no concession for forgiveness. She saw how his iris flexed orange about his narrowing pupil, and knew how the fact she disclosed had struck him. Even his own rider had lied to him, and for so long, she realized, an unbearable pain stabbing itself into her mind. Feeling more like a wretch than ever, she pressed her head against his face. "I am so sorry. I have no excuse."

He recoiled his head back, startling her. When she regained her balance, she could not read his eyes. He was staring.

Silence. Involuntarily, she felt tears begin to form in her eyes. She blinked to stop them, as she gazed up at her dragon. He'd never regarded her so, never with such dismay, never with such pain, looking at her as though she was not even the same person. Her fingers rose to be held in her teeth.

But then his nose was against her, pressing gently. With a small sigh, she held his muzzle to her chest, unbelieving. His eyes were half-lidded, and he still bore a wounded expression – but he was not shunning her. The tears almost came again. "You must understand," she said, "I would never have done it if not to keep you."

After a moment, he nodded, almost imperceptibly.

"And he was the one – that I distrusted the least."

Yonatan let out a sarcastic snort, a bitterness entering his eyes.

She smiled a little bit, and then her lips formed a short line again. "I panicked, because I was supposed to decide who I would marry, and so I chose him." She frowned. "He was not there to begin with, however, and so people got angry..." she trailed off, and then looked into his eyes again. "There was a bad man who wanted to give the King a very large amount of gold for us," she said, "of a number I never thought existed."

A quizzical precision entered Yonatan's eyes that Kefira understood as an inquiry. "The man was – well, you might remember him; the one from Hangmatana," she said with distaste.

She saw his pupils dilate.

"Why do your eyes smile whenever he is about, or mentioned?" Kefira asked, suddenly interrogative. "You usually dislike people in general, but you do not seem to mind him."

His eyes slowly returned to normal, even as his nostrils flared, and Kefira shook her head. "He is the one who – well, who I got you from, I guess…" she trailed off. "If he had his way, he'd kill me to have you, I'm sure."

These jealous words seemed to clear Yonatan's head, and the beginnings of indignity began to spread across his face. Swiftly, she spread her hands over his muzzle. "Do not worry about it. I have not seen him for days, a fortnight, I think. He is no trouble." She'd hate to see Yonatan go and tear up the palace to look for him. "He may have even returned to Babylon," she added hopefully.

He lowered his eyes back to her and breathed a quiet sigh.

"But," she said, quieter, "If he is still here, and *does* happen to come around again, I would not mind if you pretended to – eat – *him*," her voice was halting, "as you had Rakhshan."

Yonatan's resulting expression was a mixture of anticipation and mischief. Then she belatedly checked her words, and pressed her hands against the horn on his snout. "That was a jest. I do not want you to get into any trouble for it. He is an important man."

The dragon's tongue flickered out, and he seemed to accept her words, though looking as though he would not care for the man's station, only for her will.

She looked down, briefly, examining the scales that lipped his maw, and his gleaming teeth between the jaws held ajar. She had been in his mouth once, as a protected passenger, but she could not imagine the horror of passing the threshold as a victim, like

Rakhshan, even if Yonatan had released him.

"Did you know you were going to let him go, before you did it?" she asked suddenly.

It took him a moment to process the question, and then his eyes narrowed sheepishly. And then he nodded.

"I knew that." She put another kiss on his snout. "I cannot pretend I know why you did it, and I shan't make you explain. But I know you have a good heart."

Yonatan looked at her mutely, receiving the words. The conversation faded, and she realized that the morose look in his eyes persisted.

Arm slung over his muzzle, she rubbed his scales beneath her fingertips. Her own voice was sober when she said, "You need not worry. Nothing has changed between us. I have an occupation now, I suppose, that is all."

The dragon did not look as though he believed her. They stood in silence for a while. And then she knelt beneath his chin. "Why do we not pray, again?"

A gleam entered Yonatan's eye, and he lowered his head to the ground beside her.

Rakhshan watched from a distance, leaning unnoticed against an arbor. Not for the first time, he saw how tender they were with one another; it was strange, as though one was the succor to the other's soul. Love, certainly.

It was hard to see the warmth Kefira was capable of with Yonatan. Even as her new husband, Rakhshan thought sullenly, he knew that for some reason he could have no part in it.

With a wry smile, he found then that he was jealous of the dragon.

Of course, he tried not to look at the dragon, at Yonatan, as hard as it was to ignore a creature so large. Being so close – if being far out of earshot could be called close – the very presence of the dragon made his heart quicken, and his palms sweat, despite himself. His mind told him that he was not afraid, that Yonatan was still the hatchling that he'd helped raise, and not the savage beast that some might disdain his muteness to make him. But his body felt like it belonged to a skittish hare, now that he knew what the dragon was capable of. An animal fear threatened to thrash his reason, and if he thought for too long about their last encounter, he still felt ill.

The dragon's words after. The foreboding pact of some sort of brittle peace between them. Rakhshan may have Yonatan's rider now, but Yonatan could snuff out Rakhshan with one movement of whatever bodily weapon he chose. Rakhshan had never intended to let any harm to come to Kefira, but his goal had escalated: never let Yonatan think for one second that Kefira might even have the *potential* to be in *any form* of danger.

Rakhshan folded his arms, wiping sweat from his palms and rubbing a bruise that spanned his lower ribs, letting the ache hone his mind past the unease rising within him. His eyes were on the distant grass, where Kefira was kneeling.

"It is refreshing, is it not, to see such a specimen of incorruptible love?" A voice said from out of sight. "It is enough to make one believe that mankind is not completely devoid of good or god's hand."

Rakhshan started, head jerking to the sound.

The responsible figure stood, not looking at him but past, at the spectacle Rakhshan himself had been taking in. The man was tall and refined of demeanor and form, and he recognized the curled beard and the narrow, brown eyes of the Babylonian.

His stomach dropped, and he felt his face instantly go pale. But Shaza'eil did not look at him, and the four guards that surrounded him had only a mind for their vigil.

For a moment, Rakhshan just stared at him, stunned by his presence. And then, after a sickening moment, he realized that he could not reply in any form to the man. Instead, he just bit his tongue and pretended to gaze back at Kefira, all the while feeling his pulse thrum in his wrists.

"For once you seem to be tongue tied, mercenary," Shaza'eil remarked, finally sending a sidelong gaze to his subject, eyes gleaming.

Rakhshan allowed himself a bitter smile, by way of hiding the scowl that wanted to take its place. "I had not expected to see you again, envoy," he grated out politely. He now met the man's gaze, emerging from his initial stun.

"Likewise," Shaza'eil said, equally courteous. A smiled spread across his face. "Pray, how did the long journey from Hangmatana treat you?"

"Well enough." Rakhshan answered brusquely; then heard himself ask, "What brings you here?" He did not care about what brought this man here, but this was the one who would have bought Kefira for a mountain of gold, even though he wanted nothing to do with her; his resentment for him was palpable. But he tried not to let it show on his face. Just make idle talk, and eventually the man would go away, as a mosquito would after growing bored of its victim.

"A meeting," the Babylonian replied, his voice a wistful sigh. "Or rather, exemption from one."

Rakhshan was surprised. He'd actually given something beyond an empty reply. But he pretended not to be interested, as though he himself had been to hundreds of meetings in the last week, and was looking at a jilted secretary.

Shaza'eil continued, looking out over the garden. "It happens to be military in nature, no less, or so I have been informed." He said the words as though they left a bitter taste on his tongue. "The first one of such a nature for a long time, as I understand it. And Babylon is excluded, even as the quasi-envoy of a nonexistent nation is *not*."

After a moment, Rakhshan could guess who he was talking about. Certainly the Israeli man who had united he and Kefira; he was also an advisor to the King.

Then Shaza'eil smiled. "But what are my annoyances to you but amusements? I did not come here to bother you."

Then what *did* you come here for? That was what Rakhshan wanted to know. But he said nothing and sullenly looked out at Kefira, who was still speaking with Yonatan.

"But looking at her makes it difficult to feel troubled, I'm sure," the man perseverated. "I do not believe I ever congratulated you on your marriage."

Rakhshan felt his blood begin to buzz in his hands.

"It was a quick ordeal, small and quiet – hardly the celebration such a momentous occasion deserved… Two orphans found a common home in fortune, and by it a great dragon was safeguarded from those who desired him for selfish gain. A happy ending to three different tales." His lips curled upwards, in his mirthless way. "The gods have such odd ways of doing things, but despite their means, their ends are always benevolent."

The Persian did not believe a word he said. He just nodded, in hopes of shutting this oppressor up.

He heard the inquiring smile in Shaza'eil's voice. "Tell me, what god did you so please in your youth, as to be bestowed such a gift?"

"I am quite sure I have not pleased any god."

"But certainly you have," the man replied, aghast. "How else could such fortune have fallen into your lap?"

"An evil spirit must have pulled wool over god's eyes, and so he accidentally dropped some on me."

"An evil spirit must have pulled wool over *many* gods' eyes – for certainly many had come together: the Dragon Mother Tiamat," Shaza'eil's eyes went from Yonatan, to Kefira; "the Great Consort Ishtar, both conspiring with Fortuna to forge their gift," he said, "into a humble pair of silver rings."

The way his eyes slithered to Kefira, when she kissed Yonatan's nose, made Rakhshan sick. He stopped leaning against the bower and turned to face the man. "Do you have a problem with this?" he asked finally, raising his hand with the ring on it. "Is that why you insist upon needling me?"

Shaza'eil looked coldly at him. "I assure you: that ring means nothing to me," he said, after a moment.

"Why are you here?"

"*Demanded* the insignificant bandit of the ambassador of the land's greatest empire."

His sudden lack of propriety stunned Rakhshan for a moment. Then he stepped forward, fists tightening. "You cannot bear it, can you," he found himself saying. A muscle in the Babylonian's neck twitched. "That you had half the capital in Babylon to exchange for Yonatan, yet still the King was somehow not swayed by your bribery. You cannot stand the fact that *I*, of all people, without money, without prospects, without gods, was chosen, not you."

"And suppose that you are right," Shaza'eil snapped, voice bordering a hiss. "Maybe I have fleetingly envied, in my lowest of states, the fortune of a lawless little bastard." He grinned menacingly. "But I do not think I will envy you for long. Because, try as you might, you can only hope to flounder in the mire you've dived into, boy. The only achievement you can ever aspire to is foreseeing your fate a minute before it finds you. You were not meant for this place, or your newfound position. And I am not the only one who knows it.

"In the meantime, I suggest you think of what you are, the naught that you were born to amount to, and who it is that you are defying. Know that you will not be able to hold for long what you have wrongfully gained. You and that Jewish rat will leave as you came: with nothing."

Rakhshan felt his own anger, seething throughout his veins, but he was not lost in it enough to forget the four armed men that accompanied the serpent before him. His jaw was clenched so hard it hurt. Somehow, his voice was kept beneath a snarl. "You may be the voice of Babylon here, ambassador, and you may berate me all you like." He dropped the words like the condemning rocks of a stoning. "But I will not permit you to involve yourself with Kefira – *my wife* – in any way, or even talk about her, not even to say something *kind*. She is no longer a tool that can be grasped for in this court, and neither of us will tolerate anything further from you."

"Oh, you will tolerate nothing further from me?" the man sneered. "Are you trying to threaten me, boy?"

Rakhshan did not hide his smirk. "Do you *feel* threatened?"

He could see a flash of red in the man's eyes, and was satisfied when he did not speak for a moment. Then he brusquely turned his rigid back to him, and did not look back as he said, "Not as you shall."

When he was gone, Rakhshan huffed and leaned back against the arbor. He didn't believe the jackal would carry out a single thing he insinuated. The man could do nothing to harm him, anyway, not with the backing of Mār and the King. The coward's threats were empty.

But then his eyes returned to Kefira, and he wondered.

Kefira's fists healed in time, leaving small round scars where her knuckles had struck dragon scales. Leva fussed over them nonstop, and insisted she sleep with oils of coconut and lavender on her hands. Kefira did not like the feeling of once more going to sleep slick with ointments, but bore it. She liked the smell, at least, and they did not taste bad, when her hands happened to stray to her mouth.

One day at breakfast, Rakhshan asked after the nature of the new aroma that clung to her; she hid the wounds on her fists beneath the table, and disclosed to him the identities of the scents. He seemed to remember, even as she did, that one of them was the aroma she'd borne on their wedding day, and smiled.

He was at the apartment less frequently, now.

The first time she truly noticed his absence was proceeded with a courier, informing him that his presence was desired at a meeting. He would not say what the occasion was.

This confounded both of them. Rakhshan was hesitant, but he

went. When he returned, it was very late at night; Kefira woke at the sound of the door. She pretended to be asleep; his footsteps stopped by the entry to the bedroom. Peeking through slitted eyelids, she saw he was leaning against the wall, the glow of his lamp illuminating in gold the folds of his clothing and the planes of his face.

She felt he watched her for an hour before finally moving. He padded quietly closer, and she heard his breath, as he kissed her lightly on the forehead. He left afterwards, leaving her flustered and fighting to maintain a visage of sleep.

It was the first meeting of many. Kefira once asked what they were about. "Martial matters; concerning Yonatan, among other things." He was vague, to say the least.

"Do you know why you are invited?" she ventured.

He shrugged. "I found it odd that they would invite a – man of ill repute, such as I; but the Levite told me that the King fancied – how did he say it – diversity in counsel and unity in command, and so I was not at all unwelcome by him."

"Tobias was there? How come I was not invited?"

"Though they would dislike you less than I as Yonatan's delegate, I do not think you would be as..."

"As what?"

"As – eloquent, in the arena of a conference."

"And you *are*?"

"Remember, *I* have a few years training in the Asman Kāra - "

"The Sky Army? It *is* a military meeting, then."

He just smiled, and would give her no more on the subject.

Soon the man seemed to be leaving for more than these secretive discourses. Those meetings always occurred at certain time periods – afternoon to late night. But he would be gone at more random intervals now, which she assumed were visits to Mār. But sometimes when Mār was sure to be having a meal, or to be out hunting with palace dragons, Rakhshan was gone even then. She did not ask him about it.

He also received messages, through Barid. She knew they were from Parudrauga. One day, sitting at the table and leaned over a square of papyrus, he announced, "Mehrnaz, if you remember her, is going to have an egg, by Mār. Tahmour tells me Ravan wants it desperately." He looked up at her. "I think she's taking after someone."

Kefira smiled, a little sadly, remembering the place and its inhabitants. "How does the city fare?"

"The crops are sprouting. And the rest of the city moves at their pace. Everyone is still a little stunned, about our... arrangement."

She shook her head. "As they should be. It was a mad ordeal. I do not believe the most inebriated vagrant among them could have plotted a madder mess." She returned his gaze, eyes soft.

He looked as though he could not agree more.

That night there was no meeting. Yet he was absent. Kefira ate dinner alone again, and went to bed after being treated by Leva. She didn't fall asleep, and so stared in the fading light up at the white and green canopy above her. It was past dark when she heard Rakhshan return.

After a minute, the girl heard him fall onto his divan. Silence. She felt a chill and stirred within the covers. Pressing her cheek into a pillow, she shut her eyes. Now that she was certain he had returned safely, she could sleep easier.

Before she drifted off, however, a sound registered. The other room. She heard the rattle of unsettled breathing. It came almost inaudibly. She wondered if Rakhshan was snoring. It did not occur to her that he could be weeping.

Then, the next day he vanished. It was now seven days since Kefira last saw him.

That first morning, when she woke up, she thought he was freshening himself. But then, after no motion from the washroom sounded, she peeked in and saw that he was not there. She asked Leva where he was. She said that she hadn't realized he left, and then began to tell her about what a disagreeable sort of person he was, upon which Kefira only replied a vague concurrence.

For the rest of the day, she told herself that he was visiting Mār. Maybe they were hunting together – he was fond of his bow, after all. But when night came and went, and he had not returned, she went to see the dragon. Rakhshan was not there, and Mār would not acknowledge her existence.

Navid and Remus were not concerned, and expressed that she shouldn't be, either, though their reassurances weren't explicit. "He will return," or, "He is in no danger."

So she steeled herself and decided that he was at another meeting, a particularly long one. She would wait. He would return.

In his absence, the apartment seemed bigger, like a cave. The air seemed colder, and quieter; she wanted to hang fabric over the windows. Days were longer. These were things she felt as she reassured herself that she did not worry about him, or miss him. Certainly not the latter.

She would have rather liked to visit Tobias. But she could not find him anywhere. So she spent her time with Yonatan, when she could. But they could hardly be alone anymore, what with the dragon sages and tenders and guards he had. And he spent a lot of his time now with Shoala. Kefira still did not think he knew the people's intentions for them, but the she-dragon seemed quietly to know.

She was a young Gandarewa, shorter and of stockier build than Yonatan, and of milder temperament. She was not disagreeable, and apparently was of exceptional pedigree: she would never be as large as Yonatan would grow to be, but came from an impressive line that was said to ensure offspring that would bring his great size into the Persian lines.

These politics around Shoala and Yonatan did not concern Kefira, only that she seemed to make him happier.

Kefira sighed, staring out of the window of the bedroom. The sun began setting unnoticed before her flickering eyes as she stared out on the courtyard. Masons were finishing another day's work of tiling. She watched without interest. Today she was informed that Yonatan was to be united with Shoala, soon, within the fortnight. It'd finally been decided.

She'd known it was to be, and had tried to stave off the disturbing thought; though that was to no avail, now. She couldn't stop thinking about it. But she tried not to be upset. She could not allow herself to feel the same measure of revulsion that he had at her union. Yonatan's was imperative, anyway, and had never been concealed from her. She had no right to rail against it.

Dismally, she wondered if Rakhshan felt different whenever Mār decided to sow his seed. Did he feel a distance spread a little wider between them? He did not seem overly perturbed about Mehrnaz. So it was probably different for them; they were, after all, both male.

Kefira slid to her knees, and rested her head upon her arms on the windowsill. Where was he? There was no such thing as week-long meetings without respite. Certainly he would have informed her if such an occasion arose. But to be gone for more days than she could count on a hand – without word or explanation...

Food poisoning? Accidental injury? Anything could be keeping him. But why wouldn't she, of all people, be told? To keep her from worry? But then, they'd have explained away his absence at least with an excuse. Instead, now there was complete silence.

She found herself angry, suddenly. If he was hurt, and was avoiding her to hide it – what if Yonatan had harmed him again? Or there was an attempt on his life, and was he perhaps now in hiding?

Rakhshan needed to stop not telling her things. If he was here, she would give him a piece of her mind. *What are those meetings about? Where have you been? Why haven't you told me?*

But then she realized that she didn't care if any of those questions were answered. She just wanted him here.

"Kefira."

The girl hadn't heard anyone come in. She wasn't sure who the voice belonged to. She turned her head to see the speaker.

Who was it but her truant husband. She jumped to her feet. "There you are! Where've you been?" She closed the distance between them, incredulous at his sudden presence.

"Whoa," he said, and she heard him wince, right before she realized she'd flung her arms about his waist.

Just as quickly, she stepped back, abashed. "I'm sorry! You – surprised me." Her large eyes absorbed his face. He looked to be swallowing pain. "Are you alright?"

"Yes," he said. "Yes, I am." His amber eyes flickered.

Silence.

"Are you wounded?" she insisted quietly, as her eyes searched for hidden bandages.

"Not by your meaning of the word," he replied haltingly. Then he half-turned, toward the door. "Will you sit down?"

Tentatively, she followed him into the drawing room. "Where have you been?" she asked. His walk seemed stilted, slow. "Rakhshan… what is this all about? Why have you been gone so long? Without a word - "

Once she took her place on the longchair across from him, he sat. She could tell he was trying to hide the effort it took. But she saw the taught muscles in his jaw. Then he leaned forward, folded arms bolstered on his knees.

"Kefira. You know the meetings I'm going to."

"Yes – yes – is that where you've been?"

"No; but I want to tell you what all of those have been about," he explained, eyes rising from the floor to her face. "They *have* been military in nature, as you've guessed. They've concerned means, or stratagem, rather that – well…" He broke off. But then, for the first time, his gaze met hers with stolid conviction. "Kefira. To put it shortly, Persia is going to declare war upon Babylon."

Her teeth clutched her finger, before she realized she'd put up her hands to catch a cry of disbelief. "What?" was all she could say.

A smile began to spread across his face. "The King realized he wanted their land. With some prompting. Tobias," he continued, "shared writings of an old prophet, by the name of Isaiah, son of Amoz."

"Jewish names," she said slowly.

"Indeed. The prophet wrote of a king. Who would defeat the Babylonians, and deliver the Jews."

Kefira stared as Rakhshan continued, unable to breathe.

"At the meeting, Tobias had one of his scribes read the passage. It mentioned Cyrus by name. Everyone was amazed, for the date on the parchment was two hundred years before the King was even born."

His eyes looked past her. "It'd said... *I am the Lord, Who says of Jerusalem, 'It shall be inhabited,' and of their ruins, 'I will restore them,' Who says to the watery deep, 'Be dry, and I will dry up your streams,' Who says of Cyrus, 'He is My shepherd and will accomplish all that I please; he will say of Jerusalem, "Let it be rebuilt," and of the temple, "Let its foundations be laid."'*"

"It said that?" Kefira breathed.

"I cannot forget the words," he replied.

"The King was not angry?"

"At first he was perplexed; then he asked his scribes why no one has ever brought this to his attention before?" Rakhshan smiled. "His only anger was with them."

Kefira stared at Rakhshan's feet. She could not process his words. What if they were true.

"And... just like that?" she asked.

"That was the first meeting. The last have been figuring out the execution. There should be a full plan within the month."

"Rakhshan," she finally gasped. "Do you know what this means?" When she met his eyes, she was not even sure that she herself knew.

"I think you're getting your temple rebuilt after all," he replied softly.

He of all people had faith in this – it struck her; for she'd never even dared to hope. She dipped her head, to rest it in her hands, dumbfounded. "Adonai." The whisper emerged.

She felt his hand touch her elbow. "Yonatan will be able to help fight for it."

"He will," she said, eyes widening. "I've told him all I know of our holy land, and our people – but I don't think either of us... ever had any hope..."

"I know." Rakhshan leaned back. "I cannot tell you how amazed I was, and I'm – wasn't even one of your people." He explained quickly, "It would be his first official action, so beforehand, it was decided he would get some training; and you would, as well."

"Me? They'd let *me* ride? Training where?"

"Well, of course you'd go – Yonatan would have no one else, and riding Mār I could not, even if he had a mind to let me."

"Praise God – are we – we are going to the Asman Kāra, yes?" Kefira asked.

Rakhshan smiled. "Yes. And Mār and I are to finish our training there, too, so you will not be going to an institution alone."

"An institution!" Where children of high-status are educated, reservoirs of wisdom for the prestigious. "I've never even seen one before! Oh, Rakhshan..." She looked hopelessly at him. "What has happened, in the last months, that such fortune had been given me?"

His gaze returned hers steadily.

"Getting to keep Yonatan, and – well, all this amazing news you bring." She glanced at the far wall. "Sometimes I'm afraid of how the world opens up. Like now, I figure. Though I know I should not be." She looked at him. "I – I am very glad, that you will be going, too."

He smiled. "I'm glad that you're glad. Of course I would not let you go alone. Even with Yonatan watching, I'd fear the boys there might steal you away."

She laughed a little. Then her eyes fell to his legs, and she grew solemn. "Rakhshan – where have you been? I know it could not have been at a bureaucrat's, signing papers."

His expression sobered. "Indeed, no. I will – I will explain myself." He leaned forward, hands knit. "At the first meeting," he began, "I met Tobias for the first time beyond our – well, our wedding. I asked him further about Isaiah's writing, and your homeland, Hardlās, and Babylon, for the purpose of helping devise a plan for Yonatan's employment in a war. I admit, I found the Levite intimidating at first - "

"You found Tobias intimidating?" Kefira interrupted, balking.

His lips curled wryly. "I don't deny it. Anyway. He proved quite – well, he invited me to have a meal with him, and then we ended up having many such meetings. So I have been gone more frequently."

Kefira was astonished; she'd never had any expectation for any sort of amity to form between Rakhshan and Tobias. "What for?" she asked, not at all displeased by the idea.

Rakhshan shrugged. "I just... found what he said interesting. I never thought it possible, but he knows even more stories of your people than you do."

"They're not just stories," she retorted.

His eyes were almost golden in the half-light, and he said, "I know."

Slowly, Kefira stood. "Rakhshan – where were you this last week?" Her words were quiet.

He looked down, then up at her face again. "Kefira... you know only a little of my childhood; I grew up without parents, just as you did, only in a much different place." He ran a hand through his hair as he looked at the floor. "So I believed that the pantheon, all gods, were only cruel, indifferent spirits, that did not care at all that children went without fathers and mothers. That children like us were condemned to living in hunger and fear."

She watched as he edged off the longchair, and slowly knelt. "But in the last months, I – well, I saw the fingerprints of a good god at work." She saw him swallow, and meet her gaze. "I found I don't want to keep on – not trusting, anymore. Because I realized that, where God takes away parents, he gives dragons."

His face grew glassy in her eyes, and she blinked away tears, listening stunned. "What are you saying?"

"Where you go, I will go," he murmured, "And where you stay, I will stay. Your people will be my people, and your God my God. Where you die, I will die, and there I will be buried." He held her hand. "May the sovereign Lord of Israel deal with me, be it ever so severely, if I let anything but death separate you from me."

She stared at him, and he said, "Hallelu Yah, Kefira."

Kefira fell to her knees, eyes fixed on his. Not a second later, she fell forward and embraced him.

His body stiffened, and then she felt his palm against the back of her head. "Do not cry, Kefira."

"Oh, God," she sobbed. "Dear God, thank you." Not until he spoke the impossible words had she realized how much she'd longed for this, for him to say just these things, for that look in his eyes.

His hand steadied her shaking shoulders, as his other arm encircled her lightly. It took her a moment of wiping her eyes to realize that she'd fallen to kneel on his lap. When she straightened, his face was close.

But he smiled painfully. "Maybe," he said, "you might – remember the rite a newborn Jewish male undergoes," he began slowly.

She started. "Oh, am I hurting you?" Eyes wide, she withdrew from him, mortified. "I'm so sorry."

"It is quite alright," he replied sheepishly, and she saw a wince in his expression. But that soon disappeared and a grin replaced it. "The pain was surprisingly worth it."

She smiled coyly in return, and the expression melted as she looked at him. Rakhshan. Rakhshan, the wicked and perverse man, the heathen, the mercenary – Rakhshan, believing in the one true God. She could not believe it.

And so they sat, at the feet of their divans in silence. Her knees were touching his, and she was not shy of it. All she could do was stare at him. She couldn't help but blurt, "We must make a sacrifice."

Rakhshan sat up. "Tobias said the same thing. We go tomorrow."

"Truly?"

"Yes. After so many leagues, you finally get your goat."

Kefira's mind went back to when she first saw the man before her, carrying a bleating kid from the bushes. Before his lies, before his rescues. "I guess we've come over many leagues," she said, conflicting humors tangling within her. "How long ago was it?"

"You mean when we met?"

"Yes."

"About four months, I believe."

She took in a stunned breath. "It does not feel that way at all. Everything's gone by so fast."

"And I feel the opposite," he replied, melancholy tingeing his voice. "It seemed a slow march; all toward an unseen destination."

She didn't ask if he knew where that destination was, or if he'd reached it yet. She just said, after a while, "And – are you at peace with that destination?"

"I think yes." He smiled.

"I'm heartened to hear that."

His eyes searched hers. "And what about you?"

Kefira looked at his hand. She realized hers was held in it. "Yes," she said. "Yes; I think, for once, that I am."

The ram's legs took to the rocks with ease as it followed them up the mountain; it was strong, its coat of fleece shone white and unblemished, its spiral horns were unbroken, and its yellow eyes gleamed with all the intellectual spark sheepkind could muster.

Kefira led it with a rope, conscious of keeping its head under control, even as she heard the sway of Yonatan's tail behind her; it was not as disturbed by him as she'd thought, as long as it did not turn its face to look behind and see the great pillars of the dragon's legs, or look up to see the ceiling of his belly.

Beside her Rakhshan walked, guiding Tobias with an arm. They went slowly, and so Yonatan had to take a few steps and pause, and wait for them to get ahead of him. He wanted to fly them up to the ridge, but of course the ram wouldn't have stood for it, and so they went on foot.

She did not mind it though. She had not been outside of the palace grounds for many fortnights, and it was refreshing to stretch her legs again, to feel the roasting sun, the humid breeze coming off of the distant ocean. If she kept her eyes on the ground and the ram, then she could almost imagine that she was back months ago, with the little goat, outside of the shack whence the little red egg had come, before everything.

But then there was Rakhshan, and Tobias, and the dragon, and the capitol city of Persia at her back, glimmering in the afternoon sky.

She studied her husband furtively. The way he walked; it looked as though he still hurt, but his movements remained smooth as he led Tobias up an even path through the rocks and ruts.

The ram jumped as Yonatan's head came closer to the ground, when the earth around them suddenly grew level. There were no trees on the peak, just yellow tussocks and green brush; grey, rugged stones studded the landscape. Kefira looked up, into the blue above, seeing swathes of white cloud scud across the morning sky.

"I believe we've arrived," Rakhshan said, breaking the silence.

Tobias nodded, and smiled. "Let us find a place."

They located a flat spread of ground, a slab of stone jutting from the dirt of a cliff that looked over the city. Under the Levite's instruction, Rakhshan and Kefira began piling rocks the center of the earthen platform. Once more, her hands were in the dirt, and she felt fresh again, through the slow, repeated motion of bending and lifting a rock from the earth. Leva would have a fit when she saw her nails, upon her return.

Yonatan was not idle in their exertion. For a few minutes he was occupied by a large boulder; he tried picking it up, though it did not budge, until after he used his claws to excavate it. When it was removed, it left a winepress-sized hole in the ground. Dust fell away from it as he raised it over their heads, waited for them to get out of the way, and nestled it amongst the much smaller rocks.

Tobias smiled and patted his hands on the earthen table. "I think this will do just fine." He began to brush away the dirt on its surface. "Is there firewood, nigh?"

There was no tree in sight, save for in the lower hills. Without bidding, Yonatan leaped off the mountain and Kefira watched him glide down, just as the Zarek sentinels half a league off did. But he returned swiftly, a whole tree clutched in a foretalon, its frail roots still clinging to the dirt that had harbored it.

He dropped back to the mountain, causing the rocks of the altar to rattle, and deposited the dry tree before them, much to the ram's budding alarm.

Kefira tightened her grip on the animal's harness. "Ought it be in smaller pieces?" she asked, half to Yonatan, and half to Tobias.

Promptly Yonatan took it up in his talons, and began snapping the wood into human-sized lengths, and then half again, sending splinters and dust into the air. Rakhshan approached the growing pile of kindling and said, "Is there a special way the fire must be arranged?"

"Just arrange the wood in layers, as I do, and we shall put it aflame."

As Rakhshan brought the kindling to the altar, Kefira bolstered her heels into the ground to hold the ram. She looked up at Yonatan. "This is what I wanted to do the day that I found you," she found herself saying to him. "The place your egg resided had a small goat that I wanted to find a Levite for, to make a sacrifice for me. But this now is a ram from the flock of the King. I did not know I would ever…" she trailed off, as his golden gaze absorbed her. "In truth, I've never had a sacrifice made for me before, not even in my old village." Her eyes went wistfully to the ram. "It seems that after ten and six years of living," she murmured, "I should have had one a long time ago, should have had many in the past... But Tobias told me something that the old king David once said in a song."

Before she knew it, she was rubbing her eye, and realized that the altar was now burning. Tobias was kneeling beneath the growing glow. Rakhshan was beside her, flint stones in his hand, and said, "I think it is time for the ram, now."

"Is it?" she breathed. She stepped forward, and passed the ropes to Rakhshan; then she remembered when first a goat had been exchanged between them, and for once regretted Mār's absence. Her eyes went to Rakhshan's and she knew he felt the same.

Tobias stood, now, and Rakhshan presented the ram to him. "Come close," said the Levite. "Let us begin." He was a wizened silhouette against the flame behind him. The fire of the altar seemed to consume all the other light around it, as though it was the twilight sun itself.

Kefira approached with Rakhshan, feeling Yonatan move behind. "You are to each lay your hand on the head of the offering, and it will be accepted on behalf of your atonement."

She looked into the creature's yellow eyes. This was it. This creature was going to take the place of her – a place of justice that she did not have to suffer herself, that was what was said. Slowly extending her hand, she thought of the gallows, the stake that had waited to hoist her up on its tip, every time she should have lost a hand. But this was not a creature taking her punishment from man. It was pardoning her from the consequences of the Creator. Her palm rested against its wiry-furred snout as air warm hissed through its nostrils. Suddenly, she found her eyes on Rakhshan's and unseeing Tobias's, and wondered if they recognized what she did. Her husband's amber eyes shimmered, and she knew that he'd known for longer than she.

Kefira knelt, hand still on the ram's forehead. And whispered her gratitude to Adonai. Then she held its face in both hands, securing its gaze downward. Then, she looked up at Yonatan.

He seemed a little surprised at this inclusion, but slowly, he lifted a talon, and even slower, gently tapped the ram's head with a scimitar claw. The animal bleated and jerked, but Kefira held it fast.

Then it was Rakhshan's turn, and he seemed captivated by the touch, as though he was shaking hands with an emissary of a great king.

Tobias said, "Rakhshan, it is your duty to make the sacrifice."

The man looked up at him, aghast. "You mean – I?"

"You are the head of your household," the old man explained. "But worry not; I will guide you."

Kefira knelt by Rakhshan as he was handed a glinting blade. She met his eyes, and a whole new expression was in them, hard and warm. "I will help hold him still," she said. "My family had a flock."

Rakhshan nodded, and followed the Levite's direction, after Kefira coaxed the disgruntled ram into lying down. Her husband rested his knee over the creature's side, and took hold of its horn to keep its head to the ground. As she watched him bring forth the knife, she began to stroke the woolly flank, with anticipating breath unable to release. She looked up at Tobias, to make sure he thought they were not getting anything wrong, as if he could see.

When she looked back, the ram exclaimed a gurgling bleat, a final cry. Scarlet began to spread over the wool on its neck, and she saw blood had spurted onto Rakhshan's arm. And then Tobias was kneeling beside the dispatched ram as well, handing a bowl to Rakhshan. "Be certain to preserve the blood." And the sound of trickling blood met Kefira's ears; she shivered.

She saw Yonatan lower his head further to observe, as Tobias straightened, bowl in hand. For the first time since she'd known him, Kefira did not believe that he was blind. He moved to the altar with grace, and began to paint its warm rocks with blood, sprinkling droplets that glistened like dew before the fire.

"What shall I do, now?" Rakhshan asked him, wiping the blade in the grass.

"The flesh is to be divided and placed on the fire in pieces. May you add more wood, Yonatan?" Tobias emptied his bowl, and Yonatan began splintering. "Remove the head, and the fat, and the organs, and we shall wash them and burn them."

Kefira and Rakhshan exchanged glances. She smiled and whispered, "This is a little more than you thought, isn't it?" He nodded, returning the expression a little.

He carved the neck before the jaw, through flesh and bone, until the head was removed. He handed it to Tobias, who placed it on the fire. Then he slit open the stomach, and opened the ribcage. "Let me help," she said to him, "I've butchered a little before, when I was younger."

He grinned. "That is something I never thought you capable of." But he gave the knife anyway, and watched as she slit up its legs, and removed the white layers in its loins and joints. Halfway through, she realized that she was up to her elbows in red smear, but so was Rakhshan, so she did not mind. One by one, organs were removed, rinsed in a basin, and laid in the fire – kidneys, liver, heart, each individual vessel first all over in stringy flesh, before it is washed clean and gleaming. Only when she could see the yellow gleam of its spine did she realize that it was finished.

Rakhshan lifted the empty carcass, and at Tobias's bidding placed it on the fire, a woolen border to the sizzling offal.

Kefira stood, realizing she'd been kneeling for a long time, and the movement hurt her knees. The ground was purple where they'd been working. Yonatan sniffed the earth, and she gazed at it, as she rubbed her sticky hands together. Her sleeves were rolled up to hang upon her shoulders, leaving her arms bear, but that had by no means deterred her clothes from becoming stained. She was glad Leva had somehow anticipated this, in that day's less ornate wardrobe.

She walked closer to the fire, where the men now stood, and

Yonatan followed. She could feel the heat of the blaze pressing against her face, as yellow fire hissed and spat around the sacrifice. The sky was wholly dark now, and the light of the fire blotted out that of the stars and the city below.

"It has been a long time," Tobias murmured. "I have not done that in a long time. It is good to hear."

Kefira stood next to Rakhshan, and listened, and smelled, as she averted her face from the heat. It smelled like roasting meat – juicy, succulent, savory meat. *A pleasing aroma to the Lord.* There was a cindery harshness in the smoke that told of the beginning of the fleshes' incineration. Greasy black fumes took to the sky as hide began to turn to ash, and she heard the pop of boiling marrow bursting throughout the bones.

This creature's end was irrevocable, she realized. Its dissolution, its destruction, was so supremely final, so irreversible; the once noble beast of glinting eyes and strong hooves would be reduced to no more than grey dust, something to be blown away with a breath.

Kefira saw the firelight reflected in Yonatan's eyes; it was she who should have been on the altar. But she was not. Even though she was long given the promise of Zion, and it was going to be fulfilled in this very time, she had only met it with frail hope and fear. Just as Israel had not believed the prophets that foretold its doom, she had not believed in the promise of restoration. She had not believed, until now, that the events of the last months could have ever amounted to good – though, now, she was surrounded in the fruition of the pain, despite it all. And Adonai had known it was going to turn out this way all along. She'd had the audacity not to trust Him, the one in control of it all. She was weaker, she realized, than the very creature that took her place.

She was about to bring up her hands to rub her eyes, pulled up short, and then just let her red arms drop. Staring at the fire, she felt a pair of tears move down her face, painful gratitude for the king that provided the lamb that provided her atonement; and the God that provided that king. And so much more. Her eyes went to

Yonatan. And she thought of the words she'd wanted to speak to him. "My sacrifice, O God, is a broken spirit," she whispered, the verses of David, "A broken and contrite heart You, God, will not despise. May it please you to prosper Zion, to build up the walls of Jerusalem."

Then her bloody hand was enveloped in Rakhshan's. She looked up at him and he said, "I think He shall."

Chapter XXI
Moonset

"Why did you give me mercy?" Kefira asked the King one day, when he invited her to his chambers for a meal. She tried to look up at him, from the loaf of bread she cradled in her hands, but could not.

She watched from the corner of her sight as he took a drink of wine. "We are both wielders of great power. I, in the form of a nation, and you, in the form of a dragon," he replied, as nonchalantly as though he were solving a simple mathematical problem for a child. "I believe both assets merit a certain degree of mutual respect."

Kefira smiled a little, abashed. "Your goodness is without bounds." She felt dually insecure in his presence; not only was she the only one at his table, but – this was the man prophesied to free her people, and in his aura the delicious foods could only be dry in her mouth.

The King's golden eyes creased in the corners, and he smiled. "I simply do not waver from my principles. I believe that everywhere a person can," he said, "they should act as a liberator. I brought together the nations between the gulf and the northern sea into the great Empire of today, and its people I gave freedom, dignity, and prosperity, and that has brought me as much joy as it has them.

"But that is just my own people. As of yet, I have not touched the lands west of here." He leaned back. "A people in a prison of their own make."

Kefira's brow arched in a question. But the way he inclined his head suggested that he did not mind she speak. "What do you mean, my king?"

"I have read your histories, as well as heard your prophecies. Your nation of old, great Israel, affluent and prosperous, gradually lapsed into apathy, and thus fell into decline. It was not the apathy of ignorance, either; I understand that your people had received many warnings from the mouthpieces of your god. Israel was told that it would fall prey to its neighbors." The King paused, eyes growing hard, and Kefira saw disapproval unsubdued within them. Then he took another drink from his goblet. She waited.

"If it was not for you, Kefira, then I do not believe I would have considered going to battle for your people. I have always believed them deserving of their fate, their subservience to the Babylonians. Tobias was just an anomaly to me, a relic of their *old* spirit: a ghost of Israel, not a sign that Israel could be resurrected.

"But you, and Yonatan: even though generations have passed since Israel's perceived demise, you both have shown that she is not dead. Merely... sleeping. And so, as God has anointed me, I believe it is my duty to wake her up."

Kefira stared into her goblet, eyes fixed on the purple liquid, unable to look at the King for fear of showing him the tears that threatened to spill over.

Yonatan was with Shoala. Kefira's elbows ached on the windowsill. The sun was descending upon the horizon, the sky as fiery as her dragon's scales. But she did not see him outside in his distant garden. He was with his new mate, somewhere. Ensuring that the line of the Hardlās did not die.

He's growing up. He *is* grown up, Kefira decided. He was no longer the same hatchling that once could coil about her shoulders. No, that was not true – he was the same – their love was the same. She brought up her hands to rest her chin upon. He was just so much greater.

When Rakhshan opened the door, she realized that she'd been waiting for him. She turned from the window to face him. "How was the meeting?"

"I was seeing Mār, actually," he replied, removing his jerkin to drape it over a divan. "He sends his regards."

"He does?"

"He would if he was not a complete mule."

Kefira smiled bitterly, and quickly grew solemn. "How has he taken the news?"

"He was mad at you, at first – for poisoning me, he said."

"I guessed as much; I visited him once, when I was looking for you while you were with Tobias, and he – did not say a word."

Rakhshan shook his head. "He's cooled off a little, since; in fact, he acted quite indifferent the duration of our conversation, as though nothing had changed."

Kefira hugged her elbows. "I guess that is sort of a good thing."

Rakhshan pursed his lips and shrugged. "Well, it's not bad, at least. I believe he'll come around, though."

She nodded and walked closer, standing aside the table. "So, how are you feeling?" It had been a week since his return, therefore a whole fortnight since his procedure. How was he to heal?

The man sat in his longchair and knitted his hands in his lap. "Better." He glanced at her. "I – it's an odd thing to do. I still don't rightly understand it – circumcision. What Tobias told me," he continued, "was that it identifies me as someone different, as one who did not by blood come from Abraham, but by covenant. I guess that made it worth the pain." Then, as though waking from a stupor, he looked at her. "You know, this is an odd topic for conversation."

Kefira chuckled self-consciously. "It is. But you may go on. As *husband and wife*," she said affectedly, "we ought to be able to share such things with one another." She moved to sit across from him.

Rakhshan smiled at her pertly. "There's not much else – to put to words," he said. He paused, and then looked at his hands. "It just feels as though I no longer tread water, in life. That I have found – a ship."

"A ship?"

He laughed helplessly. "Or a *reason*. And a family, for once. Not like an unknown sire and a dead mother, but," he trailed off and shook his head, as though put off by his own ineloquence.

"A Father."

"Yes, a King."

Kefira tentatively took one of his hands in hers, and held it between her palms. "I think we are like Ruth and Boaz."

Rakhshan smiled, eyebrow cocking. "I was told that story. That makes me *Ruth*, does it not?"

"I suppose it does," she replied with a smile. The expression faded, and she lowered her eyes. Her hands were small in his. They used to have the same calloused as he had, but now there was only soft skin over her thin fingers, that were conscious of every small movement in the tendons of his palm. Only then did the silver bands they shared seem to register. One on her finger, the other on his, in the same place she put it those fortnights ago. "Rakhshan?" she asked.

"Yes?"

She had not meant to address him at all, she belatedly realized. And she still held his hand. But she did not drop it. "Thank you," she said.

For a moment, his palm was still. "You're welcome," he replied. "What for?"

"I just – I did not know if I've ever thanked you for saving me."

His gaze softened. "It was no trouble."

"I don't believe that. I acted rashly, yet you still - "

"It is the least I could do," he cut in. He looked down. "After I… betrayed you, twice." He tilted his head, not looking at her. "It is a good arrangement, what we have. I got you into a mess, I revealed Yonatan and you to the men that would usurp you. It only makes sense that I help secure you."

You've done so much more than that, and you do not even know it. Without him, how would she ever have gone to Pasargadae? How could she have ever otherwise inspired a King to save a nation?

Kefira realized that gratitude was not the only thing that trembled in her heart. She didn't respond to his words, unable to put together a just reply. So instead, she just stood and moved to sit beside him. His eyes gave away his surprise. She stammered, "It is not just that. It is not for those reasons that I..."

The girl looked hopelessly into his amber gaze, lost. So close to him, she had to tip her head upward to look him in the eye, even as he slouched. "You are a good man," she said. And she leaned her head tentatively on his shoulder.

"And you, a good woman," Rakhshan replied. They sat side by side for a long time, Kefira all the while feeling sweat heat her palms. Rakhshan was motionless beside her, warm and stable, as though her presence were fragile, a bird easily frightened away.

But there was no fear in her. In those minutes, the girl felt a weariness seep into her bones, like thirst. Before she realized what she was doing, she slipped beneath Rakhshan's arm and found herself embracing him.

She could tell that he was astonished. Still, he put his other arm around her, just the same. Her own forwardness astonished her, and she lowered her head to rest on his chest, to hide her blush. When she blinked, she realized how close he was; she smelled the smoky-sweet scent of cardamom, felt the texture of his clothing, and his breath stirring her shawl, and the warmth of his arms, that made her realize that she'd been cold before. Then a whisper slipped out before she could subdue it. "I am glad to be married to you, Rakhshan."

She felt him straighten in the embrace, and after a pause, say, "My dear Kefira. Are you saying that you *love* me?"

The girl was taken aback, cheek frozen against his soft leather tunic. The playful accusation struck her. Never had she ever confronted the idea. Never had she allowed herself to. But love – love, like Yonatan, like her mother and father – love. Love Rakhshan. After stunned seconds, Kefira nodded softly into his chest.

She heard the smile in his voice. "Then, I will have you know," he murmured, "that I've been glad to be married to you since even before we were wed."

Kefira shut her eyes tight, heat flooding to her face. "Thank you," she said. She felt his stubble as he kissed her forehead.

The gesture no longer dismayed her. She opened her eyes again, she realized that they sky was darkling. She recognized the divan. Slowly, she lifted her hands to touch his arms. They separated, she stood, and he looked up at her, a measure of disillusionment in his eyes. "Goodnight," he said, and began to recline.

But then she took hold of his hands again, and pulled him upright. "No," she replied, holding onto his arm, locking it close over her chest. "With me," she murmured.

"Kefira?" he began, incredulous.

She felt as surprised as he did, she realized. Had she truly just invited him – her stomach stirred, and she felt that she was blushing. But nonetheless, she found herself getting up to the tips of her toes, touching her lips to his cheek, feeling heat blossom within her once more. "My husband does *not* belong on a cushion in the drawing room," she said.

He smiled broadly. "And your husband does not dispute this judgment." Without another word, he with ardor dipped his head to kiss her back.

The apartment was soon black, unlit. But in time a golden light bloomed behind the curtain of the servant's room, Leva lighting a lamp. This light spilled into the drawing room when she passed the threshold. She shielded the flame from broaching her mistress's bedroom as she passed to reach the door, the exit. "I'm going to leave to get some…" she began, "some…"

Well, they did not hear her, and she knew it and so offered no further excuse. She fled, leaving husband and wife in the other room undisturbed.

The moon shone cold and unblinking through a window, to illuminate a grey puddle on the floor of the Babylonian ambassador's chambers, the light reflecting dimly to expose the shapes of his servants as they worked in the darkness.

Shaza'eil watched them as he sharpened his sword, but paid heed to nothing but his own designs, as they were fashioned like a spider's web in his mind.

He used to despise the brat. But his low opinion her had most unexpectedly changed into a sort of skeptical curiosity. She was clever when she spoke, for a wardu girl, possessing within her an air of insolence such as he'd never before experienced. Never had he been subjected to such covert, yet shameless disrespect. Her veiled, brazen defiance – despite himself – he found it to be intoxicating. The cut of a blade in battle.

At the thought of every avoided gaze, every double-edged word, and the way she tried to make herself to appear flat around him – he was filled with such furious pleasure that he could hardly believe that he'd once intended to kill her.

And he remembered when with all his being he wanted to. After all, she had stolen the beast that was his by birthright. And so he acted accordingly, when he saw the rat again in the garden. When her brown neck was in his hands. The stunned fear in her dark eyes. The movement of her throat, slow and deathly, as though he'd already begun to choke her.

Would he have done it, if the old man had not interrupted? Should he have? No, there would have been too many repercussions, then. The disruption on his part was providence. Now he had a better means of achieving the Hardlā. Much better. Much more agreeable for all the parties involved.

He watched languidly as servants finished packing the chests of his belongings. His eyes went to the window. Night still lay as a heavy blanket over the city.

His eyes went down again. Kefira. He spoke the name in his mind as he brought a whetstone across his falchion. He was not sure for what purpose he was keening his blade, only knew that it was a practical thing to do. The plan did not involve bloodshed – or bloodshed of a martial sort, anyway. But it did a man good to know that his blade was sharp.

Yet the refined metal that gleamed before him was not his greatest weapon. It was not a weapon at all, compared to what Kefira would be to him. He smiled mirthlessly. Who knew that someone so infuriatingly inconvenient would turn out to be his greatest asset.

He stroked the blade with the backs of his fingers. Soon.

The scent of rosemary, herbs done up by the handmaiden, hung in their chambers. Kefira got up alone while the night yet resided, walking slowly over a discarded blanket, stained, on the ground. She covered her warm shoulders in the shawl as she left the bedroom, and stood still in the drawing room, staring into its darkness.

Ought she dance? She wanted to think and breathe and sing and marvel – but as she gazed into the silence of the room, she did none of these. The only thing that occupied her mind was the warmth and the unknown that had just been shared in.

She'd managed to get up without waking him, after he'd turned in the bed – how heavily he slept – and had unthinkingly absconded. Maybe half of her did not want to be there when he woke. What could be said, after all? She imagined, mind beginning to turn as she stood, meeting his eyes again, holding his hands again, speaking with him again, when so much had already been seen, felt, and said. There was nothing else. All she could do was just blush and look away and pop pistachios into her mouth.

Rakhshan.

She found herself at the window, looking into the cloudless night; there was the faintest tinge of blue on the horizon, the hems of an impending dawn. There were so many stars in the sky. "Adonai?" she murmured, a breath.

The girl turned her head. Her husband was there. She held her shawl close against the chill, as he moved to her side to gaze out the window. She blushed, but his own expression was one of tranquility. Their arms touched, and the cold vanished as they stood in silence. She wondered if he was going to speak.

But he did not say anything; instead they both looked on as dark dragon silhouettes moved over the stars. Kefira heard the song of Yonatan and came to peace. Leaning on her husband she watched in the fading darkness, as the moon and the night fell away beneath the west and the remnants of Jerusalem.

Lexicon

Name Pronunciation

Kefira – (Kah-FEER-uh)
Mār – (Mar)
Rakhshan – (Rak-SHON)
Yonatan – (YON-ah-ton)
Shaza'eil – (Shah-zay-EL)
Tahmour – (Ta-MOR)
Sorushe – (So-ROOSH)

Arsham – (Ar-SHOM)
Mehrnaz – (Mare-NAZ)
Ravan – (Rah-VAHN)
Tobias – (Toh-BY-us)
Mahasti – (Ma-hoss-TEE)
Parudrauga – (Pa-ru-DROW-ga)
Pasargadae – (Pa-SAR-ga-de)

Geography

Al-Khaleej – the Persian Gulf.
Atrak River – a large river in Hyrcania that flows into the Mazandaran Sea.
Carmania – a verdant satrapy in south-eastern Persia.
Dahae – a Persian satrapy that borders the Mazandaran sea.
Elam – a mountainous satrapy in central Persia.
Gedrosia – a Persian satrapy that borders Al-Khaleej.
Hangmatana – the capitol city of the satrapy of Media.
Hyrcania – a Persian satrapy that borders the Mazandaran sea.
Kārun River – a large river that flows from the mountains in western Persia.
Mazandaran Sea – the Caspian Sea, in northern Persia.
Media – a mountainous satrapy in north-western Persia.
Mount Alvand – a mountain in Media, upon which Hangmatana is built.
Mount Sinai – a mountain in Israel, where God gave the Ten Commandments to the Israelites.
Parudrauga – a port city in Gedrosia.
Pasargadae – the capitol city of Persia, in Persis.
Persis – a temperate satrapy in south-western Persia.

Deities

Ahura Mazda – the chief Persian god.
Angra Mainyu / Ahriman – the spirit of chaos that antagonizes Ahura Mazda.
Baal, Ishtar – Babylonian god and goddess of fertility.
Beelzebub – Hebrew for 'Lord of the Flies,' a name for the Devil.
Jehovah-Jireh / Adonai – the God of Israel.
Molech – a Babylonian god, for whom infants are burned to death in sacrifice.
Spenta Mainyu – Ahura Mazda's benevolent holy spirit.
Tiamat – the dragon goddess and mother of the Babylonian gods.

Dragons, Military

Abraxas – a dexterous, mountain-dwelling Persian dragon.
Asman Kāra – the Sky Army of Persia, a military branch of dragon-riding warriors.
Asmanaba – a military unit of the Asman Kāra, three to seven dragons in formation.
Azdeev – an intelligent Persian dragon, white and lithe.
Azhi Dahaki – a generally un-tame Persian dragon, ruddy green in color, spits acid.
Barid – a branch of the Asman Kāra that deals in couriering and dispatch.
Gandarewa – the largest breed of Persian dragon, gold in color, with eyespots on its wings.
Hardlā – the largest breed of dragon, of Israel, gold, red, and mauve in color.
Immortals – a branch of the Asman Kāra, one thousand dragon riders dedicated to the safety of Persia's king.
Khumbaba – a fire-breathing Babylonian dragon.
Shaghāl – a camel-sized un-tame dragon, name means 'Jackal.'
Siyudūrai – the smallest and fastest Persian dragon, blue-grey, often employed in Barid.
Thu'ban – a fire-breathing Persian dragon, dark red and purple.
Zarek – a vigilant dragon ridden exclusively by Immortals.

Measurements

Cubit – length, one and a half feet, or half a meter.
League – distance, three miles, or five kilometers.
Shekel – weight, one and one-fourth pounds, or eleven and a half grams.
Talent – weight, seventy-five pounds, or thirty-four kilograms.

Other

Alalega – a narcotic substance derived from opium poppies.
Awilu – the title for a Babylonian noble.
Bride Price – a gift of capital from a groom to the bride's family.
Chai – tea.
Chuppah – a canopy over a couple while they're taking their vows, in a Hebrew wedding.
Dowry – a gift of capital from a bride's family to her groom.
Eunuch – an emasculated manservant of high position, often entrusted with guarding women.
Frawardin – the first month of the Persian year, September.
High Place – a pagan place of worship, often on a hilltop or other elevated location.
Kashrut – Hebrew laws of Kosher that concern food.
Levite – a Jew from the tribe of Levi, the family in charge of priesthood in Israel.
Sapo – Soap.
Wardu – the title for a Babylonian peasant.
Zion – a synonym for Israel, and a mountain near Jerusalem.

Acknowledgements

My first published novel, a massive project – full of tears of joy and tears of mortal agony, slaving away at my computer desk. It was a task I could not have undertaken or completed without the help of many wonderful people.

Foremost, a thousand thanks to my editor who was a Godsend: Amy Andrews, thank you for your criticism and encouragement, without which *Remnants* would be a wretched mess full of typos and inconsistencies. Thank you to my mentor and self-employed cheerleader Tonya Noon-Toledo, who helped me make and meet deadlines.

Thank you to my beloved beta readers: Ben, Lauren, Ashleigh, Jenelle, Emily, Matt, and my brothers – your enthusiasm kept me going even when I was only running off of the dregs of my coffee mug!

Most of all, I am grateful for my parents – my dad, who first introduced me to the genre of fantasy, and financed me every step of the way in this project; and my mom, without whom *Remnants* would have never gotten off the ground. Without the blessing of your constant exhortations, ultimatums, and support, I'd still be laying lamely with my face rolling on the keyboard in despair of the revision process. Thank you for your perpetual energy!

I love you all to death and look forward to working with you all again in my further pursuits in the magical world of writing!

Made in the USA
Charleston, SC
08 May 2014